**REA**

P9-BHR-321

## SASS

In the bathroom, Sass's emotions ran away with her. As always, his words of love touched her in every way imaginable. Not only did he confess to loving her, he really seemed sure that he wanted to marry her. She stepped in the hot water. So weak from the lovemaking, her emotions so drained, Sass sat down on the floor of the tub to allow the water to rain down on her.

Kristopher came into the bathroom, stepped into the shower stall and lifted her to her feet. Unable to distinguish the shower water from tears, her sudden flight made him wonder if she'd been crying. If so, was she scared of him all over again? Would she run away from the relationship? Had he put too much pressure on her too soon to get married? With the answers all locked inside of her heart, he prayed that she'd one day give him the key.

FEB 2 5 2003

# BOOK YOUR PLACE ON OUR WEBSITE AND MAKE THE ARABESQUE ROMANCE CONNECTION!

We've created a customized website just for our very special Arabesque readers, where you can get the inside scoop on everything that's going on with Arabesque romance novels.

When you come online, you'll have the exciting opportunity to:

- View covers of upcoming books

- Learn about our future publishing schedule (listed by publication month and author)

- Find out when your favorite authors will be visiting a city near you

- Search for and order backlist books

- Check out author bios and background information

- Send e-mail to your favorite authors

- Join us in weekly chats with authors, readers and other guests

- Get writing guidelines

- AND MUCH MORE!

Visit our website at
http://www.arabesquebooks.com

# SASS

## Linda Hudson-Smith

**BET Publications, LLC**
http://www.bet.com
http://www.arabesquebooks.com

ARABESQUE BOOKS are published by

BET Publications, LLC
c/o BET BOOKS
One BET Plaza
1900 W Place NE
Washington, DC 20018-1211

Copyright © 2003 by Linda Hudson-Smith

All rights reserved. No part of this book may be reproduced, stored in a retrieval system, or transmitted in any form or by any means without the prior written consent of the Publisher.

If you purchased this book without a cover, you should be aware that this book is stolen property. It was reported as "unsold and destroyed" to the Publisher and neither the Author nor the Publisher has received any payment for this "stripped book."

All Kensington Titles, Imprints, and Distributed Lines are available at special quantity discounts for bulk purshases for sales promotions, premiums, fund-raising, and educational or institutional use. Special book excerpts or customized printings can also be created to fit specific needs. For details, write or phone the office of the Kensington special sales manager: Kensington Publishing Corp., 850 Third Avenue, New York, NY 10022, attn: Special Sales Department, Phone: 1-800-221-2647.

BET Books is a trademark of Black Entertainment Television, Inc. ARABESQUE, the ARABESQUE logo, and the BET BOOKS logo are trademarks and registered trademarks.

First Printing: February 2003
10 9 8 7 6 5 4 3 2 1

*This book is dedicated to my five beloved grandchildren:*
*Joshua, Gregory III, Keraishawn, Omunique, Scott II*

*You all are the sunshine of my life!*
*May God always keep you in His tender, loving care.*

*I love you.*

# ACKNOWLEDGMENTS

Thanks to each and every one of you who contributed to, participated in, and attended the realease gala for my debut mainstream inspirational novel entitled Ladies in Waiting, BET Books/New Spirit. It was truly a magnificent evening. I was both humbled and honored by your presence.

Thanks to all of my family members who came from quite a distance to help celebrate my special evening, my one moment in time: Northern California, Las Vegas, Houston, Denver, Chicago, and my hometown of Washington, Pennsylvania.

A very special thanks to Scott Brian Smith Justified. Your musical performances were extraordinary. You are an extremely talented songwriter and recording artist. I am so proud of you. Thank you so much for making my special day an even brighter event. I love you.

A very speical thanks to the event's Masters of Ceremony, Comedian/Ventriloquist, Willie Brown, and his sassy, animated sidekick, Woody. Your performances were absolutely thrilling and awe-inspiring!

Judyann Elder
John Cothran, Jr.
Candy Brown-Houston
John Wesley

BET Books—Contributors
Brenda Bailey—Hostess, Centerpiece Creations
Ingenious Concepts—Programs and Actor's Billing
    Board
Stacy Powell—Hostess, Event Coordinator
Beverly Jimerson—Hostess
Drusilla Smith—Hostess
Derek Cohill—DJ & Lighting Technician
Victoria Rabb—Hilton Hotel Catering Services Consul-
    tant
Connie De Silva—Guest Services

# One

Seated at a table in the restaurant Le Bistro de la Gare located near the famous Champs Elysées, Sass Stephens and her co-worker, Lesilee Taft, were enjoying a light lunch and lively conversation. Employed at the same California television network, Sass and Lesilee had come to Paris for a two-week vacation.

Sass's sepia eyes sparkled like diamonds. "I'm so excited to be in Paris. I'm glad we came together. Since you've been here before, I don't feel intimidated at all. Had I come by myself, I'm not sure how far I would've ventured into this wonderful city."

Knowingly, Lesilee smiled. "You wouldn't have remained by yourself for long. The Frenchmen here would've taken very good care of you. From the moment you were spotted alone, you would've had more than your fair share of good-looking male company."

Laughing, Sass rolled her eyes. "I certainly didn't come here looking for a man. I'm here to get away from the haunting memories of one. But if a good-looking one happens along, I'll reassess my position. These few years of celibacy have been a bit too much for me already."

Lesilee leaned forward in her chair. "Well, you better start reassessing. Don't look now, but there's a very good-looking gentleman at the table right next to us. It seems to me he can't keep his eyes off you," Lesilee whispered.

Discreetly, Sass looked over at the next table. When the devilishly-handsome man smiled brilliantly at her, raising his glass in a toast, Sass quickly looked around for an exit. While nearly choking on her own saliva, her golden-brown complexion became completely flushed.

"Oh, God, Lesilee, I've got to find a way to get out of here. I can barely breathe. I can't believe my own eyes. How can this be happening to me now, of all times, of all places?"

"Gosh, he's handsome. Did you get a glimpse of those beautiful white teeth and that gorgeous smile? His mocha complexion is absolutely gorgeous. He's been looking at you for some time now with those daring sea-green eyes of his."

Sass clicked her tongue. "Haven't you heard a word I've said, Lesilee! I don't give a care how long he's been looking at me. You have to come with me right now. Please, Lesilee, let's go." Frantic, Sass reached under the table for her purse, ready to bolt for the nearest exit.

Finally hearing the urgency in Sass's tone, Lesilee looked concerned. "It's too late. Brace yourself. He's coming over to the table. Get a load of his tall, lean physique. He has to be at least six-three." Lesilee unwittingly ignored the hysteria compelling itself against Sass's sanity.

Sass felt hot, as if flaming torches bored into her back. Her hands began to tremble.

*"Bonjour, Mademoiselle Stephens,"* Kristopher Chandler greeted Sass in French. "Out of all the people in the world, I never expected to see you in this bistro." He turned to Lesilee. "I'm sorry for the intrusion, but I'm a very old friend of Sass's, Kristopher Chandler." He extended his hand to Lesilee. Though it didn't show, Kristopher was more nervous than Sass.

Having gone totally pale, Lesilee looked up, smiling weakly at the man who Sass had been desperately trying

3 1833 04038 034 4

to get over for the past couple of years. The same man she was still very much in love with even though he'd ripped her heart out and handed it to her on a silver platter. "Pleased to meet you."

He smiled broadly at Lesilee's words, but his eyes stayed glued on Sass. Blushing heavily with confusion, Sass refused to meet his piercing gaze head on. Her long, sweeping lashes instantly lowered over her sepia eyes. His breath caught, the way it always did when he looked into her heart through the exquisite beauty of her sheer eyes. He'd certainly missed seeing the world through her blushing innocence.

His eyes drank thirstily of Sass's enchanting beauty. "Sass, you still remind me of that painting, the one I told you I saw in the Louvre on a prior visit to France. I'd love to have the opportunity to take you there so you can see it for yourself."

This fabulous-looking photographer had always known exactly how to get right to the point, Sass mused. "I'm afraid my holiday schedule is full, Kristopher." Sass had no desire to get back into another thicket of emotional briars with Kristopher Chandler. Besides, she hadn't yet freed herself or her heart from the soul-tearing thorns of their torrid past.

He smiled, as though he had no intentions of being denied the opportunity to get to know the beautiful Sass Stephens all over again. Desperately, he'd been searching for her a long time now, hoping to regain her trust and win back her heart. Pulling out a chair, he installed his long, lean frame onto it. Watching him closely, Sass couldn't help noticing the elegant cut of his dark blue single-breasted suit. He still had a penchant for beautiful, expensive clothes, and the same sort of proclivity he'd had for beautiful women that had been instrumental in tearing them apart.

Sea-green eyes sank into the depths of her sepia ones. "You still don't trust me, Sass? I can be trusted in this. If you'd feel more comfortable, Lesilee is more than welcome to join us."

Sass smiled sweetly, though it didn't light in her eyes. "Monsieur Chandler, I don't think we should get into the issue of trust with one another. That could take months; I've only got two weeks of vacation. At any rate, I've had a long flight. I'd simply like to rest."

His slender hand reached up to cover his heart. "Ah, Mademoiselle Stephens, as for rest, there is no rest in the City of Light, especially when you are a tourist. For I imagine this is only your first trip to the unending allures of beautiful Paris!"

His flirting with her in a very believable French accent made her insides quiver. Sass couldn't help but warm inside at the symphonic tone of his voice. It sounded like a love ballad. She'd never forget how she'd hung on to Kristopher's every melodic word when they'd first met. But she now had to remain immune to them. He was a very dangerous man with his poetic style of conversing. "Lesilee has lived here before and has promised to be the perfect tour guide. I can assure you that I won't miss out on any part of the intrigue of Paris."

Speaking of intrigue, forever captivated by her unusual name, he once again thought of how positively sedating her sheer eyes were. "Sass, why are you being so obstinate about this?" His mesmerizing eyes appeared to seduce Sass, completely unnerving her in the process.

Her eyes went straight to his beautiful head of honey-brown hair and then dropped downward to his sensational, pouting lips. "Obstinate? I don't think so. Perhaps just a tad sassy, but you have a lot of nerve pretending you don't know why I'd have issues of trust with you."

He'd sensed that she was feisty when he'd first spotted

her a few years back; she'd proved him right on numerous occasions. "If I recall correctly, you've always been a bit impudent, more than just living up to your name." Ignoring her comment about the trust issue, he turned to Lesilee. "Do you think you can convince *our* lovely friend to have dinner with me this evening?"

Lesilee shrugged her shoulders. "I'm afraid that's entirely up to her. Sass, if you're worried about me, don't. I plan to spend some time with my friend, Gregoire. I can guarantee you I won't be lonely." Lesilee laughed from deep down in her throat, as though she held a delicious secret within. Her blue-black eyes appeared to caress the same inner secret.

Sass wasn't at all concerned about her good friend. She was worried about how the debonair Monsieur Kristopher Chandler had already affected her emotionally; more afraid of the way he looked at her and how he made her insides quiver with apprehension. "Kristopher, I appreciate the offer, but I'd like to stay on my own while in Paris. Believe me, it's nothing personal." But it was very personal, deeply. She already hated herself for actually wanting to accept his invitation. She'd have to be out of her mind to do so, all the way insane-crazy.

Though his eyes sparkled, his heart felt saddened. "As you wish, Sass. However, should you change your mind please contact me at this number." As he handed her a business card, his hand briefly grazed her softness. His sharp intake of breath was audible.

Sass had heard the disappointment in his voice. It disturbed her to know she'd caused him any distress, even though he'd caused her plenty. Without looking at the card, she stuck it in her purse. Watching him walk away from the table made her wish she'd had the courage to tell him exactly what she thought of him and his poetic baloney. Like old times, she couldn't.

Lesilee looked at Sass in disbelief. "Sass, I'm surprised you didn't take him up on his offer. He seems sincere. I didn't know you or him back then, but maybe time has changed him."

Sass sighed. "Kristopher also seemed sincere enough to me, a long time ago. He turned out to be just the opposite. I'm so afraid of my own judgment where he's concerned. We both know it hasn't served me too well in the past. I couldn't stand for it to fail me again."

Lesilee clicked her tongue noisily. "Sass, I know you promised not to dwell on the past while on vacation, but if there's the slightest chance that you could learn to trust him again, you shouldn't deny yourself that opportunity. I know you came here hoping to get over him, but I think you're making a big mistake in not getting things out in the open, to settle things with him once and for all. This is the perfect opportunity for you to tell him how much he's hurt you."

Sass looked ready to cry. "Maybe so, but it's too late now. We need to get over to the television network. You promised Gregoire we'd be there right after lunch." Sass sighed.

Lesilee got Sass's message right away; time to change the subject. Her ebony eyes grew soft and sentimental as she thought of her own ex-lover. "Sweet Gregoire. I wonder if he's still as handsome as I remember him. He was such a gentleman, an all-around great guy."

Comfortably seated in a cab, Sass and Lesilee talked over their vacation plans on the way to the television station. Twenty minutes later, the flirtatious cab driver dropped the women off at a large office complex located in one of the highest rent districts in Paris.

The building alone impressed Sass and she couldn't

wait to see what was inside. Lesilee had worked in the towering structure as a foreign news correspondent, so she knew just what to expect. They entered the double glass doors and immediately took the elevator up to the office suites. Stepping off the elevator, Sass looked around. As a lump arose in her throat, Sass gasped loudly at the magnificent decor of the massive suite housing the grand reception area.

Gregoire Bedier, the newsroom director of foreign affairs, noticed the two beautiful women the very moment they stepped off the elevator. Still madly in love with Lesilee Taft, he looked happy and thrilled to see her again. Above average in height, Gegoire had dark, velvety skin. In Sass's opinion he actually looked more Italian than French. His large, dark eyes had a slight droop, the first of his striking features that Sass noticed. Though he was a black man by color, in France he was simply French.

Gregoire held his arms out to Lesilee. *"Ma cherie, Lesilee,"* he gushed, "you are a sight to behold. I have waited forever for this very moment." He kissed Lesilee on both cheeks before landing a full kiss on her soft, ruby-red mouth. Lesilee blushed as old feelings rushed out to greet her. He then turned to look at Sass. "You must be Sass Stephens. *Vous êtes très jolie.*" He touched his fingers to his lips. Sass blushed at being referred to as very pretty. "Welcome to Paris, Sass. We Parisians are excited to have you. Paris will be very kind to one so lovely."

Gregoire kissed both of Sass's cheeks. "Come, I must introduce you both to the American man who's in our employ for a short time. He's been eagerly anticipating your arrival."

Lesilee looked surprised. "I thought I was the only American who'd ever work here!" Lesilee joked. "When did he come aboard with the station?"

"Only a short while ago. It is a temporary assignment. His two years are almost up."

Gregoire led the two women down a long corridor and into a tremendous office, where he spoke briefly with a secretary. He then ushered the women into a private inner office, an executive suite that looked to be the size of an apartment.

While staring in disbelief at the elegant furnishings, the warm masculine decor of the cavernous room gave Sass a heated feeling inside. Though the American wasn't in, he soon entered, approaching them from behind. Smelling the man's cologne before she saw him, she somehow thought the scent smelled familiar, absurd since she didn't know anyone in Paris. Turning around to take at look at the person who smelled so good, her jaw immediately dropped. Standing before her was the smiling face of a handsome African-American. World-renowned photographer Kristopher Chandler looked pleased to see who the guests in his office were.

"So, we meet again! It must be our fate." But he'd always known that Sass was his fate, even when he'd run out on her. "Please forgive me, Sass. I knew you were coming to Paris and that you'd visit the station, but I didn't know I'd run into you at an eatery. I hope you're not too terribly angry with me. I should've told you that I had a temporary photography assignment here at the station right after I approached your table. I was contracted to do a photography shoot of all the Paris attractions for an upcoming television documentary."

Sensing that these two had some sort of personal history, Gregoire was amused at how smitten Kristopher seemed to be with Sass. Recalling how he'd reacted when he first laid eyes on Lesilee, he understood the American's attraction to one so lovely. "I gather that you somehow know our American correspondents, Kristopher. I see that no introductions are necessary."

"You're right, Gregoire. I only met Lesilee today at Le Bistro de la Gare, but Sass and I met a long time ago. I must say that both were intriguing first meetings." He smiled broadly, marveling at Sass's fabulous golden-brown coloring. If only he could get her to listen to the voice of reason . . .

Sass was still in shock from seeing Kristopher again—so soon. As he lifted her hand, kissing the back of it, she nearly fainted dead away at his feet, her nerves frayed beyond repair.

Kristopher looked concerned when she nearly swooned. "Sass, are you ill?"

Sass was totally embarrassed by her adolescent reaction to the man who possessed deadly good looks, infinite charisma . . . and a lying, cheating heart. "No, Kristopher, I'm fine. I was just surprised to see you again. If I had taken the time at lunch to find out why you were here in Paris, I wouldn't feel at such a disadvantage. I should've known it had to do with your photography."

Sass saw that Gregoire and Lesilee were getting a big kick out of her embarrassment and at Kristopher's obvious pleasure at seeing her again. She fought the urge to pull a face at them.

Kristopher couldn't believe his good fortune in finding Sass again. He recalled being overwhelmed when he'd heard her name being mentioned in conjunction with a visit to the station. Although he'd learned that she was coming to Paris with a former American correspondent, Lesilee Taft, no one seemed to know the exact date and time; just that the visit was to occur within the next two weeks. "You don't need to be embarrassed. I'm glad it happened like this. Maybe this way you can feel more comfortable being around me again. We've always had so much in common and we do have a lot to catch up on."

Having formed a devious plan, Sass smiled. "Your comments have been very generous. I'd like to take you up on the dinner invitation offered earlier. That is, if it's still open."

Lesilee was surprised, but certainly pleased, at Sass's sudden change of heart. Kristopher's eyes weren't large enough to contain his excitement.

"Mademoiselle Stephens, of course the offer still stands. I'm eager to spend the evening getting to know you all over again." He kissed the back of each of her hands.

Sass blushed, feeling as though a cloud had somehow settled under her feet. "The feeling is mutual." Her smile was innocently flirtatious, but she had other things in mind for Monsieur Chandler. Promising herself to take advantage of being with this tall, dark, lethally handsome man while in Paris, she vowed to lose the horrible memories he'd given her within those sparkling sea-green eyes of his. Then she'd leave him high and dry, just as he'd left her.

Smiling broadly at Sass, Kristopher somehow knew his heart would leave Paris when she did. Hopefully, he would have the good fortune to steal hers again before she returned home. He found himself unable to take his eyes off the beautiful woman who still deeply intrigued him.

While taking the women around the offices to meet the rest of the staff, Gregoire took pleasure in making the introductions. Lesilee knew many of the staff members, but it was a treat for Sass to meet everyone. All of the employees were outwardly friendly and several of them offered to take Sass under their wing to show her how things ran in their part of the office.

At Kristopher's suggestion, the foursome split up. Personally, he showed Sass all the different departments throughout the building, patiently explaining what he'd learned about each department's function as they strolled along. Sass appeared fascinated by his every word and gesture, as she had so many years ago. But her pain would keep her wary of his indelible charms.

More than an hour later, when Kristopher finally led Sass back to Gregoire's private office, they found the couple catching up on old times. Gregoire greeted them warmly, inviting them into the conversation.

Finding herself intent on their every word, Sass thought both men were a pleasure to converse with. Both were quite knowledgeable on a variety of subjects. Regarding the media, Gregoire knew what it took to make it in the exciting world of television. With dedication and hard work, he'd worked himself upward from the news desk to his present position. He also spoke five different languages.

Chandler didn't give much information about his personal or business background, but he didn't need to. Sass knew everything there was to know about him. Having traveled the globe shooting everything in his wake with his expensive equipment, he was also fluent in many languages. Sass certainly knew that he was in tune with what went on in his own company, a very upscale photography and modeling studio. Recalling how his employees had held him in high esteem, she also remembered that he'd treated his staff with the same utmost respect.

Inside their quietly decorated suite at the comfortable Frederique Hotel, the two women sat on their beds chatting away. While going over the day's activities, they eagerly planned the itinerary for their two-week stay in Paris.

Sass curled her legs up under her. "I can't believe

Kristopher is working there at the Paris station on a temporary assignment. At only thirty years old, he already possesses wealth untold. Though very well educated, he was a self-starter in the photography business."

Lesilee pushed her tawny-brown hair away from her small, rounded face. "Sounds to me like he's a very savvy businessman. I got the impression early on that he was a man of means, even before I knew who he was. His superbly tailored suit of clothing and that gorgeous tan of his were somewhat of an indicator. Having lived here for several years, I can usually spot the elite right off, especially our countrymen." Her ebony eyes had a way of expressing themselves without any help from her generous mouth.

Sass scowled, looking a bit worried. "Lesilee, I'm horribly uncomfortable with my decision to have dinner with him." Lesilee gave her a questioning look. "It's just that our past is so torrid. There's so much I haven't told you about our rocky relationship, things I'm still so devastated by. How do I back out of this complicated situation without losing face?"

Lesilee dismissed Sass's concern with the wave of her hand. "Sass, I'm sure you're making too much of this. It's only dinner. I'm sure you're not thinking of falling back into bed with him, though I can certainly see why you'd want to. He's quite a looker . . . and that athletic body of his could set a woman's soul on fire, not to mention her bed. The man has practically insisted on spending time with you. If it's bothering you that much, you should tell him when he arrives this evening. It looks to me as though he's desperate to redeem himself."

"I doubt that, but I guess I'll go forward with our plans. We have so much unfinished business between us. That's probably why I haven't been able to move on with my life. About Gregoire, he's really drop-dead handsome. His coloring looks like it's quite deep despite his tan."

"It is. There are a lot of mixed French in this country. Gregoire is one of them. Unlike in America, where you're This-American or That-American, if you're born in France, you're simply French. In fact, America is the only country I know of that labels its citizens that way. Gregoire proudly lays claim to his French and African ancestry."

Sass's sepia eyes widened. "I got the impression that something very heavy is going on between you two. Am I right?"

Lesilee's eyelashes fluttered. "You're right. Gregoire and I had quite a romance going on when I lived here. He's the most romantic man I've ever encountered. I felt the old sparks come alive the second he touched me. He felt it, too. I'm looking forward to spending the evening with him. I'm glad you accepted Kristopher's invitation. I wouldn't have gone out with Gregoire otherwise. I meant to tell you more about Gregoire ages ago, but you know how busy it's been at the television station since you started working there. We've barely had time to breathe."

Blushing, Sass shook her head. "I still can't believe I accepted Kristopher's invite. I'm having a hard time believing he's here in Paris, period. Running into him was a total shock to my system."

Smiling, Lesilee looked at Sass over the rim of her water glass. "You really surprised me when you brought dinner up, but I was thrilled at you for showing such sass. No pun intended."

Sass sighed. "Kristopher is still the only man in the world who can say my name with such raw passion. When I heard him say it today, I felt an incredible heat wave rush right through me. His lips seemed to gently caress my name as it rolled off his tongue. But . . ."

Lesilee cut her eyes sharply as she interrupted Sass. "There's that forbidden word again! Every time you say 'but,' in reference to Kristopher, you're going to have to pay me five dollars. And I hope I don't make a dime off you." Sass got a faraway look in her eyes as the tears threatened to flow. "Sass, let it go. I know it still hurts. We're on the other side of the world now—and I know the source of your pain is here also. Despite all of that please try to have a good time during our vacation. You owe it to yourself."

Sass blinked back the burning tears. "I'm sorry, Lesilee. I'm not going to ruin this vacation for either of us. As of right now, I won't use that word again. And I'll try very hard not to think of the hurt that he's caused me for the rest of our vacation." *But I'll never forget it.*

Lesilee's smile came across the room to caress Sass gently. "Good! Now let's go put on our finery so we'll be ready when those two sexy men come a'calling." As Sass stood up and affected a believable swoon, they both dissolved into laughter.

Feeling refreshed from their showers, the two women dressed carefully, with much enthusiasm. Sass chose to wear a sexy, black crepe dress, with the flaring hemline ending slightly above the knee. The low-cut neckline hugged her shoulders. Brushing all of her heavy, sandy-brown hair to one side, she secured it in place with decorative pins. She then lightly applied foundation and blush to her nearly flawless golden-brown skin. Looking into the mirror, she saw that the sparkle had begun to return to her sepia eyes, hoping it would still be there by the time she left Paris. It certainly beat the haunted look she'd worn for the past few years.

Lesilee looked chic in an elegant black dinner suit embellished with gold braiding. The double-breasted six-button jacket had braided gold scroll detailing on its peaked collar and pocket flaps. With a slit up the right side, the skirt fell below her lower calf. Both women wore elegant gold earrings in their ears and stylish black pumps on their feet.

Smiling smugly, Sass whirled herself around in front of the mirror. "We are stunning! Gregoire has no idea of what he's getting himself into. You look ravishing, my lovely sister!"

Lesilee grinned widely. "Gregoire knows all right. Many Frenchmen have a thing for American women. They often seek their company out whenever the opportunity presents itself. If you decide not to see Kristopher past tonight, you'll surely find out."

"I already feel sought out. Kristopher has never had any problems making his intentions known. If it's romance he's looking for, he's going to be sorely disappointed. I'm still way too vulnerable for that. Thus far, I haven't been able to be romantic with anyone else since our breakup." Sass successfully curbed the urge to mention the damaging hurt he'd brought to her.

"As you said, I don't know your entire history with him, but I think Kristopher's charming. If he's half as romantic in nature as Gregoire, you're in for an electrifying evening, Sass Stephens. Keep an open mind. You owe it to yourself to at least find closure with him."


Soberly contemplating the happenings of the earlier hours of the day, Kristopher stood at the door of Sass's hotel room. The fact that she had agreed to have dinner with him had surprised him as much as it had thrilled him. But he couldn't take her decision lightly. He couldn't risk coming off as too confident. Confident, he wasn't; at least where this courageous woman was concerned. He had caused Sass undue, unforgivable, pain. Therefore, trying to win her heart back wasn't going to be an easy task. In no way could he act cocky or too sure of himself. If he knew Sass the way he thought he did, she wasn't going to let him off the hook at the drop of a hat. In fact, she may never let him off the hook. That was a grave concern for him.

A knock came on the door just as Lesilee finished her statement about Kristopher. Sass felt nervous as she watched Lesilee float over to the door with the sort of confidence she had often prayed for.

*"Bonsoir, Kristopher!* Please come in. You're looking quite handsome."

Dressed in a fashionable black dress suit, Kristopher's slate-gray tailored dress shirt hugged his gorgeously tanned neckline. His gleaming white teeth and healthy mocha skin color created the perfect picture of health. Sass sucked back a gasp of sheer pleasure.

His smile shone radiantly. *"Bonsoir, Lesilee. Vous êtes très aimable."*

Lesilee smiled back. "I'm not very kind, Kristopher, just very honest."

His eyes searched the room for Sass. His breath caught when he saw the enchanting glint in her sepia gaze, hoping it was meant for him. "Sass Stephens, you're even more beautiful than the famed Mona Lisa."

Sass found herself blushing like crazy. The melodic, fluent way in which he'd spoken French had caused her heart to tremor. *"Merci, Kristopher.* And I agree with Lesilee. You look very handsome. Would you like to have a seat?" She found it hard to be so polite, but she couldn't effectively execute her plans for him if she didn't come across as sincere.

His long legs carried him across the room easily, gracefully. Before sitting down on the oyster-white brocaded sofa, he kissed Sass on both cheeks, just one of the many French customs he'd adopted. He'd been in

France for nearly two years and it felt like home to him. In fact, he was considering moving there and opening up an international modeling agency.

"Lesilee, I hope I haven't intruded upon your time with Sass, but I've been looking forward to having her company for the evening. I'd be honored if you and Gregoire would be my guests, as well."

*"Merci,* Kristopher, but Gregoire has already made reservations for us at Jules Verne. I'm sure you know how hard it is to get reservations there. He made them weeks ago to ensure us a wonderful dining spot."

"It's only one of the most popular dining spots in Paris. The glorious panoramic view leaves one feeling out of touch with reality. Gregoire has made an excellent choice. Perhaps we can get together another time." Although Kristopher had made the offer, what he really wanted was to be alone with Sass. He felt rather relieved that the other couple had already made plans.

Kristopher got to his feet. Removing Sass's wrap from her hand, he carefully draped it around her shoulders. "Sass, are you ready to go?"

"Yes, Kristopher. Quite ready." *Readier than you can ever imagine.*

Spotting the chauffeur driven silver Rolls Royce awaiting its passengers at the entry of the hotel, Sass fought hard to hide her excitement. The look of sheer pleasure in her eyes, however, was a dead giveaway. Kristopher felt both excited and encouraged by it. As the chauffeur opened the car door for them, Sass felt exhilarated with the prospect of finally bringing closure to their very painful relationship. In time, she hoped she'd have all the answers to her many burning questions; like who was the woman in his apartment the night she'd come there to find him with nothing on but a bathrobe. And why he'd run out on her at a time when she'd needed him most.

On the way to the restaurant Kristopher inquired of her family's health. Sass told him that everyone was fine. The youngest of three daughters, Sass was born to Jason and Amantha Stephens, both retired schoolteachers. She then talked a little about her two sisters, Staci and Stephanie, both registered nurses, and their husbands, Gerald and Eugene, all of whom Kristopher had met. Staci and Eugene Roberts lived in the same neighborhood as Jason and Amantha. Stephanie and Gerald Jackson lived in a new housing development only a few miles from Sass's apartment complex.

Sass beamed. "As you already know, my sisters and I are very close. Despite our age differences people still ask if we're triplets. We still hate to admit to each other that we're nearly exact replicas. Not too much has changed since you last hung out with us. Without discussing what we're going to wear, when we go out or plan to meet somewhere, we still end up dressing alike. We still have similar tastes." *Except in men. They weren't involved with cowards.*

Both of her sisters had married wonderful, loving, very spiritual men. She was the only one who'd come out on the losing end of a serious relationship. Her parents' marriage was also filled with love and respect. Jason and Amantha still adored each other after thirty-five years of matrimony. Her relationship with Kristopher had only lasted a short time, but the deeply embedded emotional scars she carried would surely last forever.

"Now that I've told you so much about me, most of which you already knew, I'd like to hear a little about you and what goes on in your day to day life here in Paris."

"Sass, I could never know enough about you. As for me, I'm no longer one of my favorite subjects. I've been quite successful all of my life so people tend to think I'm bragging. A braggart I'm not. The most interesting parts about me are merely my accomplishments."

Sass grinned. "Oh, I somehow doubt that. I know of your glowing accomplishments, but I also know that you're a very interesting man." *Interesting beyond comprehension, my dear man, and not to be trusted.*

He touched his finger to her chin briefly. "In that case, perhaps I could rummage up a few new things to tell you about myself. Where should I begin?"

"How about what it's been like living in a country as magnificent as this one for close to two years?"

"Now that's a subject I could ramble on about for ages . . ."

# Two

As Sass and Kristopher arrived at The Laurent, one of the most refined restaurants in the city, she noticed right away his familiarity with the staff. Though too polite to ask, she couldn't help wondering if he'd brought other dates here. She then asked herself why she should care.

Standing tall and proud, Kristopher guided Sass through the restaurant, his arm draped loosely around her slender waist. Sass's eyes filled with wonder at the indescribable beauty of the place, gleaming even brighter as they took in the magnificent crystal chandeliers and silver candelabras. Marble pillars glowed in the soft lighting, ceiling-to-floor windows looked out onto illuminated shrubbery in the surrounding park, and live piano music could be heard drifting gently through the spacious areas.

By the way Kristopher was received, as they were escorted to a very private section of the restaurant, Sass saw that the employees were aware of his prestige. This very accomplished man had a definite presence about him, had a way of walking into a room like he owned it, a way of turning heads. Unwittingly or wittingly, his demeanor commanded respect.

Seated in a cozy alcove of the elegant restaurant, Kristopher stared straight into Sass's eyes. The sadness resting there disturbed him. Not knowing how to inter-

pret her mood, his smile was sympathetic as he covered
her hand with his. "Sass, is this place not to your liking?"

"This place is perfect! What in the world would make
you think I didn't like it?"

He tilted his head to one side. "You suddenly seemed
so sad. Your eyes are devoid of the sparkle they carried
earlier." He hoped the past memories weren't responsible for her sorrow.

*"Je regrette beaucoup, Kristopher,"* came her softly spoken
apology. "I was thinking of another place in time. Please
forgive me."

He smiled gently. "Your French is very good, but may
I have the pleasure of ordering for you? I've dined here
many times and I know what'll give your taste buds divine pleasure."

Smiling back, Sass nodded. "I'd love to have you order
for me. I trust your excellent taste." *And that's all.* "As for
my French, I know a little, but I plan to learn as much of
this poetic language as I can. When I studied the language, I was surprised to find that there were no
contractions. I guess that's one of the things that makes
English so hard for others to learn."

"Languages derived from Latin don't have contractions. Otherwise, it would be very difficult to conjugate
the verbs. I just started to use contractions again when
I'm speaking English, now that I've mastered French.
I've spoken a lot of the native language over the past
year and a half." Without taking his eyes off Sass, he summoned the waiter with a wave of his hand.

Sass listened intently as he spoke to the waiter in the
native tongue. His words carried such a melody, making her easily understand why French was referred to as
one of the romance languages. Throughout Kristopher's
exchange with the waiter, Sass carefully studied his dark,
riveting profile. Though extremely good looking, the

unfamiliar maturation he wore was what held her intrigue. Something about him had definitely changed. He seemed more humble.

Finished with the waiter, Kristopher turned his attention back to the woman who could still make his heart croon. "What plans have you made for your stay in Paris?"

Sass's eyes danced with excitement. "I plan to see all the famous landmarks and I'd also like to take a trip to the French Riviera. Lesilee is very familiar with the country since she used to live here. She plans to show me as much of France as we can cram into two weeks."

He couldn't help noticing how the flickering candlelight matched the flicker in her sheer brown eyes. Each time she smiled, he felt bewitched. "I took the liberty of booking us into one of the livelier night spots after dinner. A place that you won't want to miss out on."

Sass lowered her sweeping lashes to hide regret. "I hope you don't mind, but I think I'd like to return to the hotel after dinner. I'm exhausted and jet lag is also starting to kick in." Awaiting his response, nervously, she played with her napkin.

His eyes fell softly on her face. "I do mind, very much. But I understand. I hope you'll allow me to show you some of the city during your stay. There are so many exciting places off the tourist route. Very few travelers are fortunate enough to experience such secret treasures."

His eyes felt like a soft cloud against her skin, making her face feel flushed. "I can't promise anything right now, Kristopher. I don't want to be tied down with schedules and commitments during my vacation. However, I'll give your offer every consideration."

A curious expression settled in his eyes. "Very well, Sass. I'll be hoping to hear from you on the matter. Do you plan to come back to the television station?"

Sass shrugged her shoulders. "Not unless Lesilee feels

the need to do so. She wanted me to see the station and she wanted to see Gregoire again, her dear friend. The station is really something else. It seems that you've made quite an impression on everyone there."

"I hope so. How do you like your job at Los Angeles Broadcasting Systems?"

"I love it! I've been working there as a full-time employee for almost two years. I finally earned my degree in communications. I interned at LABS and was offered a job immediately after I graduated. Right now I work a lot behind the scenes, but I hope to land a job as an entertainment correspondent one day. I love the dazzle of Hollywood. I'd do almost anything—that is, within reason—to be able to interview Denzel Washington. The man has a presence like no other." *No other man besides you,* she mused with a smile, wishing she could completely surrender herself to his exotic charms and outrageous good looks. If only they were meeting for the very first time . . . As the waiter appeared with their meals, Sass abruptly ended her thoughts.

Entrees of tender veal and chicken bathed in saffron butter sauce were placed before them. Rice pilaf and fresh vegetables, steamed in a delicate wine sauce, accompanied the main entree. For dessert Kristopher ordered *reine de Saba,* a delicious chocolate fudge–like cake with English custard.

The meal was devoured in complete silence, yet Kristopher could see by Sass's expressive face how much she enjoyed her food. He'd bet his fortune that her lips were still as delicious as the sinfully tasty meal they dined on. His heart pounded every time she licked them.

Sass laughed. "You were right. The food was divine. I'm going to have to be very careful with my diet. A person could gain weight just by looking at these delightful dishes."

He seemed amused by her comment. "I'm glad you're pleased. The French diet is quite different from ours. Since they eat a lot of heavy sauces and creams, plenty of exercise is required to keep the fat at a minimum. I work off rich food with my avid jogging."

"It's true that our diets are quite different, but the African-Americans' diet is even more loaded with calories. With my father being from the South, I was raised on a lot of southern dishes." She sounded breathless, hating herself for it. Cautiously, she dared to look into his eyes, hoping not to be affected by their beauty. She was immediately transformed, deeply intrigued.

Folding his hands, he placed them on the table, never batting an eye. "I'm sure you haven't forgotten how much I used to enjoy eating your father's cooking." He smiled mischievously. "I don't know how you could forget that I got hooked on his black-eyed peas, collards and cornbread. Jason Stephens definitely knows how to throw down in the kitchen."

"No, I hadn't forgotten. You did everything but lick the plate clean." He laughed heartily at this. Sass still found his deep laughter captivating, downright seductive.

A look of understanding blazed in his eyes. "Is that why you always seemed so embarrassed after I finished eating? I often wondered why you had such a funny look on your face when we ate together. Now I know why. Apparently I'd embarrassed the hell out of you."

"Let me assure you, you didn't embarrass me one bit. I was just amazed by such a healthy appetite. It was like you had a bottomless pit for a stomach. You ate like that all the time, not just at my parents' house." *I saw everything about you through my heart, back then. The eyes of the heart are always blinded by love; completely blinded to treachery at its best.*

"I don't know if I've ever told you this, but my great-grandfather was West Indian, via the Motherland. My grandmother taught my mother to cook a lot of spicy Caribbean style dishes, but I prefer southern food, good old soul food." Frowning, he looked closely at Sass. "Are you sure you're okay?"

Sass nodded. "I'm fine. Why do you ask?"

"You don't seem very comfortable with me. You also looked scared."

"I guess I'm a little shocked at us sitting here together like this. It's been a long time since we've seen one another, let alone go out on a date. There's so much history between us, but I'm not trying to deceive you. Being with you may take a little getting used to, but I'll be okay."

"Lovely Sass, I don't believe you're capable of deceit. You've always been pure at heart. I'm going to hate for the evening to end. I'd hoped the night wouldn't end and that we could welcome in the sunrise from the magnificent view from the roof of the high-rise I live in." As her eyes blinked incessantly, he saw the same sadness he'd seen earlier. Not only did it disturb him; it nearly broke his heart. "Sass, did I say something to upset you?"

Momentarily, she looked distracted. "I've heard similar words from you before. They turned out to be words of insincerity. Kristopher, I have to be honest with you. I'm still trying desperately to completely recover from our horrendous love affair. Though it's been over for a long time, I've yet to come to terms with all the devastation my heart had to endure. We had a very complex relationship, which ended on an unpleasant note."

*My whole life's one huge complexity.* Her thoughts were even painful. In attempting a believable smile, she failed dismally. Her heart had simply forgotten how to laugh or smile.

"Your offer is so inviting, but it scares me to death. I

don't ever want to get hurt again . . . and certainly not by you. Since you're living here for the time being . . . and I live on another continent, I don't think it would be wise for us to engage in any romantic adventures."

Feeling her pain, he took her hand. "This assignment is only temporary. I still reside on the same continent as you, at least, the last time I checked." Hoping to lighten her somber mood, he laughed. "In fact, I'll be back home in Los Angeles in a month or so. But we're in Paris now. Why do we need to worry about what's so far into the future?"

She saw the sincerity in his eyes, but she also remembered seeing that very same look before. Sass tried to put her gloomy mood in check. "After all we've been through, why would you want to see me again?" *Pray tell, why in the world would I want to see you again?*

He smiled brightly. "Mademoiselle Stephens, I'm a man who knows exactly what he wants. At one year shy of thirty, I'm hardly a fickle adolescent. If it's any comfort to you, I've also been hurt by what transpired between us. I thought I'd never get over it. And I won't, until I can figure out why I let things happen the way they did. Don't you believe in trying to make amends for horrible injustices?" Reaching across the table, he placed his hand over hers.

As he squeezed her hand gently, Sass pulled away, as though his touch repulsed her. She immediately felt terrible for her outrageously rude reaction. But he understood it more than she'd ever realize. Regret flashed in her eyes. "I'm sorry, Kristopher. I'm still so vulnerable to your touch, to any man's touch. I used to believe that we could make amends, but that was long ago. I'd like to go back to the hotel now. I'm feeling really tired."

He frowned. "You apologize way too much. I understand your reaction. Your entire body probably feels like a huge open wound and that no amount of healing ointment can soothe the gouging pain. If it was within my power to heal your heart, I would, but only you can cure those open gashes." He decided to risk another stab at intimacy. Tilting her chin slightly, he placed an airy kiss on her full lips. "I can only help you through the transition."

She touched his face ever so gently. "We can't do this. Ever."

Her comment hurt. "I understand how you feel. *Voulez-vous faire une promenade?*" he asked, testing her French skills, wondering if she'd understood his question.

She grimaced. "I'm afraid you're going to have to translate that last comment for me. However, I did understand the word 'walk'."

"I asked if you'd like to take a walk. The gardens here are breathtaking. If only for a short time, I feel that you need to have your breath stolen away."

"*Merci.*"

"*Pas de quoi, Sass.*"

She had never before heard 'you are welcome' sound so seductive. *If it'll heal the pain, please, by all means, take my breath away.* As he touched a sensuous kiss into her palm, her inner thighs trembled. "I'd love to take a walk in the garden, Kristopher."

Her acceptance of his offer lit a fire in his eyes. Spreading like a firestorm, the heat from his eyes warmed Sass's broken heart. "I'll take care of the check now." When Kristopher summoned the waiter back to the table, he appeared at his side within seconds. "*S'il vous plait apportez-nous l'addition.*"

Sass understood that he had asked for the check, happy she'd taken the short course in conversational French. Once he'd signed the check, he stood, pulling Sass's chair out. Tucking her arm in his, they strolled from the restaurant and out into the romantically lit park.

Sass had a wonderful vision of what the Garden of Eden must be like as they strolled through the illuminated park. She felt so much peace here. Her soul had been restless for so long. Having already tasted the bittersweet fruit from the Tree of the Knowledge of Good and Evil, she wondered if she'd see the Tree of Life here in the garden. That would be a welcoming site, a comforting one.

A few minutes into the walk Kristopher stopped abruptly and turned to face his companion. Placing both of his hands on her shoulders, he gazed into her starlit eyes. "You're as beautiful as the midnight sun." He pointed to the silver moon. "You don't deserve to be unhappy. I don't know how I could've broken your heart the way I did. I wasn't worthy of you back then." He slid his forefinger down the side of her face. "You were too young to have to endure so much pain. I was just a little over twenty-one when my heart was broken to pieces, but by an older woman. The heart heals slowly when we're young. As we get older and grow in our wisdom, the heartaches will get much, much easier."

Trying hard to hide her anguish, Sass frowned. "I don't want it to get easier. I just want it to never happen again. Perhaps my heart is different from yours, Kristopher. I don't believe it will ever fully heal." Tears stung her eyes.

Taking out a handkerchief, he dabbed at her watery eyes. "Don't cry, Sass. No man is ever worth your tears, especially me. I'm the one responsible for them. Tears should be saved for joyous and passionate occasions." Pulling her closer to his lean body, he gently directed her head onto his chest. Slowly, cautiously, he wrapped his arms around her.

The tension she felt began to melt away as she relaxed under his touch. When unexpected images from the past swooped down before her, she tried to pull away from his loving embrace, startling him in the process.

As he regained his calm, he only held her tighter.

"Don't pull away. I won't bring further harm to you. Everyone needs to feel warmth and protection at one time or another. I'm only offering you a bit of comfort," he whispered against her cheek. Feeling the coldness of her face, he relaxed his hold on her long enough to remove his jacket and place it around her shoulders. "Are you cold?"

She nodded. "I'm a little cold but also very tired. Will you take me home now?" She really didn't want their tender moment to end. It was crazy, but she somehow felt safe and secure in his powerful arms, arms that now seemed to possess divine healing powers.

He pressed his lips to her temple. "The car is out in front waiting for us. I hope I didn't offend you. I don't intend to bring you a moment of unease."

She gave him her brightest smile. "You've been a perfect gentleman, but the time difference is catching up with me. I haven't slept since I deplaned at Charles de Gaulle early this morning. Lesilee is probably worried about me, as well."

His eyes grew sympathetic. "I can see that you're tired. But if I know Gregoire, he and Lesilee will be out the entire night. He loves the nightlife. And Paris is always alive and jumping until dawn."

On the drive to the hotel, Sass fell asleep. Lifting his arm, Kristopher gently slipped it around her shoulders, bringing her head against his chest. As he lightly traced her lips with his finger, the urge to kiss her was almost demanding. She looked like a small child who had lost her way. But he was the one responsible for her pain. He had to have been a lunatic to hurt her so deeply. Sass had needed a real man to love her, and he couldn't help hoping that she'd one day bestow the honor on the man he'd become. Although they'd been apart for a long time, he'd never been able to release her memory from his heart and soul. If he had his way, she would always be a part of him, forevermore.

As the Rolls Royce came to a smooth halt in front of the hotel, Kristopher awakened her with gentleness. "We're at your hotel, Sass. Get your things. I'll see you safely inside."

Her eyes opened slowly and she shook her head. "That's not necessary. I can make it alone." She sounded drowsy and her eyelids drooped heavily.

His brow creased. "In France, a gentleman always sees the lady to her door. You're in another country. That's the way it's always done here . . . and should be done at home."

She opened her mouth to object, but he quickly placed his mouth over her lips, quieting her protest. The kiss was slow, tantalizing. Genuinely surprised to find herself relaxing her mouth against his, she savored the moment. The taste of him was as sweet as the chocolate cake they'd had for dessert. His lips felt as soft as a whisper on her mouth.

As she entangled her fingers in his thick honey-brown hair, he moaned. Her touch had somehow reached right through to his soul. Briefly, he held her away from him, piercing her composure as he united his eyes with hers. His seductive gaze held her spellbound. Crushing his mouth against hers with an almost ferocious hunger caused her to gasp with pleasure and fear. Her knees nearly turned to water as her breathing came fast and shallow. To lose control now was to once again lose the battle to him. That couldn't happen now or ever.

Feeling that the situation was spiraling out of control, she placed her hands on his chest and gently pushed him away. "I've got to go now. Thank you for a lovely evening."

Before he could respond, she was out of the car and

halfway into the hotel. Though he desperately wanted to run after her, it would only upset her and possibly ruin his chances of ever seeing her again. She was much too vulnerable for him to put any pressure on her. He had two weeks to try and at least attempt to make amends for breaking her heart . . . and risk getting his own crushed. But just a few minutes of time spent in her intriguing company would be well worth it. All he needed was just a little more time to make her see that he was a changed man.

Sass let herself into the dimly lit room. Closing the door behind her, she gave her emotions their freedom. Strangely enough, she felt sorry for not letting him see her inside. That's the least she could've done after he showed her such a great time. She felt a tad disgusted.

Even though it seemed he'd changed, she didn't think she could ever trust him with her heart again. So sure she had grown totally immune to his charming ways, she hadn't meant for things to go so far. Needing him like she once did scared her to death. She may have gotten away from him tonight, but it frightened her to know that she still needed his comforting ways more than she'd ever thought possible.

Sass still felt uncomfortable with all the difficulties from their past. She hadn't told Kristopher too many personal things about her life after they were last together. She hadn't mentioned Justin on purpose, the only male who had exclusive rights to her heart. In her mind, this was the last date she and the unforgettable Kristopher Chandler would ever have.

In the wee hours of the morning Lesilee let herself into the darkened suite. After turning on the light, she glanced over at Sass, immediately noticing the unrest on her friend's face. She also found it strange that Sass was still dressed in the clothes she'd worn on her date.

Lesilee knelt down in front of Sass's bed and shook her gently.

Moaning, Sass began to stir. She finally looked up and smiled weakly at Lesilee.

"Sass, you need to get into your night clothes. You're ruining that gorgeous dress."

Sass sat on the edge of the bed and began to remove her pantyhose. "I was too exhausted physically and emotionally to undress. I barely made it up to the room. How was your evening?"

As Lesliee quickly stripped out of her clothing, her smile was like a bright beam of light.

"It was fantastic! Gregoire has not lost a drop of his romantic nature. He makes me feel so wanted, so desirable. I can't believe the spark between us is as strong as it was in the very beginning. I'm not sure anymore why I decided to leave Paris." Lesilee sighed deeply. "How was your evening with Kristopher?"

"It was pretty sensational, but when my insecurities set in, I cut the date short. He'd made plans for dancing and watching the sunrise from his apartment, but I couldn't get into it. I'm going to have to pay you five dollars after all, but I couldn't get the hurt Kristopher caused me out of my mind. I guess that makes it ten. But everything he said reminded me of the things he used to say. Oh, dear, I may as well go for broke. Kristopher has the same romantic spirit as before, but I'm not sure his morals are any different. I can't stop making the comparisons, especially with him acting like we've never been apart." *Oh, if only I could tell it all. If only I dared to reveal all the pent-up secrets.*

"Sass, you have it bad. Honey, I really feel for you. I

hope I never fall in love again, at least, not as deeply as you have. You remind me of how much it hurts. I can actually see how much you're hurting inside. Did Kristopher ever realize how much pain he'd caused you?"

Sass dug her heels in deep, determined not to cry over him ever again. "I think so, but I guess he just didn't care then. He's never really explained why he had a change of heart. He was so good to me at first. Then, all of a sudden, he changed. I was warned he'd probably hurt me, but I didn't listen. The times I felt strong enough to leave him, he wasn't trying to hear it. I can think of several times I wanted out, but my love for him was so strong I'd always give in. I was almost naive enough to think being with him again might chase all those bad memories away. I don't think anything can block them out. It still hurts like hell."

"I guess I shouldn't ask if you plan to see Kristopher again."

Sass shook her head vigorously. "Not if I can help it. I'm too vulnerable right now. I think he knows it, too. Even though he was so sweet tonight, I told him how uncomfortable I felt. He was more than understanding, but I fear that he'll turn out to be just like he was before." Sass felt so dispirited. "I know I shouldn't judge him by his past character flaws, but I do, harshly."

"Take a time out, Sass. Don't badger yourself anymore. Things have a way of working themselves out. Please don't turn him away until you have all your questions answered. Bringing closure could turn out to be your saving grace. Paris is one of the most romantic cities in the world. You still need to give it a chance to weave its magical powers over you."

Sass blew out a ragged breath. "The way I ran out on him, I doubt if he'd ever want to see me again, which is probably for the best. I'm such a coward around him.

His kiss may have left me trembling with desire, but it also scared me back to reality."

Amusement played around in Lesilee's eyes. "Don't put any money on it. He doesn't seem easily deterred. If I'm correct in my assessment, he *will* find a way to see you again."

Sass shrugged her shoulders. "Maybe so. But every time I've tried to get close to someone else I think of the pain that comes with falling in love. I was kissing him back tonight, but then I was reminded of all of our yesterdays. Instead of losing myself in his kisses, the way I wanted to, I ended up feeling his betrayal of me. I'm a one-man woman, yet I know with certainty that Kristopher isn't the right man for me. But he's the one and only man I've felt deep down in my soul." Sass buried her head into the pillow.

Lesilee felt deep concern for her friend. "Sass, it appears you're never going to get over the pain of yesterday."

Sass wiped her nose with a tissue. "My therapist said the same thing. I guess I don't want to forget any of the bad things, so as not to repeat them."

"From some of the things you've gone through, I have to wonder how you get through each day. I often wonder if I'd be as strong if it happened to me. I can easily see how you fell in love with the guy. According to the few accounts you shared with me, he really showed you what romance was all about. But it appears that he also deceived you in the worst way possible."

With thoughts of Gregoire pushing their way into her mind, Lesilee decided to change the subject. "To get us on a more pleasant note, Gregoire showed me an incredible evening. We went through all the old memories of the tender moments we once shared. This trip is going to bring a lot of joy to my withered soul. I've missed Gregoire more than I realized. He wants to take up where we left off, but I'm worried I'll run scared again. Like yours, Sass, my pain was unmanageable from a previous relationship. Even though I eventually got over it, the thought of it happening again is close at hand. But we're not in this beautiful city to think about the dark shadows of past . . . and I've somehow got to help you chase away yours."

Sass rolled her eyes. "I can't see that happening any time soon."

"Getting everything out in the open with Kristopher Chandler is a perfect solution to the problem. But you're going to have to let him in first. I know how awful it is to kiss someone without being able to forget all the pain they've caused you. Maybe that's the only way we know how to cope with our heartache. Paris is going to be good to us." *It has to be.* Lesilee didn't think Sass could live through another heartache, but she needed to face the past, head on.

When Sass didn't respond, Lesilee noticed that her dear friend had fallen off to sleep. Noticing the wet tears still visible on Sass's lovely face, Lesilee pulled the covers up over her brokenhearted comrade. After turning off the light, she slipped back into her own bed.


The two women slept late into the morning. Even then, they only awakened to the sound of the telephone. Lesilee sat on the side of the bed and picked up the receiver. *"Bonjour."* Lesilee sounded weary as she rubbed the sleep from her eyes.

*"Bonjour.* Kristopher Chandler here. Is this Mademoiselle Taft?" It had to be someone other than Sass. He'd never forget the sound of her beautiful voice.

"It's Lesilee, Kristopher. *Comment allez-vous?"* Her French was perfect.

Sass stirred when she heard Kristopher's name and heard Lesilee ask him how he was doing. Sitting up in the middle of the bed, Sass looked inquisitively at Lesilee.

*"Très bien, merci, et vous?"*

"I'm fine, Kristopher." The look in Sass's questioning eyes had caused Lesilee to switch to English so that she could follow the rest of the conversation without the difficulty of translating. Sass smiled, grateful that Lesilee had made the change.

"That's good to hear." Kristopher had followed Lesilee's lead in English. "How was your evening with Gregoire?"

Lesilee's eyes sparkled at the mention of Gregorie's name. "We had a glorious one. There's no other type of evening to have in Paris."

"You're so right!" There came a slight pause. "I'm afraid Sass didn't have a good time. I'd like to talk with her, but she may not want to. Do you think it's best that I don't pursue her?"

"I'll let you ask her that question, Kristopher. Hold on."

Sass shook her head wildly. Lesilee ignored her objections, stretching the phone out to her anyway. Reluctantly, Sass took it, shaking her fist at Lesilee. Sass then gave Lesilee a warm smile to soften the threatening gesture.

*"Bonjour, Kristopher."* Sass tried hard to sound cheerful.

*"Bonjour, Mademoiselle Stephens.* It's good to hear your voice. You disappeared pretty quickly last night. You left me feeling bewildered and lonely."

Sass smiled. "I'm sorry, but I was feeling a little insecure."

"Do you want me to back off, Sass?" He held his breath as he waited for her response.

Sass was embarrassed by the question. Unsure of how to answer it, she crossed her legs under her, fidgeting in discomfort. "Kristopher, there's so much I haven't told you about myself. After you hear everything, you may not want to spend any more time in my company."

He laughed. "As long as you're not going to tell me you're a transvestite, I don't think there's anything you could say to change my mind about wanting to continue seeing you."

His statement drew the rose-petal laughter from deep within her throat. "I can assure you I'm not a transvestite! I'm one hundred percent woman. Other than taking my word for it, I don't have a clue how to convince you otherwise." *As if he didn't know that already.*

"I can think of a few ways for you to convince me. However, I'll keep my thoughts private for now." The memory of their hot, sensuous nights came with ease.

Sass began to enjoy their flirtatiously animated exchange. Drawing her knees up, she rested her head back on the pillow. "I won't insist on hearing your private thoughts, but there's so much new stuff that you don't know about me . . . and I'm not sure where to begin."

"Why don't you begin by letting me show you around the city today? We can discuss the things you want to then."

"Kristopher, I don't . . . know about . . . today. Lesilee and I have yet to finalize our plans for this morning." Sass looked at Lesilee with questioning eyes. When she motioned for her to accept the invitation, Sass still seemed somewhat reluctant.

"May I call you back shortly?"

"Of course. I'll be patiently waiting for your call. Sass, there are no strings attached to my offer. No strings whatsoever."

He called out his home phone number to her and she quickly scribbled it on a note pad. After hanging up the receiver, Sass threw her head back, covering her face with the pillow.

"Sass, what are you thinking?"

Slowly, Sass removed the pillow from her face. Lesilee saw the uncertainty flashing there in her eyes. "To be honest, I really don't know. It's the strangest thing I've ever encountered. I want to see Kristopher, but I'm very much afraid of him. He knows my heart so well. I won't be able to hide my feelings for him much longer. Revealing my heart to him again could prove disastrous for me."

"I understand what you must be feeling. But, girl, we're in Paris, one of the most romantic cities in the world! You need to start living each day as though it was your last! None of us are promised tomorrow . . ."

# Three

On this fine morning the Paris weather couldn't have been better. Busy readying herself for the date, Sass had accepted Kristopher's invitation, but only after much prompting from Lesilee. Lesilee and Gregoire had also accepted the invitation from Kristopher to accompany them. They'd decided on a tour of the city and an outdoor picnic for later in the afternoon.

Sass wore a fuschia-colored summer suit of pure linen. The cute ensemble consisted of tailored pleated shorts, and a fitted sleeveless jacket with four abalone shell buttons and flap pockets. As she stood before the mirror tending to her hair, she tightly braided a strip of natural rawhide leather through her long tresses, fashioning her hair into one thick plait.

Lesilee looked darling and quite comfortable in a domestic rayon challis yellow romper, printed with a soft blue floral. Three decorative buttons dotted the front yoke while the darts through the waist opened into relaxed, easy fitting legs.

Through with her own hair, at Lesilee's request Sass brushed her friend's hair back from her face until every strand was in place. After twisting a large portion of Lesilee's hair, she wrapped another thick section of hair around the rest of it. Sass finished Lesilee's casual style by sticking yellow-flowered pins all around the upper portion of the ponytail.

The chauffeur of the Rolls Royce whisked his passengers through the heavy and crazy Paris traffic destined for the Eiffel Tower. Pierre was a very interesting-looking person, but Sass wondered if he had a tongue. The only greeting she'd ever received from him was a curt nod, just before he'd promptly open the door with his white-gloved hand. A stout man who wore his gray uniform with pride, Pierre Gauthier's azure eyes carried an amusing twinkle and his rosy cheeks shined like new money. Pierre's height helped to disguise his slight obesity quite well.

Both Kristopher and Gregoire looked comfortable dressed in casual but popular name-brand clothes. Kristopher's emerald green Ralph Lauren polo sweater lent additional color to his sea-green eyes. Wearing crisply creased white pants that looked as though they'd been recently purchased, his overall appearance showed off his expensive taste in clothing.

Gregoire looked strikingly handsome dressed in loose fitting khaki slacks and a navy blue open-collared shirt. His burnished-brown hair was neatly combed. Amused, Sass watched his ebony eyes flirt madly with Lesilee's blue-black ones. In Sass's opinion, Gregoire was not as debonair as Kristopher, yet he was sophisticated. He possessed his own special persona.

Pierre pulled up to the curb and parked near the front entrance to the Eiffel Tower. Rapidly exiting the car, he opened the door to allow his passengers to disembark. Sass giggled inwardly as the chauffeur gave his usual curt nod.

Sass looked all around her in amazement, having a hard time believing she actually stood right in front of the famed Eiffel Tower. However, she seemed disappointed in its color. She'd always believed it was golden, rather than the smoky-black color it actually was. Still, she was impressed with the size and height of the magnificent structure.

Sass looked to Kristopher. "I always thought the Eiffel Tower was gold. But before I actually saw the Golden Gate Bridge in San Francisco, I thought it was gold, too."

Kristopher grinned. "Sass, everyone thinks it is golden, but it only reflects the gold color at night when it's lit up. There are three platforms from where we can see the city. On a clear day you can see many miles in any direction." As Kristopher explained things to Sass, Gregoire and Lesilee followed close behind.

Lesilee pointed up to the top of the tower. "Sass, Gregoire and I dined in the upper tier of the structure. There's an exclusive private elevator to reach the restaurant. We'll have to dine there before we leave. It's an experience one mustn't pass up. When you have an excellent conversationalist like Gregoire as your date, it can be a little taste of heaven." Gregoire kissed Lesilee softly on the mouth to show his pleasure at her compliments.

Sass's eyes glistened with excitement. "I can't wait! I bet dining at the top of the Eiffel Tower will be the highlight of my trip. That is, if I can stay conscious." Everyone laughed.

Kristopher's arm encircled Sass's waist innocently. She felt instant discomfort, but said nothing. "Not if I have my way," Kristopher responded. "The places I'd like to show you will leave you breathless and remain in your memory forever."

While chatting away, the foursome entered the spectator elevator and Kristopher selected the floor. When the car lurched forward as it made its ascent, Sass slightly swooned. Kristopher tightened his arm around her waist to steady her.

"In all my excitement, I forgot that I'm somewhat fearful of heights. I guess it's too late now. Since I wasn't afraid in a private plane, I thought this would be a piece of cake." She laughed nervously, silently praying that she wouldn't pass out.

Kristopher smiled sympathetically. "I'll take very good care of you, Sass. Just lean on me." He saw doubt on her face, which said, *you didn't take very good care of me before.*

Gregoire laughed. "Kristopher, if Sass is afraid of heights, taking her to the rooftop of your apartment is out of the question."

"Don't worry about me, Gregoire. I have an adventurous nature. I've found myself doing things I never thought I'd even think about, let alone try." *Like being here with him.*

Lesilee smiled warmly. "Once you get to know Sass, you'll see that she can be very daring indeed. She has surprised me so many times."

At the top of the tower, the bird's-eye view of Paris was magnificent. Sass felt like she did on the private plane ride that Kristopher had taken her on so long ago. Eagerly, she anticipated the rest of the tour and the remainder of her stay in Paris.

The next stop was the Arc de Triomphe located in the middle of Place Charles-DeGaulle. Sass learned from Kristopher that the landmark, the brawniest triumphal arch in existence, stood above the Tomb of the Unknown Soldier. The top of the arch offered another spectacular view of an amazing Paris.

At the Louvre Museum, the two couples entered through the glass pyramid designed by I. M. Pei. It stood seven stories over the subterranean Welcome Center. Inside the Louvre, Kristopher showed Sass the painting that reminded him of her. Though she saw very little resemblance to herself, she was gracious enough not to disagree with him. The woman in the painting was so stunning, Sass was flattered he'd put her in the company of such rare beauty.

Keeping Sass close to his side, Kristopher held her hand tightly. Patient and very articulate in explaining some of the history of France, Sass saw that he was quite knowledgeable about the most important and the unimportant, especially for someone who wasn't a native.

Located on a hill above the left bank of the Seine was Park Saint-Cloud. Designed by Le Notre, the park offered them yet another fantastic view of Paris. There, they lunched on finger sandwiches of different meat fillings, fresh fruits and cheese. Gregoire had brought along a fine French wine for the group to drink, but only two sips of the wine put Sass in a silly mood.

"The meal was very tasty," Lesilee complimented. "Now I'm ready for a deadly French pastry. Kristopher, do you think you could get us into Jules Verne later? The desserts there are to die for." Lesilee licked her lips. Everyone laughed as she rolled her eyes to the back of her head with a divine expression.

Kristopher threw his head back in laughter. He kissed Sass's hair before he stood up. "I believe Mr. Laurent has quite a bit of pull at Jules Verne. Excuse me. I'll give him a call and see what arrangements I can make."

Sass watched his confident stride as he made his way back to the car. Wow, she thought quietly, her sepia eyes snapping shots of his firm, superbly rounded derriere. *The brother still has the body of an athletic wonder. But has the condition of his roguish heart changed for the better?*

Amused by her friend's expression, Lesilee followed the direction of Sass's eyes. "Sass, you look as though you see something you like."

*"Chaud!"* Sass shook her hand out to stress just how *hot* she thought Kristopher's body was. Her companions laughed and Gregoire even blushed. A brief sadness suddenly touched Sass's eyes. She quickly warded off of her dark mood, scolding herself inwardly.

Gregoire noticed the odd look in Sass's eyes. "Sass, are you enjoying yourself so far?"

*"Oui, Monsieur Bedier.* So far your city is holding my heart prisoner and it doesn't seem to want to break free." Sass sounded breathless.

Gregoire laughed. "If you stick with Chandler during your stay, I can assure you that you'll have the experience of a lifetime. He's a premier entertainer."

"I'm sure of that." The underlying sarcasm in Sass's tone wasn't lost on Lesilee. "He certainly seems to know his way around all the Paris attractions. You'd think he was born and raised here," Sass continued.

Kristopher returned and confirmed the plans for having dessert at Jules Verne.

After the group herded into the car for the trip to Montmartre, Pierre guided the Rolls through the heavy traffic with ease, confident in his abilities to maneuver the large car in the safest manner possible.

"Montmartre is often referred to as the real Paris," Kristopher explained to Sass. "The streets are made of cobblestone. The area is also noted for the many artists' hangouts. It's surrounded by lovely squares. Place du Terte is the most picturesque."

As the group continued their walk through the narrow streets of Montmartre, Sass was terribly impressed with the old houses standing along the streets. A few minutes into the tour, much to her dismay, Sass had to go to the bathroom. Discreetly, she told Lesilee of her plight. Lesilee excused herself and directed Sass to a small nightclub close by.

Both women nearly gagged when they walked into the establishment. The smoke was quite thick and the smell of alcohol reeked on the air. Once Lesilee asked for the ladies' room in French, they were directed to the back of the joint. The jazz music that played sounded rather nice to Sass.

Sass nearly croaked when she saw what she had to do to use the toilet. A large, gaping hole stared up at her from the center of the floor. Sass looked at Lesilee in horror. Lesilee just laughed and shrugged her shoulders. Nature's urgent call wouldn't allow Sass to turn down the seedy accommodations. Frowning heavily, she positioned herself over the primitive hole. How ridiculous, she mused, scowling with certain displeasure.

The two women laughed about the bathroom incident all the way back to where they'd left their companions. The men couldn't help wondering what they found so amusing.

Kristopher raised a curious eyebrow. "Care to let us in on your amusement?"

Sass's face immediately flushed with embarrassment at his question.

Either Lesilee didn't catch the warning in Sass's eyes, or she chose to completely ignore it. "Sass just got acquainted with one of the city's oldest form of toilettes." Lesilee tried but failed to stifle her laughter.

If looks could kill, Lesilee would've met with an early demise. Unaware of Sass's distress over the situation, Gregoire joined Lesilee in laughter.

Kristopher was sensitive to Sass's embarrassment. Pulling her close to him, he kissed the tip of her nose. "Don't mind them. They have no tact," Kristopher whispered into Sass's ear. "You don't need to feel embarrassed with me."

"Don't worry, I'll have my revenge on Lesilee. We work together and hang out quite often. So I'm in no big hurry for payback."

Kristopher smiled down at her. "If there's anyway I can assist you, we can plot against both of them."

Suddenly, Sass realized she was beginning to feel somewhat comfortable with Kristopher. Standing on her tiptoes, she planted a kiss on his cheek. Her gesture surprised but pleased him thoroughly. "We'll have to find something devilish to do to them," Sass whispered.

Amused by her wicked expression, Kristopher smiled his approval of her plan.

The last stop on their tour was the Notre Dame cathedral. The beauty of the old cathedral caused tears to well in Sass's eyes as Kristopher gave her a history lesson about the cathedral she wouldn't soon forget. While staring up into the ceiling at the exquisite lighting fixtures, she saw the famed rose window, a spectacular vision of loveliness.

"The paintings and art objects of this cathedral are precious and rare," Kristopher said.

The group mounted the tower to see the bells. They stepped outside on the roof platform, where a view of the Seine and its bridges was in clear sight. Once the inside tour was over, they walked around the areas outside of the cathedral.

Though she tried desperately to hide it Sass was so tired. All she wanted to do was drop down to the nearest soft spot and slip into darkness. Instead, she rubbed her arms briskly, trying to keep herself somewhat alert.

Kristopher noticed the heavy droop of her eyes, amused by her failure to keep her eyelids open. "You *are* very tired." He kissed both of her lids. "We can go if you like. If we're going out tonight, you should get some rest." Too tired to object, she simply nodded. "Gregoire, Lesilee, Sass has had about all she can take for right now. Do you have any objections to us returning to the hotel?"

"You two go ahead. Lesilee and I will make our own way back. We'll meet with you at the restaurant at eight-thirty. Pierre doesn't have to pick us up. We'll take a cab there."

"*Au revoir.*" Kristopher waved his hand in farewell. Sass looked back at Lesilee for a fleeting moment, as if she wasn't sure about being alone again with Kristopher.


At the door of Sass's hotel suite, Kristopher used her key card to gain entry. Picking Sass up with ease, he carried her over to the sofa. Surprisingly, she didn't raise any objections. Positioning her comfortably in the center of the sofa, he dropped down next to her. Lifting her legs across his knees, he removed her shoes and began massaging her feet tenderly.

"That feels good." She closed her eyes and laid her head back against the soft cushioned sofa. She then willed herself not to think of the unpleasant parts of the past.

Kristopher nudged Sass. "Do you need any other pleasures?" His feigned French accent gently teased her ears.

Opening her eyes, Sass flashed him a brilliant smile. "Too numerous to count."

"What about this?" He brushed her lips lightly with his.

"That's nice." Surprised to find herself surrendering to his sweet advances, she sighed inwardly.

He seduced her ear with his tongue. "And this?"

Her murmurs came as soft as cotton and her eyes began to glaze over from his impassioned caresses. "That feels delicious, Kristopher. So gentle."

Not wanting her to run scared, he wrapped her up in his arms. Fervently, he searched her open mouth with his tongue. Pulling his face closer, she swallowed his sweet kisses, running nervous fingers through his honey-brown hair. Slowly, he unbraided her silky hair until it fell loose in his hands. Gripping her hair gently, he entwined his fingers in its thickness.

Kristopher pulled his polo sweater free from inside his slacks. Taking her hand, he slid it under his shirt and rested it against the hairy expanse of his muscular chest. With his hand closed tightly over hers, his other hand spread across her back and tenderly rubbed her tight muscles. He guided her hand over his chest, moving it in slow motion.

"Your touch is like a bonfire. It's burning its way into my soul. It feels wonderful," he whispered against her lips. "Trust me. I'll never again bring harm to your heart; never intentionally hurt you in any way. Please try to trust me again, Sass."

*Where have I heard that before?* She wanted to pull away, but the urgency for his intimate touch outweighed her desire to flee. She hadn't been touched this intimately in a very long time. In fact, she hadn't been touched like this period since Kristopher had left her.

"I don't know why, but I somehow believe you, Kristopher. Since my heart is already broken into a million pieces, I guess no more damage can be done to it, anyway."

He captured her eyes within the depth of his own. "If you'll let me, I'll help you put those pieces back together, permanently. They'll never break apart again." His heart became filled with the same sort of emotion he'd felt with her before. It felt so good, so right for them to be together like this again. "I promise you."

Having him so near frightened and thrilled her all at once. "That would truly be a miracle. I'm always so afraid my heart will remain broken."

He kissed her gently on the mouth. "No, Sass, not with me around to help it heal."

Pulling back from him, she looked up into his eyes. "I've only known broken promises from you. I wanted so much to believe that there was someone out there to love me unconditionally. Someone that can accept the unconditional love I was capable of giving."

Her eyes blazed with uncertainty. "I don't know if I can hope that way again. In my mind I've created so many visions of the way I thought love should be. At one time, you were at the very core of those imaginative creations. In fact, you were once the center of my universe."

He winced, exhaling a deep sigh. "I can't stand the pain in your eyes. I know I've been insensitive to you. By the look in your eyes, I understand why you believe I've hurt you beyond repair. I hope that you'll give me the chance to help your heart heal."

Expressionless, she shrugged her shoulders. "I don't know about all that, but you were very insensitive to me." *No, I will not get any deeper into this painful subject, not tonight.*

Kristopher knew they'd gotten onto a rocky path. Looking for a safer topic, he remembered what she'd said to him on the phone. "You mentioned earlier that there were some things I need to know about you. We both know you're not a transvestite, so do you care to share the rest?" He laughed in hopes of lifting the dark clouds from her eyes.

She laughed at his humor. Swallowing hard, she prepared herself for yet another painful rejection. Suspecting it to come soon after she told him the more personal details of her life, life after him, her heart began to tremble so hard she had to inhale deeply. "I have a child." She was unable to keep from smiling at just the thought of her precious bundle of joy, her darling baby boy. A sudden chill invaded her body as a sorrowful look crowded its way into her eyes.

Kristopher rubbed her arms, as though he could feel the coldness suddenly taking hold of her soul. He knew exactly what had turned her mood dark, but he wasn't going to explore that part of the past any further. "A boy or a girl? What's your baby's name?"

"I have a son, Kristopher. His name his Justin Brian. He lights up my world and makes me feel truly loved and needed. Watching him grow has brought me lots of joy." She instantly recalled how Kristopher had never wanted children, just another painful reminder of the past.

"I used to think that I didn't want children. But now that I have so much to offer one, I've thought about it a lot lately. How old is Justin?" The fact that another man had fathered a child with Sass made his heart wrench with grief. Thinking of what she'd already gone through with him hurt like hell.

She smiled at the way Justin's name rolled sweetly off his tongue. There was such tenderness in his voice when he'd called her child by name. "Justin will be four in a few months. My parents are keeping him while I'm away. I have a lady that comes in and cares for him when I'm working. I spend as much quality time with him as I can. We have lots of special places. There's a local pizza parlor that we love to go to and I can't leave out his love for playtime at McDonald's. I'm not crazy about the food there, but he's chicken nuggets insane."

The age of her child gave him a moment of deep concern. The time frame was definitely an issue for him even if she'd gotten involved with the new man right away.

"The story of my son is another chapter in the never-ending saga of Sass Stephens." She looked away, unable to bear the saddest memories of all. Memories of why he had left her so long ago was something she still couldn't accept.

He gently turned her face back to him. "Are you in love with Justin's father?"

"I've only been in love once, but I can't explain anything more than that. It's too complicated and too painful to discuss. Especially when someone is supposed to be on a joyous vacation. Trust me, it's not a happy story. My life wasn't a happy story until Justin came into it."

"I want to understand you much better than I did before. Maybe that'll come with time. Thanks for sharing it with me. Perhaps one day you'll trust me again. Sass, none of what you've told me changes my opinion of you. We all have something in our past that has caused us much unhappiness. I've never married, nor have I ever been pregnant, but you know I'm not free of blemishes. In fact, I'm far from being blemish-free. I'm the last person in the world who needs to judge someone."

Sass appreciated the humor in his statement once she finally realized he'd been trying to cheer her up. However, she didn't have the strength to reward him with laughter.

She touched his cheek for a brief second. "Kristopher, you've been understanding about this. Thank you for not judging me harshly."

He gave her a tight squeeze. "I never want to be harsh to you again. It's no longer in my nature to do so." Bringing her even closer to him, he draped his arm around her trembling shoulders. "I bet you're a wonderful mother. I can see in your eyes the love you have for your son. I hope I'll one day have the pleasure of meeting young Justin."

In the next instant, he glanced at his watch. Sass's heart fell. She felt so sure that he wanted to get away from her . . . and she couldn't blame him. The desire for kids was the one thing they'd never had in common.

That not-so-little revelation had later become the source of her deepest pain.

"I'm going to go now, but I'll be back at eight. Paris is waiting to be further introduced to the most beautiful and honest woman that I know."

Though he kissed her tenderly, Sass was sure she'd never see his handsome face again. Within seconds of the door clicking shut, Sass moved over to the bed and threw herself on top of the flowered blue bedspread. She looked around at the decor of the room, really noticing it for the first time. The wallpaper was done in the nuances of spring and the suite looked cheerful and quite comfortable. The well-maintained European furnishings offered a home-away-from-home like atmosphere, but did nothing to wash away her dark despair.

Sass saw a need to do some soul-searching, as she normally did when she was troubled. She loved this city, but there was one thing missing. Love. Lovers have been known to take this beautiful city by storm. Why did life have to be so unpredictable? It was truly unpredictable, especially when you hadn't yet learned to become the master of your own destiny.

Allowing her thoughts to take her completely over, she closed her eyes.

The only man Sass had ever been able to fully trust was her father. In fact, she'd become scared to death of men after her affair with Kristopher. He had earned her trust and respect and then he'd trashed both, yet she really couldn't be angry with him. She constantly asked herself why she was so forgiving to those who had hurt her deeply.

Anger and bitterness were not in her heart. There were times when she wished she knew how to be angry and bitter. She'd like to know exactly how revenge worked, how it felt not to be on the receiving end of it.

But what good would that do? Probably none, but it might be a lot more fun making other people miserable, rather than them causing her to feel so disconsolate.

Sass felt guilty about the intimacy that had just occurred with her and Kristopher, but she didn't understand why she had to feel that way. Why did kissing him back bring on such feelings of remorse, especially when she had welcomed his sweet mouth on hers? Was she really still in love with him? Since doubt existed, she needed to find out for sure. She owed it to herself to at least finally bring closure to this seemingly endless saga if nothing else. Besides, there was no future for her with anyone else until she did. If only she could make Kristopher Chandler hurt in the same way he'd devastated her.

No way was she going to let some evil force take control of her ever again. She didn't even remember all the unkind things she'd said or done to Kristopher in reaction to her pain. She had pretty much taken everything on the cuff, but her subconscious mind had taken her over, engaging in acts that had been totally out of character for her. Of course doing horrible things to others was out of character for her since she had such a gentle nature. She never thought she had a dark side, but she'd learned differently. She'd never forget the day she slapped him across his smug face for disrespecting her. She had to admit that it had felt good to even the score.

Sass's subconscious always seemed to be there when it came down to protecting her from the dark side of others. She didn't even know why she allowed herself to engage in thoughts of hurting him. She was still too soft, still didn't know how to be tough, nor was she willing to learn. The idea of her loving him and then leaving him high and dry was just wishful thinking on her part. She'd probably fail at that, too.

Boy Wonder had definitely possessed a dark side, but

Sass had refused to see it for such a long time. But she just couldn't figure out how he could've been so loving and kind if he had intended to hurt her. Why had he told her he loved her only to end up breaking her heart?

Sass had somehow convinced herself that in his own way that he did love her. For sure, he'd never find someone else to love him the way she did. He had at one time admitted to Sass that she represented the marrying kind and that he feared marriage and children more than anything else. Sass knew she was a hopeless case where her love for Kristopher was concerned, but she couldn't let herself believe for one second that he hadn't loved her on some level. It was too ominous to think otherwise.

It all boiled down to the fact that she still wanted and needed him, plain and simple. Like Kristopher, she'd never admit to him her desires and needs. The truth of the matter frightened her. He hadn't wanted to face the truth of what she'd meant to him in the past and she hadn't been able to face the future without him. He had been frightened of what he felt for her in the past and she was now terribly afraid that her feelings for him still existed in the present. They were really a great pair; both were cowards. Perhaps there was hope for them after all.

Tiredly, Sass raised herself from the bed and entered the bathroom to shower. Her every intention was to slip into nightclothes and sleep the pain away. She no more expected Kristopher to return than she expected him to appear before her in the shower. Her faith in men was no longer than her thumbnails. Since she had taken to biting them off to the quick, one could say her faith in men was nonexistent. But that wasn't how she wanted it to be; she needed to love again.

The steaming hot water beating down over her nude body mingled with the hot tears streaming from her eyes. As Sass remembered the first kiss she shared with Kristopher, her heart released a joyous laugh. Nervously, she twisted around on her finger the gold friendship ring that Kristopher had once given her as a present. She put it to her lips, kissing it tenderly. It was now time to let go of the painful memories of yesterdays and yesteryears.

When she suddenly felt white-hot hands all over her body, she closed her eyes. The hands pushed her back against the cold tile and gently fondled her breasts. A warm mouth closed over hers, deeply sucking the breath from her very being. The body attached to the hands moved seductively against hers, drawing a torrid response. The same hands gripped her firm buttocks, roving heatedly, squeezing, massaging until she trembled under the intense pressure. Her body began to shudder uncontrollably as the shower ran out of hot water. Her heated mood was instantly frozen by the splurging cold liquid.

"Oh, no," she cried, "I was almost there! Kristopher, I so desperately wanted you to be the one to take me there. I should be coming into shore. You should be right here with me."

Physically drained from the imagined rendezvous with Kristopher, she dried her body off with a soft towel and slipped into her bathrobe. The phone jingled loudly. Sass stared at it for several seconds, trying to decide if she wanted to answer it. Thinking that it might be Lesilee, she picked it up.

*"Bonsoir."* Sass's greeting lacked her normal enthusiasm.

*"Bonsoir.* I am calling for Mademoiselle Stephens. My name is Francois Deligne," the strange voice said. The Frenchman's tone sounded formal and somewhat clipped.

A puzzled look besieged her expression. "This is Mademoiselle Stephens. What can I do for you?"

"Mademoiselle Stephens, I am an associate of Kristopher Chandler."

The noticeable pause gave Sass a pretty good idea of what he would say next.

"Monsieur Chandler has asked me to give his sincere regrets for being unable to keep his commitment for the evening. He has been called away on unexpected business and will ring you when he reaches his destination. He is quite sorry for the inconvenience."

*I'll just bet he is. "Merci, Monsieur Deligne.* I understand perfectly. *Adieu."*

Sass only understood that Kristopher had done it again. He had badly bruised her heart once more. After hanging up the phone, she sat quietly, staring into space. She had wondered if her being a mother would turn him off, but it hadn't stopped her from hoping that it wouldn't matter. She was glad she hadn't gone any further into her complicated story with him. Out of frustration and anger, she picked up a magazine and threw it across the room.

At seven-fifteen Lesilee and Gregoire entered the hotel suite. Lesilee excused herself and walked into the bedroom. Surprised to see Sass asleep, she wondered why she wasn't dressed for the evening. She hoped that Sass hadn't cancelled out on Kristopher.

Lesilee stood over the bed. "Sass," she whispered softly. When Sass didn't respond, she shook her gently. As Sass slowly opened her eyes, the acute pain Lesilee saw there caused her to flinch. "Why aren't you dressed for the evening?" she asked, not knowing what else to say.

Sass sighed. "Monsieur Chandler cancelled. He was called away on business, but I suspect that it has more to do with the things I told him earlier." Sass propped herself up in bed. Taking up a pillow, she placed it across her chest.

Lesilee frowned. "When did all this come up?"

"After he left the hotel. Someone named Francois Deligne called to give Kristopher's regrets. He didn't even have the decency to call himself." Sass's tone was rather cool, belying the heated anger she felt inside.

Lesilee sat on the side of the bed. "Honey, you may be jumping to the wrong conclusions. From what I've been able to learn about Kristopher through Gregoire and what you're suggesting just doesn't seem to fit into his style or character."

Sass turned down her bottom lip. "I guess that remains to be seen. But, Lesilee, you have no idea what Kristopher can be like. When he left here, I had the feeling I'd never see him again. To be perfectly honest, I'm somewhat relieved. I don't think we can ever go back."

Lesilee shook her head. "I don't think you mean that. You're just disappointed. When you find out the truth, you're going to feel differently."

Though it came hard for her, Sass managed a weak smile.

Lesilee gently kissed Sass on the cheek. "Sass, Gregoire is in the other room. I'm going to cancel our plans and stay in with you. I'll be right back."

Sass grabbed Lesilee's arm before she could move away. "No! I won't hear of it. You and Gregoire go and have yourself a wonderful evening. I'll be fine here. I'm learning to deal with my disappointments. I don't want to spoil a minute of your vacation."

"Sass, you're not spoiling anything for me. We came to Paris together and you surely didn't expect your past to venture into your present. I know it's been a long time since your affair ended, but I know that life isn't a walk in the park for you."

Sass affected a brighter smile. "Lesilee, I want you to get dressed and get out of here. I need to be alone. I know I'll be lousy company and I don't want you to have to endure it."

Lesilee frowned. She wasn't going to argue with Sass because she remembered feeling the same way when she'd been in her position. "Okay, honey. I won't turn this into a battle of wills. Somehow I get the feeling yours might be a little stronger than mine." Lesilee laughed lightly as Sass hugged her friend and smiled her approval of Lesilee's final decision.

Lesilee rushed through her preparations so that Sass could have her space. She felt guilty at leaving but she knew that Sass was serious about wanting to be alone. Being well acquainted with the Sunday-straight-through-Monday blues, Lesilee understood perfectly.

All alone in the room, Sass ordered a light meal from room service. Settling herself down comfortably in bed, she began reading the magazine she'd thrown across the room earlier. Interestingly enough, it was a European magazine written in English. As she leafed through it, she spotted a special feature article on Kristopher Chandler. *Will wonders never cease?*

The article addressed his temporary appointment at the Paris Television Station, mentioning him as a world-renowned photographer. Sass couldn't believe her eyes. While the article gave a brief history of his personal and professional background, a few pictures of the inside of his apartment were also featured. She was astonished at what she saw. As she flipped the pages, Kristopher smiled at her from the arm of one of the decorative sofas in his home.

She outlined his smile with her finger. *You may have a trusting smile, but I wonder if you can really be trusted this time around? Why did you have someone else call me, especially when your cell phone would've easily allowed you to communicate your plight?*

The doorbell rang before she could turn the page. Looking totally distracted, she slipped into her robe and quickly ran to the door.

Expecting her meal, she threw the door open in haste. Kristopher stood before her, wearing the same trusting smile he'd worn in the article. She eyed him with cold suspicion. Not only did he know why she displayed such coldness in her normally warm eyes, he understood.

"Sass, are you going to invite me in?"

"I wasn't expecting you. I was told by your associate that you were away on business." When she didn't move aside to allow him to enter, he moved closer to where she stood.

He took her hand and looked into her eyes. "Sass, when it dawned on me what the phone call may have caused you to think, I rushed through my appointment to get back here to you. It appears my fears weren't unfounded. Please let me come in and explain."

Even more wary of him now, Sass searched his eyes intently before stepping aside. The apologetic look made her curious about what he had to say for himself. "Kristopher, come on in. Please allow me a few minutes to slip into something."

Pulling her into his arms, he ran his fingers through her disheveled hair. "You look beautiful just the way you are. Come on, Sass, let's sit down."

She pulled her robe tighter about her body as he guided her into the sitting area, where he politely stood until she was seated. Though she couldn't explain it, she felt embarrassed by the whole episode. "I was under the impression you were going to phone later."

He brushed his hand across her cheek. "A phone call

wouldn't have been enough in this situation. You deserve better. I was called into an emergency meeting with some of my colleagues. There was no time to make the call myself. I only asked Francois to call because I didn't want to leave you waiting. During the meeting it came to mind what you might be thinking. I pushed things along as quickly as I could. You've had enough disappointments. I have no intentions of adding anything else to that list. I meant the things I said to you earlier. I hope you'll forgive my lateness." Deep regret came through his eyes with crystal clarity.

Sass slipped him an uneasy smile. "I'll admit that I did jump to the wrong conclusions. I loudly expressed my feelings to Lesilee. But she didn't believe this was your way of doing things, even though she has no idea what we've been through. However, I'm glad she was right."

Moving closer to her, he put his arms around her shoulders. "I'll have to thank *Mademoiselle* Taft for having faith in me. The night's still young. If you give me the opportunity, I'd like to fulfill my promise of a wonderful Paris evening."

"You're on. I've already showered and it'll only take me a few minutes to get dressed. As you know, I'm not one who takes forever to get ready. Less is more. I'll be right back." Surprising him, she kissed him lightly on the mouth.

Kristopher took the liberty of answering the door when room service came with her meal. After tipping the service man, he set the food aside for her to consume later. So far so good, he thought. He hoped she could forgive the horrible things he'd put her through, the unconscionable things he'd done long before he'd learned what it took to be a real man.

\* \* \*

Lesilee's statement came to Sass's mind as she dressed. *You were right, my friend. I'm feeling quite different.* In acknowledging how lonely she'd felt, Sass was glad he'd come back.

Looking vivacious in a svelte ivory-white knit suit, Sass walked into the living room. The halter-style top with covered buttons and decorative pockets skimmed her slender body like a passionate lover. Because the mid-calf skirt had a side slit just above the knee, Kristopher got a great glimpse of her smooth brown leg. Copper jewelry added a deeper hint of glitter to her sepia eyes.

His broad smile of approval caused her to blush. "Sass, even the most beautiful women in Paris are no matches for you. You're fascinating!" He stuck his arm out for her to take and she easily slid hers into his.

# Four

The couple reached the highly polished Rolls Royce, where Pierre waited patiently. "Mademoiselle Stephens, you are especially lovely this evening! I see why Monsieur Chandler is so enchanted. The night life in the City of Light eagerly awaits your arrival." Pierre's warm azure eyes smiled brightly at Sass, who was totally stunned by his verbal greeting.

Sass was shocked that Pierre even knew her name; more astonished that Kristopher might've discussed her with the French chauffeur.

Kristopher's eyes twinkled merrily with laughter. "Pierre is a man of few words, Sass, but your gentle beauty wouldn't allow him to be silenced any longer."

Comfortably seated in the back of the car, Sass laughed softly. "I've often wondered if Pierre even had a tongue. He normally just nods his head and goes about his business."

"He rarely talks with any of the company guests. Pierre has been with the station owner's family, the Laurents, for a long time. When Andre's parents were killed in one of their private planes, Pierre became like a father to him. I've come to respect Pierre greatly."

Though she'd never met the owner or his parents, their death somehow caused her to feel grieved as she voiced a silent prayer in their behalf. "Have you discussed me with Pierre?"

Kristopher kissed the tip of her nose. "Sure I have. Just guy talk, so to speak. Pierre started that particular conversation by telling me how beautiful he thought you were. So that's how he knows I'm so enchanted with you."

*Maybe so, but how long will the enchantment last this time? All that glitters isn't gold.* She really didn't think any of his renewed fascination with her would last beyond Paris. Sass decided it was best for her not to even think further than this evening about anything to do with him and her.

"Are you ready to paint the town red, Sass?"

"Any color but blue, Kristopher. My sad moods have already done enough of that."

"If given half a chance, I'll chase all of your blues away." To keep from responding with a sarcastic comment, she slipped her head against his shoulder. Without hesitation, he rested his hand in her silky hair.

As they stepped out of the elevator at the top of the spectacular Eiffel Tower, they found the action inside Jules Verne quite animated. Easily, despite the crowded conditions, they were led through the throng to the reserved table. Lesilee and Gregoire were so into one another they didn't even notice their friends approach.

When Lesilee finally did look up, she saw Sass smiling at her. Kristopher, on the other hand, was beaming all over. Tickled pink, Lesilee quickly left her seat and embraced Sass with warmth. "I'm so happy to see you! I felt so guilty about leaving you all alone."

Sass's eyes glowed with mischief. "You didn't look like you were feeling guilty to me. It looked to me as if you were in paradise." Lesilee laughed, embracing her friend again.

After pulling out Sass's chair, Kristopher took the empty seat across from her. Reaching across the table, he extended his hand to Gregoire and the two men shook hands.

Gregoire's eyes drank in Sass's glowing complexion as he kissed the back of her hand. "What you saw just now was me trying to take Lesilee's mind off the guilt."

Sass suppressed a giggle. "Gregoire, you obviously think as fast sitting down as you do when you're on your feet." Everyone laughed.

"Sass is here now, so no one has to feel guilty. I was able to rush through my business affairs. We're going to have a night to remember," Kristopher assured everyone.

"Sounds good to me," Lesilee stated.

"Have you been here long?" Sass asked.

Lesilee looked at her watch. "Not more than an hour or so."

Immediately, Kristopher summoned the waiter and ordered a bottle of Dom Perignon champagne. Sass could tell that Kristopher was as much revered in this establishment as in The Laurent. She still hadn't found out if he frequented it, but it ceased to matter or be a question for her. While finding Kristopher more and more attractive with each passing moment, she was also beginning to realize that there just might be a chance that he'd truly changed his bad-boy ways.

Her older sister had her cracking up the first time she'd referred to the bad-boy image as the "Billy-bad-ass syndrome." Staci often said that every woman thought she wanted one, but once she got him, she didn't have a clue how to handle him and his bad-boy ways. In Staci's opinion, none of the guys into that macho-man sort of image were worth a plug nickel.

Sass took a few minutes to look around the popular restaurant. As she glanced out the window, her breath was whisked away. Though rendered speechless, the look in her eyes was easy enough to read. She was unable to believe how much the interior decor perfectly matched the exterior of the Eiffel Tower, and was just as magnificent.

Wondering what it would take for him to have her back in his life, Kristopher studied Sass. He had grown even more enchanted with her eyes. While he had traveled all over the globe, he'd never seen a lovelier pair of eyes. The eyes of sheer nudity allowed him to see into her soul. If he could have Sass back in his life, he'd finally be complete. For sure, he never wanted to disappoint her again. If only she could love him half as much as she'd loved him before he'd broken her heart, he'd be a deliriously happy man. A bright light appeared in his eyes as he came up with a brilliant idea.

"I'd like all of you to come with me to Monte Carlo as my guests," Kristopher announced. "We can leave as early as tomorrow or as soon as it's convenient for everyone. If you'll agree, I can make the arrangements with Mr. Laurent for the use of his condo."

"That would be wonderful," Lesilee gushed. "Sass wanted to see some of the Riviera and your offer would provide her the perfect opportunity. What do you say, Sass?"

Sass's smile was enthusiastic. "As we say in America, count me in." Surprised yet relieved that Sass had accepted the offer Lesilee released a breath of sweet relief.

Kristopher was more than pleased. For the rest of her stay in Paris, Kristopher hoped to convince Sass that he was a changed man, a man who loved her more than anything in the world.

Shortly after enjoying the exquisite meal and panoramic view at Jules Verne, the two couples had been

led to their reserved seats inside The Lido; the largest
and most spectacular dance revue show in Paris, located
in the Normandie Cinema Building.

The numerous showgirls easily danced their way into
Sass's heart. Lesilee had seen this particular show more
than once, but she was still as taken as her friend. Sass
appeared embarrassed by the semi-nude dancers, but
she seemed to get over it rather quickly. Very little was
missed from their ringside tier seating. Just before the
sun came up, the foursome escaped the club and made
their way to Kristopher's high-rise apartment to watch
the sun mark the beginning of a new day.

The magazine pictures Sass had seen earlier of Kristopher's apartment were lifeless in comparison to the real
thing. Wealth and class permeated the fine furnishings
and tasteful accents. While admiring the fantastic view
from the edge of the sky-high balcony, the fear of heights
was no longer a problem for Sass; Kristopher held her se-
curely in his arms.

In all her excitement, with no recent thought to her
planned mission of vengeance, Sass pulled his head down
and covered his mouth with her own. Savoring the warm
kisses from her sweet lips, he responded ardently to her
sensuality. Kristopher and Sass appeared to be locked in
their own time and space. Lesilee and Gregoire slipped inside to give them time alone. It looked as if something
wonderful might reignite between them after all.

Monte Carlo, a district of Monaco, was named for
Charles III in 1866. The popular French Riviera city had
served as a playground to the rich and famous for centuries; the azure waters and terraced hills were sought

out each year by millions of tourists. The economy had grown by leaps and bounds. Tourism and gambling made up only a small percentage of the revenue, which was surprising to Sass.

The luxuriously decorated condo looked out on the Mediterranean, and Sass found it to be breathtaking. Soon after they'd settled into the exquisite guestrooms, the couples had split up to take excursions around the area.

Seated on the lovely open terrace of L'Escale restaurant, located in the port area, Sass couldn't help thinking about the Laurents' condo. Besides the magnificent view, the more than two thousand square feet of living space boasted expensive European furnishings throughout. The guestroom she was assigned was nothing less than exquisite.

Sass looked over at Kristopher and smiled. Seated across the table from her, he sipped on one of the refreshing drinks he'd ordered for them. She took a sip from her drink and then set down her glass. "Kristopher, why didn't Monsieur Laurent purchase the Monte Carlo station?"

Sass was especially interested in the television station, Tele Monte Carlo, where one of the most powerful transmitters in the world was located. Lesilee had been to Monte Carlo but she'd never had the pleasure of seeing the station that mesmerized Sass. Unlike her friends the world travelers, Mexico was the only placed Sass had ever traveled to outside the United States.

"It wasn't for sale. I don't expect it ever will be since France owns a large percentage of it. Monaco owns the rest. That particular station is pretty much heard throughout the Continent."

"With Monte Carlo being such a small place, I had

no idea of the importance of the television station until now. I'm flabbergasted."

Kristopher laughed. "You can't always judge things by size. Look how small you and Lesilee are and you both pack a pretty mean punch. You two are leading Gregoire and me around by the ring in our noses." He couldn't help remembering a time when he was in the lead, the leading man in her life. But he'd thrown it all away because of useless fear and his desire for amassing riches over spiritual gain.

Sass was amused by his comments. "I'm going to have to speak for myself on that one, Kristopher. It appears to me that you're the one leading." *Just like before. Am I now the hunter, only to be captured by the same slick game?* She found herself praying that it wasn't a game at all to him. Her heart couldn't survive another landslide or more of his selfish games.

"I'm not sure I would've seen Monte Carlo if it wasn't for you. *Merci, Monsieur Chandler,*" she flirted.

"As for Gregoire and Lesilee, I think they've been leading each other around by their nose-rings for years now. It appears they may be ready to melt those rings into one."

As she smiled up at him, Kristopher felt his senses deserting him. Smiling back at her, Kristopher looked at Sass in disbelief. "Are you saying what I think you are? Are Lesilee and Gregoire talking about tying the knot? She's only been back in his life a few days now." But he understood that perfectly; he felt the same exact way about Sass after a long separation. Kristopher had never stopped loving Sass, but he hadn't been able to find her to tell her how sorry he was about all the dreadful mistakes he'd made in the past.

Sass grinned. "They've been in love for a long time, but I'm afraid Lesilee has been the one putting the decision off. I've heard about love and Paris in the spring, but they add new meaning to it!" Sass couldn't help wondering if love could blossom for her again this spring.

"I guess congratulations may be in order. Have they decided when and where the ceremony will take place?"

"Congratulations may be a bit premature, Kristopher. They're just in the planning stages. Lesilee needs more time to make sure this is what she really wants this time around."

Kristopher looked at Sass with adoration. "I see. Sorry if I spoke out of turn." He seemed embarrassed that he'd misunderstood Sass's comments.

"I'm the one who spoke out of turn. I should've waited until their plans were firm."

Sass touched Kristopher's face gently, glad that he'd shown sensitivity in the matter. In turn, he kissed her full on the mouth. Both grew flushed at the sensuous contact, but Sass felt herself color each time Kristopher came near her. He had the ability to make her blush all the way down to her toes. She didn't know how this holiday excursion was going to turn out, but she had made up her mind. Sass Stephens wasn't going to shackle her feelings and inhibit herself in any way. It was a different time and place for them. After all, Paris was the world's lover's lane.

The next two days were spent touring and uncovering the treasures of famed Monte Carlo. The beautiful city was steeped in history and Sass found every bit of it interesting, to say the least. At times she felt totally out of her element, making her wonder how she'd gotten from a small coastal city back East all the way to the dazzling world of Monaco. When alone, she'd take a minute to put herself in check. Sass Stephens had gotten where she was by tenacity and unyielding faith. With all the horrendous things that had happened to her, she hadn't given up her dreams. Her painful past was always near, but she'd like to see it move on and leave her free as a bird. There were times when her unmanageable pain threatened to be her undoing. But she was doing her best not let it threaten whatever was happening between her and Kristopher.

Kristopher tried to be there for her and to help screen out as much of the pain as she would allow him. He was very tentative and their time alone was spent learning more and more about the people they'd become. Nothing she'd told him about her present life seemed to turn him off. He had fallen in love with her all over again, even deeper than before, according to him.

Sass and Kristopher had separate rooms but were apart very little. The couple spent hours lazing on the beach, talking until the wee hours of the morning, only separating long enough to shower and change clothes. Discreetly, Lesilee and Gregoire gave Sass and Kristopher every opportunity to be alone since both were hoping something beautiful and long lasting would recur between their two dear friends.


Since Nice was only twelve miles west of Monaco, and Cannes only a short distance from Nice by auto, Kristopher was able to give Sass the parts of France she was most interested in touring. Gregoire and Lesilee had stayed in Monte Carlo to relax and enjoy one another's company. Together, they'd already explored both areas and were content to just indulge themselves in each other. Sass had to admit that she liked spending time alone with Kristopher.

In Nice, Sass and Kristopher walked along the Promenade des Anglais, before touring the Museum of Shells and Chagall Museum. Later, they walked through the flower market. As this was the last day of their stay in the south of France, they were only able to stop briefly at the many attractions of Nice.

At Cannes, famous for its film festival, they strolled down the Boulevard de la Croisette, which served as the main boulevard. Cannes was also noted as the fashion center of the Riviera. Kristopher led an excited Sass through the fashion shops, the Castrum Canolis houses and the Museum of Mediterranean Civilization. He found great pleasure in guiding Sass through the Antibes Museum. She was thrilled to experience, first-hand, the Picasso exhibit.

The couple practically rushed through lunch at the Carlton, located seaside at La Croisette. Kristopher was eager to get back to Monte Carlo, where he planned to give Sass one more fantastic night filled with glitz, glamour and whatever else her heart desired.

Very still and quiet, seated on the big bed, musing over the day's activities, Sass smiled as the tender moments between her and Kristopher engulfed her mind. Their drive along the beautiful coastal areas, the sightseeing and shopping sprees in Cannes and Nice had left them very tired but more intimately familiar. They'd also grown much closer to each other.

Kristopher's warmth and sensitivity toward Sass was providing her with the spark she needed to begin a new chapter in her life, which she hoped would help her begin the process of healing. Kristopher was very much a part of her soul, but she had to try very hard to release her tightly clenched hold on the past and on the unmitigated pain he had caused her. He'd been so sweet to her. What surprised her most is that he was so informed about France. There wasn't a question she'd asked of him that he hadn't been able to answer.

Sass suddenly closed her eyes to remember the smell of him. Falling in and out of love with Kristopher was becoming an everyday occurrence. Lately she was finding herself more in love with him than out. It was confusing at best, but Sass just didn't know if they could have the kind of future that he seemed to want for them.

Earlier, when his mouth had touched hers, she'd felt such calmness. Then the wind driven storm of passion had arrived, leaving her insides quaking when she'd discovered how much she wanted to make love to him without cessation. Though he'd become highly aware of her desire, he'd refrained from responding irresponsibly, knowing she would only regret it later. She had felt a sense of rejection, but it had only lasted a few moments. Once he'd carefully explained his reasons why they shouldn't go there, she knew he was right, but it hadn't eased the pain of her embarrassment. His sensitivity had only made her want him even more. One day, she mused dazedly, she'd be able to give herself to him again, fully—without guilt, without regret or shame.

Frustrated because she didn't think any of her clothes were appropriate for the Monte Carlo casinos, Sass wondered what to do about it. She had brought along many fine dresses, but from what she'd seen in the fashion center her wardrobe was totally inadequate. She would've bought a dress while they'd shopped, but when she'd looked at the price tags there was no way she could've afforded any of the fabulous merchandise.

A knock came on the door just as she was about to go to Kristopher's room to cancel, hoping he'd agree to a quiet evening inside. When she opened the door, she found one of the housekeepers standing there. In fairly good English, the fair-haired young lady explained that her mission was to deliver the large decoratively wrapped package she held to *Monsieur* Chandler's special houseguest.

Bewilderment beamed in her eyes as she smiled knowingly at the young woman. Sass accepted the package and thanked her for making the delivery. She carried the box into the room and sat down on the sofa, where she carefully removed the wrapping. When she discovered the contents of the gift box, her laughter filled the air.

*How could Kristopher have possibly known?* Laughing uncontrollably, Sass lifted out of the box the most exquisite dress in all of Europe. The sexy, black formal evening gown held her spell-bound. Strapless, with a fitted bodice, the material of the dress was silky-soft and clinging. She loved the way the delicately beaded gown swirled softly to the floor. Sass eagerly opened the card that lay on top of the hot pink tissue paper.

A BEAUTIFUL DRESS FOR A MOST BEAUTIFUL LADY. I SIMPLY CANNOT WAIT TO SEE YOU IN THIS STUNNING DESIGNER'S ORIGINAL. LOVE, KRISTOPHER.

Dancing around the room with the dress held up to her body, Sass felt exuberant. Then her enthusiasm quickly changed to apprehension as stinging questions prickled her mind. *Did Kristopher think the clothes she'd been wearing were too shabby? Was he ashamed of her attire? Maybe he had somehow noticed the longing for the dress in her eyes when they'd shopped.*

Sass immediately dismissed her concerns. Whatever he thought, she felt grateful for the gift. She was going to wear this fabulous dress like she was born into it. The rose petals were once again evident in her laughter as her mood brightened. After checking the time, she immediately ran into the bathroom to prepare for the evening.

The next problem arose when Sass didn't feel that any of her jewelry was elegant enough for the dress. She hoped Lesilee would come to her room before Kristopher knocked so she could borrow something nice from her. Lesilee had excellent taste in clothing and she also possessed many expensive pieces of jewelry. Sass had to stop a minute and give herself a reality check, something she found herself doing a lot lately.

"You have to put the insecurities away," Sass berated herself. She should be telling herself that she was as every bit as beautiful as any woman in this country instead of doubting who she was. What she wore was only a fraction of herself. What was inside of her was what counted most. If she didn't think she was beautiful, no one else would either. She had to accept herself for who she was and learn how to trust in her most basic instincts.

Sass knew that she could try to run away from what was happening between her and Kristopher, but she couldn't hide, especially from herself. Her inner voice, known to her as the Holy Spirit, would always be there to tell her the truth regardless of the outcome. It would also fiercely protect her from any harm when she got into difficulty. She had to trust that Kristopher had come back into her life for a reason. But if she ran away before she discovered the truth of why he was there, she could miss out on a valuable lesson or even a divine experience of some sort. Nothing in this life occurred by happenstance.

Patting her heart gently, she smiled lazily. "Sass, hang on in there, girlfriend. Don't ever lose sight of love for self and never forget to appreciate that love to the fullest. Kristopher can't possibly break your heart again unless you give him permission to do so."

Seated in a comfortable chair in the guest bedroom, dressed in a dashing black tuxedo, Kristopher impatiently waited until it was time to knock on Sass's bedroom door. The short time he'd been away from her had him feeling lonely and in need of the smile that gave his heart wings. As he thought about the imminent departure to Paris, he was aware that he hadn't quite accomplished his mission, but he wasn't finished yet. He still had time before she left France to hopefully convince her that they still belonged together.

Reaching for the velvet case on his dresser, he opened it, smiling down at the dazzling jewels nestled there. "Mom would want me to give these to the woman I love."

Sass took a deep breath before knocking on the door to his suite. He suddenly appeared in front of her, his smoldering eyes roving from her sexy, sophisticated hairstyle down to the gold evening sandals on her feet. Then his eyes moved upward and flash-danced across her satiny soft complexion. Completely mesmerized by the way the dress clung to her slender curves, he prayed for an angel of mercy to deliver him from the heat akin to the Gobi Desert burning in his loins.

His intense scrutiny made her feel shy, yet her breath caught as she saw how handsome he looked in his evening attire. The man was simply breathtaking; no two ways about it.

"Sass, there are no words in any language to describe the way you look. You're driving me to distraction. All I want to do is devour you. As I've said time and time again, you should be gracing the front of a highly respectable fashion magazine. You could demand any amount of money for your photograph—and receive it."

"Thanks."

As he reached for her, bringing her into his arms, he noticed that she wasn't wearing any jewelry. That observation only lent more credence to his plan to share the jewels with her. He had brought them to France to use on the international models during the special fashion show events that would eventually be featured in his extraordinary photography layouts.

Lesilee hadn't come to Sass's room. Because Sass hadn't wanted to disturb the couple if they were together in Lesilee's room, she'd decided that the dress was just as beautiful without any accessories.

His stiff white dress shirt tickled her chin as he kissed her mouth. "Please come inside. I have something to give you." He sounded mysterious, piquing her curiosity. As she stepped further into the room, he closed the door behind her. "Close your eyes. I want you to feel this magnificent surprise before you actually see it."

Sass laughed nervously. "I could take that remark a couple of ways. Maybe I should see it before I actually feel it." If her memory served her right, his male endowment was nothing less than marvelous. It had certainly fulfilled her on the numerous nights they'd spent together.

Kristopher laughed at her suggestive comment. "I see what you mean, but I'm fully dressed. So your virtue is safe." Eagerly awaiting the surprise, she closed her eyes.

Walking over to the dresser, he carefully removed the sparkling brilliant diamond choker from its case. Standing behind her, he encircled her neck with the jewels. While fastening the solid gold clasp, he decided to afford her the pleasure of putting the matching earrings and bracelet on herself. The expensive jewelry was an age-old heirloom. Before telling her to open her eyes, he covered them with his hands and guided her over to the mirrored dresser.

As she opened her eyes and looked into the glass, her mouth fell open in wondrous awe. Sass lightly fingered the choker. Her brain felt as if it had been numbed from the blinding reflection bouncing off the mirror. He then handed her the earrings and bracelet.

Filled with excitement, she carefully put the other jewels on, barely able to wait to see the effect. But she had no intentions of allowing Kristopher to give her such expensive gifts. The dress was too much as it was. Theirs wasn't the type of relationship that would even allow her to think for a single minute that she could take the jewels without consequence.

"Well, what do you think?" Her expression was so soft, but her eyes were fiery. He hadn't seen this type of fire in her eyes ever before; so fiery he could light a candle from their flaming embers. His breath caught.

"The problem is I can't think! My vocabulary eludes me. Kristopher, this is a lovely gesture, but I can't accept such a gift. I'm not deserving of something this exquisite. These jewels are far too precious for me to accept on a mere whim."

Her inner voice gave rise. *You are deserving of the Crown Jewels . . . and so much more.* She laughed inwardly when she thought of what her sister Stephanie would say. She had more words of wisdom for Sass and their other sister than their parents did. *Never, ever look a gift horse in the mouth.* She could almost hear Stephanie's advice. *If he breaks your heart again, you can live comfortably on the profit from these jewels alone, should you decide to hock your memoirs. The price you'd get from these jewels would pay for more than Justin's college education.* In this instance, Stephanie wouldn't want her to be with Kristopher again, period.

"Indulge me for tonight. They have belonged to several generations of Chandler wives, including my late mother. Yet I'm sure no Chandler woman ever wore them as well as you do."

As she thought about his comment, her eyes appeared to stare straight into his being. Then she smiled brightly.

She wasn't a Chandler wife, nor did she think she ever would be, but she was going to honor his request. "Just for tonight! Do you keep these precious jewels in your apartment?"

"Before moving here, I had all of my important and expensive personal effects transferred to France. I've used the jewels for a couple of photography shoots. The models love to wear them. I removed them from the bank vault before we left Paris. I'm always prepared should a spontaneous photography session present itself."

Sass smiled. "Thank you for this act of kindness and extreme generosity." Entwining her arms around his neck, she thanked him with a hot, moist kiss. Her body, as hot as her kiss, melted into his. Her evil plan to pay him back had failed at every turn. This man still had the same affect he'd had on her from the moment she'd first met him. How could she have even thought that she could resist him? Resisting him was not an easy feat; it hadn't been in the past nor was it any less uncomplicated in the present.

"You're welcome, Sass."

In the Principality of Monaco, the ever-famous Monte Carlo Casino, which first opened in 1856, more than exceeded all standards of excellence in beauty and the definition of first class. Its dazzling array of entertainment and extraordinary ultra-plush interior lay in wait to cater to the world's elite.

Arriving with Sass Stephens on his arm, Kristopher Chandler proudly basked in the envious stares from his wealthy counterparts. Heads craned from every direction as he strode through the casino with what he thought was the most beautiful woman in the world. While Sass believed the gaping stares had to do with the beautiful diamonds she wore, Kristopher knew that the jewels had nothing to do with it. There was no comparison. She looked exquisite.

Kristopher's personal and professional prowess had been featured in several European fashion magazines. Knowing that the American photographer was one of the most sought after bachelors in his circle of wealthy and powerful people, a few women looked on with envy. Those who dared to stop and stare soon went about the business of indulging themselves in whatever their pleasures. Kristopher's immaculately tailored clothes, Sass's expensive dress, and the magnificent jewels easily made them the most stunning couple in the room. His pride in her showed in the way he held her so near as he gracefully guided her through the casino.

Sass leaned in closer to Kristopher. "I'm nervous," she whispered.

Amused by her confession, he kissed her forehead, hugging her closely to him. "No need for you to be on edge, Sass. You're with me. Do I make you anxious?"

"Of course not." Her lie hadn't come with ease. Butterflies lived in her stomach whenever she was anywhere in the vicinity of him. "I'm becoming comfortable with you again. I'm glad we're building a new friendship." To reassure him, she telegraphed him a dazzling smile.

Her description of their relationship disheartened him a bit, but he didn't take exception to it since genuine friendships often made for the best loving relationships. In his recently acquired wisdom, he now thought that any serious relationship should begin with a sincere friendship. He and Sass had nearly become instant lovers, missing out on what should've come before all else: friendship.

He squeezed her hand with affection. "I'm honored that you're starting to consider me a friend. I've heard that when friends turn into lovers it's rewarding and long lasting. Don't take that as pressure to become my lover again. You're the master of our destiny," he whispered softly into her ear.

Sass was pleased with what he'd said. Well aware that she didn't have the power to be the master of anyone's destiny but her own, Sass sighed inwardly.

"Have you ever gambled before?"

She laughed openly at his question. "Sure, if you call penny-ante poker and nickel tonk gambling. I've been to Las Vegas a couple of times, but I never did anything more than play the small change slots."

He still found her innocence charming. "Sass, you're about to see people bet some of the highest stakes in the world. Monte Carlo is not for the faint at heart when it comes to gambling. Come on, we'll go to the gaming tables. You'll find the players fascinating. I'm not a seasoned gambler but I've been known to flirt with chance a time or two." He laughed. "You can be my Lady Luck this evening. No matter what, I can't lose with you here beside me." With her, he had always felt like a winner. Too bad he hadn't honored her value in the past.

She had to admit that she actually liked the new him, but since she'd brought friendship into the conversation she now had to grin and bear it. "If you use me as your lucky charm, you might be flirting with disaster! If it weren't for bad luck, I wouldn't have any luck at all." She briefly felt disenchanted with herself for being so enchanted with him all over again.

"Sass, I got a feeling your luck is about to change. Stick with me and you'll see."

Watching the high stakes betting with fascination registering in her eyes, Sass was amazed at the amount of money wagered. Even though it was done in French francs, and she couldn't convert it to dollars quickly enough, she knew it was an exorbitant amount. Kristopher lost money the first couple of times out, but it wasn't long before his pile of chips had begun to grow. When he asked her to roll the dice for him, she was scared out of her wits. Sass shrieked with joy when she rolled a seven on her first roll. Elated, he kissed her softly on the mouth.

Entering the Monte Carlo Casino, dressed in stunning fashionable evening attire, Lesilee and Gregoire turned many of heads as well. The strapless bodice of her ivory-white evening gown shimmered with dainty mother-of-pearl sequins and the scarf wrapped seductively around her neck flowed down the back. Her sequined slippers matched the gown perfectly. Diamond teardrop earrings dangled gracefully from her ears.

Gregoire looked suave in his formal white dinner jacket and ivory-buttoned tuxedo shirt. His glimmering cummerbund and bow tie nearly matched the color of the sequins in Lesilee's dress and his black formal dress shoes shined like polished lacquer. The couple walked hand in hand through the casino searching for Kristopher and Sass, who watched their grand entrance from the gaming table. While waving at the arriving couple from near the center of the room, Sass could almost feel their positive energy from her position.

"From the look of things, I'd guess that their love is on a winning streak," Sass told Kristopher.

"Lesilee has really lit a fire under Gregoire. In the short time I've known him, I've never seen him this animated."

"Nor I her. She's been worried about how she'd handle some of the issues from a previous relationship, but I don't think she can deny what's happening to her now. They are a striking couple!"

"Lesilee's an incredible looking woman. I don't think she needs to worry about a thing. She and Gregoire both look very happy. They also seem good for each other. If she decides to marry him, I think he'll make her an exceptional husband. He's a very sincere and generous man," Kristopher informed Sass. *The same type of man I should've been for you.*

"Lesilee is glowing. In a few days we'll be returning home. I can't help but wonder if she'll make that all-important decision before we leave. They appear to be deeply in love with each other." Sass silently wished that she'd once again be able to trust in love that deeply.

Gregoire gently touched Lesilee's hair as he gave her forehead a light kiss. Putting her arm through his, they proceeded to the gaming table, where Kristopher and Sass eagerly waited for them to make their way through the lively throng.

Kristopher extended his hand. *"Bonsoir, Gregoire et Lesilee!* We've been waiting for you two to get here."

Sass smiled as Gregoire and Lesilee took turns kissing her flushed cheeks. *"Bonsoir,* my dear friends! I'm so glad you made it. I watched your grand arrival. Lesilee, you look fantastic and I love your dress," Sass gushed. "Gregoire, you're looking rather dashing yourself. You two make such a lovely couple."

As soon as all the greetings were out of the way, Sass got back to her wagering, screaming when she rolled another winner. She turned around and smiled knowingly at Kristopher, Lesilee and Gregoire.

Staring wide-eyed at the jewels around Sass's slender neck, Lesilee couldn't believe the beauty of the gems or the person wearing them. "Speaking of lovely couples, you and those jewels make a perfect pair. You're both beautiful." Lesilee's eyes were full of questions about the expensive finery, but she didn't voice them out loud.

"These gems have been in Kristopher's family for years. He was kind enough to allow me to wear them for the evening," Sass stated, satisfying the burning curiosity in Lesilee's eyes.

"Sass, you and the jewels compliment each other beautifully," Gregoire said.

The couples quickly settled in at the casino while moving from table to table. Gregoire was very knowledgeable about the games as he continuously gave the two women several pointers. Sass could see that Lesilee wasn't exactly a stranger to the tables as she made bets comfortably, easily learning the unfamiliar games.

The evening held many untold surprises. Sass and her companions enjoyed themselves tremendously. Kristopher was falling more and more in love with Sass, yet at times he saw an overwhelming sadness in her eyes, an image that he couldn't get out of his mind.

# Five

At evening's end, mired in happiness, Sass and Kristopher walked hand-in-hand along a quiet stretch of beach. Sass smiled sweetly at her companion as their eyes locked together in an embrace that spread delicious warmth through each of their bodies.

"You've been a wonderful host," Sass said softly. "I thank you for all the generous attention you've lavished on me." She looked at him in an inviting way, and he eagerly took her up on the offered invitation.

Bending his head, he softly whispered kisses against her parted lips. "You're welcome, Sass, but all the thanks should come from me. From the moment I saw you at the bistro, I knew fate had finally decided to work with me. In a few days you'll be returning home . . . and I'm feeling rather sad about that." *When you go, you'll take my heart with you.* "Is your leaving Paris the end for us?"

Sass sighed heavily. She had hoped this particular conversation wouldn't take place. Taking both of his hands, she swung them lightly. He halted the motion by gently placing their laced hands behind his back, which brought her in closer to him. "Kristopher, I don't want our relationship to end, but I don't see how we can keep it going from this distance." He closed his eyes in dismay. She stood on her toes and kissed his eyelids. "I really don't know where we *can* go from here."

He opened those beautiful eyes and caressed her cheek with the back of his hand. "Distance isn't a problem for me. I can see you often. I'm used to flying the friendly skies. Knowing that you'll be waiting on the other end will make it all worthwhile. Sass Stephens, I'm still in love with you, have always been in love with you. I want to spend the rest of my life proving that to you. My immaturity is what kept us from a life together. I take full responsibility for all that went wrong."

His confession surprised her even though he'd already told her as much without saying the words. Whether he was actually in love with her, she wasn't sure, but he certainly made her feel as if it were true. In fact, he made her feel treasured. "In such a short time of us getting reacquainted, how could you possibly know that you want to spend the rest of your life with me? I have a child you haven't met. Basically, you and I are from totally different worlds."

Dropping to the sand, he pulled her down onto his lap, giving no thought to ruining the expensive dress that she wore. "As I mentioned before, I know exactly what I want. I've always wanted you. I wanted you back then and I want you now. And I know that we still have a lot of issues to resolve. Justin's a part of you so that means I want him, too. As for the two different worlds, with love there's no such thing. Love transcends different worlds and lifestyles. Perhaps you don't think you can love me again, but once you get to know the person I've become, I think you'll feel differently. Please allow me to remain in your life beyond Paris. Please give us a chance to go forward from this moment on. I've made a mountain of mistakes, but I'm ready to chip away at whatever barriers that stand between us making a serious attempt at trying again."

She shook her head from side to side. "Not to discount your feelings, but I no longer imagine anyone wanting to always be with someone who might not love them in return. I've already been there, done that. Remember? I once loved someone that couldn't love me back, namely you. I was sure I knew what I wanted, too. I have no idea what I want anymore."

His eyes searching hers, he held her hands tighter. "How long did it take you to fall in love with me when we first met?"

Sass blinked hard. Just the memory of that feeling hurt like the dickens. "That's an unfair question."

"Why? It's not much different from the question you asked a few moments back."

"I fell in love instantaneously." She saw him wince. "Did my answer somehow hurt you, Kristopher?"

His eyes darkened for a brief moment. "In a way. Only because I know the precious gift of your love wasn't appreciated by me, nor did I deserve it. If I had, you'd no longer be single and available." He smiled gently. "Forgive me for walking down memory lane. But you're more than a mere mortal woman to me. You're a precious work of art. Lots of love and compassion was poured into you during your creation. The angels have smiled on you in many ways."

His tender words reached inside to capture her heart. Sass suddenly felt a kindred spirit for him come alive. His words were sweet and generous. "Kristopher, I'll try to give us every conceivable chance. But I have to tell you. I don't know if I can handle another hurtful episode as graciously as I did before. I don't want to wake up one day and find out that you've split on me again. Can you promise me that it won't happen like that a second time?"

"Not only can I make the promise, I'll keep it. Unlike

before, I promise to be open and honest with you, Sass. What else can I do to reassure you?"

"Kiss me." *God, how did I get from the pain of the past to the joy of here and now?*

Before pulling her into his arms, he smiled. Resting back in the sand, he drew her mouth down over his, kissing her thoroughly. Their mouths caught fire, sending the heat to the depths of their most intimate body parts. Feeling scared, her emotions spiraling out of control, she turned away and walked down the beach. Leaping to his feet, he followed after her and reunited their bodies in an impassioned embrace.

"Don't be afraid of this. I'd never do anything you don't want," he whispered huskily into her ear. "Trust me, Sass. I won't hurt you again. I can only prove myself worthy with time."

She wanted so desperately to believe him, but she'd heard these very words before. Time would tell all. It sure had in the past. Fear once again gripped her, especially when she remembered all the things she hadn't told him about her life and those she'd vowed never to tell anyone, ever.

Hoping to wipe her fears away, he kissed her again. Enjoying the delicious assault on her senses, she relaxed and allowed him to fill her mind and heart with the colorful attractions of things to come with him by her side. Briefly, he held her away from him, his eyes engaging hers in a passionate coupling. As his love was revealed for her to see, she had only one question: *Was it real?*

As they neared the Laurents' condo, he halted their forward motion, turning to face Sass. "It's still early here, Sass. I know a private club where we can dance the sun into existence. It's right near the end of the beach. Do you have enough energy to play for a few more hours?"

* * *

The Jazz on One was filled to capacity. Kristopher showed how much pull he had when he got them through the door just by giving his name. Sass was impressed, but she could see that he hadn't wielded his power just to show off. David T. Walker, one of his favorite jazz guitarists, was performing there. He also knew the owner of the club very well. Kristopher patronized the club regularly when he stayed at the Laurents' condo. The Laurents' influence helped to earn him VIP status.

Seated in the back of the club, away from the stage, they could talk more easily and also have a clear view of the bandstand. Sass and Kristopher's formal clothes didn't quite fit in with the casually fashionable crowds frequenting the club, but neither of them seemed to care. As far as Kristopher was concerned, they were the only two people existing in his world or in any world. He desperately needed Sass Stephens back in his.

"David T. Walker has been off the American music circuit for years," Kristopher told Sass. "He came to France many years ago to showcase his still very viable talent. Listen carefully to his style. You can tell me what you think of his performance later."

Sass was fascinated with the African-American guitarist. He had a way of making his prized guitar talk—she almost believed the electric guitar was talking to her in particular. As the sweet chords of music wooed her, she fell in love with the guitarist's soul-stirring style.

"I don't think this night can get any better, Kristopher."

"My plans for you in months to come will make tonight pale by comparison. I'm going to dazzle you in more ways than one."

Sass was getting an excellent education in how a lady

should be treated. Kristopher seemed intent on becoming the master educator. But he'd treated her like a queen the first time she loved him. Then he'd betrayed her trust. Sass smiled despite her thoughts as she felt the jazzy music right down to her feet. All of the people in the club were absolutely fascinating, but one handsome African-American in particular captivated her more than anyone else. Her enchantment was with the man who sat intimately close to her, the same one who held on to her hand as if it were an extension of his own.

"You look as though you're having a wonderful time. I can read the music from your sheer eyes. I see a spicy but soft melody, which can also be written as a very romantic ballad."

She squeezed his hand gently. "I *am* having a good time. Thanks for bringing me here. I've missed out on so much over the past few years. Maybe you can be instrumental in helping me make up for lost time. I'd really appreciate that." A delicate expression fell across her face. The soft lighting from the candle lent her an angelic appearance, yet no one would suspect that a war with the devil raged within her.

"When I think of the things I've already put you through it makes me shudder. You weren't even twenty-one when we first met. I get the feeling you've been through far more than I suspect, but I'll never again cause you any kind of grief."

"I can't imagine going through that kind of pain. I know now that I'm someone special. I don't need someone to make me feel that way. I had such a wonderful time growing up. I was popular in school, my grades were great, and I got to travel a lot throughout the United States. My family had such high hopes for me."

*Then I fell into the ultimate trap: loving someone who didn't love me back.* What was so sad about all of it was that she couldn't ever go back and change her past. As she lowered her head onto his chest, he kissed the top of her head.

As David T. Walker began to play "Never Can Say Goodbye" on his guitar, Sass went wild over her favorite song. She knew that although it was sung by Michael Jackson it had been written by Clifton Davis. Sass pulled Kristopher out of his seat and nudged him toward the tiny dance floor.

Drifting back in time, Sass did all the dances she could remember from her old high school days. She and her friends went to every dance, party and anything else worth attending. That was a time in her life when everything was as bright as ribbons and bows.

Kristopher pulled her into his arms. "Sass," he whispered into her ear, "we may not be able to go back, but we can move forward. Believe in us. Just consider the past few years a minor set-back in the major-league life we're about to embark on. It's clear to me that I took gross advantage of you back then. Let me take the responsibility for hurting you. Let me carry the guilt. Free yourself. Free your spirit. Only you have the power to do that."

Sass kissed him, wondering if she'd ever be free. "We're here to have a good time. Let's talk about something else. I know. You can give me the four-one-one about the trip back to Paris."

Kristopher guided her back to the table, quenching his thirst from her mouth before they were seated. "Four-one-one?" He looked totally perplexed by her request.

Sass cracked up at the look on his face. "Information. I can't believe you've never heard that expression before. Brother, you'd better start hanging out with some real sisters and brothers! Seems like you've been abroad a little too long."

He grinned, feeling like an idiot. "I should've at least

gotten that one, but I got it now. As for our flight plans, we leave for Paris tomorrow, in the early afternoon."

Their last days together in Paris were spent sightseeing and sharing spectacular nights out on the town. Sass, Kristopher, Lesilee and Gregoire spent most of the remaining time together. Their tours included many of the colorful markets. They also took a tour down the Seine on a Bateaux mouches, on which they dined and danced the evening away. Kristopher later surprised Sass by arranging a night tour of the city by limousine.

The most exciting part of the sightseeing ventures for Sass was the tour of Louis XIV's Palace of Versailles, where the French king and his court had resided after leaving Paris. After strolling through the many formal gardens designed by Le Notre, they visited the Royal Apartments and the beautiful Hall of Mirrors; a single image could be seen several times over. The two couples dined in quaint bistros in the Latin Quarter and in some of the most elegant restaurants in the city.

Kristopher had given Sass a special gift of perfume, called Starlit Sass, before leaving Monaco. The delicate scents had been blended just for her. Sass's eyes had become his starlight, lighting him up like a sky full of midnight stars. He'd been given a special number to reorder the fragrance at will. She was so taken by the special gift she cried every time she looked at the delicately designed crystal vial. Kristopher had once again become very important to her, making her both fearful and enchanted with him; the fear, however, had finally begun to diminish.

Inside Kristopher's Paris apartment, Sass lay sleeping in the guestroom, but nightmares filled her head with terrifying images. A faceless stranger was pulling Justin from her arms and she fought like a tigress to hold on to him. The stranger finally managed to wrestle Justin from her arms. All she could do was scream as she watched her baby being carried off into the night. Her loud moans and groans had reached Kristopher's ears, where he'd been laying awake thinking of her—and how he was going to work hard at making things right for them.

Rapidly, he got up from his bed and moved stealthily across the hall to her room. Opening the door quietly, he slipped silently inside. As Sass had begun talking in her sleep, he didn't know whether to awaken her. Her sleep-filled voice cried out Justin's name.

"Oh, my sweet Justin, they've come to take you away from me. Now you'll never know love . . . and I'm the only one you'll have to blame. You'll think it's my fault because I can never tell you the truth. Justin, please forgive your mommy . . ."

Unable to stand the pain in her voice, Kristopher laid down beside her, gathering her tense, damp body into his strong arms. "Sass, I'm here to protect you. It's only a nightmare. Please tell me why you're so upset?"

As her eyes fluttered open, she stared at him through haze-filled orbs. Remembering her dream, she gasped in horror, wondering if she'd spoken aloud.

"Was I talking in my sleep?" she asked breathlessly.

He kissed away the tears rolling from her eyes. "Yes, Sass, but it's okay. You were just having a bad dream." He didn't dare question the things he'd heard, but Sass couldn't deny the chaos she saw in his eyes. It seemed to express what he felt inside.

She took his hand. "It's not okay. I remember most of my dream. You more than likely want to know what it meant." She swallowed hard before continuing. "I've already told you many things about myself, but there are still a lot of things I can't tell you. Not because I don't want to—I do. It's just going to take more time. We've only been back together for such a short time." *That's not enough time for any person, especially one's who's already been fatally wounded by love, to trust that completely.*

"There are some things that have gone down in my life that my own family's not privy to." Her body sagged under the tremendous weight of the things she held inside. She'd never shared these burdens with anyone, not even her therapist, Dr. Ford. She'd taken a vow not to. Kristopher struggled to maintain his composure, but his breath was cut off by the ache in his heart for her.

"Sass, each time we have one of these conversations it helps me to love you even more. You've been brave. I don't want you to feel any despair. I intend to help mend your broken heart by any means necessary. Please let me help you get through whatever is killing your spirit. It took me a while to realize how much I damaged your soul."

She pulled the creamy-white satin sheet over her bare legs. "You've already helped me. You'll never know how much. I'm trying desperately to move on, but I realize I have a long way to go. With you here, I'll make it through this. There's just been so much to try and get over. The thought of leaving today fills me with a different kind of despair."

Pulling back the sheets, he slipped under them to be closer to her. "I needed to hear that you're going to let me be there for you. That's encouraging. I'll come home in a few weeks. Since you've been here in Paris, I've left a few things unattended. As soon as my business is straight, I'll come. I can't wait to meet Justin." He noticed that the mention of Justin had instantly placed laughter in her eyes.

"Oh, Justin. I miss him. I can't wait to feel his chubby

little arms around my neck and his hands in my hair. He's my world and I'm his."

"And you are mine."

His statement made her smile. Laying her head on his naked chest, she pulled his head down and crushed his mouth against hers. He wanted her in the worst way, but he needed her to decide when the time was right for anything more intimate. For now, he would content himself with just holding her, kissing her sensuously.

Sass looked up into his eyes. "It's in the wee hours, but can we have a heart to heart?"

He shrugged. "Any ground rules?"

She laughed softly. "Only that I get to ask you all the questions. You're already pretty much caught up on the happenings in my life and I've already told you a lot about Lesilee. But I want to know all there is to know about this new and improved you. I suddenly realized that we haven't dug into your personal cache of tell-all yet. And I don't want to save it for later."

He rolled up on his side. "Fire away, Sass, but make sure you want the answers to the questions you ask."

She saluted him. "I haven't heard you speak of any recent experiences with the fairer sex. You're so handsome and charming. I can't imagine that the women aren't still falling all over themselves to get to you. Have you had many love affairs since ours?"

With her expression so delectable, Kristopher couldn't help laughing. He thought she had such an engaging way of probing into things that were really none of her business. "Have you ever heard it said that the good guys always finish last?"

Sass sat straight up in the bed. "I have, but what's that got to do with you?"

Kristopher stroked his chin thoughtfully. "How should I say this? Let's say that most of the women I'm attracted to preferred the roguish type of male, the great pretender. You know how some women like their hero to be the macho, virile sort. They even fancy the strong but silent type, the one that never reveals his true feelings; the one who wouldn't dare to wear his heart on his sleeve. The same type of man I used to be."

"Kristopher," Sass interjected, "are you saying that women aren't attracted to you because you're one of the good guys?" She had a hard time believing that one, especially the part about him being the good guy. He was one of the exact images of the definitions he'd just given, a bad boy. But he did admit it.

"Rarely does the good guy get the girl, especially when he has her best interest at heart. Some of the women I've known love to play the subservient role. They like to be commanded and demanded of. Otherwise, they don't feel loved. It's interesting. When I changed into something worthwhile, the women's attitude toward me soured."

Sass was astonished. "I would've never guessed that you'd have any sort of problems with women, ever. When we were out together, females fell all over themselves just to get a glimpse of you. It's unbelievable, but it doesn't answer my question about your love affairs."

Kristopher grinned. "Sass, I've had a few affairs, but that's all they ever were. Nothing I could ever take seriously. Please remember that a lot of women are first attracted to a man's financial portfolio. Money alone is enough for some of them to consider a lifetime in the bed of a successful man. It's funny, but I used to think they were only interested in me. What a blow to my ego. All a part of growing up, I guess."

"Sorry, bud, but the ladies don't have a monopoly on applying for that gig. There are plenty of gigolos in the world. Is it easy to figure it out when someone's only after the money?"

"Extremely easy. It usually comes on the initial date or just a simple first encounter. The questions are pointed and have everything to do with your finances. It's so transparent."

Sass stifled a giggled. "I never asked all those questions, did I?"

Kristopher stroked her leg with his hand and his eyes caressed her face with his love. "No, you didn't ask a single one. In fact, you weren't at all impressed with me. That's one of the things that sparked my intrigue. However, there's one thing I've always been puzzled by. It's when a woman says that a man is too good to be true, that they're too nice. Why do some women take kindness in a man as a weakness?"

"That cuts both ways, too. Men also see kindness in women as a weakness." *Just the way you saw me.* "I guess I've never really thought of things from a man's point of view. Anyway, that would be impossible for me to accomplish since I'm a female. In this instance, I like the fact that you've become kind and considerate. It rather turns me on."

His eyes narrowed. "Is that because you've seen the other side of the coin with me? Or have you always liked nice men?"

Caught off guard by his directness, Sass bit into her lower lip. Slowly, her eyes drifted across his handsome face. "Hey, I'm the only one who's supposed to be asking the questions. Don't you remember the ground rules we set?"

"You didn't stop me on the last one so I assumed it was okay. You're not going to respond?"

"You were a very nice man. You treated me so well in the beginning, the same as you're doing now. You were respectful, thoughtful, and generous. That was the Kristopher I fell in love with. Then you changed drastically, for the worse. I've often wondered if it was a change at all. Maybe you camouflaged your true self until you won my heart. But isn't that the way it always happens? Are there really happy endings in romance? I've yet to find out."

Kristopher outlined her full lips with his forefinger. "According to the romance novels."

Sass raised an inquisitive eyebrow. "When did you start reading romance novels?"

"When I started missing you like crazy. They got me through some pretty dismal nights. I remember how much you loved them. Now I love reading them. Does that surprise you?"

"Yeah, it does. I didn't know men read great stuff like that, especially men like you."

"The ending is always a happy one, but I focus on the conflict. The why and how the conflict comes about can often determine the outcome. In a personal relationship there'll be conflicts, but there can also be resolutions. The resolution depends on how badly each party wants to heal the conflict. Nothing in this life is easy, but isn't it worth the struggles we endure in order to live our lives fully? Do you see what I mean, Sass?"

Sass looked perplexed. "What do you do when there's no conflict to speak of, yet your relationship sours anyway?"

Kristopher shook his head in the negative. "There's *always* conflict when something goes awry, even if it's only inwardly felt by one or the other party involved. Conflict usually starts deep within an individual, but it'll eventually spill over into the relationship. Say, for instance, that you didn't like the type of clothes I wear. You might internalize it to keep from injuring my feelings. Though that's not such a big deal, you still feel conflicted. If brought to my attention, I might agree with you and change my outward appearance, thus, the conflict is easily resolved. If I don't agree, the conflict deepens. You follow me?"

"Perfectly."

"Good. Let's look at the heart. Rarely are we attracted for very long to someone when we discover we don't like that person. The heart will speak to that conflict of interest in an instant, but we often choose to ignore the signals, the red flags so to speak. But what happens when we don't like ourselves?"

"Conflict!"

"Correct. We're now faced with the biggest conflict of all. How do we dupe people into liking us when we don't like ourselves? If a person doesn't like himself, it's a safe bet that he won't know how to like others. I didn't like myself, Sass, and I liked the way I treated you even less. I just didn't know how to control a foreign emotion: love."

His analogy was making perfect sense to Sass so far.

"The quality of man's character lies within his heart. If he doesn't know his own heart, he can't hope to know the heart of another. Sass, it all begins within the heart of man. The heart is where the spirit of love dwells. I'm afraid I just recently opened up my heart to myself. In doing so, I learned to love me. Unlike before, I'm now capable of loving someone back. I'm capable of opening up and pouring out my feelings without fear. I can love you without holding back because I now love me. I was at odds with myself. That produced constant conflict within."

Sass was scared to respond. She'd never heard Kristopher sound this passionate, so emotional. He had her stunned. She took a minute to regroup. "So what happens when a man's heart gets broken?" She heard how stupid she sounded but it was the only thing she could think of to say. Sass was still reeling from his comments.

"Deep, emotional conflict. The worst kind, Sass."

She laid her head back in the well of his arm. "That

was a lesson I hope I'll never forget. It seems that I stay in conflict, but it's usually with myself. I'm at odd with myself about leaving today, but I have to. I'm going to miss the special times we've shared. It seems like you've made it into the age of wisdom. What you said was profound. I learned something from you today."

"We can continue to learn from each other. For starters, I'll teach you to become fluent in French and you can teach me the meaning of some of those crazy sayings you use. Like you said, I've been abroad too long, too long out of touch with the real brothers and sisters." They both laughed. "There's a lot of room for growth if we sow the seeds. Do you want to go back to sleep for a short time? We won't have breakfast for another couple of hours."

"Will you stay here with me?"

His heart thundered inside his chest for the woman he loved endlessly. "There's no other place I'd rather be."

The sun seemed to shine with an extraordinary brilliance on yet another beautiful Paris morning. Smiling at one another from across the table, Sass and Kristopher sat outdoors on the roof of the high-rise complex. Breakfast consisted of only fresh fruits and juices.

Kristopher picked up a chunky piece of honeydew melon and placed it up to Sass's mouth. She bit into it and licked her lips. Without taking her eyes off him, she fumbled around the fruit plate until she speared a juicy wedge of pineapple. She took a bite of the golden-yellow fruit before feeding the rest to him.

The busy streets below bustled fervently with the fast paced movements of early morning traffic and job-bound pedestrians, yet Sass and Kristopher were oblivious to any of the sounds echoing about. The rhythm of the early morning breeze sang a lustful, melodious song. Soft and gentle, the sun danced around in the sky to the music of the wind.

"It's peaceful here. I hate to leave. As it's been said before, all good things must come to an end." Her deep sigh announced the regret of her imminent departure.

Kristopher's eyes gently scolded her. "Our good thing's not coming to an end. We have many wonderful days ahead of us. Perhaps we'll have meals on this very terrace again, among many other beautiful places. We may even be blessed enough to have Justin with us the next time."

Sass placed her right hand over her heart. "You make my heart rejoice. When you mention my son's name, you make it sound like a treasure you hold near and dear. That pleases me." It also surprised her in ways that she couldn't express.

"I aim to please you, Sass. I was born to please you, but I just didn't know it before. However, I'd never use your son as a way to get to your heart. You and Justin are one. As I came to love you, I'll come to love Justin. You don't know what it feels like inside my chest. There's wild music, dancing, thumping, and a trembling that comes over me each time you speak of your son, whenever you smile, every time I look into your eyes from where I can see into your heart. You're so beautiful. I can't wait until we're together like this again."

Briefly, Sass covered his hand with hers. Raising her hand level with his lips, he kissed each of her fingertips.

Daring to steal a look at the view below, Sass moved over to the ledge of the terrace. Cautiously, she looked over the edge but pulled back quickly. To fight off the dizzy spell, her hands coiled up into her hair, ruffling it with wild abandon. "This is heaven. It's what I'd like the rest of my life to be like. The sun is warm and bright from way up here."

As his hand encircled her waist from behind, the coolness of his breath fanned the side of face. "It's done. Your life can be as pleasant as you want. Whether you're with me or with someone else always remember that you chart your own course in this life. Even if it's raining outside, you can command the sun to shine inside your heart. The master controls are within. You should be the only one that flips the on and off buttons to your desires."

She turned so that her body made contact with his. "You've said many things that I would hate to forget. I'm going away with a lot of the wisdom you've shared. I thank you from deep within my heart." It seemed that Kristopher really had changed. He was no longer Billy-Bad-Ass of long ago, she mused with sheer relief.

Although she was sure she could forgive him, in time, for his misdeeds, she wasn't so sure that her family would ever absolve him. Her father and brother-in-laws were going to have a difficult time with the fact that she'd gotten involved with Kristopher Chandler again—an extremely difficult time. She cringed at just the thought of their reaction to what they'd consider her not-so-good news. Allowing Kristopher back in her life would bring about family opposition.

The moods at the airport were rather melancholy as Sass and Kristopher stepped away from Gregoire and Lesilee to have the last few minutes alone. Kristopher guided Sass to a seat in the departure area, where they sat down next to each other.

Kristopher lifted her left hand and touched her fingertips to his lips. "I'll be lost without you. I feel like I'm suffocating. The sun won't come out for me again, not until I'm face to face with your sun-filled eyes. I love you, Sass." Reaching into his inside jacket pocket, he drew out a slender jewelry box. "Wear this and know that you're loved," he whispered softly.

Taking the box from his hand, she opened it. Her eyes began to water as she removed the solid gold bracelet delicately engraved with one name: SASS.

After kissing the letters, she held it out for him to put on her wrist. *"Merci beaucoup!* I'll wear this beauty twenty-four hours a day, every day of the year." Putting her arms around his neck, she tenderly kissed his mouth. "You've blessed me in so many ways. I hope I can come to trust you again. I sincerely want this new Mr. Nice Guy to finish first, though I can't imagine you ever finishing last at anything."

"Love and trust can happen for us. I'll be home soon. Wait for me. I do love you."

"I'm beginning to feel your love, Kristopher."

Taking her in his arms, he slipped his tongue gently into her mouth. The kisses grew urgent, making her want to make love to him right on the spot. *Why had she waited?* She moaned inwardly. Now they'd have to wait so much longer. But that was the best thing about it all. She hadn't given in to him completely. Perhaps that meant she had truly learned something from the pain of the past—and that she wouldn't make the same serious mistakes with him all over again.

As he had a hard time keeping his manhood from rising to the occasion, his muscles grew taut. Feeling her need for him, he imagined how things might be for them when they were together again. However, he'd made up his mind that he wouldn't make love to her until she agreed to be his wife. *There'd be no more disappointments in Sass Stephen's life. He would personally see to that.*

Sass saw that Lesilee and Gregoire seemed to be hurting over their separation too. Lesilee wore a beautiful Tiffany diamond ring, their engagement now official. A smile came to Sass's eyes as she watched them kissing each other passionately.

As the two women departed to board their aircraft, Sass looked back at Kristopher. What she saw in his eyes sent her fleeing back to him. With open arms, he waited impatiently for her to reach him. Gathering her full against his body, he kissed her fervently.

With great reluctance, he released his hold on her. "Until we meet again. *Au revoir, Sass.*"

*"Au revoir."* Sass slowly moved away from Kristopher. Turning back for a last minute glance at the man she'd never stopped loving, the one who'd hurt her so deeply, she blew him a kiss as she entered the international departure area.

# Six

Settling back into her old lifestyle and returning to business as usual was difficult for Sass. Her only reasons for being happy to be back in Los Angeles were Justin and the rest of her family. As her job had become even more demanding, she'd been assigned a lot of research duties for several upcoming television documentaries. Documenting the tragic events of September 11 was the most challenging for her.

Arriving home late in the evening, Sass felt extremely tired until Justin greeted her at the door, his eyes shining brightly with love. Lillian was right behind him. Sass greeted the housekeeper warmly, elated that she had someone so reliable to care for her adorable son.

Sass's three-bedroom apartment, large and beautifully furnished, held rattan furnishings that graced the living room, the dining area, and master bedroom. Solid-colored cushions rested on the sofa and the chairs. The hardwood floors in all the rooms were covered with large tapestry rugs. The antique accents scattered about here and there added to the comfortable ambience of the room.

Picking Justin up, Sass carried him over to the rattan sofa. "How's my boy today? Mommy missed you." She pressed her nose gently into his and he giggled.

Justin smiled at her in the way that always made her

heart pound with happiness. "I missed you too, Mommy. Can we go to McDonald's?"

She laughed at his question. He loved McDonald's. She loved him so much she couldn't refuse him anything, proud that he spoke exceptionally well for his age. "We can go to McDonald's, but let me look at my mail first."

Lillian was surprised by his request. "Sass, Justin couldn't possibly be hungry. I just gave him a good, healthy meal." Lillian rubbed Justin's stomach, making him laugh.

Sass smiled. "It's okay, Lillian. Justin likes to go to McDonald's for more than just the food. We know how he loves to play on the toys. I'm tired, but I don't mind taking him out."

Lillian's warm brown complexion was smooth and clear. As her toasted-almond eyes laughed merrily, she pushed a few strands of her mixed gray hair behind her ears. "I can take him for you. I have nothing planned for this evening. Just going to read and continue to be lonely." Lillian's husky laughter swept through the room like a magic melody.

"Thanks, but I'll enjoy the outing as much as Justin will. Lillian, we have to find you a man. You're too young to be spending all your evenings alone. When you're not here working, you should be out having a good time. It would also be nice for you to have a companion visit you here, especially when I'm away and you have to stay over."

"If you call nearly sixty-four young, then I guess I'm still in my youth. A companion would be nice, but I haven't met anyone I'm interested in."

Sass grinned. "I have the perfect person in mind. Mr. Wesley Jones does some carpentry work at the station. I happen to know he's been widowed for some time now. He's handsome, too. He has clear, smoky skin, is average in height, and has a strong, healthy looking body. Mr. Jones has all of his hair, mixed gray like yours."

Lillian was delighted with Sass's description of this Mr. Jones. "I'm afraid he might not be interested in me and I'm simply not interested in being rejected. That's a kind suggestion from you, Sass, but I think I'll pass. I've been out of circulation for so long it really doesn't bother me that much anymore. He sounds tempting, but I might not be his type."

Sass sensed Lillian's insecurities about meeting Wes. *So, I'll just have to figure out a way to get them together on my own.*

Sass looked around for Justin when she didn't hear his happy chatter. She smiled when she saw him curled up in the chair asleep. Her heart grew full with the love she felt for her only child. "It looks as though I've just lost my date for McDonald's. He's probably so full from eating the dinner you prepared for him that he couldn't stay awake." Sass laughed heartily.

Lillian smiled at the bundle of joy who'd brought new meaning into her lonely life. "I'm on my way out, but I'll put him to bed first. You go ahead and read your mail. Justin will be fine with me."

Sass blew Lillian a kiss. "Thanks, Lillian. I don't know what we'd do without you around here."

Settling herself back against the pillows on the sofa, Sass began rifling through her mail, searching for postmarks from France. When she didn't find anything from Kristopher, she lost interest, but then decided to open everything anyway. She'd been home for a couple of weeks now. Even though Kristopher had called several times, she'd expected a letter from him.

Included in her mail was a fancy invitation with gold embossed letters, an invitation to a black-tie fashion show to be held at the Bonaventure Hotel. Sass got invitations all the time, but she didn't have a clue as to who'd sent this one. There was an RSVP number, so she'd find out who the host was when she called in to confirm her intended presence.

She frowned when she noticed that the affair was next weekend, wondering why the invite had been sent so late. She was even more puzzled when she saw "Until We Meet Again" written at the bottom. Those were the same words Kristopher had used when she'd departed Paris. She smiled, hoping he had sent the invitation. *Could the fashion show be one of his events?* She doubted that he could've put together a fashion show of this magnitude from Paris. But if so, that would mean he was already scheduled to come to Los Angeles. Giggling happily, she prayed that she'd guessed right. Then she dismissed the idea of the show as one of his.

With Lillian gone, Sass suddenly felt lonely. She and Lesilee hadn't gotten together much in the evenings since their return because Lesilee was busy tying up loose ends for her future return to Paris. Sass missed her friend already, wishing she was going back to Paris with her. Los Angeles had begun to pale next to the City of Light. Ready for a hot shower and a good night's sleep, Sass pulled herself up from the sofa and started down the hallway.

The bedroom furniture was done in a lighter rattan than that in the living room. A lavender and yellow comforter set graced the queen-size bed, lending a cheerful but restful ambience to the ivory-white walls. Pleated scarves draped the lavender and white sheers in a dramatic fashion. A chain of white and lavender silk flowers hung from decorative brass holders on each side of the wall above the windows.

Sass stepped into the bathroom. Large and plush, the room carried the same color scheme as the bedroom. Instant memories of Kristopher joined her in the shower. She smiled when she thought of his delectable mouth taking her breath away. Imagining him lathering her body with soap and rubbing her intimate self with tender loving care made her feel hot all over. Sass wished that she'd had the courage to give herself to him in Paris, yet she was glad that she hadn't.

The bad-boy memories of Kristopher tried to push the recent good times with him out of the way, but she wasn't having any of it. Sticking her hand out of the shower, she reached for her towel and began drying herself off. After stepping out of the shower stall, she dressed in an ivory-white silk chemise. Picking up the crystal vial that held the Sunlit Sass perfume, she sprayed it lightly over her body.

Once she'd checked on Justin, she went back to her bedroom. The firm mattress felt so good under her tired body as she slid into bed, relaxing in a matter of seconds. Just before she drifted off to sleep, Kristopher slid in bed next to her.

Curling up against his warm, solid body, she closed her eyes. His long fingers began to play in her wavy hair. Lowering his head, he kissed her body all over, drawing soft moans from her parted lips. When he touched his lips to her navel, she screamed out in ecstasy.

Gently pushing her gown away, he lowered himself against her nude body. The hardened contact made her weep with joy. Entering her tenderly, he drove her insane with his sultry manhood. After rolling over, he drew her on top of him. While mingling her tongue seductively with his, she rubbed his thighs with passion-heated hands. As her fingers went on a trip through his thick head of soft hair, she moved over him with impassioned motions, giving herself up to him the way she'd wanted to in Paris.

With their bodies sweating heavily from the hot furnace they'd been thrown into, Kristopher and Sass wished for a cool pool of rippling waters to douse their flaming fires. Bathed in her own sweat, Sass rolled over on her back. Discovering that Kristopher had been a mere figment of her lust-filled imagination, she moaned softly into her pillow.

Kristopher's touch had felt so real to her. *Why did she have this crazy imagination?* As sure as she breathed in air, she had felt his body inside of hers. Her imagination was no crazier than the next person's, she decided. She was just in dire need of the type of intimacy that could only be given to her by a man. His touch had felt so real to her simply because she wanted him so much. She also needed to admit that the love bug has once again bitten her. She didn't fully trust him. Even though he seemed more sensitive to her, the jury was still deliberating.

Although Sass was alone in the bed, she was embarrassed by her heavy sexual fantasy. This was certainly no party for her, since a get-together consisted of more than just one person. She thought about giving Kristopher a call so they could fantasize together. Phone sex had become a fast growing craze from what she'd heard.

Sass decided that she needed to go back to sleep. "Try to lighten up on the sexual fantasies. The heavy erotica is draining you. You have to pull yourself together for your appointment with Dr. Ford tomorrow. You also need your beauty rest." Sass laughed at herself. Talking to herself like this made her feel as if she were a few sandwiches shy of a picnic.

Hearing a shuffling noise, she looked in the direction from where it came. Standing in the doorway was Justin, rubbing his eyes and smiling lopsided at her. He looked so cute in his Disney pajamas with the padded feet. Sass felt her heart rejoice with the power of her love.

"Who you talking to, Mommy? I don't see nobody."

Sass laughed out loud as she pulled Justin under the covers with her. "Mommy was talking to herself. Sometimes grown-ups do crazy things. Sleep now, my precious."

While holding Justin close to her, they both gave in to the summons of the sandman.

Kristopher had been in his office for hours. Seated behind his desk, he was rushing to get through a mountain of proofs. For the first time ever, he'd allowed himself to get behind in his duties. Since he'd begun seeing Sass again, he hadn't kept his nose to the grindstone. Being with her made him realize he'd been working far too much. After careful consideration, he'd decided to hire someone to assist him in finishing the photo shoot, another professional that he could trust to take over in his absence.

Kristopher's new game plan included getting back home to L.A. as often as he could. He had high hopes of one day marrying Sass and perhaps moving both her and Justin to Paris. If she wouldn't move to France, there'd be no other choice for him but to move back home and stay there. He was more than willing to stay in L.A., but he also had the desire to open a studio in Paris. But that might have to go on hold until their future together was decided.

Kristopher's financial resources would allow him to take excellent care of a family. He'd worked hard to bring his photography modeling studio to a successful end. Besides revenue from the studio, he was heavily invested in several successful Fortune 500 companies. But for now, he wanted to concentrate on getting Sass to trust him again with her heart. He wanted to be in a position to give her and Justin his undivided attention. He had so much to make up to Sass. He had the rest of his life to do so.

Wanting to hear Sass's sweet voice was almost more than he could bear. With the significant time difference, he knew she'd be sleeping at this hour. He wondered if she'd gotten the letter he'd sent by special delivery. If Sass was a character out of a mystical, magical romance novel, he never wanted to stop reading her story. He'd already summoned her a million times in his dreams. Each time she appeared in one of his fantasies, his lonely, aching heart was soothed by the reality of what she meant to him: everything. Running into her again was an answer to thousands and thousands of desperate supplications.

Fondly, he remembered the days of the relaxed ambiance of the Cote d'Azur with Sass by his side. They'd grown closer together there. She'd begun to let down her guard, loving all the treasures of Monaco. At times he'd felt like he was with a small child. Her honesty had overwhelmed him many times over. That alone nearly made him weep with sheer pleasure.

Her tears of happiness had vitalized him on the day she'd received the perfume named especially for her. It seemed that he could feel her tears running down his very own face. If Kristopher couldn't have her as his own, he didn't know what he'd do with himself. He didn't want to imagine a day without her; it would be like imagining a lifetime without smiling. He hadn't gone to her yet because she needed time to digest all the feelings they'd begun to share anew. But he had to go to her. The very day she'd left Paris wouldn't have been soon enough.


Sass stood at the door waiting until Justin and Lillian disappeared from sight. Lillian was taking him to nursery school. Sass closed the door at the same time the little red Nissan Sentra turned the corner. She then retreated to the kitchen where she opened the refrigerator and poured herself a glass of orange juice. As she sat down, she noticed a special delivery on the table. She smiled brightly at the French postmark. Lillian must have taken delivery of it and forgot to tell her, she mused, ripping the letter open. Resting her head against the back of the chair, she began reading, her heart thumping with eager anticipation.

"Sass, I wrote this letter after we talked on the phone last evening." She looked at the postmark to see which evening he was talking about. "I miss you. My mouth craves for the sweet taste of honey lying in wait on your sensuous lips. My own are but shrinking violets without your generous mouth to tenderly shower them with the moisture from your kisses. My lonely eyes long to have the sun in yours to come out to play, to light me up." She shrieked out loud at the words lighting up her insides. "I've wanted to come home from the moment you left, but I know you need more time. But I don't know how much longer I can wait. The City of Light is in dire need of the light in your lovely eyes to continue to shine so brilliantly. So, you see, if I don't come soon and borrow a spark of light from your eyes, Paris will grow dismally dim."

*Oh, Kristopher, you're missed, too.* In urgent need of his tender touch, she wanted to feel his mouth against hers as much as he needed hers against his. Sadly enough, she had to come to the conclusion that the fancy invitation hadn't come from him.

Glancing at the clock on the kitchen stove, mentally, she counted the hours to see where Kristopher could be reached at this hour. With the letter in hand, she walked from the kitchen and into the bedroom, where she picked up the phone. She first dialed the country code and then the number in Paris. Within minutes Kristopher's deep voice came over the line, causing her to smile brightly. Her heart raced at the sound of his sexy voice.

"Kristopher, Sass. You sound close. We have a good connection."

"Sass! You can't imagine how much I wanted to talk to you. You must've read my mind. How are you and Justin?"

She loved the fact that he always remembered to include Justin. "We're both fine. Justin has already gone to nursery school but I still need to finish getting ready for work. I just discovered your letter. I've been reading it and exacting pure pleasure from your sweet words."

"I'm glad you're both fine; happy you received my letter. Sass, I'm thinking of coming home next week. Is that too soon for you?"

"These arms of mine don't know how you're going to get here, they just need you to get here soon. Kristopher, my arms ache for you. It's already been too long." She winced, unable to believe the words she'd just spoken. She was exposing her feelings without reservation, and way too soon, an absolute no-no. *The hell with all that crap.* Lots of rules, especially dumb ones, were an agitation to her anyway.

He couldn't believe his ears. "In that case, I won't wait until next week. I'll fly out in the next day or two. It may even be tomorrow if I get any more anxious to see you. Sass, I'll contact you as soon as I get to my place. Is that okay with you?"

"I can live with that, but if you had wings, I'd demand you get here today." She laughed. "By the way, bring your evening attire. We have a black-tie fashion show to attend." She paused, waiting for any indication that he might've sent the invitation.

"I'll come well prepared. I'm also looking forward to meeting Justin and reacquainting myself with your family."

She grimaced at that. In no way would they be waiting to meet him again. All they were going to do was flip out. Then they'd get into analyzing to death her new relationship with him, she thought with apprehension. Since no response came regarding the invite, she let that thought go. "I have to go now, Kristopher. I'll wait patiently to hear from you. Have a wonderful flight!"

"Knowing that I'm coming to you will make the long hours easier to bear. *Au revoir, Sass.*"


Seated in Dr. Ford's office, patiently waiting for her to enter, Sass thought about Kristopher being there with her within the next forty-eight hours or less. She couldn't wait to see him, but it didn't stop her from being anxiety ridden over his visit, knowing that her family wasn't going to welcome him with open arms. So afraid of someone insulting him, she hadn't yet shared anything with her family about seeing him again. But that had to happen, and soon.

Dressed beautifully, as always, thirty-something, tall and slender, with coffee-brown skin and cinnamon-brown eyes, Dr. Elise Ford walked into the office and around to her desk. Sass stood out of respect for the striking woman.

"You can sit back down, Sass. It's okay." As her eyes openly examined her patient, she was pleased with what she saw. Sass looked more rested. Her face and eyes looked healthy with color again.

"Before we get started with the session, I'd like you to know there's been another major upheaval in my life. A strange twist of fate occurred while I was in Paris. The past is dead for me now and I have an urgent need to bury it."

Sass's comments surprised Dr. Ford. "I'd like you to explain to me how the past died so suddenly. Just a couple of weeks ago you were buried beneath it."

"It's dead because I'm not the same old Sass anymore. I don't like her and I don't ever want to go back to being the way she was."

There was a definite emphatic coldness in Sass's voice

that Dr. Ford hadn't heard before. It concerned her. "What makes you think you're so different from the old Sass Stephens?"

Making direct eye contact with her therapist, Sass crossed her legs. "The old Sass was timid and scared of her own shadow. The new Sass has grown more confident, eager to get on with the rest of her life. Finally, she wants the past to remain in the past."

Elise Ford held steady eye contact with her patient. "Sass, did something out of the ordinary happen to you in Paris? You seem a little cold to me."

"I'm sorry, I don't mean to sound like that. Maybe I'm taking my new self-confidence a little too far. But, yes, something did happen to me in Paris, something wonderful and exciting. I met Kristopher Chandler in France. He and I spent a lot of time together over there. I no longer think that all men are alike, that they can't change. I'm not afraid to take risks anymore. Suddenly life is worth living. I now intend to live in the real world with all its ups and downs."

Dr. Ford stared at Sass in amazement. "That all sounds well and good, but are you saying that you've put your past with Kristopher Chandler behind you?" Dr. Ford seemed eager to hear Sass's response, amazed that Sass could now speak of him with such calm.

"No, I'm not saying that at all. I've just realized that my past will present itself now and then. What counts is what I decide to do with it when it does. I'm not going to run from it any longer. I'm going to control it instead of it controlling me. Dr. Ford, I'm tired of blaming myself for Kristopher Chandler's numerous imperfections. And I now believe that he has changed for the better. He's not the same man that broke my heart. I'm almost sure of it."

Dr. Ford didn't try to hide her concern. "Do you know why you've put the blame of the soured relationship on yourself? Was there something you think you may have done wrong?"

"I did nothing wrong in that relationship but dishonor myself. I thought he would see the pureness of my love for him, instead of the disrespect I showed myself. You see, I chose loving him over the love I should've been giving to myself. At least, that's the way I think he saw it."

"How do you see it all in hindsight?"

"I actually didn't think I was dishonoring myself. That is, not until it was over between us. All I know is that I loved him. I've always equated love with forgiveness because that's what I was taught. If that was wrong, then I stand accused. I was honest, loyal, and would've given my life for him. To truly love is to forgive without question or thought. Unfortunately, he saw it as a sign of weakness. It was a vicious cycle. In short, he disrespected me, I disrespected myself, and then we seemed to lose respect for each other. Though the pain was extraordinary in getting me to this point, I now understand that he just wasn't ready to deal with his real feelings. What's been the hardest for me to admit, even to myself, was that he just didn't love me."

"You seem to have come to grips with a lot of truths, but have you come to terms with the kind of man Kristopher Chandler actually was back then . . . and not what you thought or hoped for him to be?"

"I know he was a cheating liar. He didn't deserve my faith and trust. But I've forgiven him even though the memories sometime bring anger and bitterness into my heart."

"Wow, Sass. I'm rather stunned. I'm hearing you, but I'm having a hard time believing it. Just a few short weeks ago you were in here ferociously attacking Kristopher Chandler's honor . . . and now you suddenly seem able to put the past in proper prospective. Forgive me for having such a hard time digesting all this. Yet I do believe you're finally on the road to recovery. Or you've fallen so deeply back into denial that'll you'll never be able to see the truth."

"I need someone to believe me, to believe in me. I've had so many conversations with my inner voice that it's not even funny. I realize those voices are my very own, that they're there to protect me, to keep me from harm's way. Still, I continue to fight them, though I know they're there for my own good."

Dr. Ford arose from her seat and embraced Sass warmly, trying hard to keep her cinnamon-brown eyes free of the fear she felt for her patient. "I can't help being somewhat concerned for you. Though you seem to be doing just fine, I don't think you're out of the woods yet. I really need to understand what happened in Paris to bring about this sudden change in you. I want to hear about your latest dealings with Kristopher." With a look of worry on her face, Dr. Ford returned to her seat.

"I ran into Kristopher at a quaint little bistro. In just a short time of seeing him again, I found him to be warm, caring, and ever so sensitive. He believes he's still in love with me and that he wants to take care of Justin and me for the rest of our lives. His sea-green eyes still remind me of precious jade stones and his devastatingly cool aura is bathed in confidence and quiet strength. But his spirit now seems to be more at peace. It somehow seems purer, calmer."

Ready to push the panic button, a red flag immediately went up in front of Dr. Ford. "The new Kristopher sounds divine, but do you imagine yourself in love with him again?"

"I imagine myself in key with him. The same key I've used to unlock the door of my past, to allow myself the opportunity to love him again. He knows that I still have issues with the old Kristopher, just as I know it. But there's room in my heart to love him again. I just have to remember to keep the old Kristopher out of the future. I think I can do that now.

"The good part of my relationship with Kristopher has shown me what I should expect from a man . . . and demand no less from one. The bad portion taught me what to never tolerate from anyone. I have to be grateful for that. Kristopher came into my life at a very vulnerable time for me. With no malice intended, it's possible I could've been confusing gratitude for love. I was willing to explore that possibility, but I don't think that's the case at all. I love him. For sure, I love him for the things he wittingly or unwittingly taught me. Kristopher filled my world with the fantasy and wonders of how love could be, but he left my heart empty and shattered. He left without writing the happy, fairytale ending. That made the story incomplete. Now there's a real chance for healing, for closure, for completion."

Dr. Ford neatly folded the red flag and tucked it away until further notice. She also took her finger off the panic button. "Sass, you've matured so much in just a short time. If you strongly believe all the things that you're saying, you have to constantly practice self-control in life's up and downs. You can have the world at your fingertips. It's all up to you. Above all, you have to continue to believe and trust in yourself."

Sass exhaled deeply. "Thank you, Dr. Ford. You've helped me so much. If you hadn't gotten through to me, hadn't given me the assignments about remembering my past, I wouldn't be in recovery. There's so much about my past that I just blocked out. I thought that if I could tuck it neatly away I'd never have to come face to face with it. Meeting my past, seemingly for the first time, has been a gut wrenching experience. If I deal with things as they come up . . . and not stuff so much garbage inside, perhaps I can handle the world being at my fingertips."

"Sass, you did most of the hard work. I planted some seeds and you simply cultivated them. Very well, I might add. You should be rewarded with a new crop of wonderful experiences. Keep the cultivation up. Don't allow any more new weeds to take root."

"I promise that I won't. And I know I need to continue seeing you. I have a long way to go. We make a great team." Sass laughed. "We both know there's an important element of my past that I'm not ready to explore." *The most horrific part of it.* "However, it'll take an act of congress to remove me from my newly acquired position in life. My confidence is back."

Dr. Ford smiled with understanding. "I can see that. I'll let you go in a few minutes, but I want to discuss your relationship a little more. Is Kristopher living in France? If so, how do you plan to handle a long-distance relationship?"

"Certainly not by osmosis. I've been having quite a few fantasy-filled dreams about him and I'm becoming familiar with the art of hypnotic suggestion." Sass pulled a face, making Dr. Ford laugh. "Seriously, Kristopher plans to fly home whenever he can. I'm sure I'll go there when time permits. His assignment is only temporary. In fact, Kristopher will be here within the next forty-eight hours or so. I don't plan to allow him to pressure me into anything. I'm just cracking the door. Whether I open it up completely still remains to be seen. He's been very patient with me and I've told him a lot about my present life."

Dr. Ford was once again taken by surprise. "My girl, you're really dealing with things in an effective manner. It seems you've been quite busy. And here I've been worried that you were going to keep putting your problems on hold. I'm glad you've been up front with him. Does he have any problems with you having a son? I remember you telling me that he never wanted kids."

With her legs beginning to cramp, Sass stood to relieve the ache in her joints. "None whatsoever. He wants to meet Justin but I don't think I'm going to allow that to happen yet. I have some concerns there. I don't want Justin to ever be hurt by something I've done because I didn't clearly think things through. I need to give myself more time to get used to the idea of having Kristopher back in my life before I go getting my son's emotions involved here."

"I think you're wise to take serious precautions where Justin is concerned. Don't rush back into a relationship with Kristopher. Give yourself as much time as you need. Don't be surprised if reality starts to set in after the blush comes off the newness of the blossom." Dr. Ford picked up her appointment book and looked over her schedule. "I have a conference to attend next week so I'll see you the week after. I hope you have a wonderful visit with Kristopher. I'll be looking forward to hearing all about it. One more thing: What will happen if he decides that he can't accept Justin? Have you thought about that possibility?"

"Do you really need to ask those questions? Justin is my child. Anyone that can't accept him can't possibly be with me. Kristopher is excited about meeting Justin. He even asked if I had a picture of him, but I didn't show him one. If they do meet, I'll closely study Justin's reaction to Kristopher. Children are able to judge a person's character better than some adults are. At any rate, I won't let him get too close to Justin, not until I'm sure of where we're going."

Dr. Ford laughed. "You keep surprising me. Your attitudes are very mature. I'm not going to worry about you any longer. Just listen to your inner voice. It'll keep you on the straight and narrow."

Proud of the way she'd handled herself, Sass waved as she left the doctor's office.

# Seven

Sass had dropped in at a local newspaper office to do further research for the story regarding September 11. Only a couple of hours had passed, but she'd read so many newspapers that the words had started to run together. It was past the time to take a break.

After walking a couple of blocks from the newspaper office, she stopped in a coffee shop to eat. As it was well after lunchtime, she expected to get in and right back out. Surprisingly, the coffee shop was packed. As she turned to leave, she heard someone call out her name. Sass turned around and saw an old friend approaching, Dr. Daniel Davis. She smiled broadly at the thin man with the warm-beige complexion and dark-brown eyes.

Daniel greeted Sass and kissed her cheek. He then took her hand and guided her to his table. "Look at you." Daniel beamed at her. "You look like a sunny day in the countryside."

"Thank you. It's so good to see you. Dan, I feel guilty for not keeping closer in touch. You've always been such a good friend to me. It's been too long. I've been so busy. And that's no excuse."

"You don't have to feel guilty, Sass. I'm just as busy as you are. I heard your name announced on television one night. Then, when I saw it come up on the screen after the story, I felt such pride in you."

Sass blushed. "That's sweet of you. Thanks. Dan, how's your private practice going?"

He placed his hand over hers. "Honey, if my practice was doing any better, I wouldn't have time to go to the bathroom." He laughed. "I have a lot of elderly patients who I enjoy working with. So many of our elderly are left to fend for themselves with few resources. They barely manage on such scant incomes. It has always been my desire to give something back, so I do a lot of free medical care. I even make house calls. Fancy that in this day and age."

Feeling great sentiment for this kind soul, Sass smiled. "Dan, the world needs more people like you. You've always been dedicated and caring. I'll never forget the help you gave me when I was in desperate need of a friendly face and a reassuring smile."

"I would do anything for you. You must know that." Sass nodded in agreement. "How are things working out for you, honey? I was so scared for you . . . and now you seem to have pulled it all together. I can't help remembering your pain. You look happy now. Are you?"

"I'm doing just fine. Dr. Ford has worked wonders on me. I'm glad you recommended her. She's been so patient. We've finally begun to clean out the human garbage disposal." She gave a sigh of relief. "In fact, I had an appointment today. She's pleased with my progress."

"I'm ecstatic for you, Sass. Have you gotten that low-life out of your system?" When the lights dimmed in her eyes, he was sorry he'd asked.

Sass took a moment to effect composure. When Dan kept looking over at another table, she wondered what held his interest. "Dan, Kristopher's not a low-life. He was just scared. I don't think he really knew what he wanted back then. His inability to commit may've been the problem. He thought running away would solve it.

I've rejected that idea so many times, but since there's no other explanation, I have to believe that that was it. He wasn't ready to settle down, so I guess it got a bit overwhelming for him. His lifestyle called for him to take off at a moment's notice, which was another problem in settling down. He was also immature."

Dan frowned. "You're much more generous than he deserves. I guess it's not in your nature to be vindictive. You have to react the only way you know how."

"Oh, I wasn't as calm as you seem to think. I let my alter ego take over. It waged a fierce battle against Kristopher until I was able to get it in check. I didn't even remember all the things that went on, not until they started coming out in my therapy sessions." Sass felt a twinge of deep regret. "What happened in the aftermath has changed both of our lives forever."

"Since your alter ego didn't kill him, I'd say he got off pretty lightly. But let's put all that away. It's in the past. Tell me what's going on in your present life."

Sass took a minute to catch her breath. Fearful of his reaction, Sass decided not to tell him she was seeing Kristopher again. She'd save that for a later time, a time when she was sure of what she was doing. "My job is fantastic and I just returned from vacation in Paris!"

Dan raised both eyebrows. He then became totally distracted by something or someone at another table.

Sass grew impatient with his divided attention. "Dan, what has you so distracted? I keep losing your attention."

He smiled at the irritated expression on her face. "I'm sorry, Sass. There's a beautiful woman over at the next table, but I can't tell if she's looking at me or you." He seemed embarrassed at being caught at something so juvenile. "It's been hard to concentrate with her staring at us so hard."

Sass stole a glance at the next table. She had to force

a smile to her lips when she saw the woman who had caused her so much grief. "That's Grace Chapman. She's one of Kristopher's top fashion models. Would you like to meet her?" Sass nearly gagged while swallowing the nastiness that had almost escaped from her tongue.

"I don't mind meeting her, but I can tell you now she's not my type. Too, too obvious. From what I can see of her eyes over here, I wouldn't trust her as far as I could throw her. She looks like a hungry panther about to strike out at its prey."

Sass was shocked at his comment since she'd never heard him speak ill of anyone. That is, anyone other than Kristopher. "Well, it's too late now. She knows I've seen her. She's coming toward us. I'm having a flashback of a similar situation in Paris." Sass remembered how Kristopher had approached her. However, his approach had turned out to be a pleasant experience. An encounter with Grace would be anything but pleasing.

Grace's polished mahogany legs neared the table. Long and willowy, her lower extremities appeared neverending. "Sass, girl. How are you? I haven't seen you in a dog's age." Grace giggled like an adolescent, which came across as false. "I've missed seeing you around the studio."

Sass instantly saw the insincerity of Grace's statement in her calculating amber eyes, especially since she hadn't been at Kristopher's studio in years. Uninvited, Grace hugged Sass as she plopped down next to her. The phony affection made Sass want to throw up.

Sass then introduced Grace to Dan, telling her that he was a highly respected physician.

"So, you're in love with a doctor now. I hope he's treating you better than K.C. did."

A flicker of deep pain skipped across Sass's features. "Dan and I *are not* lovers, Grace. We're old friends who

used to work at the same hospital while I was in college."
Sass grew angry at Grace's rude assumption.

Grace looked apologetic. "No harm intended. What
have you been doing with your bad self? It's been over a
year since I saw you last."

Sass hated brash slang, especially when it had been
played-out for umpteen years. She frowned heavily at
Grace's comments. "Three years," Sass corrected. "Just
working hard and trying to stay out of trouble." The agitation in Sass's voice couldn't be disguised.

Looking amused, Grace turned her attention to Dan.
"Good doctor, what type of doctoring do you do? I'm in
need of a good plastic surgeon. K.C. says my breasts need
to be augmented. I was against implants but he seems to
think they'll enhance my appearance."

The look Dan gave Grace in return was far from
amusing.

Sass couldn't help wondering why Grace kept mentioning Kristopher. It was as if she were trying to draw
some sort of reaction from her, or worse, hurt her even
more than she already had. Sass suspected that Grace
had had a lot to do with the way things had unfolded between her and Kristopher.

"I'm an internist. I don't *do* breasts. When you do find
a plastic surgeon, just make sure he's board certified.
Check his credentials out well. It could save you a lot of
unnecessary grief."

The same type of grief you're trying to heap on me,
Sass mused painfully.

Grace's catlike eyes flirted boldly with Dan. "Thank you
for the advice. How can I pay you for services rendered?"

"As a friend of Sass's, the advice is free." A definite
chill had clipped his tone.

*Now, why don't you go play in traffic on the 405 freeway.*
Sass knew she was being churlish but she couldn't help

it. Being in the company of Grace wasn't the least bit pleasant.

Grace pushed her chair back and stood up. "Sass, it was nice seeing you, but I have to run. And, doctor, it was definitely a blast meeting you. I hope I'll run into you again." Grace kissed Sass on the cheek, causing Sass to cringe. Before departing, she dropped her business card in front of Dan. "Perhaps we can do lunch or dinner so we can get better acquainted."

He looked at it as though the gold-embossed card carried a deadly disease, but he didn't bother to pick it up. "It's people like her who give women a bad name." He looked at Sass with concern. "You haven't touched your sandwich since she sat down. She upset you, didn't she?"

"Grace has a way of rubbing me the wrong way. She was so rude to me the first time I met her. It all stemmed from jealousy. She ostentatiously referred to me as Kristopher's bunny of the month." *Unfortunately, she turned out to be right.* "She stayed out of my face after that initial encounter, once I put her in her place. Yet I picked up on something today that I had often considered but really wasn't that sure about."

"It wouldn't take a rocket scientist to pick up on what she was doing here today. She was trying to hurt you. Grace is *not* your friend. Don't ever let her convince you otherwise."

"She had the hots for Kristopher from the very beginning. After that little demonic display we just got from her, I'm now wondering how much of a part she really played in the problems in our relationship." Sass was now glad that she hadn't told Dan about her and Kristopher renewing their relationship. He wouldn't like it in the least, especially after witnessing the annoying episode with Grace.

"Honey, whatever part she played, you can be sure it was a starring role."

"Probably so, but that's old history now." *Or was it?* Sass had to wonder.

After strolling hand-in-hand back to the newspaper office, Dan saw Sass safely to the front door, where he kissed her on the cheek. "I'm serious about us getting together again."

Sass hugged Dan warmly. "I'll see what I can do, Dan. I promise to keep in touch. Don't hesitate to call me whenever. I'm sure we can find some time to hang out."

Dan had once been crazy about Sass, but she'd never seen him as anything more than a good friend. That was the reason he'd never told her how he felt and why he'd settled for friendship. Even now, he felt that any man in Sass's life would play second fiddle to Kristopher Chandler. Sass had been so in love with Kristopher, so deeply in love with him that it had totally impaired her better judgment.

Having spent several more hours at the newspaper office reading and writing, Sass was exhausted by the time she exited the building. She didn't have to worry about Justin; Lillian was dropping him off at her parent's place where she'd later pick him up.

Only a few minutes had elapsed when Sass used her cell phone to make a quick call back to her office. The station operator answered and she asked to speak to Wesley Jones. She was immediately connected to the engineering department.

"Wesley Jones here."

"Hi, Wesley, it's Sass Stephens. How are you?"

"I'm fine, my dear. What can I do for you?"

"Could you please do some work for me at my apartment? I need a few extra shelves installed in the walk-in closet in the master bedroom. I've already gotten the okay from the owner of the complex."

"Sure, young lady. When would you like me to take care of it?"

She felt a little guilty about what she was doing, but it was too late now. "Whenever you're available. Why don't you drop by and see what I need first. Then you can give me an estimate."

"I'll give you a call before I come over to your place, Sass."

"Good. I'll expect to hear from you soon."


It had only taken Sass a couple of days to put her covert plans into action. The evening had been filled with lots of fun activities. Sass had successfully pulled off her match-making between Lillian and Wesley. Her parents, two sisters, and their husbands were also in attendance. Over dinner prepared by Sass's two hands, the seniors had become instantly charmed with each other. They'd even made plans to see a movie together later in the week. Sass felt satisfied with the outcome of her efforts.

Her workload had been a little easier this day. Before her company had arrived, she and Justin had spent an hour in the park across the street from her apartment. Justin had gone home to stay with his aunt Stephanie for the next couple of days. Sass hated the thought of being in the apartment alone.

Lying in bed, but having a hard time getting to sleep, Sass wondered why she hadn't heard from Kristopher. He should've been here by now. She hoped nothing had happened to him. Get rid of the negative thoughts, she scolded herself. When the phone rang, her heart began to beat wildly. Before answering, she prayed that it was the man with the sea-green eyes.

"Hello." Sass held her breath.

"Sass, it's Staci. Did I wake you?"

*No, but I'm disappointed.* "Hi, Staci. I thought you might be someone else. I was expecting a call from a friend."

"I called to see if you wanted to go shopping with me tomorrow. I forgot to ask you when I was there earlier."

"I'd love to, but I've already made other plans."

"With whom?"

"Why do you need to know every little thing about my business, Staci?"

"It must be a new man! Otherwise, you wouldn't have your big butt up on your shoulders. Who is he, what does he look like, and what's his occupation?"

Sass grimaced. "I need to talk to you, but I need you to listen. The things I'm about to tell you are for your ears only. I know you can make a promise not to breathe a word of this to anyone, but can you keep it?"

"Oh, Sass, sounds like you've gotten yourself into something you're not too sure about. I hear it in your voice. But I promise not to utter a word, baby sister."

Sinking her teeth into her lower lip, Sass closed her eyes to gear up for the fireworks. "I'm seeing Kristopher Chandler again."

Sass chewed on her thumbnail as several moments of uncomfortable silence ensued.

"Could you repeat that? Cause I'm sure I didn't hear you say that you're seeing the man who broke your heart into millions of microchips and scattered them across mother earth."

"That's exactly what I said."

"You got to be out of your damn mind! Have you forgotten what you've already been through with him? No, this mess of a man ain't happening in your life again."

"Will you please listen, Staci? You promised."

"No! I promised to keep your secret. I didn't promise not to read you and to magnify this situation like fine print. You have to be sick to even consider allowing him back in your life. Mom and Dad are going to have a hissy-fit when they find out about this. And you can rest assured that I'm not the one who's going to bring this kind grief to them. You're on your own on that mountainous feat. You're not surprised by my reaction, are you?"

"Hardly! I understand it perfectly. But I need you to understand that I have to bring closure to this situation . . ."

"How are you going to bring closure by seeing him again? That's not going to bring the outcome you think. You're only going to fall into his trap again and possibly fall back in love with him at the same time."

"I can't fall back in love with someone I've never fallen out of love with. I've never stopped loving Kristopher. He's changed, Staci. So much so that I find it hard to believe myself."

"If you find the change in him hard to believe, how are you going to convince the rest of us that he's changed? Kristopher wasn't honest with you in the least bit. He didn't treat you right or with respect. How can you just up and forget about all that, Sass Stephens?"

After switching over to the portable phone, Sass began to pace the room like someone on speed. "What about forgiveness, Staci? Isn't that what we were taught?"

"Forgiveness is one thing. Getting back involved with him is another matter entirely. What do you see happening between you two? Do you honestly believe that you have a future with that career Casanova?"

Sass took a deep breath. "I know what you're saying. I only decided to start seeing Kristopher so that I could pay him back for what he did to me, but I no longer feel that way. He has really changed. Please just be there for me. It's difficult to do this without having someone I love around to talk to about it. I'm not asking you to accept Kristopher. I'm just asking you to accept the decisions I've made where he's concerned. Staci, I know all the pitfalls before me. But what am I supposed to do with the love that my heart overflows with for him? What am I supposed to do with the love Genie that's been bottled up inside of me for the past several years? Love wants to, needs to break out of solitary confinement, Staci! And I fully understand that the consequences, good or bad, are mine alone to bear."

Staci wiped the tears from the corners of her eyes. The undisguised pain and desperation in her baby sister's voice was too loud for her to ignore. Although the family would be terribly divided on this matter, especially the men, she couldn't turn her sister out if she wanted to. "I'm here for you, Sass, whatever your decision. As for the consequences, they *are* yours to bear, but not alone. The family will feel them, too, simply because we love you. Now what can I do to ease the anxiety of this situation?"

Sass quickly filled in her older sister about the details of Paris and beyond. She then told her she'd like for her and Stephanie and their spouses to attend the fashion show with her and Kristopher. Though somewhat reluctant, Staci finally agreed to go, promising to talk the others into it even though she knew it was going to be a tough sell.

"I know it's going to be awkward for all of us. But I think it's the best way for us to break the ice."

"Or get Kristopher's neck broken! You know you got two hotheaded brothers-in-law."

Sass moaned. "I know. I hope the guys will go easy on him. I hope they don't embarrass him or me. I'm really more worried about Gerald and Eugene than you and Stephanie."

"You're right to worry about them, but Stephanie and I know how to put them boys in check with ease. I'm

going to do my best to be happy for you despite my negative feelings about this matter. Now, I want you to stop
the agonizing already."

Sass sighed in relief. "Thanks. I don't know how to
stop worrying about it, but I promise to try." Sass
laughed anxiously. "I'll call you in the morning, Staci."

"Goodnight, Sass. Get some rest, baby sister. I got your
back."


Hurriedly, Kristopher put his clothes away in the
spacious closet of the lavish master suite at his Hollywood Hills home. All he could think of was his reunion
with Sass.

Seconds later he sat on the bed and carefully studied
the new area map of Los Angeles, to pinpoint her street.
Though he knew his native city like the back of his hand,
he wasn't familiar with the newly developed area that
Sass lived in. Having made up his mind not to call her,
but to just present himself at her door, he hoped she
wouldn't be angry with him. With his Mercedes Benz
now parked in the circular driveway, he rushed outside
to begin his journey. Had his flight not been delayed in
Paris, he would've been in the states hours ago.


Still unable to sleep, Sass's worry pricked at her like
tiny pins. Please don't let anything happen to him, she
prayed in silence. She thought about calling the airport,
but she didn't have an estimated time of arrival nor did
she know a flight number. In fact, she didn't even know
which commercial airline he was flying on. Getting out
of bed, she grabbed her satin robe and headed for the
kitchen. After turning the fire on under the teakettle,
she sat at the table to wait for the whistle to blow. Reach-

ing into her robe pocket, she pulled out her letter from Kristopher and began reading it over again. It was only about the tenth time she'd done so. Still, she basked in every sweet word written on the expensive stationery.

Although the teakettle was whistling, she continued to read the last couple of lines.

Wearily, Sass got out of her seat and poured a cup of tea. Before she could sit back down at the table, her doorbell rang. Looking at the clock on the stove, she wondered who could be ringing her bell at this time of night. When Kristopher entered her mind, her feet sprouted wings. After setting her cup down, she ran for the door. She felt his presence before she ever opened it, but she still looked out the peephole first.

Swinging the door wide open, she rushed into his arms, nearly toppling him over in the process. "Kristopher, Kristopher! I've been so worried about you. What happened?"

Her enthusiastic greeting made him feel good all over. Not bothering to answer, he crushed his mouth down over hers. They stood out in the hallway kissing, until Sass felt the drafty air creeping up under her robe.

He held her away from him. "Sass, you're still as beautiful as I remember. I'm sorry I'm so late. I'd never fly commercial again if I could help it. It has taken far too long to reach you. Let me look at you." He turned her around and around. Bringing her back to him, he studied her beauty with a large smile on his face. "How much have I missed you? You can't possibly know."

Her skin grew flushed. "I think I might have some idea. Let's go inside. I'm beginning to tremble from the cold, but now I have you here to warm me."

He grinned. "Yes, I'll warm you with the hot blood pulsating through my heart." Picking her up with ease, he carried her inside.

She noticed his attractive attire as he carried her over to the couch and set her down. For several minutes, he lost himself in her sepia eyes. The diction of their liquid orbs seemed to tear down all the barriers that once stood between them.

Sass couldn't help but notice that his light blue silk shirt was still immaculate despite his long flight. The charcoal gray suit still looked impeccably pressed. "Your clothes are flawless. What did you do, fly in the nude?"

He threw his head back in laughter. Enchanted with the sound of his laugh, she ran her fingers through his slightly tussled hair. "Had I tried that, I would've been arrested. I'm a little wrinkled but not much. I was rarely in my seat. I must've paced the entire jetliner." He took a minute to look around the room. "Where's our young Justin?"

The "our" was especially noted by Sass. "He's with his Aunt Stephanie. He'll be home in a couple of days." Sass scowled. "Could we take a minute to talk about Justin?"

"You look troubled. What is it?"

She wrung her hands together. "I don't think it's a good idea for us to bring Justin into our relationship right now. It wouldn't be fair to him emotionally. Do you mind if we wait a while and see how things go? I think that would be the best for all of us."

With no emotion on his face, Kristopher nodded. "I'm disappointed in your decision, but I respect it. I have no desire to cause you or Justin any discomfort. I didn't want to leave home again without meeting him, but hopefully there'll be other opportunities."

"How long will you be here?"

"I can stay for a week or two, I can leave sooner if you get tired of me. I don't want to be an unwanted intruder in your life."

"A week or more! How exciting. I can assure you that I won't tire of you. I hope you won't tire of me either. An intruder? Please! I also hope you're not even a tiny bit angry with me over my decision regarding my baby boy."

"How can I be angry at the woman I want forever with?"

"You flatter me, Kristopher Chandler. But before we even begin to discuss forever, are you prepared to face my angry family? Staci is the only one who knows I'm seeing you again. I must tell you; they'll have many questions you might not want to answer."

"I've got nothing to hide. I'm prepared to answer any questions they might pose. I can supply them with references and financial statements if necessary." His mood grew somber despite his joking reference. He knew all too well the daunting opposition facing him.

She loved how he never backed down from anything or anyone, especially a challenge. Unloosening his tie, she opened the first two buttons on his shirt. "If you think I'm trying to seduce you, you're right. As for my family, you'll have a hard time earning their respect."

Looking at her with adoration in his eyes, his teeth lovingly nipped at her lower lip. "Don't worry. You earn respect by giving it. Back to seducing me, I won't let you. Not until you agree to carry my surname."

She saw that he was much too serious for her playful mood. A combination of devilment and defiance flickered in her sheer eyes as she narrowed them at him seductively. "You want to bet? If I wanted you in my bed, you wouldn't be able to turn me down. Forgive me for calling it like it is. Men will be men."

He was amused by her devilish behavior. "If you're trying to live up to your name right now, you're succeeding." His eyes grew sober. "Sass, there's no doubt that I want to be in your bed. I can never forget the wild passion we once enjoyed. However, I'm content to wait until we share one bed, together, forever, on the continent of your choice."

His gentle, loving words struck her dumb. He'd made

her an offer that she might have a hard time refusing. That alone was incredible. Was he really asking her to marry him? He'd talked of forever in Paris, but this time it was a bit more direct.

Sass kissed him on the mouth passionately. "I don't know what to say, Kristopher, and I'm not really sure I know what you're saying."

He kissed her back. "I think you do. Like I told you when we first met, I now know what I want. Rarely does it take me long to figure out how to get it. For you, I'm willing to wait, as long you need me to. No pressure for now since you're such a sweet challenge."

"So I am. I appreciate your patience. Thanks. Are you happy to be back in your home?"

Pulling her head down, he flicked his tongue over her outer ear. "Extremely happy. As the old saying goes, there's no place like home. Finding you again makes it even more appealing. I've been away a lot since we split up. I now have a wonderful reason to stay here in Los Angeles as much as possible. In fact, I have a brand new home up in the Hollywood Hills. Are you familiar with the newer home developments in that area?"

Sass grinned. "I know where they're located, but I'm not familiar with them. Besides, I couldn't afford to buy a house up there if I wanted one. You're in a big money neighborhood."

"If you agree to be with me that'll quickly change. Not only will we have a beautiful home to live in, we'll do lots of traveling and stay in hotels just for the thrill of it. The finest hotels all over the world will cater to us. There's nothing you could hope for and not receive."

"Stop, Kristopher! You're tempting me to run away with you and never look back. How I love traveling to exotic places."

Putting his hand on the nape of her neck, he tilted

her head back and stared deep into her eyes. "That's the intention, my lovely Sass."

Every time he called her that it made her body tingle all over. She whistled inwardly, sizzling from his intimate touch. To cool things down, she stood to her feet. "I was drinking a cup of tea when you rang my bell. Would you care to join me in the kitchen?"

Pulling her back down to him, he drank deeply from her mouth, holding her captive until she needed to breathe. Finally, he released her. Sass, wanting more, wasted no time in engaging him in another hot, wet kiss.

Her kiss left him totally breathless. "Once we have our tea, I'd like to see the rest of your place." Arising from the couch, he draped his arm loosely around Sass's waist, allowing her to guide him into the kitchen.

After pulling out a chair for him to sit down, she reignited the fire under the kettle. "Since Justin will be gone for a few days, would you like to stay here with me?"

With amusement twinkling in his eyes, he smiled brightly at her. "Are you still trying to win the bet you challenged me with earlier?"

She wrinkled her nose. "No. I'm serious. You can sleep in the guestroom, or in Justin's crib bed. Whichever you prefer."

He was completely taken by her charming sense of humor. "Did you get Justin's approval for me to sleep in his bed?"

Her rose petal laughter bounced off the stark white kitchen walls and he loved the lilting sound of it. The teakettle whistled, startling her. Now it was his turn to laugh. He did, from deep within his throat.

She stared openly at his dancing eyes. "I almost forgot that your laughter is like none other that I've ever heard. I hope I'll hear it often. Even if you are laughing at me."

He laughed again just to bring her pleasure.

Sass fixed two cups of tea and set one in front of him. She then pulled out a chair and sat down. Thrilled at being together again, they looked into each other's eyes from over the rims of their cups.

After finishing their tea, Sass led Kristopher through the entire apartment, which she thought was absolutely seedy compared with his magnificent place in Paris. But he thought it was absolutely charming . . . and told her so.

While standing in the center of Justin's bedroom, Kristopher looked all around the gaily-decorated space. Stuffed animals and toys were everywhere but neatly arranged. The bedspread with the balloons and clowns all over it made him feel happy. Two small California football team sport jerseys were pinned to one wall and a small football sat on a red plastic tee atop the oak dresser. A miniature basketball court and a small basketball sat next to the dresser. Carousel night lamps held brightly painted horses and other animals normally seen on a merry-go-round.

The room reminded Kristopher of a theme park. It was both colorful and cheerful. A large wall-photo of Justin captured his eye. His breath caught. He'd seen this baby boy before. Justin was the spitting image of pictures of him when he was that age. His heart rate went berserk.

He drew in a deep breath to regain his composure. "Sass, you must've decorated this room. It smacks of your cheerful, animated personality." He had to drag his eyes from the photo.

"I did. I think a child's room should be as bright and colorful as Disneyland. Their life should reflect the same. You're only a child for a short time. Once you become an adult things should be just as vibrant, yet it doesn't work out that way very often." She thought of all the deep pain she'd endured at the hands of others, especially at Kristopher's.

He felt her sudden anguish. "I always thought you had a great childhood."

"I had a wonderful one. My teenage years were even better, but it ended too quickly. It seems like right after you finish college it's bright lights out, but Justin has turned the sunbeams back on in my world. I get as much of a kick out of this room as he does. As for fun, we both love to go to amusement parks."

"We'll go to Disneyland as soon as you allow me to meet Justin. How does that sound to you?" Kristopher had felt her change in mood. Although he wanted to shelter her from any sad feelings, he knew she had to feel her pain before letting go of it.

"I'd love to go to Disneyland with you. I bet you're a bigger kid than I am." Theme parks hadn't been one of the places they'd gone together. She turned out the light as they stepped from the room.

"I'm hilarious at amusement parks. You'd think I'd never been to one. I had a wonderful childhood, too. My parents took me to every amusement park in the U.S. of A." Thinking of those days brought moisture to his eyes. When missing his parents deeply, he often thought that he could smell his mother's perfume and feel her gentle fingers in his hair.

Sass looked at him with concern. "Kristopher, are you okay?"

"I'm fine. I just miss my mother and father. They've only been gone a few years. It's been hard for me to get past that horrible event. Their tragic death still haunts me. They died when their house caught fire as they slept in each other's arms."

She reached out to him in his grief. "I'm sorry, Kristopher. I had no idea. Come over here. Let's sit down."

Putting her arms around him, Sass lowered his head,

holding it tightly against her breasts. *Share your pain with me, Kristopher. We can deal with it together.*

"I only know a fraction of how you must feel. When I lost you, it was like someone close to me had died. I didn't know what I was feeling at the time. I never realized I mourned you until recently. Dr. Ford, my therapist, explained to me what I had gone through. She surprised me when she told me that the mate opposing divorce would much rather lose a loved one to death than to divorce. With divorce one of the partners makes a conscious decision to leave the other. In death, only God can make that decision. I found the concept very strange in the beginning, but now I understand it. If it's any comfort to you, your parents died together, still in love, in each other's embrace."

Kristopher stroked her hair. "It's the only comfort to me, Sass. Dr. Ford's right. No person wants to be left behind by another. I can see how it would be easier if it were not a decision made by only one partner. But please know this, I don't ever want to cause you grief. I didn't know how deep pain could run until I lost them. I'd never been on the receiving end of it. But I knew how to dish it out." His parents' death was largely responsible for the change in him.

"I have grieved all these years, especially when I have to discuss our past in therapy. I'm sure I haven't completed the healing process entirely. But while I was in Paris, so many things became abundantly clear to me. I always blamed myself for our problems, but now I know I didn't do anything to make you behave the way you did. These are your problems. I need to let you own them. I don't want to claim them as my own anymore."

"Good for you. I'm happy to hear you reasoning everything out so well. I was your first love. Though I know you'll never forget the past entirely, it's time to chase away the winter from your heart. It's time to fill the void with spring and summer. I pray that your heart can re-open and eventually reserve a permanent spot for me."

Lying her head in his lap, Sass pulled his face down to hers, melting her mouth over his.

Swept away by her gentleness, he savored the sweet honey from her lips. As the night slowly slipped away, they stayed in a heated embrace.

At midnight, Sass stifled a yawn. "I can hardly keep my eyes open. I'm ready to go to bed."

"I'll go on home now, but I plan to return with the sun. While I'm here you'll have to show me all your new special places in the City of Angels. I'm sure you have many. You love L.A. as much as I do."

She felt bitterly disappointed. Though he'd never answered her about staying over, she'd rather thought that he would. Perhaps he'd thought she was just joking. "Okay, I'll walk you to the door."

Though he saw the disappointment in her face, he knew that he should go. His hormones were raging for release as they clung together at the door. He didn't want to pull away, but he did. She quickly turned her head so he couldn't see her disappointment. Closing the door behind him, she ran to her bedroom.

In less than a minute, the doorbell rang again.

Looking around to see what he may have forgotten, she ran to the door. Upon opening the door, he swept her into his arms. He then carried her into the bedroom, where he pulled the crisp white percale linen farther back and laid Sass in the center of the bed. After removing his jacket and shirt, he laid down next to her. Under the sheets, he slid his pants off, throwing them on the Brentwood rocking chair situated in one corner of the room.

With her heart trying to make its way out of her chest, she suddenly felt frightened.

Seeing the fear in her eyes, he laid his head back on the pillow and pulled her into his arms. "Sleep, beautiful Sass. We're both tired and we need our energy for later in the day. If you have a bad dream, wake me up. I still sleep like a log," he whispered against her forehead.

So grateful for his generous, reassuring words, she buried her head onto his chest and curled up her fingers in his hair. *"Bonne nuit."* He didn't hear her tell him goodnight because he was already asleep. She closed her eyes and nestled in closer to him.

Kristopher awakened at three A.M., his arms aching for the feel of her. Sliding up behind her, he wrapped his arms around her waist. Massaging the soft flesh at her nape with his fingertips, he kissed the back of her neck. Awakening from his touch, she turned to face him and softly caressed the slight stubble on his handsome face. Pulling her on top of him, he held her tightly against his arousal. Locked in a loving embrace, they fell back to sleep.

The phone bell awakened Sass. By the time she picked it up, the caller had already hung up. Her annoyance rapidly turned to bewilderment when she discovered that Kristopher wasn't beside her. She then noticed the note lying on the pillow where his beautiful head had lain earlier. She picked up the sheet of paper and slowly perused it.

SASS, I'VE GONE HOME TO SHOWER AND CHANGE CLOTHES. I'LL RETURN BEFORE YOU HAVE A CHANCE TO MISS ME TOO TERRIBLY. There was a happy face before the note continued.

I'LL TAKE YOU TO BREAKFAST. WE CAN THEN SPEND THE REST OF THE DAY MAKING EXCITING NEW MEMORIES. LOVE YOU, KRISTOPHER. Sass kissed his signature. Feeling happy and extremely exhilarated, she jumped up and ran for the shower.

# Eight

Sass looked chic dressed in a delightfully feminine black and white polka dotted sundress. Short in length, fashioned with back laces, the style showed off her beautiful golden-brown skin. Large white buttons ran from the fitted bodice to the hemline. Black and white dotted earrings complimented her attire. Sass's hair fell in soft waves onto her shoulders. The bold, gold highlights streaking through her sandy-brown tresses added a dramatic finish to her already stunning appearance.

The doorbell rang just as she slipped her feet into black crocheted sling-back sandals. Sass dashed out of the room. Catching her breath, she calmed down before opening the door.

Wearing white jeans and a coral short-sleeved polo shirt with a gold insignia on the breast pocket, Kristopher looked handsome. His sunny smile lit up his eyes when she reached up to hug him. Kristopher leaned into her and planted a lingering kiss on her mouth. Before stepping completely inside, he reached around the corner and picked up the large gray and pink stuffed elephant he'd purchased for Justin.

Sass squealed in delight when he presented the toy in front of her. "Oh, thank you. It's so beautiful. I have the perfect spot for it in my bedroom. When did you purchase this? Nothing's open this early."

He felt slightly embarrassed by her assumption. "I purchased it at a gift shop at the airport. Sorry, Sass, but the elephant's for Justin."

Momentarily, she looked stunned. Then she laughed heartily. "And here I thought I was your favorite." She kissed his mouth to show her gratitude for the sweet gesture toward her darling Justin. Sass picked up the large elephant and hugged it to her breasts.

He kissed her forehead. "You're so much more than a favorite. I'm deeply in love with you." He felt his confession inwardly as he smiled broadly. "Will Justin be afraid of the elephant?"

Sass laughed. "It's probably bigger than him, but he's not afraid of anything. Why do you think I don't have any pets around here? With Justin around, a poor puppy would never know what to expect." His deep, throaty laughter rang sweetly in her ear.

She stretched out her hand. "Come with me. We can put this in Justin's room. I can't wait to see his mahogany eyes light up when he sees his new friend!"

Kristopher followed along behind her, thrilled that she was so pleased with the gift, hoping Justin would be, too. He also wanted to be there when she gave the gift to Justin, but he wasn't going to push the envelope. He'd just have to wait until Sass decided to let him meet her baby son, hoping she'd change her mind real soon. He was curious as hell about her baby boy.

The phone rang just as they entered Justin's room. Sass left him alone while she ran back to the living room to answer the call.

"Hello." Sass was practically out of breath as she spoke into the mouthpiece.

"Sass, it's Staci. Is everything okay over there? You sure are breathing hard. Are you alright?"

"I'm fine. I had to run to the phone. I was in Justin's

room where there's no extension. Kristopher is in the other room as we speak . . . and I'm not letting him out of my sight after this phone call."

Feeling an instant let down at Sass's news, Staci sighed. "Excuse me, but when are you going to tell Mom, Dad, and Stephanie that you're involved with Mr. Casanova again?"

"In due time. I'm keeping this all to myself for the time being. We'll talk later." Sass said her goodbye, hung up the phone, and ran back to Justin's room.

Standing in silence outside the door, Sass noticed that Kristopher appeared deep in thought. As she watched him run his fingers haphazardly through his hair, she wondered if he was having second thoughts about their relationship. While she studied his body language, he picked up Justin's football and tossed it up in the air. Then his bright smile suddenly charged the air with an electrical current, causing her to breathe a deep sigh of relief.

She stepped back into the room. "Are you having fun? For a moment I thought you looked unhappy. I was thrilled to see a smile reappear on your handsome face."

The smile he tossed her way gently bruised her heart. Pulling her further into the room, he looked around for somewhere to sit. Spotting the rocking chair, which was a replica of the one in her bedroom, he sat down and lowered her onto his lap. "There's something we have to discuss." His tone was no-nonsense.

His mood frightened her, especially when she saw sadness in his eyes. "What is it, Kristopher? You're scaring me."

He gently massaged her hair, kissing her cheeks softly. "It's nothing for you to be frightened of. I just need you to know that I'm aware of how difficult this is going to be on you when you tell your family about us. I don't want you alienated from them." He frowned lightly.

Glad that it wasn't something she couldn't deal with, her breath escaped. "Kristopher, I'll handle my family when the timing is right. And they'll come to accept it. If we find that we really do love one another, what we have in each other is all we'll need."

"Sass, they've been there for you through all your trials. We have to take their feelings into consideration. I felt you should know how aware I am. I fully understand how they feel about me and why they feel that way. You've always been so honest about everything in your life and I want you to know everything about mine. I don't want you short-changed like before."

*Hardly,* she mused, hating the fact that she couldn't quite share everything with him.

"I won't be. My family loves me. They may not like my choices, but they won't alienate me for a second. Like any loving family, they want what's best for me. They may not think you're it at the moment, but they'll play fair. If nothing else, they'll respect my decision."

"Okay, so we won't worry about that for now. But let me assure you that I'm ready to face them and I'm ready to apologize for everything I've done to hurt you." He pressed his chin into her shoulder. "When you hurt, they hurt. Perhaps we should go have breakfast now. Then I'd like to do some serious shopping before the day is over."

Sass got up from his lap, grabbed his hand, and pulled him up from the chair. Nearly dragging him through the house, she stopped in her bedroom for a lightweight sweater. Hand in hand, they exited the front door.


The bright yellow sun and the pastel clouds were a perfect romantic backdrop for anyone lucky enough to be in love, or imagining themselves so, Sass mused, as she got out of the midnight blue Mercedes Benz. A cool, light breeze added another wonderful ingredient to the much sought-after Southern California's nearly-every-day-is-a-beach-day type weather.

Sass had directed Kristopher to the closest Waffle House. They were seated as soon as they stepped inside, a highly unusual occurrence. This time of morning, this particular chain of restaurants were normally very busy. The wait for a seat could be up to thirty minutes or longer. The booth they occupied faced the streets of the busy shopping district. Kristopher and Sass enjoyed their conversation with one another as they patiently waited for their waiter to arrive. The waiter appeared, took their order, and hurried away.

They had both ordered the old-fashioned buttermilk pancakes with traditional maple syrup. For beverages they'd chosen freshly squeezed orange juice. Sass didn't drink coffee, but Kristopher ordered a cup for himself. In France, coffee was enjoyed from bowls, but Kristopher was home now, where he was well acquainted with the coffee cup.

When the delicious-smelling breakfast finally arrived, they couldn't wait for the waiter to leave to dig in. Very little was said during breakfast, but a lot of heavy eye contact passed between the two of them. Not much time had passed before they'd devoured everything in sight.

"Where are you taking me shopping, Sass? I'd like to know your favorite places."

"That all depends on what you're looking for. There seems to be as many shopping centers in California as there are people. I personally like to shop in the Wilshire District or Hollywood. When I'm really short on money, I go downtown to the garment district."

He smiled. "You don't have to worry about being short on money. As I told you earlier, there's nothing you want that you can't have. That also includes anything for young Justin." As her eyes sparkled for him, he thought they looked like exquisite jewels.

"No offense, but I won't accept your money. I have a budget that I stick to. Thank you for your generosity. If I let you spoil me, and it doesn't work out between us, where will I be?"

He reached across the table and took her hand. "Things will work out between us. There's no reason for them not to. I love you. I know it's going to take some time for you to love me back." Under the table, he stretched his leg out, rubbing it against hers playfully.

She rewarded him with soft laughter. "You know, you just might be right. I feel so good about you that I really can't imagine you not being here with me. I'm beginning to trust you again, which is something that I thought I'd never be able to do with any man, especially you."

"Winning your trust is very important to me, Sass Stephens."

"Winning it may not be the hardest part. Can you keep my trust? That's what worries me the most. I trusted you before but you weren't able to maintain it. I'd hate for that to happen again since it's a very important element in any relationship."

"I know, Sass. Just keep in mind that I'm a different person today than I was years ago. Once you really get to know the new and improved me, you'll see how much I've changed."

"I really hope so, since I've decided that I want our relationship to work this time."

As they arrived on Sunset Strip, the stores were just beginning to open their doors. Sass was glad they'd beaten the crowds. After securing the car, Kristopher took Sass's hand. Both appeared ready to embark on a pleasurable shopping journey.

While darting in and out of stores, they laughed at some of the strange clothes on the racks, having the time of their life. Sass tried on a bunch of silly looking hats and he thought she looked adorable in each one.

Inside a men's fashion boutique, Sass sat quietly eyeing Kristopher as he came in and out of the dressing room wearing an array of different sports coats and expensive suits. The fine tailored dress slacks hugged his muscular thighs and she fantasized heavily about making love to them with her hands and mouth.

Over an hour later, just for the heck of it, she indulged Kristopher in his fancies by trying on many different elegant day and evening dresses and several types of fashionable sports clothing. Sass came out in one indescribable formal evening gown that made him sweat. His brain felt like it had been scrambled like a raw egg. He couldn't begin to think of how he was going to convince her to let him purchase the gown; he just knew that she had to have it.

Since they'd both had such a good time trying on clothes, he begged her to walk on the wild side by going to Frederick's of Hollywood and then on to Rodeo Drive in Beverly Hills. She finally agreed, after she saw how much he really wanted to go to the places where he loved to do his shopping.

The numerous purchases that Kristopher made would be delivered to his home, along with the evening gown that he'd fallen in love with. With the upcoming black-tie affair, he wanted to be seen with Sass wearing the dress.

Before ending up at the Farmers' Market to enjoy a late lunch, they'd lived up to the popular saying "Shop until you drop." They'd already walked through the entire colorful market trying to decide what they were hungry for. Sass ended up with pizza and Kristopher had ordered a huge chef's salad. She felt guilty about eating the pizza while he only ate a salad, but it hadn't stopped her from buying a second slice.

"Where's the new wine tasting shop you spoke about last evening, Sass?"

"It's right across the parking lot. We can walk there. Are you ready to go?"

The check was quickly settled.

Sass guided Kristopher to the wine shop where they did a little wine tasting. The few sips she'd consumed left Sass's head feeling like cotton. The urge to fall asleep was overwhelming. Even with all the traveling Kristopher did, the time difference had finally caught up with him, making him feel a lot like Sass did. They had also stayed up quite late the previous evening and had awakened very early. Neither of them mentioned their fatigue to the other.

Driving high up into Mount Hollywood, they viewed the city from above. They later took in the late afternoon planetarium show that produced the night sky indoors and offered many special effects replicating celestial phenomena. Nestled together in the darkened planetarium, Kristopher kept Sass's body warm by keeping her close to him.

Sass was overly excited about the fashion show even if she didn't know who'd invited her. She'd just finished her shower and was about to get dressed. Kristopher was at home and would return within the hour. Although she was worried about what would happen between Kristopher and her brothers-in-law, she had come to terms with the fact that they'd eventually come face to face. Maybe she was pushing everyone too quickly, but time wasn't in her favor. She wanted her desire to be with him out in the open before he returned to Paris. All hell might break loose, but she wasn't about to let Kristopher get burned beyond recognition.

Sass picked up the dress she'd unsuccessfully tried to refuse from Kristopher and looked at the designer label. It suddenly dawned on her how much he'd shelled out for it. When she'd tried the clothes on earlier, she hadn't even bothered to look at the price tags. It wouldn't have made any difference what the price tag read. It would've taken a month's salary to pay for any of the dresses in the exclusive fashion boutique. Nonetheless, anyone would be able to understand why Kristopher wanted her to have this dress. Sass wasn't too amazed at his benevolence since he'd lavished her with wonderful gifts and trips before.

Shimmering and flashing sparkles of dazzling light, the gold lamé gown would've been proper attire for any First Lady attending the Inaugural Ball. The gown boasted a sweetheart neckline and long sheer sleeves; slender golden threads with tiny gold beads hung from the attached choker. The back was left open to the waist and the side thigh split was cut high. All Sass wore under the dress was gold and black bikini panties. Three rows of yellow gold rhinestones attached together were Sass's choice for her ears. The matching bracelet accented the dress beautifully.

Kristopher arrived promptly at seven-thirty. When she opened the door, he covered his eyes with his hands, peeking through his open fingers. Removing his hands from his face, he kissed his fingertips, pulling them away quickly. His dramatic gesture made her laugh.

"*Magnifique!* You were indescribable in the dress earlier, but I'm afraid I still can't find the right words to express myself. In all its glory, you look as splendorous as the Eiffel Tower at night. I just want to hug you tight."

His expression was that of a little boy, which made him look several years younger than his actual twenty-nine years.

Kristopher's honey-brown hair had been recently cut, shaped, and edged to perfection. His white dinner jacket fit him to a tee. Just in case she accepted the dress, to match it, he'd purchased a gold lamé bow tie and cummerbund. His patent shoes were highly polished. Solid gold cuff links were crested with the initial C. Emitting flickering flecks of golden highlights, his sea-green eyes meshed with the gold of his bowtie.

Sass smiled brightly. "I'm all for that hug." Drawing him from the hallway, she stood on her toes and hugged him tightly. Noticing that she hadn't put her evening slippers on yet, Kristopher was careful not to step on her delicately painted toes.

"I'm glad I convinced you to accept the dress. It was made for you, Sass. No woman in the entire world could wear the dress the way you do." His voice was packed with emotion.

Reaching into his pocket, he pulled out the slender case containing the diamond bracelet she'd worn in France. Deeply touched by his sentimental nature, she couldn't have refused to wear the jewels again if she'd wanted to. In fact, she didn't think she'd ever be able to refuse him anything again. Long ago Kristopher had won a special place in her heart, a permanent place. But was she now ready to re-reserve the ultimate spot for him, a place deep down in her soul? After taking her own bracelet off, she put his on.

"I'm glad you purchased this gown even though I objected vehemently. *Merci beaucoup, Kristopher.*" He followed her into the living room and dropped down beside her on the sofa.

*"Je t'aime, Sass."* He pulled her back into his arms. It was the first time he'd said he loved her in French. His confession utterly mesmerized her as his kisses came tender and warm. She never wanted him to stop kissing her, but they needed to get to their destination. Sass indulged him in one last kiss before breaking the enchanted spell.

She hugged him before pulling away. "My sisters are meeting us at the hotel. I don't want to keep them waiting. I need to put my shoes on and drench myself in Sunlit Sass. I'll be right back." He stood until she left the room and then he lowered himself back down onto the sofa.

As he thought about meeting up with her family again, his eyes became troubled. There was no doubt in his mind that their reaction to him was going to be anything but polite. He'd got along very well with Sass's sisters and her brothers-in law in the beginning. But after he'd hurt Sass so deeply, he'd received quite a few unveiled threats from the male in-laws.

When his thoughts unexpectedly turned to Justin, he found himself beyond excited. There'd been many times that he'd longed to hold a small child in his heart, but his raging desire had only come in recent months. He hoped Sass would give him the chance very soon. He couldn't help wondering if Justin would take to him. Remembering all the children that had taken to him over the years, especially during family photo sessions, he dismissed his concern.

A family was something he'd never really thought of having. He couldn't help wondering if Sass would ever truly forgive him for what he'd asked her to do. Was she really past that horrendous time or were they just tricking themselves into believing otherwise?

* * *

Sass and Kristopher arrived at the grand Bonaventure Hotel located in downtown Los Angeles. He drove into the valet parking lane and handed the keys to the attendant as he got out of the car. He then walked around to the other side. Patiently, he stood by waiting until the attendant helped Sass out of the car.

As she emerged, Kristopher immediately took her arm and tucked it possessively through his, smiling into her eyes. "Your most loyal court awaits its beautiful queen," he teased.

Her smile was no less radiant than a ray of summer sunshine. "It's a pleasure to have my handsome King as my most loyal and trusted escort." He kissed her cheek in appreciation of her sweet compliment.

They floated gracefully into the beautifully decorated ballroom. With the model's runway built in the center of the room, the stunning couple could've easily taken front and center. Everyone present would've undoubtedly believed that they were part of the show.

Sass had left her sister's names with the attendant at the door so they could gain access as her guests. Even as she and Kristopher were escorted to their table, she still wasn't sure who had invited her. Since she'd been too busy with Kristopher and her work to get around to it, she'd had Lillian call in her attendance at the last minute.

If Kristopher hadn't encircled her slender waist as they walked to the table, she would've fallen on her face. Grace Chatman sat at the table reserved for Sass and her guests. Seeing the model, with her arresting beauty, made things all too clear. Sass's body immediately tensed up.

Kristopher felt the tension in Sass shoot through him. She had also turned pale. Remembrance of past conflicts flashed in his eyes as he looked at the woman seated at the table. His lead model was the same woman who had toyed with Sass's emotions every chance she got. How could he have forgotten the hatred that Grace carried in her heart for the woman he loved?

Sass dug her nails deep into Kristopher's jacket. As she looked at Grace in amazement, her heart fluttered and her palms felt sweaty. When Grace raised her six-foot-plus frame from the chair, Sass almost turned and ran away. Kristopher's tender touch on her arm let her know that she could handle this tenuous situation.

"Good evening, Sass Stephens." Grace's greeting had come husky with contempt. "You are the last person I expected to see here tonight. I guess you didn't bump your head hard enough the first time. I never imagined that plain stupidity was one of your major weaknesses."

Glaring at Grace, Kristopher pulled out a chair for Sass to be seated. "That's enough, Grace! Please go backstage and get ready for the show. This table is reserved for my guests."

To make sure Sass knew that she still had a thing for Kristopher, Grace kissed him on the cheek before sitting back down in her chair. "I'll do as you wish, K.C., as soon as I finish my mineral water. Way too expensive for me to waste."

The malignant look Grace gave her made Sass's insides recoil with disgust. Sass had tolerated her at the restaurant, but not tonight. Burning inside, Sass turned a stunned gaze toward Kristopher. "So this *is* your event? Why didn't you tell me?"

Sass felt like she was inside one of her nightmares and couldn't find her way out. Desperately, she tried to awaken from it. Sass's inner voice whispered softly inside her head to offer encouragement. For once, Sass was grateful for her subconscious mind.

Though he saw her anger, Kristopher's eyes couldn't

keep from drinking in her exquisiteness. "I wanted to surprise you, Sass. I have to say that I didn't give any thought to the history between you and Grace. I'm sorry for exposing you to her ugliness again. It's been so long since all of that chaos occurred. I never dreamed something like this might happen."

*Was he daring to be facetious with her?* She felt like screaming as she got to her feet, moving out of earshot of Grace. "Damn you! I'm leaving. How could you dare to disregard all of what I went through with Grace? Perhaps you haven't changed at all." Sass turned to look back at his lead model. "For sure, she hasn't."

In all her rage, Sass still bewitched him, especially as her anger reached her see-through eyes. "I have changed, but you'll never know that if you run away from this now. I planned this special evening with only *us* in mind. It took a lot to pull it together in such a short time. I wanted this night to be perfect for us. Please don't bring our night to a bitter end. It's been a long time since you've attended one of my fashion shows with me."

"It hasn't been long enough. And you've somehow managed to deceive me again." She then thought about Grace, who hadn't mentioned a thing to her about the fashion show when they'd met at the restaurant, another indication of how vengeful she could be. Had Grace mentioned it she would've known who had invited her. Sass hated the position she was in.

"This isn't something you should keep as a surprise. Because my family will be arriving, I'll stay. I'm not ready to deal with those I-told-you-so looks they're bound to give me. Even though I detest the position you've put me in, I won't have Grace thinking that I left because of her. I intend to give her a good dose of her own medicine. But after tonight, no matter what happens at this show between you and me, I never want to see Grace's face again. Is that clear, Mr. Chandler?"

His eyes narrowed with sadness. "Couldn't be any clearer."

To show Grace that she hadn't won this round, Sass turned to Kristopher and flashed him a loving smile. As he led Sass back to the table, the adoring way in which Sass now looked at Kristopher sent chills up Grace's spine. Her expression said that she didn't care for it at all.

"Sass, do you want something to drink before I go backstage?"

Sass gently squeezed his fingers. "I'll wait until later. Thank you."

Sass saw how Grace looked green with envy, sure that she'd love for him to call her by endearing names. Grace looked as if she was wondering how he and Sass Stephens had hooked up again. It was probably a day that Grace never thought would come since she was aware of how much Kristopher had already hurt Sass. She figured that Grace was already thinking of ways to keep them from staying together permanently. No matter what Grace thought, Sass knew that Grace couldn't mistake the love Kristopher had in his eyes for her. Sass decided that her best course of action for her was to remain unpretentious and to be her usual charming self. Grace needed to know that she didn't in any way feel threatened or intimidated by her presence.

Sass spotted several people she knew as she took time to look around the room. She enjoyed looking at all the beautiful flower arrangements and lighted candelabra stationed on each table. Though particularly pleased and surprised to see Daniel Davis, especially at a Chandler event, she wasn't able to catch his eye before she noticed her sisters at the door.

"Kristopher, Staci and Stephanie are at the door. I'd like to speak to you in private. Please excuse us, Grace."

"So, he's back with the family, too," Grace mumbled.

Sass heard her cunning remark but ignored it. "I need to talk to my sisters before they come to the table, especially Stephanie since she was good enough to come tonight. I'm sure they've already talked to their husbands about you and me; otherwise I don't think any of them would've shown up. This is also one of those surprises that shouldn't be sprung on anyone."

Sass had barely looked at him when she'd spoken. He knew that he couldn't look into her heart when she had ice chips in her eyes, but she had gotten hurt again. He'd certainly be glad when this night was over. He never dreamed that Sass and Grace would clash this way after all this time, but he couldn't deny Grace's feelings for him, even though she knew there was no hope for them. She'd professed her love for him too many times for him not to know.

"Okay. I need to go backstage and check on things, anyway. Good luck." Intently, he watched as Sass made her way over to the door.

Raging inside with anger at Grace, Kristopher walked backstage to check on his models. Grace Chapman met him at the door of the dressing room. She'd left the table right after he and Sass had walked away. Jealously burned her from within as she thought about him being with Sass. Even though she saw how unhappy he already looked, she decided to harass him anyway.

"I see that you and Sass are back in touch. Guess who I saw her with a short time ago?"

"I don't have a clue. To be honest, I couldn't care less." If Grace weren't one of his most sought after models, he would've dumped her a long time ago. Besides himself, he blamed her for a lot of his trouble with Sass.

"Oh, you care alright. But from what I've heard and seen, she doesn't."

Her statement got his attention, but she didn't like the cold stare he gave her.

"Okay, so you have my curiosity aroused. Who did you see with Sass, Grace?"

Her amber eyes glistened with pure liquid devilment. "I saw the lovely and vivacious Sass Stephens as she was having lunch with her handsome new love interest, Dr. Daniel Davis." Grace had seen Daniel seated at a table on her way backstage. That just might back her up story.

"FYI, he's not her lover. They've been friends a long time. Don't you ever tire of stirring things up?"

She flashed a look of innocence his way. "I wasn't trying to stir things up. They were holding hands so I assumed they were a heavy item." She pretended injured feelings.

He threw the papers he held across the room, glad that he hadn't been holding one of his expensive cameras. Walking over to her, he put his finger in her face, shaking it back and forth. "I don't ever want to hear Sass's name come out of your vulgar mouth again. You're not worthy of saying it. You did everything you could to pull us apart—and succeeded, I might add. If she knew how you'd betrayed her, she'd chew you up and spit you out with just a glance. You hated her before you ever laid eyes on her. She had something you hadn't thus far been able to attain. Me."

Angry as hell, Kristopher paced the room like a wild animal that had been caged for the first time. Abruptly, he stopped pacing and turned back to face his lead model. "I made one mistake with you, but I'll never make it again. You lied about her to me. You lied about me to her. Thank God she showed up before anything could happen between us that night. Therefore, she'll always be two up on you; she's had my physical love and she'll always possess my heart."

The anger in Kristopher's eyes frightened Grace as she just stared at him in utter disbelief, knowing she'd better keep her sultry mouth shut. Without so much as a backward glance in her direction, he stormed off.

Sass kissed her sisters and their husbands, smiling cheerfully. "Hey guys, I'm glad you all made it. Eugene and Gerald, our table's right over there." She pointed it out. "I need to go to the ladies' room. I'd like for Staci and Stephanie to come with me." Strong feelings of exasperation had taken a hold of Sass and she needed to dispel it before she exploded.

Stephanie and Staci followed Sass out of the ballroom and into the ladies' room. The second the door was closed Sass began stomping her feet like a spoiled child. The two older sisters were surprised to see their sophisticated younger sister acting out her anger.

Sass's cheeks were stained with embarrassment. "Staci, does Stephanie know what's going on?"

Staci frowned. "Everyone knows but Mom and Dad. And it wasn't easy getting any of them here. But why are you in such a rage, stomping your feet and carrying on so?"

"I'll explain that in a minute, but I need to talk to Stephanie first." Sass turned to her other sibling. "I know how you feel about Kristopher, but I'm glad you came tonight. I know how much this is costing everyone. I just have to see if I can find some sort of closure with us. We never really ended things in the right way."

Stephanie stroked Sass's back. "Don't start crying. You don't want to mess up that beautiful face. Sweetheart, you're the only one who has to understand what you're doing. None of us like it, but this is your life and you have to live it how you see fit. Mom and Dad may not understand your decisions or motivations, but they certainly won't stop loving you because of them. This family has always stuck together and will continue to do so. Now tell us what has you so upset?"

Sass hugged both her sisters. "Thank you. I need you both so much right now, not that I haven't always. You two are not going to believe this, but this is one of Kristopher's modeling shows. He wanted to surprise me. As if that wasn't enough, Grace was seated at our table when we got here."

Looking so much alike it was uncanny, the three women stared at each other in disbelief. Each was about equal in height and had close to the same skin coloring.

Staci laughed out loud. "Boy, this is going to be one interesting evening. The sparks are going to fly in this room tonight."

Sass shot her a smug glance. "The only sparks flying tonight will be between me and Kristopher. I have no intentions of letting Grace upset my evening. He invited me here; she's just here to work. She's just going to have to swallow it . . . whole." She wasn't ready to let it be known how angry she was with Kristopher over this last act. But a premier performance was what she'd have to give to keep her family from guessing that her newly blown bubble had already burst. "I told you so" were hard, bitter words to swallow.

Stephanie raised an eyebrow. "He may have invited you here, but it sounds like Grace may not have known that. I wonder, what's her motivation? Of course, she's in love with him. She's never really kept that a secret."

Sass leaned against the gold-veined marbled counter. She looked none too happy, yet she smiled when she noticed her sisters' elegant gowns. "You both look sensational, but did you have to choose the same electric blue color?"

Stephanie shook her head. "How can you fix your mouth to ask that question, Sass? This happens to us every time we don't discuss what we're going to wear. It has certainly happened to you enough times. At least the styles of our dresses are completely different for a change. By the way, that's some dress you're wearing. A present?"

Sass clicked her tongue. "What do you think? Have you ever known me to own something that costs what I make in a month?" The three sisters all laughed at the same time. "We'd better get back in there," Sass said. "I'm not worried about Gerald, but Eugene may have already been arrested for killing Kristopher." Sass laughed nervously.

"Honey, don't laugh, you could be right," Staci warned as they herded out the door.

Back in her seat, Sass was glad that Kristopher hadn't made it back to the table yet. As she thanked her brothers-in-law for coming, she also asked them not to show any signs of anger toward her date. Although they didn't understand her reasoning for seeing him again, they'd promised to maintain control of themselves and not to say or do anything to embarrass her.

A few minutes later, Sass excused herself to go and speak to Dr. Davis. Before she could reach him, she spoke to several people that she knew, chatting only briefly.

As she finally reached Dan's table, he stood up to greet her.

"Wow, Sass Stephens, you're a sight for sore eyes. Honey, you grow lovelier every time I see you. You look like a million bucks in that dress. It must have nearly cost that much." Dan turned to his attractive companion. "Sass, this is Denise Lawson. You may not remember her, but she worked on the nursing staff in the emergency room."

Denise smiled with a genuineness that warmed Sass. "Hello, Sass. It's nice to meet you. Dan, Sass wouldn't have any reason to remember me. I worked nights. However, I saw her a couple of times when I came in to pick up my paycheck during the day shift."

Sass touched Denise's hand briefly. "Well, now that we've met, let's not be strangers. Maybe we can get together sometime soon. Dan, I guess I should warn you that I'm here with Kristopher Chandler. I hope you and Denise will stop by our table." Sass frowned at the rancorous expression on Dan's face. "I don't have time to explain right now." Sass saw that the lights had dimmed. It was time for the show to begin. "But, Dan, we'll talk about it later."

Sass slid easily into her chair. Only seconds had passed since Kristopher had returned to the table. Sass was glad to see that everyone was still alive. She was so intent on Kristopher and how he might feel being under the microscope that she totally forgot her anger.

Using discretion, Sass leaned into Kristopher. "Did you miss me?"

His passionate kiss showed her just how much. "Yes, Miss Stephens, I missed you. My heart and eyes missed you too. Your family told me you were talking to friends. I was worried about you. You're here now and seem to be no worse for wear. I can relax now and enjoy the rest of the evening with you." He inhaled deeply of her delicate perfumed scent.

Sass touched his cheek with her fingertips. "Kristopher, maybe we should cool the affectionate displays. I don't want to make them uncomfortable. They were kind enough to come here for me. They need more time to get used to the idea of an 'us.'"

"Sass, I only know how to be myself. Touching you is a

natural reaction, one that I can't control. But I'll keep your suggestion in mind."

Her smile was wan. "If I come off unaffected, just know that I'm only putting on an act."

"Only acting? But, of course. At any rate, we'll make it through this night. Tomorrow, that's up for debate. Just know that I'm here to stay. Remember that it's always darkest before the dawn."

That would've been comforting a short time ago, a time when my arms were opened wide to receive the dawn because I'd had enough of total darkness. Tonight, you were supposed to be my rising dawn, Sass whispered inwardly. Then Grace appeared. How much darker can it get?

Unable to help himself, Kristopher put his hand in Sass's hair and pulled her head closer. As if on cue, soft music drifted into the vast room. The only light in the room came from the candles and the lighted runway. But Kristopher Chandler could only see the light in Sass's eyes, eyes that owned his heart.

# Nine

Summer had just begun but the fashions on display were for fall. The golds, oranges, rusts and other shades of brown, and greens were well represented in the gorgeous fashions. The long-legged African-American models owned the runway as they gave a stupendous performance.

"We are such a beautiful group of people," Sass whispered to Kristopher. "Look at all the different fantastic skin colors we lay claim to. Their complexions, from creamy beige to dusky black, only serve to enhance the beauty of the clothing. So many different eye colors are present in our people. Why do we get such a bad rap? This room is full of some of the most intelligent men and women in society, yet we're so often put down. We're often called lazy and shiftless."

Kristopher patted the side of her cheek to calm her. "Ignorance should never be an excuse, but it's at the core of the problem, Sass. I'm sorry our people have been hurt by the ignorance of others. A country like this couldn't have been built on the backs of lazy people."

"There are doctors, lawyers, professors and many other professionals in this room, but we're still considered unable to be uneducated. I don't get it. None of those who put us down can explain it with any reasonable amount of intelligence," Sass said.

"There's no explanation for it, my beautiful lady. We just have to keep moving forward."

As Grace stepped onto the runway, Sass saw that she demanded her audience's undivided attention. Looking exotic and sexy, she turned and twirled, stopping only briefly to make several seductive stances. So far she'd received the loudest responses . . . and she lapped it up greedily.

Sass closely studied Kristopher through hooded eyes, watching his every reaction to his lead model. He was as good looking as ever and he hadn't gained so much as a single gram of fat anywhere on his body. His beautiful eyes appeared blank while Grace modeled, but Sass had definitely seen light in them for some of the other gorgeous women.

Grace threw a kiss to Kristopher as she modeled in front of their table. Sass didn't miss the look of disgust on his face, but it made her wonder if something romantic had ever gone on between the two of them. She would pay any amount of money to find out. Nonplussed by their strange behavior, she turned her attention away from Grace and Kristopher and back to the other stunning models. In a matter of seconds, she found herself staring at him again.

Feeling her eyes on him, Kristopher lifted her hand and put it to his lips. There was no one in this room more beautiful than his female companion. She should've been up there giving an even more spectacular show. Though confident that she'd eventually get over seeing Grace, he knew an emotional showdown between him and Sass was imminent, sure that it would happen in the near future. There'd be no closure for Sass where Grace was concerned, not until she openly confronted him about his past and present relationship with his lead model.

Very much in love with Sass, Kristopher was sure that his

love for her was evident in the way he looked at her, visible in his body language. If she should decide not to stay with him, he knew his heart would break. But he loved her too much to let her go without fighting for her. Her happiness was important to him and he'd continue to pray for their relationship to survive. He also knew that her family would hate for her to marry him, but her happiness was just as important to them as it was to him.

The fashion show finale began with a gorgeous bride and handsome groom entering the room through a cloud of white smoke. While the orchestra softly strummed everyone's ears with sweet music perfect for a wedding day, audible gasps could be heard around the room. The special effects had taken everyone by surprise. Though Sass didn't appear to notice, Kristopher gave her a knowing look, extremely pleased with her enthusiastic response to his brilliant ideas. This was his artistic vision of their wedding day.

The beautiful bride wore an ivory silk shantung creation with long sleeves slightly puffed at the shoulders. An extra touch of lace detailed the back of the gown, featuring a drop waist bodice of Guipure lace and a V-back embellished with the same lace design. A stunning elbow-length veil was fashioned in the same lacy material. The bride's dainty ears were decorated with pearl earrings. Her eyes were large, dark, deeply set, and her flawlessly made up earth-brown complexion carried a healthy, California-sunshine glow.

The groom wore Christian Dior black full dress complemented by a white pique shirt, white vest and white gloves. Tall, lean, and handsome, his rich raven-black skin was smooth and as clean-shaven as his head. His strut was proud, confident, as he purposely dazzled the ladies.

The couple then took the runway in a show of pomp and glitz, flaunting their stuff, which came as easy to them as breathing. Thick smoke in a rainbow of soft colors wafted through the air and the loud gasps were once again evident. As Kristopher stole a glance at Sass, the tears shining in her eyes made his desire to kiss them away nearly insuppressible.

A thunderous applause filled the room and a standing ovation followed. The models bowed and curtsied before leaving the stage in a flurry of electrifying turns and twists.

The runway was quickly broken down and the floor readied for an evening of dancing.

"Kristopher, that was a spectacular show," Staci praised. "You really outdid yourself with this one. You should be very proud." Though Sass's male family members showed some reluctance, everyone finally nodded in agreement.

His pride in his work was visible. "Thank you, Staci. I *am* proud of this fashion show. I put a lot of work into this one and in a very short amount of time. I can already see how much it's paid off. The audience was captivated."

"You have a fantastic ability for showmanship. Your models radiated and oozed with confidence," Stephanie remarked with sincerity. She had to give the brother is due.

"I thank you from the depths of my heart." *However, one person was missing up there. The lovely Sass Stephens, my adorable lady-love.*

Feeling the music in her soul, Sass turned to look at her brother-in-law, Gerald. Without her uttering a word, he knew that his sister-in-law wanted to dance. Getting to his feet, he pulled out her chair. As they floated onto the dance floor arm in arm, the others watched. Stephanie wasn't much for dancing but it always pleased her when her sisters obliged her husband. Gerald loved to show off his fancy moves, even if they were somewhat outdated.

Sass frowned when she saw Eugene turn his chair to face Kristopher. Scared that things might heat up between the two of them, she brought her head close to Gerald's ear. "I think Eugene is about to go on the war path," she whispered. "I hope it doesn't get too ugly."

"You want to go back to the table, Sass?"

"I can keep my eye on them from here. Facial expressions will indicate how things are going between the two of them. This whole evening has been kind of scary, Gerald."


"Kristopher, now that we have a chance to really talk, I have some questions." Eugene's demeanor was cool. Kristopher nodded, encouraging Eugene to continue. "Why did you invite Sass here this evening knowing her history with Grace? Why the mystery behind the invitation?"

Sass saw Staci and Stephanie exchange nervous glances. Nonchalantly, Kristopher shrugged. "Even though I planned this event some time ago, I decided to go ahead and orchestrate this show for us from Paris after meeting up with Sass again. As for the surprise, I simply wanted to show her a fantastic evening. Sass and I still have a lot to talk about. I thought after the fashion show would be a good time for us to really open up."

"The time to talk to her was when she was lying somewhere bleeding to death from a hemorrhaging heart that you caused." Eugene didn't try to hide his irritation. "My wife begged you to come and talk to Sass then, but you refused. Why?"

Kristopher looked a tad disheartened. "I honestly can't answer that question. I've asked myself that same thing a hundred times. Maybe it was shame, guilt, fear or any number of things. I don't know." Kristopher began to look weary, hoping the confrontation would end soon.

"Eugene, this is not the time or place to discuss this.

Maybe you should let it go for now. Kristopher has to answer to a much higher power than any of us," Staci said.

Eugene gave his wife a soft, expressive look. "You're right, Staci. That's one of the reasons I love you so much. You keep my head screwed on straight. But I have to say one more thing before I let it go. Chandler, Sass has her life back on track. She's found some happiness. I don't want you to interfere in her life in any way." Eugene's tone was nonthreatening, but he kept his dark brown eyes fastened on the man who'd nearly destroyed Sass.

"Eugene, I can understand where you're coming from, but I still love Sass. I never stopped. I have every intention of making things up to her. If she tells me that she doesn't want me in her life, then and only then will I honor her request." Kristopher's response reeked with a strong air of defiance.

His anger aroused to near boiling, Eugene looked at Kristopher through narrowed eyes. For his family's sake, he decided not to react in a physical manner.

Seeing the malevolent look on Eugene's face immediately brought Sass and Gerald off the dance floor and back to their seats, where the tension was obvious. Sass looked at everyone with questions in her eyes. No one volunteered a response, but Gerald made a joke to lighten the mood. Then a slow tune that had been a favorite of Sass's and Kristopher began to play. The tension grew tenfold when Sass and Kristopher's eyes met in an intense, knowing look.

"Sass, dance with me?" He was almost sure she'd refuse to appease her family. It seemed that Sass had always aimed to please everyone but herself, including him.

Though she didn't want to admit it, she loved the adorable way in which he looked at her, the way he turned her knees to water with just a glance. To keep the peace, Sass was prepared to refuse, until she saw a barely noticeable nod from Stephanie. Her older sister's approval was confirmed for her when she lowered her eyelids and gave another slight nod.

Sass stood up, holding out her hand to him. That pleased Kristopher.

Eugene thought the man had a lot of nerve and Gerald hadn't yet formed an opinion about it. Everyone watched with mouths agape as they took to the dance floor.

Calmly, Kristopher watched her every movement, closely studying Sass's body language. His own body had turned cold as ice when she'd left his side earlier. His only hope was to speed up the process of them getting back together, even though he might possibly end up in critical condition from a massive broken heart. Either way, he wanted to know his fate. If Sass was not his lot in life, he'd rather know that now as opposed to later.

Kristopher stared into Sass's sepia eyes. "Sass, I'm happy you agreed to dance with me. I know I shouldn't have asked for the sake of your family. I asked because I couldn't control the desire any more than I can stop my heart from beating at will. 'The Heart Never Forgets' was once our favorite song. And my heart was unable to forget you, though my head tried to."

Sass gave him an impatient glance, totally unimpressed by his intent-to-flatter statement. "Kristopher, you've been able to do anything else you've wanted to do at will. I'm sure you could've controlled yourself this time, too." Despite the look she gave, he'd melted her heart.

He held her slightly away from him. "I'll accept that from you. Now for the truth of the matter, I simply wanted to hold you in my arms, feel your heart beating next to mine. For that, I won't make any excuses. Sass, we have so much to talk about. Many things are left unsaid between us. Neither of us will be able to resolve much of anything else until we do. Don't let the incident with Grace keep us from finding love again."

"I won't. I remember a time when you didn't want to listen to anything I had to say, especially anything akin to the truth. I can see a big change in your ability to communicate. You now open up a lot more. I'm glad you can do that."

She wrapped her arms tightly around his neck. The same tune played as she and Kristopher finished it out in each other's arms. The revelation that she needed to feel Kristopher's arms around her, to have his body next to hers, came without warning. His outward and inner strength had suddenly become her refuge.

Kristopher laid his cheek against the warmth of hers. "You're remarkable, Sass. I'm glad you came back into my life. I've been miserable and lonely without you."

Unable to fight her desire for him, she held him tighter. "You won't be lonely anymore. I'm here. Thank you for giving me the courage to try this, even though I'm still confused about my feelings. I need to know so many things, things that neither of us has dared to explore. But I'm grateful that I've learned to act assertively instead of reacting negatively."

He smiled warmly. "Assertive action is much better for the soul than negative reactions. You've handled yourself like the lady you are." Tilting her head back, he slowly, deliberately drew her mouth against his. His kiss nearly drove her crazy with desire. Kissing him back wasn't an act. His mouth on hers was one of the things she'd missed terribly throughout the evening.

Sass and Kristopher finally returned to the table, only to find that an unwanted addition had appeared: Grace. Though still irritated with the beautiful model, Sass decided to leave well enough alone. Making a scene in front of her family wouldn't go over too well.

As was her way, Grace monopolized the conversation, irritating everyone in the process. She seemed to be trying to impress Kristopher, but she failed miserably. The only person Kristopher was interested in was Sass Stephens. Grace's colorful expressions and her obvious self-centered ways didn't at all amuse him. Grace really got vocal when Daniel Davis appeared at the table with his companion.

Grace batted her amber eyes wildly at Dan. "So, it's the good doctor. I've been waiting for your call, but I guess you've been busy doctoring some other unsuspecting female patient." Grace eyed Sass with suspicion, as though she was the woman in question.

Kristopher became so disgusted with Grace's behavior that he left the table, the last thing Grace wanted to have happen. It seemed that her main objective was to try and make Kristopher jealous, but it wasn't working.

Daniel shook his head in dismay. "Grace, I see you haven't learned any manners since the first time we met. You're a beautiful woman, but your mouth leaves a lot to be desired." Ignoring her petulance, Dan introduced his companion to the others. Grace openly snubbed Denise when Dan tried to make the introduction between the two women.

Sass thought she'd better take control of the situation before Dan lost his temper.

"Denise Lawson, I'd like you to meet my family." Sass called each of her family members by name. Everyone knew Dan. "I was lucky enough to have them join me this evening for that fabulous show." Sass smiled sweetly at Kristopher as he returned to his seat, causing his heart to sprout wings. The intimate party seemed to be ever growing, Sass noted with a mixture of amusement and dismay. What would happen next was anyone's guess.

Kristopher stood to shake the hand of the doctor. He then kissed the back of Denise's hand. "Enchanted,

Miss Lawson. Dr. Davis, it's nice to see you again after all these years."

"It has been a few years, Mr. Chandler. I'm glad Sass and I ran into each other, but Denise is the reason for us being at the show. She loves your creative energy. Sass told me you're now living in Paris. How long are you back here in California?"

Dan's forced politeness wasn't noticeable to anyone but Sass. From the expression on Denise Lawson's face, Sass could see that she was utterly taken by Dan. She was also glad that Denise had completely ignored Grace's blatant snub.

"I'll be here for two weeks or so. The time has already gone by too quickly. However, I plan to return home permanently within the next few months. My assignment in Paris is only temporary. I can hardly wait for it to be over." Kristopher smiled at Sass with adoration.

Daniel could clearly see that Kristopher appeared to be more than just infatuated with Sass. But he was more surprised to see that she seemed so comfortable with the man who'd practically left her for dead. A little quirk of fear for Sass stabbed at Dan's heart.

"I hope you have a pleasant visit," Denise chimed in. "I imagine it's very exciting to be living in Paris. If I was an envious person, I'd envy you that."

"Paris is exciting. It's different and it does grow on you in a hurry," Kristopher said.

A song with a funky cha-cha beat suddenly whisked into the room, causing a wave of people to rush toward the dance floor.

Kristopher looked at Sass and nodded toward the floor. Smiling, she got up from her seat. Kristopher politely excused himself and Sass just before he led her away. When the beat of the music became to tempting for anyone to stay seated, Grace found herself all alone at the table.

Showing off a fantastic display of his dancing talents, Kristopher led Sass through many different cha-cha steps. She kept up with him easily. As he dipped her lightly, her wavy hair swayed along with the rhythm of her body. Their laughter and playful nudging was somewhat of an indicator of their happiness at being together, but was somewhat exasperating for her family.

After several fast paced songs, the music slowed and Kristopher whirled Sass into his arms. Holding her tightly against him, his hands massaged her waist tenderly. Laying her head against his broad chest, she surrendered to his gentle moves, letting him take the lead.

When the music picked up a faster pace again, Dan cut in on Kristopher. He turned Sass over to her friend without hesitation. Gerald offered to dance with Denise, and she accepted, but only after Sass assured her that Stephanie wouldn't mind. Denise didn't want to disrespect his wife.

It was easy to see that Grace sulked over the obvious affection between Sass and Kristopher, but she was glad to have him back at the table all to herself. "Would you like to dance with me, K.C.?"

He refused to even acknowledge her presence.

She looked injured. "K.C., what don't you like about me?"

Sighing heavily, he looked down at his watch. "I don't have that much time. To make a long story short, it's your attitude. If you can't be the center of attention, you have to find a way to become the hole in the middle. You've been trying to draw Sass into some type of competition since we entered the ballroom. Her attempts to thwart your efforts were futile. There's no contest, Grace. I'm not a prize for someone to try and win. I can't seem to get you to understand that. Sass has been hurt enough. I won't allow that to happen again—by me, you or anyone else."

Grace sneered. "In case you haven't noticed, she has a new knight in shining armor."

He shot her a warning look. "If you're making a reference to Dan, don't. He's not a love interest and has never been. Denise seems perfectly comfortable with their friendship, so maybe you should try and do the same. Regardless of what your feelings for Sass are, there's no reason why we shouldn't be able to get together without any dissension. It's possible, you know."

"You amaze me. I know Sass dancing with that doctor-man has you chomping at the bit. You may think they're just friends, but I find it hard to believe. You didn't see them at lunch, but I did, and they were carrying on like lovers." Grace's intent was solely to be malicious.

"Sass being with any man drives me crazy. I wouldn't care who it was. Sass isn't the type of woman that uses a man to make another man jealous. I doubt seriously that you saw anything out of the ordinary. But I'm sure you'd like nothing better than to see them become lovers. Give the idea up. It's not going to happen. Grace, you're simply misery out looking for company. Hope you find it. To me, you're just my lead model, nothing more, nothing less. Nothing physical or emotional will ever happen between us."

"I'm sorry. I shouldn't have said those things."

"That's the most intelligent statement I've heard you make all evening." He drew in a deep, calming breath. "Grace, just try to tone down the volume in your voice. Carry yourself with some finesse. When you're up there modeling, you're the classiest woman around." He took another deep breath. "Let's get one thing straight, once and for all. We made that one mistake, but there can never be anything between us but business now. I don't like it when I'm mean and rude to you, but that seems to be the only way to get my point across."

"It wasn't a mistake on my part. You used me that night to get a point across to Sass. You were too much of a coward to tell her how terrified you were of being in love with her. You knew she'd come there and you wanted her to find us together. You had no intentions of making love to me. Even though I didn't figure it out until later, had I known up front, I still would've taken great pleasure in bringing about the most devastating night of her life."

His eyes glared with contempt. "You found pleasure in Sass's pain, but the rest is a lie."

"That's what you keep telling yourself. You set Sass Stephens up for the worst kind of heartbreak: intimate betrayal. We both know it. But I'm sure you still haven't had the guts to tell her the truth. I can only imagine what she'll do to you if she finds out what really happened that night: that I was the woman you were in bed with. You staged the whole damn episode." Not wanting to hear anything else he had to say, Grace jumped up and rushed off in a huff.

Once everyone was back at the table, Sass announced her desire to leave. When she learned that her family wanted to stay on for a short while, she hugged each of them and bade them a good evening. The moment became awkward when no one said goodnight to her date.

Ignoring the cold shoulder he'd received, Kristopher pondered Sass's announcement, wondering if she was going to let him come inside for a while. Just the thought of dropping her off at the door made him unhappy. They had to talk, had to dive into deep waters, muddy waters, and swim or drown. There was no two ways about it.

With his mission confirmed, Kristopher pulled Sass closer into the sanctuary of his arms. "Goodnight, everyone. Thank you for coming. The rest of the evening has been taken care of so please don't hesitate to order whatever you like."

Sass leaned her head on his shoulder and they floated out of the room the same way they'd come in. Those still seated at the table watched with uncertain eyes until they disappeared into the long corridor.

Carefully, Kristopher pulled the powerful car into traffic, glancing at Sass with anxious eyes. Regardless of her excellent display of valor, he knew she was having a hard time with all the incredible events that had occurred over the course of the evening.

He covered her hand with his free one. "Sass, how are you feeling?"

Looking over at him, she smiled weakly. "I don't know. I'm having all sorts of mixed emotions. If I'd known for sure that you had sent the invitation, though I had wondered, I'm not sure I would've come this evening. Any fashion show presented by you would certainly include your lead model. That alone would've been enough to keep me away."

"Then I'm glad you didn't know. I didn't want you to miss that show for anything in the world. I designed it long before you came back into my life . . . and I did it with you, with us in mind." He braked at the stoplight and looked over at her. "Can you honestly tell me that you didn't have a great time tonight?"

She pressed her lips together. "For the most part, I had a wonderful time, but that's not the issue. I mentioned to you several times that I didn't know who had invited me to this fancy shindig, but you never once let on that you were the one."

"That's the whole point of a surprise, isn't it?"

"What about Grace?"

"What about her, Sass?" Though he knew this topic would come up, he still wasn't ready for it. Especially after the things Grace had said to him earlier. *Had he wittingly set up Sass as Grace had suggested?* That was something he found hard to believe, yet . . . no, it wasn't possible.

"You know how much she hates me. That should've at least earned a warning of some kind from you. You knew she'd be there. In fact, she was practically the whole damn show."

"Okay, I see your point. But let me ask you this. You've seen Grace since you returned from Paris. Am I right?"

Sass eyed him with suspicion. "What's your point?"

"The point is, you didn't tell me that you'd seen her. Perhaps if you had, I think I might have seen the need to tell you about the show and that she'd be in it." He eased the car forward.

"So it's my fault that the cat-woman hasn't learned how to sheath her dangerous claws?"

"This is no one's fault. For sure, not yours or mine. It's been a few years already. I didn't know you'd react this way to seeing Grace again."

"But you knew how she might react to seeing me. Case in point!"

He gave a look of concession. "I see what you mean. All I can say is that I'm sorry. I don't know what else I can do about it."

"Apology accepted."

Though stunned by her easy acceptance, he smiled. "Thank you. Now, for the big question, are you going to allow me to come in for a while? Sass, you know that we need to dive into some deep waters, the kind with serious undertows. I have questions and so do you. And we both need the answers before too long. What I want is for us to be together, free of the past. What I don't want is for us to have separate futures."

Sass sighed. "I know you're right, but I'm going to see my therapist, Dr. Ford, before I get into any type of serious waters with you about all this." She suddenly felt emotionless. That somehow frightened her. "I'm sorry, but I still haven't learned how to deal with this very real presence of the past. Kristopher, you can come in for a little while, but I don't want to talk about the past, at least, not tonight. I'm bone tired and I just want to relax. Okay?"

"Okay. It's your call."

Seated on the sofa, sipping hot tea and listening to jazz vocals, Sass began to yawn. They had talked about a lot of things, had shared a few experiences regarding funny things that had happened to them over the years. Though it was in the back of their minds, weighing heavily on their hearts, neither of them brought up the past, a tumultuous past that neither could forget.

Sass yawned again and Kristopher brought her head against his chest. "I think you're ready for bed. I want to stay with you tonight, Sass. I don't want sex from you. I just want to have another awesome experience with you lying in my arms throughout the quiet hours of darkness. Let me sleep next to you tonight, Sass?"

Though she knew she'd been running hot and cold, sending mixed signals, this was what she wanted, too, even if it was crazy. She was in love with this man. To deny that fact was simply impossible. But could she lie next to him without wanting him to make love to her? Would that be so bad? How many times had they slept together already? It wasn't as if they'd never been physically intimate before. Besides, she'd been dreaming of a night like this ever since they first parted. Not wanting to analyze her feelings another second, fearing the possibility of overkill, she got to her feet.

"It's going to take me a lot longer to get ready for bed simply because I have more to remove than you do. You can make yourself comfortable in my bedroom. I'll join you in a few minutes." She turned and walked away. Pausing, she turned back to him. "I know that I probably shouldn't let this happen tonight, but I think it'll be okay for both of us. However, it may take me a little longer than you to get to the point where I can take our relationship to a higher physical level. I know we had many intimate moments in Paris, but you saw the need to hold back then—and I now see the need to practice caution. Grace has never done anything but irritate me, but she also helped me to see that I still need to be extremely careful with my heart."

He got to his feet. "I can understand that. I won't tell you your heart doesn't need guarding against me, because I know you can't accept that as truth until I prove myself to you. I'm prepared to take only what you offer. I'm in no hurry to rush or force things."

"Thank you for that, Kristopher. Excuse me while I get ready for bed."

Carrying a smile in his heart, he headed for Sass's bedroom. She was totally removed from his sight as the bathroom door closed shut, yet her perfume hung in the air. Closing his eyes, he began to savor the unforgettable moments she'd spent in his arms on the dance floor.

After a quick warm shower, Sass dressed herself in a full-length emerald silk gown designed with spaghetti straps. Done in a tassel print, the robe she wore was splashed with rich hues of emerald, gold and purple. Sass slipped into the cool silk, patted perfumed talc on her neck and ears, and then left the bathroom.

Kristopher was already undressed and in bed, completely surrounded by soft satin linens in the same emerald color as her gown. She was glad that Lillian had changed the bed earlier. He appeared to be asleep, but as soon as Sass entered the room, his entire being came alive with arousal. The exotic smell of her was branded into his olfactory nerve, wildly signaling him of her presence. He sat up in bed and reached his hand out to her.

As she gently slid her hand into his, he pulled her across his lap. Cradling her in his arms, he probed her mouth hungrily. A fiery response came from deep within her as he reached over and turned out the lamp.

Without any traces of fear to warn her, she allowed him to explore, to arouse her starving body, to kiss her neck and ears. Lowering the straps on her gown, he showered warm, wet kisses over her bare shoulders. Lifting her, laying her alongside him, he used his hand to tenderly rub the soft, firm flesh of her thighs. Then he gently massaged the delicate tissue between her legs using only the tips of his fingers. Sass purposely blocked out her earlier comments completely.

Moaning with undeniable pleasure, she looked up into his eyes and smiled. "Kristopher, I want you to make love to me," she whispered softly. "I need you and I know you need me. We won't worry about any after-effects. I'm mature enough to handle this."

His heart leaped at her whispered request. Rolling over on top of her, he completely covered her with his fully aroused, overheated body. "I'll make love to you, my love, though it won't be in the physical sense. I have something in mind for your lovely body that will make you believe you've been truly possessed. I have other ways to satisfy you and keep you content until you're ready to experience the sensuous and deeply satisfying lovemaking that we've shared in the past. But we're waiting until you're able to handle all the other unsettled elements of our relationship, not just our physical love."

Happy that he was being considerate of her, she trembled under him in response to his promising words. "That sounds like a promise I'm going to have to hold you to."

"You won't have to hold me to it, nor will you ever want it with anyone but me. Now, I'm going to risk sounding a bit arrogant. I'm holding back only because I know that's how is has to be. But once I completely possess you, you'll never leave me again. I want to be sure you want me and not my body." Their laughter put Sass more at ease.

Hypnotized by suggestion, Sass fell awake to a new horizon. Laying her head on his bare stomach, her eyes drooped shut.

On and off, all through the night, Kristopher watched Sass sleep. This had been their magical night of mystery in the making and he had no intentions of allowing her to retreat back into the private hell from which she'd come, from where he'd sent her.

While turning over on her stomach, Sass's nightgown got twisted under her. The tops of her thighs were left exposed. His sexuality responded the way it had earlier. Inhaling deeply, he tried to sedate the throbbing in his loins, futilely so. Bending his head, he traced feathery kisses up and down the back of her thighs.

A slight smile played around the corners of her mouth, which he took as encouragement to continue. Pushing her gown up even farther, he outlined the softness of her firm buttocks with agile fingers. Smiling invitingly, she opened her eyes.

His manhood broke free of its restraints. Gently pulling her into his arms, he savored his early morning breakfast from her honey-colored lips. Amorously, he fondled every part of her, reducing her to silly putty. Tenderly, he molded her into a love goddess. She responded in ways he hadn't dared to dream of.

His eyes were full, his heart and soul were hers for the taking. "Sass, you have me at a loss for words. Until my sanity returns, please don't move. Just hold me."

Unable to speak, and to indicate such, she touched her fingers to her lips and shook her head from side to side.

Her smile came gently as she located her voice. "You've certainly lived up to your promise, *Monsieur* Chandler. In breathless anticipation, I can hardly wait for us to actually make love. I'll be waiting for you to possess me completely. It's been so long for us that I'm too scared to even try to imagine it."

"Correction, *Mademoiselle* Stephens. We did make love." Drawing him even closer, she used universal body language to convey her heartfelt response. Fusing sepia and green eyes together, they embraced their quest to rediscover true love.

# Ten

Arising to a beautiful sunny morning, fully sated from Kristopher's kept promise, Sass looked at the sleeping figure of the man lying next to her. His honey-brown hair was wildly disheveled. The urge to smooth it caused her fingers to itch, but the yen to delve into her inner workings was demanding. Laying her head back against the satin pillow, she probed deeply into her subconscious mind.

Had she make a big mistake last night by letting him stay with her overnight, by giving him hope for an *us*, when none may exist?

*It's too late to ask that now, don't you think?* However, she was none the worse for the experience. She couldn't have handled things any better than she had. As for how she'd handled the entire evening, she thought her performance was in a class all by itself.

She had to admit that she was feeling more comfortable with him. It was as if he didn't expect anything from her. *Was that possible?*

*Everyone expects something. His intentions may be honorable, but he expects something from me, even if it's only my love.* It seemed that he was definitely in love with her, but it had appeared that way before. That was something she had to be sure about this time, had to be sure for the sake of her sanity. She didn't need to be reminded of what had happened the last time.

Sass had begun to think that the change in him was a miracle. He was so different, so considerate of her feelings, in spite of the situation with Grace. She knew that she loved him, but she actually liked him now, too. She liked the new person he'd become. People could love someone without liking them. He was more like the man she'd fallen in love with.

Despite the fact that he was loaded, she wasn't interested in his wealth. She was only interested in him as a person. A gold digger she wasn't. As it was right now, she simply couldn't agree to marry him. She had a way to go in completely forgiving his past deeds.

The only person Sass was sure about was Justin. Then she thought about the one question she'd had to wrestle with. Had she been wrong to agree for him to meet Justin this one time?

Though she'd thought it was still a little early in the game to bring Justin into it, he had convinced her otherwise before they'd fallen asleep. In wondering what had happened to her plans to hurt Kristopher she had to laugh. Sass had come to the realization that she could never cause pain to someone as an act of revenge. Her heart had dictatorship over her. She just wasn't a cruel person.

However, there had been times back then when she had acted totally out of character, but she'd reacted to the deeply inflicted pain. The fact that Kristopher was still very much alive proved that she hadn't lost total control of herself. A lot of women might've killed him for even less than what he'd put her through. But there had been times when she wished she were capable of doing him in. People were capable of anything when they'd been caused insurmountable pain.

An undetermined amount of time with Kristopher, so that they could talk, talk and talk was what she needed to get truthful answers to a lot of puzzling questions. It was only the truth that would set them free. Only then would they be able to let go of the past.

Sass realized that talking things over was a much better alternative to making love since that wasn't going to eradicate the past, yet she'd come pretty darn close to it last night—and she'd even allowed him to charm her right into a trip with Justin to Disneyland. She already knew that making love with that gorgeous creature was akin to finding the many mansions in the sky, not to mention living among the angels. She would definitely be walking the streets paved of gold and she could just imagine going to bed wearing only diamonds for a blanket.

On the other hand, if she made love to Kristopher prematurely, she'd never be able to move on. It would only create new memories and revive the old pain. Since the new Kristopher seemed to be in love with her, she had to decide if and when it was right to take their relationship to yet another level. Kristopher may turn out to be worthy of her and her love this time around. Even so, there was no better love than that for self.

Totally confused, Sass moved closer to Kristopher, tracing his bare back with powder-soft kisses. As she planted kisses further down on his anatomy, he awakened to her soft touch.

Turning over, he pulled her into his arms. "I've never forgotten how beautiful you are when you wake up. You're even prettier without a hint of make-up. *Il fait du soleil dans tes yeux,*" he said huskily.

"I caught sun and eyes, but you'll have to translate the rest." The way he spoke French reeled her senses. Before he could speak further, she planted a brief kiss deep onto his mouth.

"Translation: the sun is shining in your eyes. Before long, you'll know French as if it was your own language. I have many things to teach you. The one thing I long to teach you again is the true art of lovemaking. The way it should be executed can only be taught by a man who's truly in love with his woman." He laughed from deep within. The waves of his laughter rolled over her, covering her with an electric blanket of warmth.

"I've always heard that people who brag about their abilities in bed are usually quite inadequate." She stifled her laughter.

Refusing to acknowledge her comment with a verbal response, he gave her over an hour-long encore of the physical side of the previous evening. By giving her more than before, he hoped to quickly change her slanted point of view of his sexual prowess.

The smug look in his green eyes generated dangerous volts of electricity. "Dare to challenge me further?"

"Not a chance. Though I don't like to admit it, my memory of your capabilities is still very much intact." She batted her eyes wildly at him.

His electric eyes burned into hers. "I thought you'd eventually see it my way. Imagine what I just did to you and then magnify it twenty times over. After that, you'll stay in my life and in my bed until death us do part. I've also matured in many other ways."

"Oh, you haven't begun to feel what the new me is capable of doing to you! I'll cause you to lose more than just your mind. If the opportunity should arise, before you leave for France, you'd sell your soul to the devil to keep from leaving here without me."

"I can see that we're in for one hell of a night. I, for one, can't wait!"

Sass laughed at his comment.

"Now we need to get ready for Disneyland. At last, the time has come for me to meet Justin." He felt enthused about all the fun the day promised to bring. His attitude about wanting children in his life had definitely changed.

Sass still felt somewhat apprehensive about the decision she'd made regarding Kristopher meeting Justin, but his enthusiasm kept her from calling the whole thing off. "You can shower first, Kristopher. I need to make a few phone calls." She had to prepare her parents.

His smile was devilish. "I'd prefer us to shower together, but I know that's courting temptation. Temptation is one of the strongest, deadliest sins, you know."

"Yeah, I *do* know. That's what worries me."

Lifting her out of bed, he planted her firmly on her feet. "In time, I'll erase all your worry. You'll soon come to know that I'm not the callous rogue of a few years back."

Kristopher parked the Mercedes Benz in the driveway of the Stephens home. He looked apprehensive about what lay ahead, but he knew it had to come. To calm himself, he kissed Sass before they exited the car. She had a way of bringing about serenity.

Hearing laughter coming from the kitchen, Sass guided Kristopher into the large, cheerful room. Justin's mahogany eyes lit up when he saw his mother. Scrambling out of the chair, he ran toward his mother's open arms. When he ran right past her, she turned around and saw Kristopher's arms full of Justin. Kristopher and Jason Stephens, Sass's father, exchanged strained but polite greetings. Jason looked on as Justin familiarized himself with Kristopher.

Kristopher kissed the beautiful little boy, with the blond-tipped curls, on both cheeks. He couldn't help thinking how much Justin looked like him as a baby. Holding the back of Justin's head, he laid it on his shoulder, rocking him from side to side. As if he'd always known the comfort of Kristopher's arms, yawning, Justin closed his eyes.

Kristopher pecked Justin's baby-soft cheek. "You *are* quite a looker. Your mommy has told me a lot about you, but you're more beautiful than she described." *And you look just like me, even though you're not my son.* He then said something to Justin in French.

Pulling his head back, Justin looked at Kristopher strangely. His eyes appeared to ask: *Who taught you to speak English? You sound different from the people I'm used to talking to.* Kristopher laughed at the puzzled expression he saw in Justin's large mahogany eyes.

Sass thoroughly enjoyed the introduction between Kristopher and Justin, but Jason Stephens wasn't sold on the idea that Sass's ex-boyfriend had changed. Amantha Stephens, Sass's mother, had just come down the stairs. Standing at the kitchen door, she looked on with slight disapproval, but Amantha wouldn't think of voicing her opinion one way or the other.

"Sass, he's such a happy boy! I was surprised when he came to me. I'm glad he feels comfortable in my arms."

*Damn you, he's not the only one that finds comfort there,* Sass mused.

Hugging Justin close to him, Kristopher walked over to the table and sat down.

Sass also took a seat at the table. "Justin doesn't go to everyone. He's very arrogant around some people, but you seemed to have made him a fast friend. I'd say that it's quite an accomplishment." Sass tried to imagine the three of them in a family photograph. It wasn't a hard thing to conjure up, not hard at all. She could even see a resemblance.

Reaching for Justin, Sass extracted him from Kristo-

# An important message from the ARABESQUE Editor

Dear Arabesque Reader,

Because you've chosen to read one of our Arabesque romance novels, we'd like to say "thank you"! And, as a special way to thank you, we've selected four more of the books you love so well to send you for FREE!

Please enjoy them with our compliments, and thank you for continuing to enjoy Arabesque...the soul of romance.

Karen Thomas
Senior Editor,
Arabesque Romance Novels

Check out our website at
www.arabesquebooks.com

SPECIAL OFFER!
4 FREE BOOKS

ARABESQUE ®
A PRODUCT OF
BET BOOKS

# 3 QUICK STEPS
## TO RECEIVE YOUR "THANK YOU" GIFT
## FROM THE EDITOR

Send this card back and you'll receive 4 FREE Arabesque
novels! The introductory shipment of 4 Arabesque novels – a
$23.96 value – is yours absolutely FREE!

There's no catch. You're under no obligation to buy anything.
You'll receive your introductory shipment of 4 Arabesque
novels absolutely FREE (plus $1.99 to offset the costs of
shipping & handling). And you don't have to make any
minimum number of purchases—not even one!

We hope that after receiving your books you'll want to
remain an Arabesque subscriber. But the choice is yours to
continue or cancel, anytime at all! So why not take us up on
our invitation to receive 4 Arabesque Romance Novels, with
no risk of any kind. You'll be glad you did!

Call us
TOLL-FREE
at 1-800-770-1963

## THE EDITOR'S "THANK YOU" GIFT INCLUDES:

- 4 books absolutely FREE (plus $1.99 for shipping and handling)
- A FREE newsletter, *Arabesque Romance News*, filled with author interviews, book previews, special offers, and more!
- No risks or obligations. You're free to cancel whenever you wish... with no questions asked.

## BOOK CERTIFICATE

**Yes!** Please send me 4 FREE Arabesque novels (plus $1.99 for shipping & handling). I understand I am under no obligation to purchase any books, as explained on the back of this card.

Name _____

Address _____ Apt. _____

City _____ State _____ Zip _____

Telephone ( ) _____

Signature _____

Offer limited to one per household and not valid to current subscribers. All orders subject to approval. Terms, offer, & price subject to change. Offer valid only in the U.S.

*Thank you!*

AN023A

Accepting the four introductory books for FREE (plus $1.99 to offset the cost of shipping & handling) places you under no obligation to buy anything. You may keep the books and return the shipping statement marked "cancelled". If you do not cancel, about a month later we will send 4 additional Arabesque novels, and you will be billed the preferred subscriber's price of just $4.00 per title. That's $16.00 for all 4 books for a savings of 33% off the cover price (Plus $1.99 for shipping and handling). You may cancel at any time, but if you choose to continue, every month we'll send you 4 more books, which you may either purchase at the preferred discount price. . . or return to us and cancel your subscription.

THE ARABESQUE ROMANCE CLUB: HERE'S HOW IT WORKS

PLACE
STAMP
HERE

ARABESQUE ROMANCE BOOK CLUB
P.O. Box 5214
Clifton NJ 07015-5214

pher's reluctant-to-let-go arms. As she showered her prince toddler with kisses, he hugged her neck tightly in return. "You look so handsome this morning in your coverall jeans and red shirt! Mommy has a surprise for you. This nice man is going to take us to Disneyland." Sass laughed at how big Justin's eyes had grown.

"I see Mucka Mouse, Mommy?"

Sass always laughed at how he pronounced the Disney character's name, but it was her duty as a parent to correct him. "Yes, sweetie, you'll see Mickey; Minnie, too. Look at this other big surprise."

Justin clapped his hands in excitement when Sass showed him the large elephant and told him that it was a gift from Kristopher. He shook his head up and down vigorously. Jumping up and down, he hugged the pink elephant.

Kristopher got to his feet. "I'm sorry, Mrs. Stephens. I'm at your table and I haven't spoken to you. I'm afraid I was all into Justin." Kristopher was embarrassed over such a major social blunder; the awkward circumstances made it an even worse one.

He shook Amantha's hand. "I still can see where your daughter gets her beauty."

Not at all charmed, Amantha only nodded in response.

*Ease up on the charm, Kristopher,* Sass's eyes warned him. *Yours is not a welcome presence. Don't undo what I've worked so hard on the phone this morning to accomplish.*

"I have four beautiful girls," Jason boasted. Hoping to ease her tension, Jason smiled at his wife. "From the looks of things, Justin is pleased with the gift you brought him," Jason said.

Glad that Jason had said anything to him at all, Kristopher smiled warmly at Sass's father. Justin's love for the gift also thrilled him. "I'm certainly happy about it."

Justin reached for Kristopher to take him and his

heart swelled with joy at the loving gesture. Taking Justin from Sass, he snuggled him onto his lap. He couldn't help thinking that Justin's golden-tipped hair was near the color of the highlights in his own. With Justin's complexion between Sass's and his own, no one who didn't know better would think Justin wasn't his biological child. In his heart, he wished it were so. Still, he had just cause to wonder.

Amantha forced a smile. "Sass and Kristopher, would you like some breakfast?"

"We've already eaten. We're anxious to be on our way, but thanks for the offer, Mom."

Only moments later, Amantha and Jason stood at the door waving to their departing guests, both feeling awkward about the way Kristopher and Justin had taken to one another. Amantha laid her head on Jason's shoulder, watching her daughter and grandson go off with the man her daughter had never gotten over. It looked to her as if he was back to stay, to possibly change Sass and Justin's lives forever . . . and not necessarily for the better.

The Disneyland Theme Park was just opening as the happy threesome arrived. After Kristopher purchased the tickets, they strode through the gates, eyes ablaze with excitement. As this was Kristopher's first time to Disneyland in many years, he felt like he did when he was a small child. He found amusement parks fun and exhilarating. Today was even more so because he had two special friends to enjoy it with, a beautiful woman and a male child, to spoil with toys, love and affection. Taking out the map they'd been given at the entrance gate, Sass and Kristopher sat down on a park bench to map out their day.

It was quickly decided that the first stop would be rides for Justin to enjoy.

\* \* \*

Waving to Sass and Kristopher as he rode around on the kiddie rides, Justin smiled happily. A serious driver at the wheels of the cars, he turned them sharply, laughing sweetly. When there was something that could honk or make noise, he jabbed at it with enthusiasm. Kristopher began taking pictures of Justin. From the first moment he saw the camera, the toddler turned into an absolute ham. His wide-toothed grins and animated poses were delightful.

They spent the better part of the day amusing Justin, but Kristopher was the one who acted like the kid in a candy store. The first ride they took together was the boat ride through It's a Small World. The universal characters in native costumes warmed Kristopher's heart. Looking over at Sass, he saw the laughter in her eyes as Justin clapped along happily with the music. His enthusiastic response was a thrill to both his mother and Kristopher.

Kristopher was patient in running after Justin as they walked the park. He clearly understood and saw what Sass meant about the energy level of her almost-four-year-old.

"Justin is a handful, just like you said, Sass. How do you take care of him all by yourself?" After picking Justin up to carry him, he draped his arm loosely around Sass's shoulders.

"I haven't done it by myself. My parents have been a Godsend. They've helped me with Justin tremendously. I can count on them any time I need to, but I try not to take advantage of their benevolence." With Justin squirming to get down, Kristopher looked to Sass for the answer.

She nodded her approval.

Kristopher smiled. "He'll be so tired when he gets home, he'll probably sleep the entire night. I know I can't stay with you tonight, but can we see each other after you get off work tomorrow? I'll miss you both."

Sass took his hand. "I've made arrangements for my parents to take care of Justin while you're here. You can stay with me as often as you'd like." She had to know if it could work. Being around him was the only way to find out. Besides, for some unknown reason, she felt like she didn't want to be away from him for a second, admitting helplessness against his allure. She had thus far rejected the invites to his home. This had to play out on her turf.

Smiling with adoration, he pulled her close, kissing her gently on the cheek. "I'd like that very much. But I'll go back and forth from your house to mine just in case you need some time to yourself. I don't want you to get tired of me."

"I won't. I know I've said a lot of hurtful things, but I'm starting to feel happy and content. I know I've been wishy-washy the whole time, but I do get confused about what I want. Thanks for bearing with me. It seems that I sometimes take my anger for Grace out on you."

Justin suddenly spotted several of the Disney characters. Jumping up and down, he screamed their names.

As Mickey and Minnie Mouse walked up to him, he went berserk with joy.

"Mucka Mouse, is that you? Is that really you?" Justin screamed excitedly.

Kristopher snapped pictures of Justin's enthusiastic face with his camera. Like Sass, he could hardly contain his laughter at Justin's animated expressions.

"He talks so well for three years old," Kristopher marveled.

"We rarely talk babyish to him. He's mostly had older people around him. I think that contributes largely to his well-developed vocabulary. Besides that, he's a very smart toddler." Sass smiled at her son with pride.

"While you've mentioned some of your experiences since we parted company, you haven't said a word about Justin's father. How does he treat his son?"

Sass grew pale. Instantaneously, Kristopher saw that he'd stepped into sacred territory, where the toddler's father was concerned. Sass looked ready to burst into tears.

Swallowing the lump in her throat, Sass frowned. "That's something I don't want to get into. I'd like to tell you about him, but I can't, for lots of reasons. I'm sorry, Kristopher. I guess I keep disappointing you. Just when you feel at ease with me another mysterious aspect of my life presents itself." *You hid things from me before and now I'm guilty of the same.*

Kristopher lifted her chin with his forefinger. "I thought you'd started to trust me, Sass Stephens. If you marry me, I'd want to meet Justin's father."

Sass looked puzzled. "For what reason?"

Kristopher's expression was sober. "The most obvious one. If Justin's going to live under the same roof with us, I should meet his father. I want him to know I'd treat his son very well."

Sass was astonished by his positive attitude toward the baby's father, but she couldn't ever discuss the father with him. She'd vowed to never reveal the circumstances of Justin's birth. Knowing how the old Kristopher had felt about kids, she couldn't believe what he'd suggested.

"That's a very generous offer, Kristopher, but I don't think it'll fly."

Kristopher looked totally confused. "You don't think he'd agree to meet me. Wouldn't he want to know the man who might raise his son?"

Her rose petal laughter drifted into the air. She thought he looked so adorable when he was baffled about something. Then, seeing that things had gotten too serious, she managed to contain herself. The stern look on his face was an indicator of how he felt.

"I'll take care of it, if the need arises. Don't worry about it. I'm ready to go on The Pirates of the Caribbean ride." She was anxious to change the subject. Though he wasn't ready to drop it, he didn't want to spoil the day, nor did he want to pressure her. He'd done enough of that.

"If we can possibly tear Justin away from his friends, Sass, we can jump on the ride."

Justin didn't make a bit of fuss when Kristopher picked him up. In fact, he smiled warmly, showing his pretty little teeth to the man holding him with such gentleness. The line was long for the ride. While they waited patiently, Justin fell asleep in Kristopher's arms.

Later that night, with everyone seated in the comfortable living room, the Stephens' household buzzed with noise and juicy gossip about Kristopher's fashion show. Jason and Amantha sat on the love seat while the others sat on the matching sofa, with the exception of Eugene. He lounged in the leather recliner. Staci, Stephanie and their husbands laughed at Jason's shocked expression after telling him that Kristopher Chandler had been the host.

Jason's eyes grew wide with amazement. "I can't believe it. That guy must manufacture nerves somewhere. How did Sass react when she found out she'd been duped again?"

"She tried to be really blasé about it, but I think it was eating her alive. To top it off, his lead model unleashed her hawklike talons. All of a sudden, Sass finds herself sitting at the same table with Grace Chapman, a woman who hates Sass's guts," Staci offered.

Amantha laid her hand across Jason's knee. "How did Sass really handle all of this?"

"She couldn't have been more of a lady, but I almost lost my cool when I found out Sass didn't even know he was the host until they got there." Eugene shook his head in dismay, remembering how angry he'd felt at Sass being tricked again by Chandler.

Kissing her husband on the cheek, Staci laughed. "I had to cool this big guy down."

"I thought we were going to have a free-for-all," Stephanie interjected. "But cooler heads prevailed throughout the rest of the evening."

"Thank goodness for that." Amantha looked relieved. "Eugene, you always were a hot head. I know you love Sass dearly, but it wouldn't have helped matters. My youngest daughter has finally come into her own. I think she can now handle Kristopher Chandler, admirably so."

"You're right, Mom," Gerald said. "Sass has really matured. While I understood what Eugene was feeling, I also understand Kristopher. The guy made a lot of bad mistakes and he's paying for them. We don't have to add to his grief. I watched the expressions on his face when Sass danced with Daniel Davis. Their closeness didn't appear to upset him. I think he has matured as much as Sass has, if not more. I think he's coming correct this time."

"Man, you going to champion that brother? If this was happening to Stephanie, you'd have been on the guy like white on rice," Eugene said haughtily.

"You better believe it. This is my wife," Gerald said. Laughing loudly, he pulled Stephanie into his arms to hug her. She responded by kissing him on the mouth.

"You boys are really wild," Jason said. "I remember those days when the boys from out of town came messing with our girls. Talking about free-for-alls. Those were good old-fashioned whippings we used to give those arrogant guys." Jason's eyes shone bright with mischief. "We used to kick out-of-town butt practically every weekend. Didn't need to open no can of whoop-ass back then. We were it. The word got out pretty quickly after a few saloon-style brawls."

Amantha clucked her tongue, sounding like an old hen. "Oh, Jason! Don't encourage them to resort to violence. I'm glad everything worked out okay and that Sass is fine."

Having heard every bit of the family conversation, Sass poked her head inside the door. "So glad to hear it." Everyone was surprised by her sudden appearance. "It's not good to talk about people behind their backs," Sass reproved. "When I heard the subject, I decided to wait outside the door. I think our parents taught us never to gossip and also about how we should always practice the spirit of forgiveness. Didn't you teach us those things, Mom and Dad?"

Looking abashed, Amantha and Jason both nodded.

"If you weren't eavesdropping, you wouldn't have heard it." Stephanie pulled a face. "At least we weren't saying anything bad about you. You should be grateful for that. Where are Kristopher and Justin?"

Sass dropped down on the floor in front of her parent's seat, tugging playfully at Jason's hand. "He wanted to put Justin to bed so I showed him the bedroom. You guys were making so much noise, you didn't even hear us come in. I would've gone up with him but I heard my name mentioned, so I thought I'd listen to what was being said."

Worried looks passed from one family member to another.

Sass looked at them with mocked disgust. "You guys need to relax. I'm in control of me. The only person I can have power over. I'll be right back. I need to check on those two men—and put Justin's pajamas on him."

Everyone in the room exchanged uncomfortable glances as she retreated from the room.

Climbing the stairs with ease, Sass went to her old room where Justin slept when he stayed overnight with her parents. She was surprised to find Kristopher putting on Justin's pajamas. Though Justin was asleep, Kristopher was whispering softly to him. Sass listened intently, but he was speaking in French and she couldn't follow that quickly. However, she was able to pick up the words 'my son' and something about 'love.'

Emotionally full, she watched as Kristopher picked Justin up and put him in bed. Tears came to her eyes as he kissed Justin's forehead before covering him up. Sass walked into the room. Unable to stop herself, she circled his waist from behind. Together, they looked down on Justin as he slept.

"You've been wonderful, Mr. Chandler! You were patient with us the entire day." The way Kristopher had so lovingly tended to her child's every need still amazed her.

Reaching over his shoulder, he took her hand and pressed it against his heart. "I have really enjoyed this day. We'll have to plan more events to include Justin. Sass, I adore him. We've taken to each other so quickly. He brought sunshine into the day. Like his mother, he's very sweet."

When Justin rolled over and clutched the pink elephant, Sass's heart wept with sadness for the little boy who would never know his natural father. A pang of guilt hit Sass's heart. "Kristopher, maybe you shouldn't get too attached to Justin. If our relationship doesn't work out, both of you could get hurt."

"Sass, our relationship will work out if you want it to. It's entirely up to you. Please don't deprive me and

Justin the pleasure of getting to know each other," he pleaded. "I'll be extremely careful with his tender emotions. Justin and I can always be friends, regardless."

"I can see that you're still very much determined, just like my son. I can't seem to refuse you anything, either. If I'm not careful, you two will be conspiring against me at every turn. However, I don't want Justin involved in our relationship at this point. You asked for this one time meeting and I gave it. Please don't make me regret it by pressing for something more."

Kristopher nodded. "I'm sorry. I shouldn't have pressured you. In the meantime, I guess we should just concentrate on us and see where we go from here. Hopefully, we can be a real family one day."

"Speaking of family, my entire group is downstairs. So we'd better join them, or their overworked imaginations will have to be paid overtime. You know how they feel about us seeing one another, so please don't overdo it on the charm. And be careful not to take anything for granted. You are definitely going to be under the microscope."

"I'm with you." Bending his head, he kissed her mouth before they descended the stairs.

The rest of the evening was spent with everyone spinning yarns about different subject matters. When Amantha served chocolate cake and ice cream, Kristopher was careful not to rave too much about her cooking abilities, as he'd done in the past. While telling the group many stories about his upbringing, also the story of how his parents had died so tragically, Sass's family did their best to make him feel comfortable. In order to try and recognize the change in him that Sass had talked about, everyone listened intently to his every word.

There was definitely sympathy for him regarding his parents' death. His heartbreak over the loss was apparent.

Switching gears by telling many funny stories about being a teenager, Kristopher could be quite the comedian when he had an audience. After confessing to the many incorrigible things he'd done, he talked about his day in the park with Sass and Justin with excitement. His enthusiasm for his subject was obvious as he boasted about all the adorable things Justin had said or done.

The brothers-in-law kept a watchful eye on Kristopher, careful not to say anything that might upset Sass. If she married him, it would be difficult to make him a welcome addition to the family, but their deep Christian values required that they at least try.

Justin and Amantha did their best to make Kristopher comfortable in their home. As Christians, they would never disrespect him in any way. However, they were gravely concerned about Sass getting involved with him again. By the way Kristopher talked about Justin, they could tell he planned to be very much involved in their grandson's life, their biggest fear. Justin's little heart getting broken was a major concern for them. Jason would talk with Chandler about that at another time. For now, he just wanted to closely observe the interaction between Sass and the man that seemed to strip her of all rational thought.

On the drive back to the apartment Sass and Kristopher conversed about the wonderful day, their times of deep trouble, the personal changes he'd made, and the supporting role her family had played in helping her pull her life together and keep it that way.

"Despite their feelings about me, your family was very

warm. I know it was a struggle for them to make me feel comfortable, but they managed to do it."

"They're very good people. They've been through a lot with me and have always been supportive. None of them really knows the full story of our relationship. I kept so much bottled up inside. When I nearly had a nervous breakdown up in San Jose, everyone thought my weakened mental condition was over losing you." *But they'll never know the whole truth . . . and neither will you.*

"From what you've told me, more so from what you've refused to tell me, I know it wasn't all about me. Why don't you want anyone to know your issues regarding Justin's father and what else you've been through? It would certainly help me to understand things better." He was bewildered by her need for so much secrecy yet he understood it on a certain level. He, too, carried a deep secret, the truth about him and Grace.

"I really can't talk about all of it. What may seem obvious on the surface isn't always as it appears. I'm just coming to grips with all the reasons why I once felt like I didn't want to live. There were so many factors involved. I moved into a new place, into a new profession. Too soon after that, I fell in love with a new man: you." She sighed heavily.

"As if all that wasn't enough, I later found myself carrying a child that you didn't want. When I learned that you wanted me to have an abortion, that's when life started to become so unbearable for me. The one thing I could never get over was you wanting me to kill our own child." The most horrific part was finally out in the open, but she didn't feel any relief. That surprised her. But there was still so much more for her to reckon with.

Kristopher sucked up the searing pain, his expression one of deep sorrow and regret. Sass had told him she'd have the abortion. Then she later she told him she wasn't even pregnant. Now he wasn't so sure about any of it, especially after seeing Justin. "Sass, those are the same troubled waters that we need to dive into. What we're not discussing is what's standing between us; it's what's keeping us from moving ahead into the future. Are you up to talking about it tonight?"

Sass winced from the pain in her heart. "Can we do this later? I feel as though I've tackled enough issues for one day. Please let me off the hook for now? I can only do this a little at a time. It's easier for me to bear that way."

Kristopher couldn't keep from smiling at how easy it was to surrender to her wishes, even as his heart felt both of their pains. He didn't want to further complicate matters by pushing her into something she obviously wasn't ready for. "Of course, Sass, but only if you promise to try harder at trusting me. I won't betray you a second time."

She reached across the seat and took his hand. "I'm afraid it's me that I don't trust. I made a promise to someone a very long time ago, one that I must keep. That's the only issue that has nothing to do with trusting you."

He believed her. However, he wished she'd just open up and let her troubles flow from deep within, flow from where they lay dormant, silently screaming out to her whenever her troubled past threatened to collide with her future.

"Sass, you've come a long way from those dark times. We both have. It's time to move on. With the support of your family and myself, perhaps you'll soon forgive me for hurting you so badly. In time, I pray that you'll forget."

"I think I've already forgiven you, but I'll never forget how I was made to feel. Remembering how I got to where I am is a very important part of my recovery. I've already buried too much, too deep. Once I get everything out in the open, I don't plan to bury another ache or pain without dealing with it first. Remembering my pain helps me grow stronger."

"You've grown very wise in so few years. Once you've fully learned how to put the blame where it belongs—squarely on my shoulders—you'll recover completely. You didn't ask for these hurtful things. You're a very giving, compassionate person, but you were that way with the wrong person, namely me. I didn't appreciate your wonderful qualities back then. I'm afraid I didn't know how to have or show appreciation for someone like you."

She looked at him with a soft expression. Perhaps he did understand, she mused, amazed by his ability to cut right through to the core of the matter. "Do you ever have conversations with your conscience?" She felt silly for asking such an idiotic question.

"Of course. We all do. Sometimes it's what makes the difference between sanity and insanity. We need to reason things out. Our inner voices are there to assist us in making decisions for our life. I now know that it's God talking to me."

She laughed nervously. "Now I don't feel so crazy. I talk to myself a lot. I know it's my conscience, but it still makes me feel silly after the conversation is over. God talks to me, too, but in a different tone of voice. He whispers his commands to me."

"You're just getting in touch with that side of yourself. In time, it won't feel silly. In fact, you'll feel comfortable. We need our inner voices for guidance and direction." He laughed. "I'm in need of a slice of pizza! Got any recommendations?"

Sass smiled at the enthusiastic way in which he'd shifted conversational gears, sensing that it was more for her benefit than anything else. "There's a small pizza parlor right around the corner from my place. It's a favorite for Justin and me. If you're not careful, you're going to go back to Paris with excess baggage. The airlines charge for extra bags, you know."

He roared with laughter at her comment. "I had hoped to go back to Paris with more baggage than I came with. However, I don't consider it excess since I was hoping the bags would be yours and Justin's."

Sass didn't comment, but she'd heard him loud and clear.

After pulling into the parking lot of the pizza parlor, he got out of the car. Seeming to be in a hurry, he ran around to open the door for Sass. Seeing his love for her in his eyes, she wondered if she'd one day be able to completely fulfill all his yearnings. Doubt still ruled.

The tiny restaurant with windows that looked out onto the street was practically empty, just the way Sass liked it. She dragged Kristopher over to the cozy corner booth, where she and Justin always sat. The decor was the usual pizza kitchen style: red checkered cloths draped on square tables, glass dispensers filled with Parmesan cheese, dried crushed hot pepper, salt and pepper shakers. A lot of gaming machines, more pinball than anything, were lined against the walls. An old jukebox with mostly outdated tunes sat in one corner. It was a far cry from Monte Carlo.

Kristopher ordered a medium pizza with a variety of fresh vegetables. While talking and laughing, they waited for the meal, as though they hadn't eaten all day. Neither of them could believe how hungry they were after all the food they'd eaten earlier. As soon as the waiter left the table, Kristopher broke off a slice of pizza and held it out to Sass.

"Smells wonderful! Here's a napkin for you, Sass."

Sass made a bib out of the paper napkin and stuffed it

inside her shirt collar. Kristopher laughed out loud. "You look like Justin right now. And you are just as adorable."

Sass giggled. "Justin hates for me to put a napkin up to his clothes. He tells me he's a 'big boy.' He may be one, but by the time we leave here Justin looks like a human tomato. He gets the sauce everywhere. But that's part of the fun of eating the pizza."

"Really? Let's find out." Before Sass knew what he had in mind, her mouth was covered with tomato sauce. "Hmm," he moaned, tasting the sauce from her lips. "That's the distinct flavor missing from my slice. You're so spicy. I love to taste you. Can't wait to taste all of you."

Sharing her tomato sauce with him, Sass sought out his mouth, flicking his lips with the tip of her tongue. "We're going to get put in jail for lewd conduct. I guess making out in a restaurant in Paris is par for the course. I saw some heavy stuff going on over there during my vacation."

Kristopher's eyes blazed with passion. "You haven't seen the half of what goes on over there. They definitely do some things in public that would be against the law here."

"Oh, that racy, huh? Americans are such prudes, anyway. We're practically morally bankrupt, but our laws don't coincide with some of the strange things we see on television and in the movies." Sass looked over at the gaming wall. "Do you still like to play the pinball machines?"

"It's what I like best. Want to play a game or two? I must warn you. I'm still very good at it, Sass."

"I'll play if you're not a sore loser, because I'm going to win," Sass taunted him, racing for her and Justin's favorite machine.

As they played the various pinball machines, Sass surprised him by the skillful way she'd learned to handle the levers. But she wasn't quite good enough to best him. She finally gave up after he beat her four games in a row.

\* \* \*

At home in the big four-poster bed, Sass cuddled up next to Kristopher, teasing his inner ear with her tongue. He savored the delicious pangs of passion coursing through his body. She then straddled his back and gently massaged his tired muscles. Once she finished with him, he turned her over on her stomach. Getting on his knees beside her, he showed her the true meaning of massage, tenderly touching places that she didn't even know were muscles. As he rubbed and kneaded every inch of her, she found herself wanting his soft touch to go on forever.

When he quickly jumped out of bed, she was puzzled, until he returned with a bottle of oil from his shaving kit. After lifting her soft pink gown, he poured the oil in his hand and rubbed her back and thighs until she practically screamed out his name in ecstasy.

"Does that feel good?"

"Wonderful!" she responded breathlessly.

"This should feel even better!" Turning her on her back, he rubbed the front of her thighs and then tenderly kneaded her firm breasts. Slowly sucking a rounded breast into his warm mouth, he continued the massage with his moist tongue. As her rose-colored nipples stood erect, he teased them gently with his teeth. She squirmed against him until he rolled over and pulled her full against his body. With the side of her face against his chest, they talked for several hours before falling asleep.

# Eleven

Dinner had been long over, but Kristopher and the Stephenses were just getting heavy into their conversation. They'd made light conversation over the meal, but Kristopher had a lot more to say and Amantha and Jason seemed eager to listen to every word.

Still seated at the formally decorated table, the three looked somewhat relaxed, sipping on hot coffee. Inside the very expensive Beverly Hills establishment, where Kristopher had asked them to meet him, he lavishly wined and dined Sass's parents. They were all on a first name basis, yet Kristopher was terribly uncomfortable calling them by such. They'd insisted and he hadn't wanted to offend them in any way. It was important to try and gain their respect.

"I want to tell you face to face how much I love your beautiful daughter. I want Sass for my wife and Justin as my son. I know I've done a lot of emotional harm to Sass, but I can assure you that I've changed. I promise you I'll do my best to make them happy." Glad to have that part of the conversation over with, he sighed. "If Sass agrees to become my wife, will we have your blessings, Jason and Amantha?"

Jason shifted his position in the soft velvet chair. "Anyone who can bring happiness to Sass has my blessing, but I'm not sure you're the one to do that," Jason offered matter of factly. "However, I could be wrong. Although I don't know each and every detail of your past relationship with Sass, I do know that my daughter was terribly crushed after it was over. Even then, you and Sass had only known each other for a short time. And now you've only been back in her life for a brief spell, so how can you be so sure about marriage?"

Kristopher smiled warmly. "Your daughter asked the same question. I can only answer honestly. I'm a man who knows exactly what he wants, when he wants it, and how he's going to get it. I fell in love with Sass at first sight, a long time ago, but I wasn't the man I am now. In that same moment, I knew I wanted her, but I wasn't ready to commit to marriage then. I know exactly when I wanted her to become my wife, but it came immediately after she was gone. Then, in Paris, at the same moment she looked at me with her sheer brown eyes, the second I saw them filled with the heartache and sadness I'd caused, I knew my feelings about her would never change. I'm still working on how to get us to forever."

Amantha was nearly in tears by the time he finished making his statement, but only because she was a romantic at heart. This man hadn't convinced her that he loved her daughter or that he even deserved another chance. But she had to admit that her heart had softened up a little.

"I'm not completely satisfied with your answers about Sass, but I'm not the one that you have to convince. My daughter is an adult and she makes her own decisions. While my wife and I aren't thrilled that she's seeing you again, we have no intentions of trying to sway her in one direction or another. If our Sass is happy, we'll be happy for her. The matter of our grandson, who has no voice in this, is our main concern. So I have to ask if you can really accept another man's child. Justin is not a pawn in a game of chess. I'd hate to see him being used as such. His welfare is and has always been first and foremost with my wife and me. Sass has learned to fend for herself, but Justin can't. We won't sit idly by and see our grandson get hurt."

Kristopher saw an opening to inquire of Justin's natural father, but he thought better of it. It would be disrespectful of him to pry into Sass's private affairs. "Justin's a light that shines brightly. I'll love Justin as if he were mine. He'll never want for anything. Sass and I will make a home for him. We'll do our best to teach Justin how to love and be loved. We'll create a family bond for him that'll never be broken. He'll learn family values and moral ones. He'll be raised in the religion of Sass's choice. He'll have the best education offered. The most important of all I've mentioned is the love. I can give Justin as much love as I'm capable of giving his mother. I can't change the past wrongs, but I can make the future right. I fully realize that these are my dreams. They all hinge on whatever Sass decides."

Jason nodded. It seemed to him that Kristopher Chandler just might be capable of all the things he'd mentioned. For sure, he'd pushed all the right buttons. Did he truly mean Sass well?

Looking anxious, Amantha rubbed her hands together. "We know Sass has decided to at least see if you two can make this work, but what if she decides that it can't? Will you respect her decision and not try to force the outcome you might want?"

A brief flash of pain coursed through Kristopher's body. "Amantha and Jason, I knew Sass wasn't ready for me to come back into her life in Paris, yet I pursued her. I know she's still not sure about me, but I am hopeful. If and when she decides she doesn't want me, I'll let go. It'll be extremely difficult, but I want her happiness. If it's not with me, so be it. I just need a chance to prove myself to her, to her family. Sass doesn't want any of us to be at odds. Neither do I."

It was easy to see that Kristopher's convictions ran very deep.

"Kristopher, I pray that you'll abide by whatever Sass's decision is. You two have a profound history between you, though you only stayed together a short time. It won't surprise me if she tries to make a life with you, but you both must consider what's best for Justin," Amantha said. "You're the only man Sass has ever exposed Justin to. For you to get back together and then decide that you can't make it would be the worse thing that could happen to our grandson."

To offer her comfort, Jason placed his hand over Amantha's.

"Believe me, Sass is taking all that into consideration. Seeing Justin was just a one-time occurrence—and she's not going to let it happen again until our future is decided one way or the other. Sass has no intention of compromising Justin's heart."

Jason looked relieved. "Sass is a smart girl. She'll make the right decision. I think she's already made it. It's my guess that she just doesn't know how to talk about it yet. Sass has always had this need to please others but damn near forgets to do what makes her happy. I have to admit that I've really seen a change in her, especially since her return from Paris." Jason had thought the change in her was for the better, but now he wondered if it would last. He wasn't as confident about Sass making the right decision as he sounded. He knew how much Sass had once loved Kristopher, how much she still loved him. Still, he had to give the man a fair chance.

"Kristopher, if Sass decides to make her future with you, is taking them to Paris your intention? It'll hurt to have her and Justin move so far away from us." Amantha voiced.

"I've thought of moving my business to Paris, but my home is still here. Should Sass and I stay together home will be wherever she decides. Her family will always be welcome. I know this isn't going to be easy on anyone, but I'm going to do my part. I do love Sass."

Jason extended his hand to Kristopher. "You've answered most of our questions satisfactorily. I still have some doubt. However, we wish you the best of luck. We might not be your strongest allies, but neither will we be your opposition. I respect you for asking us out to face our issues. It's late and we should be getting home. Stephanie's there with Justin. She has to work tomorrow. Thank you for the evening."

Amantha surprised Kristopher when she took his hand and squeezed it gently. "Go with God, son. He'll never steer you in the wrong direction," Amantha kindly remarked.

"Thank you for that. Let me take care of the check and I'll see you out."


Kristopher saw Sass's parents to their car. After getting into his own, he checked the time before starting the engine. He then phoned Sass's apartment.

It was nearly midnight, but the phone just rang and rang. He felt an icy pain grip his heart, hoping her failure to answer didn't mean that something had happened to her. Feeling somewhat dispirited, he ended the call. As he drove along slowly, as a way of killing time, he didn't know whether to go over to her apartment or move on toward home.


Stuck on the side of the road, far from her apartment complex, Sass waited for someone from road service to come and fix the flat tire on her green Acura 3.2 TL. Feeling exasperated, she was ready to call AAA again when the tow truck showed up. She'd been lucky the tire hadn't blown on the freeway. Running over to the service vehicle, she let him know how happy she was that he'd arrived. Sass was sure that Kristopher's dinner with her parents was over and that he was beside himself with worry about her not being home at this hour.

She had gone out to dinner with Lesilee and a few other co-workers just to give her something to do while Kristopher met with her parents. The anguish would've been too much for her had she opted to sit at home and wait for his return. There was no doubt in her mind that her parents hadn't made things easy for Kristopher. They had a lot of negative feelings about him, which weren't going to change overnight. She hadn't told them all of the real serious things that had gone wrong in their relationship because it would've been a bitter pill for them to swallow. Since she needed time to realize all the changes in Kristopher, she had to give them time to do the same. If the changes in him were indeed permanent ones, they'd come to accept him.

After checking the tire for nails, the service man removed the spare from the trunk. Then he jacked up the car up, fixing the tire in no time. Advising her to get a new tire and not to delay in doing so, he waved as he pulled off. Sass shouted her thanks.

Sass got back into the car and headed for the Hollywood Freeway, home to the man she hoped to one day have the ultimate future with. But there were still so many things to take into consideration, Justin's happiness and welfare being the main one.

* * *

Using his cell phone, Kristopher tried Sass's apartment again. There was still no answer. Worried, he paced the spacious master-suite in his home, his heart nearly shattering into a million pieces at the thought of something happening to her. Or could she still be with her friends just enjoying a girl's night out? Perhaps she was at home and had convinced herself not to see him again. Maybe she wasn't answering the phone because she didn't want to talk to him. Was it too late for amends? Had too much water passed under the bridge? Had reality paid her a visit?

Kristopher had been so sure that she was falling in love with him again. Maybe he'd been much too confident in the matter, but he was the type of man who never left room for disappointment or failure. To do that would be like setting himself up for disaster before it had a chance to happen. For the most part, that was the philosophy he lived by.

Seated at the desk, he began composing a letter to Sass, just in case she'd decided not give him another chance. At times he couldn't see what he was writing for the tears, yet he felt every word that he penned. By the time he finished up with his signature, he had convinced himself that Sass had changed her mind about them. After tearing up the note, he picked up the phone to call the airlines to check on availability for the earliest flight to Paris.

Stunned to find out that Kristopher wasn't at home at such a late hour, Sass picked up the phone to call her parent's home, aborting it when she realized everyone would be asleep. Her parents were never up at this hour. *Where can Kristopher be?* Icy fear reached into her heart, nearly freezing it solid. Could he have had an accident? Picking up the phone, she hastily dialed her parent's home. Her concern for him was greater than her desire not to awaken them.

Amantha grabbed the phone on the first ring. Sass knew she'd been asleep by her voice.

"Mom, please tell me if you know where Kristopher is. He's not at home. I'm more than just a little crazy." Frantically, Sass paced the room as she talked.

"Sweetheart, we left Kristopher hours ago. Have you been with your girlfriends all this time? It's really late."

Sass frowned. "No, I haven't. I had a flat tire. It took the tow truck next to forever to arrive. I can't imagine where he could be."

"If you've already checked his home, I don't know what else to tell you. Could he be at his studio?"

The doorbell rang simultaneously with Amantha finishing her statement. Sass's heart skipped a beat. "Mom, Kristopher's at the door now. I'll see you all tomorrow. Kiss Justin for me as soon as he gets up. I'll be there early."

Sass ran for the door. Upon opening the viewing window, her heart soared when she saw Kristopher standing there. After wrestling with the locks, she snatched the door open and leaped into his arms. Mashing her mouth against his, she greedily robbed him of his breath.

"I thought something terrible happened to you." She was relieved at seeing him still in one piece.

Picking her up, he carried her to the sofa, never taking his eyes off her. "Something did. I thought you'd changed your mind about us. I've been calling here for hours."

Her eyes misted. "Oh, ye of little faith. I'm sorry if I've given you reason to feel that way. Just when I was drowning in my fears, you've appeared to rescue me."

Boring his sea-green eyes deep into hers, he searched them for answers. The love she felt for him was clear to see. *Was it the lasting kind? Had he found the answer he was looking for?*

"Thinking that something terrible happened to you made me realize I'm wasting precious time being indecisive about our future. *Je t'aime, Kristopher!* I want to be your wife. I want to live wherever you live for the rest of my life!" Sass cried against his lips.

"I love you, too, Sass! I thought I'd never again hear those beautiful words come from your lips to me. I'll make you happy. Sass, you've made my life complete. We'll have a warm, loving family." Kristopher felt like crying, too, but he saw that Sass needed his strength right now. This was more than he'd hoped for. Though overjoyed at her words, he'd thought she'd still want more time to think about marriage. For him, her timing was perfect.

Flexing her fingers in his thick honey-brown hair, she pushed his head back against the sofa. Climbing onto his lap, she unbuttoned his shirt and trailed kisses from his neck down to his hard, flat stomach. He moaned softly as her fingers tugged anxiously at his belt. Assisting her in her explorations, he loosened the buckle.

His smile was deliciously taunting. "Are you back to trying to seduce me?"

"Trying is not the appropriate word," she whispered against his lips. "You said once I made the decision to marry you, you'd teach me the art of lovemaking, the kind of loving that can only be taught by a man who truly loves his woman. In case you weren't listening, the decision has been made."

"I thought I said, 'once you married me,'" he challenged.

"Let's pretend. Then we'll be officially authorized to play house. Or would you rather play doctor?"

Kristopher's brows came together in a slight frown. "I'd rather tell you what went on between your parents and me. Then we won't have to talk about it again."

Sass stood up and pulled at his hand. "I talk much better in bed. When we're finished, we won't have anywhere to go but into each other." She took off for the bedroom, laughing wildly.

After turning off all the lights, Kristopher followed after her, finding her already in bed when he entered the room. He quickly removed his clothes and dove under the comforter with her, cradling his head in her arms.

She kissed his forehead. "Now you can tell me your story, Kristopher."

Lifting her hand, he kissed the back of it. "Surprisingly, it didn't go too badly. I told your parents what my intentions are. They aren't thrilled with us getting back together. But they're not going to try and sway you one way or the other. We talked about Justin and what us getting together meant for him. He's their main concern. Sass, we have to do everything in our power to be fair to that little one. I was relieved to get so much out in the open. I know they still have reservations. I was honest and they were the same in return. At least we all know where we stand with each other. I have to be totally honest with you. I didn't think it could ever be anything but an uphill battle with your family. For a moment there, I expected them to tell me to stay away from you. But that didn't even come up. In fact, your parents' aren't going to oppose our relationship. We actually ended the evening on a pretty good note. A mutual respect was established. We'll have to wait and see what happens from here on in."

She stroked Kristopher's hair. "Speaking of honesty, I've heard the only truth I needed to hear. That you love me is all I need to know. The rest is easy. My family will come around in time. I'm sure of it. They may never become chummy with you, but neither will they be bent on vengeance. I left Lesilee and the other crew at the restaurant. Then I had a flat tire. That's why I was so late getting home. Now, is it going to be house or doctor?"

He laughed with joy. "All of the above . . . and so much more."

"One more question, Kristopher. What made you think I'd changed my mind about us?"

He ran his thumb over her eyebrows to smooth them. "Just an odd feeling. I drove around the city aimlessly. Then I came to the conclusion that if you'd decided not to make a life with me, I needed to hear it from your lips. I stopped and had coffee. Then I drove here. I half expected not to find you here since there was no answer when I called. I was planning on sitting in the car until you arrived. But you're here. I'm here with you. Together, we'll fight the issues of the past whenever they rise up in battle."

Sass kissed him hard on the mouth. "I'm so glad you came. I know I planned on seeing Dr. Ford before making any decisions, but it has turned out the way it should have. I feel at peace now. Those two little repeated words of yours, 'I'm sorry,' have removed most of the bitter feelings I had. Now, Monsieur Chandler, I'm waiting for Lovemaking 101 to begin."

Climbing out of bed, Kristopher walked over to the dresser and lit the votive candles. He turned on the television and tuned it to the DMX station that carried soft hits. After retrieving two glasses and the bottle of French wine from the corner table, he climbed back into bed with Sass, smiling broadly.

In the romantic setting Kristopher had created, he began teaching Sass the first lesson in the art of lovemaking. Holding her in one arm, he lifted the wineglass of sparkling liquid up to her lips. Before she could swallow it, he covered her lips with his and shared in the wine from her mouth.

Eyeing him adoringly, she held up the glass for him to drink from. She returned the sensuous gesture by drinking from his slightly parted lips. Their tongues mingled together in tasting the lightly fruited wine.

Kristopher first undressed her with his smoldering eyes. He then removed her nightgown with slow deliberation. Touching her softly, caressing each part of her with his warm hands, he made her hunger for more. With expert manipulation, he aroused erotic zones she never knew existed. From her head to the tip of her toes, he nipped, fondled and kissed her tenderly with moist lips. His heated touch set her body ablaze.

Stealing her heart and soul like a thief in the night, he brought her unspeakable delights, receiving the very same pleasures from her avid responses. His body was already on fire, but when Sass poured the warm wine around his navel area, licking it away greedily, he became a white-hot inferno. Taking a few pages from his lesson book, she straddled his chest, teasing him with her ravenous mouth and tongue.

Rolling Sass away from him, he stared deeply into her eyes. "I'm insane with wanting to be inside of you, but we can stop now if you're the least bit uncomfortable. It's up to you."

Sass's wild desire for him burned in her eyes like a raging fire. "I've already made up my mind. No matter what, this is one decision I won't ever regret. If you stop now, you're risking the loss of more than your sanity. I won't be responsible for what happens to you if you don't relieve my burning desires," she said huskily.

He nipped at her lower lip. "And I won't be responsible for what happens with us from this moment on. I'm going to put out your lake of fire if it takes all night." He quickly sheathed himself with a condom.

Her pulse raced as he hovered over her. Lifting her buttocks gently, kneading them softly, he brought her up close to him. Cherishing her body, as though it were a precious gem, he flowed gently into her warmth. Before the entry was entirely completed, her body went into spasmodic contractions.

In a smooth, easy style, he filled her with rapture, creating a frenzy of her mind and body. Encouraging her to open her eyes and look at him, he made love to her with the passion in his own. Coveting her body as if were a national treasure, his deep thrusts and wild gyrations sent Sass to the end of the universe. She joined him with the force of the compelling wild motions. Bewildered with fulfillment, they stayed locked in an impassioned embrace, re-igniting the desires to voyage to parts unknown, over and over again.

Stealing a ring from Saturn, Kristopher gave it to her as a token of his love. Landing on Jupiter, Sass removed streaks of brilliant light, presenting them to him to as her token to light his way until they were together forever. They made love in cool dark caves, in fields of yellow daisies, and red poppies, on lush green islands in paradise. After making love on the soft pillows in the sky, they drank from the fountain of eternity. Before departing, they left behind a sample of the love they felt for each other. With their hearts no longer afraid of breaking, souls no longer fearful of dying, Kristopher and Sass lay close to one another making plans for their future.

Sass felt that love was capable of bridging the gap between all the people of the world.

To him she was like a diamond whose brilliance was nearly lost; its edges roughened by his careless treatment of her. He promised to fully restore her luster and smooth out her rough edges with tender, loving care. She in turn promised him that she and Justin would become the family he'd been sorely missing. While discussing some of the problems that might arise in marriage, they seemed prepared to deal with any obstacles put in their way.

\* \* \*

Sitting quietly, waiting for Kristopher to get off the phone with a colleague in Paris, Sass was curious as to why Carmel, California, had been mentioned in his conversation. Her thoughts briefly turned to the last few days she and Kristopher had enjoyed while lazing about the house after she got off work. He had been so attentive to her. The change in him was miraculous.

When she'd spoken with her parents earlier in the week, Amantha and Jason announced their upcoming trip and they wanted to take Justin with them. As much as she would miss him, Sass wasn't about to let Justin miss out on anything that contributed to his social development. Her parents had always taken their children on vacation with them every single year, so they'd be well traveled and well rounded. It was good that he was with them since Kristopher was still in town and Sass had only allowed Justin to spend limited amounts of time with him and her.

Kristopher hung up the phone and sat down next to Sass. "I have a proposition for you, Sass. How would you like to go with me to Carmel? Before you answer, I think you should know your answer determines whether I keep up with my business obligations or ignore them. It'll also keep me here with you a bit longer, maybe another full week."

"How's that?"

He grinned. "Because I'm not going without you. If I don't go, I neglect my business interests. On the other side of the coin, it means I'd have to return to Paris right away."

Her eyes filled with joyful laughter. "That's no proposition. It sounds like blackmail to me. Is there any ransom involved?"

He laughed at her bewildered expression. "None for you to pay. Instead, I'll pay the ransom of ten-thousand laughs, seventy-two hours of tender moments, a million and one kisses. How does that sound?"

"I'd love to go, but it's not that simple. I have Justin to think about. I'd also need to see about taking more time off from work. When are you leaving?"

"In order to relax and unwind after my meeting, before fulfilling my dinner obligation, I should leave early in the morning. When I come here on Monday, I'll stay another couple of days. Then I really have to get to Paris. Justin is with Jason and Amantha, but we'll be back before they return. I understand your need to see about time off. Maybe you could land an assignment up in Carmel. This elitist party should be the talk of all the gossip columnists. You're interested in becoming an entertainment correspondent, aren't you?"

She brightened at his last comment. "You may have something there. I'll talk with Mandy and see what she thinks. Give me a name I can drop on her. It has to be a name with a lot of money and power behind it in order for Mandy Wells to go for it."

Kristopher rested the palm of his hand in her hair. "Try out Steven and Reva Anders on her. If she doesn't know who they are, LABS isn't keeping up with the money and power people. Stephen Anders is one of the richest men in television communications. When he says jump, how high is the next question asked."

Sass rested her head on his shoulder. "I've definitely heard that name a time or two around LABS. I'm sure Mandy knows him. She stays on top of everything. Do you think he'd allow me to submit an entertainment commentary on his party?"

Kristopher laughed. "The man has an ego larger than the solar system. He loves to hear and see his name highlighted in any form of media. His wife is an interesting woman. I won't tell you much about Reva. I'd like you to o your own assessment of her. I've shared many evenings with them; there's never a dull moment with the Anders. And I know you won't have a boring time with me."

Reflecting back on the wonderful things Kristopher had said to her during the last couple of days, her heart became full. He often made simple, everyday words sound like a poetry reading. What was different about him from before was that his entire attitude had changed.

Concerned with the faraway look in her eyes, he nudged her. "Have I lost you to some distant land? What's going through your mind?"

Sass looked at him and smiled. "I was just thinking of some of the things you've said to me since I've known you. You have such a beautiful, poetic vocabulary. Where do all those beautiful responses come from?"

His expression turned soft. "From the dictionary I keep shelved in my heart. The poetic words only appear when I look into your lovely eyes."

"Kristopher Chandler, you are quite the Romeo." There were many women who had come and gone, before and after her. Would the time come for him to leave her again? The sad thought briefly crossed her mind, but she warded off the defeatist thinking. It wouldn't work between them if she didn't stay positive.

With mischief dancing in his eyes, Kristopher squeezed her hand. "Since your parents didn't name you Juliet, I'll have to say I'm only a Romeo to my Sass."

She laughed. "That was a pretty flimsy line, brother. I see that I still have to be very protective of my heart around you. If I'm not careful, you'll have me believing the moon is made of green cheese."

"It is! Didn't you taste it while we were on it?"

Her gentle laughter filled the room with soft, tantalizing music. "Kristopher, hold me." She suddenly felt very vulnerable despite her desire not to give in to her fears.

The vulnerability in her eyes cut into his heart like a newly sharpened surgeon's scalpel. He guided her head against his chest. "Talk to me, Sass. You can trust me."

"I can't explain what comes over me. At times I feel a little fearful." *There's still so much you don't know.* She was so fearful of him finding everything out.

"Nothing to fear but fear itself, sweet Sass."

Dressed in a fresh pair of jeans and a T-shirt, Sass went into the kitchen to make breakfast food for dinner. Kristopher still felt the effects of their all-afternoon love affair as he lay across the bed to await her call.

"Kristopher, how do you want your eggs?" she yelled from the kitchen.

"Scrambled," he shouted back in response.

Opening the refrigerator, she pulled out all the ingredients to make a pleasant meal. Sass first made a pan of white hominy grits with butter. She then fried four eggs, over easy. After buttering some brown bread, she stuck the bread under the broiler pan of the oven. When everything was ready, she went back to the bedroom, only to find Kristopher sound asleep.

A powerful beam of glowing light suddenly flashed in her eyes. This was the dawn of a new horizon. Kristopher wasn't the same man who'd hurt her so deeply. The new him hadn't been inconsiderate of her once and she didn't think he'd ever be again. Bending over the bed, she outlined Kristopher's ear with her tongue.

Turning over onto his back, he reached up and pulled her down on top of him.

"Dinner-breakfast is ready." Hungry for the taste of him, she kissed his mouth.

"I prefer to eat in bed, but I'll come to the kitchen."

Swinging her off her feet, he kissed her thoroughly. He then went into the bathroom to wash up.

Looking at the neatly set kitchen table, he smiled. They bowed their heads for the blessing.

Kristopher kissed her before picking up his fork. "You taste as good as the food smells." Putting the fork to his mouth, he closed his eyes. "Mm, this is great! Sass, I have a question for you." She nodded for him to proceed. "Why did you ask me how I wanted my eggs if you were just going to fix them the way you wanted to?" He smiled devilishly.

She poked her lower lip out. "I wanted fried so I made it easier for myself. If you have a problem with it, there are plenty of restaurants in the area." The softness in her eyes belied the challenging tone in her voice.

Laughing, he arched an eyebrow. "*Pardonnez-moi!* Jason must have had a crystal ball present when he decided you were going to be sassy." He looked down at his plate. "Where's the meat, *Mademoiselle?* I have the appetite of a hungry bear."

"I'm sorry, I didn't have any. I usually only buy meat the same day I plan to cook it. I should've thought to get some for your visit."

"It's no big deal. If you need money for groceries, just let me know. I'm not around to mooch off you."

"Kristopher, you haven't given me a single reason to think that. You have spent an exorbitant amount of money showing Justin and me a wonderful time. I'm grateful for that, but I'd never ask you for money unless I was absolutely destitute. Thank you for all that you've done for us so far."

He rested his elbows on the table. "Our relationship should be based on give, take and share. Sass, you don't have to be destitute to come to me. What good am I to you if I refuse to help you out? It would kill me to know that you and Justin needed something yet you wouldn't come to me. Money is for spending. Who better to spend it on than someone you love deeply?"

She smiled gently. "Thank you for your graciousness, Kristopher. I'll remember that for the future."

"Make sure you do, precious. With that settled, are you ready for that helicopter ride up to Carmel tomorrow?"

Her stomach grew a little queasy. "I'd rather fly in a regular plane, but since the flight arrangements have already been made, I guess I have to be ready."

Kristopher came around the table. Kneeling before her, he pulled her forward into his arms. "Don't look so frightened, Sass. The flight will be fantastic. If it'll make you feel better, I'll hold you all the way."

"Promise?"

"Promise." He kissed her, lighting a spark that kept them clinging together for the next several minutes.

# Twelve

The morning was bright and clear with blue skies prevalent in the heavens. As the helicopter carrying Sass and Kristopher glided through the air, the conditions for flying couldn't have been any better. Light winds and good visibility made for a perfect flight in the small, four-passenger Bell helicopter. From the moment of take off from Los Angeles International Airport, Sass was in awe of her surroundings, not to mention the pilot's expertise in handling the state-of-the-art flying machine. She couldn't believe how unafraid she was.

It was obvious to her that Kristopher had flown this route many times. He was also familiar with the pilot. She felt like she had her own personal tour guide as Kristopher explained everything interesting there was to know about the route.

The beautiful scenery kept her breathless. Imagining herself as a bird, she relaxed and enjoyed her journey through the Master's magnificent creations.

A short time later, when they'd finally landed safely, Sass was already eagerly anticipating the trip back.

The trip in the convertible down what was known as Seventeen-Mile Drive was an experience Sass would never forget. Seeing through the innocent eyes of a child, she celebrated in the illustrious natural surroundings. Continuously stopping along the way, the beautiful SR1 highway took them from one wonder to the next, through numerous magnificent points of interest.

Sass felt as though she could smell the sun on her golden skin, feel nature tenderly strumming her once broken heartstrings. The best part of the trip for Kristopher was watching the changing expressions in Sass's eyes that charmed, dazzled, and captivated him through Seal Rock, Cypress Point, Spy Glass Hill, through the entire scenic route from the Monterey Peninsula to Carmel. Reaching across the seat, he planted a soft kiss on her wind-blown cheeks.

"Kristopher, I haven't been this happy in a long time. To be able to touch nature in all its splendor is an experience that's unmatched in my soul."

"I can see your happiness. It's quite intriguing. I'm happy I could share this entire splendor with you, but I have to warn you. This is only the beginning. I plan to share a whole new universe with you, if you let me."

"Kristopher, I'm happy just being with you," she said honestly. "Over the last month, you've made waking up each day a real treat for me. You've filled the worst void in my life. The one thing I'm not going to question any longer is if I'm still in love with you. I loved you back then and I love you now. In fact, I'll never stop loving you. But as we both know, love isn't always enough to make a relationship work. If love was all it took, we wouldn't have to worry. If something should happen to our marriage plans . . . and this is as far as its goes, I'll be okay. I'm learning not to expect too much."

"Don't worry about how far it's going to go. Let's enjoy wherever it takes us. As far as what to expect, you should demand no less than the best of everything." No verbal response from her was necessary since he felt her thoughts.

Offering spacious units with spectacular ocean views, private balconies, and wood burning fireplaces, the quiet and gracious Tickle Me Pink Inn was nestled on a jagged cliff in Carmel, high above the ocean. The pounding surf down below could be heard and seen from the balconies way upon high.

Kristopher led Sass to their room to settle her in before his meeting. Once they hurried through getting their things unpacked, taking Sass by the hand, he guided her from the bright decorous room and out onto the private balcony. The rare beauty of the seascape below mesmerized Sass.

Her enthusiasm for what she saw was refreshing and exciting to Kristopher. As usual, the bewitching sparkle in her eyes left him breathless.

Back inside the room, Kristopher hung up their evening clothes and stored the suitcases in the closet. He went into the bathroom, dropped off his shaving kit, and came back out in a matter of seconds.

Stretching out across the bed, he looked over at Sass. With amusement glimmering in his eyes, he patted the spot bedside him, inviting her to lie down next to him. Smiling, she laid down next to him.

He grazed her cheek with gentle lips. "Sass, I want to make love to you before I go to my meeting. It'll either give me a fresh perspective, or cause me to think of nothing but you waiting here for me. Either way, I want to be inside of you," he whispered.

"I want the same, desperately."

To show him how much she wanted him, she stripped out of her white polo top and removed her denim jeans.

Throwing one of her legs across his hip, she reached for his zipper. With their eyes locked together, making heavy eye contact, they took great pleasure in stripping each other until every article of clothing was removed.

Once he'd started a hotter-than-hell fire on her lips, he traveled up and down the length of her body, torturing her pleasurably with his mouth and hands. Squirming under his expert touch, on one of his trips up to the top, she pulled his head down between her breasts, lacing her fingers through his hair. Burying his head into her soft flesh, he kissed and nipped wildly at her skin.

Her eyes were bright with pure passion. It drove him crazy to see such ecstasy burning there, knowing it burned for him. Rolling over on his back, he gently pulled her to the end of the bed. Tenderly, he nudged his muscular thigh between hers. Looking into his eyes, she placed a comdom on him, then lifted herself up and came in direct contact with the swollen tip of his thickened manhood.

"Hold on to me, sweet Sass. As I promised, I'll take you there. Touch me, sweetheart. Yes, right there," he whispered against her neck. Gripping his buttocks, she pulled him in closer to her. Switching back and forth from tender to rough, she massaged his muscles, sending hell's fire down his back.

He tried to roll her over but she completely surprised him by pushing him flat on his back. Feeling wild and free, she moved over him in ways, exotic ways, ways that would've brought him to his knees had he been standing. Keeping him locked deeply inside her, she moved on top of him like a wild bucking bronco, drawing strangled sounds of passion from deep in his throat.

The desert was hot from the blazing sun. With the sweat from their bodies as the only liquid available to them, they drank thirstily from each other. Using their tongues, they lapped every drop of moisture from each other's bodies. The salty taste of their combined sweat revived them, giving them new energy to withstand the blazing heat of the sun.

An unexpected sandstorm suddenly whirled around them, sending powerful, gusty winds ripping through their bodies. With frantic screams penetrating the silence, their arms tightened around one another, trembling from the force of the wind as they united in climax.

Spent, tired, totally fulfilled, Sass fell away from him. Throwing her head back against the pillow, she drew his head into the well of her arm, wishing this moment never had to end.

"Sass, did I take you there?"

She smiled smugly. "Are you needing your ego stroked?"

"Honestly? Not even. I just want to make sure you're fulfilled."

"If you can't tell that by what we just felt, Kristopher, then I don't know what to say."

"I can only imagine what you felt, Sass, and I know what I experienced. But I want you to *tell* me what you were feeling, my love."

"That's a little hard to do since there are no words in the English language to describe it, but I'll give it my best shot." Her voice sounded deeply tranquil. "I felt a wonderful, powerful rush of molten heat." She closed her eyes. "Then I saw the end of the earth right under my feet. When I tried to stand on its surface, I couldn't. I became like a feather, blowing, falling forever into the distance. As I spiraled toward the center of the universe, it felt so wonderful that I actually climaxed from the sheer pleasure of the fall. The dramatic descent brought me into the safe haven of your arms, where I was destined to dwell forever." She kissed his brow. "Now it's your turn." Sass couldn't believe she wasn't the least bit embarrassed by what she'd just said, especially the part about her reaching a climax. This conversation was more than a little hot.

He looked up into her eyes. "I spotted a deserted island with lush greenery and an emerald green oasis in the center of it. Out of the corner of my eye, I saw you coming through the dense foliage. But the closer I got to you, the farther you moved away. Then you suddenly turned around and looked right at me. What I saw in your eyes took my breath away. The look of love caressed your eyes like a blanket of fire.

"Without warning, you snared me. After taking me captive, you made me your slave, wringing every drop of energy from my body. You then ran from me and I chased after you. That's when you began to fall off the end of the earth. I caught you as you floated downward. Embracing each other with the strength of our love, we floated into eternity, where we would reside forevermore."

Sass couldn't keep from giggling, nor could she keep her inner thermometer from rising. His stimulating story had her wanting him all over again. "Kristopher, I've never felt like this before, even though the intimacy we shared before was fantastic. I hope to experience these same feelings over and over."

Passion glistened in her eyes and his were filled with the amazing love he felt for her.

"I love you, Sass Stephens," he confessed. "I can't wait to marry you."

Sass couldn't have responded if she'd wanted to. Her throat felt like it was closed. Even though she was now completely sure of his love for her, the issue of trust wasn't settled in her heart. Shuddering from her desire to be completely free to love him without reservation, she gasped for breath. Veiling her eyes with her lashes, she let the cool tears soothe the burning sensation. Unlike before, these were happy tears.

"It's time for you to get ready for your meeting," she said, choked up with emotion. "I'm going to shower, climb between these sheets, and dream about nothing but you while you're gone."

Emotionally full, she ran from the room before he could respond. Her flight caused him concern, but he decided to give her the space she seemed to need.

In the bathroom, Sass's emotions ran away with her. As always, his words of love touched her in every way imaginable. Not only did he confess to loving her, he really seemed sure that he wanted to marry her. She stepped in the hot water. So weak from the lovemaking, her emotions so drained, Sass sat down on the floor of the tub to allow the water to rain down on her.

Kristopher came into the bathroom, stepped into the shower stall and lifted her to her feet. Unable to distinguish the shower water from tears, her sudden flight made him wonder if she'd been cyring. If so, was she scared of him all over again? Would she run away from the relationship? Had he put too much pressure on her too soon to get married? With the answers all locked inside of her heart, he prayed that she'd one day give him the key.

Sleep came easy for Sass, though it soon became filled with nightmares from the past. Anger and rage possessed her mind as she fell victim to her pain. Kristopher was in bed with the faceless woman, the woman she now suspected of being Grace. Just as Grace turned to look at her, Sass awakened with a start. The evil look of triumph in Grace's eyes shook Sass down to the core of her heart and made her tremble with a mixture of fear and fury.

As she thanked God that it was only a horrible dream, she grabbed her robe and climbed out of bed. Outside on the balcony, she sat on a chair. Just as a sharp pain soared through her, the white surf crashed against the rocks far below. She gasped in horror when she conjured up an image of her broken body thrown among the jagged rocks by the swirling waves.

To ease the pain, she imagined several seagulls swooping down to carry her to safety. The gulls would build a nest of flowers for her to sleep upon and cover her broken body with sweet honeysuckle nectar. The white and gray birds would then care for her until her broken body was completely healed, until she could once again fly free on her own.

Back inside, the room seemed to spin as Sass walked around in a daze. As she searched every corner for her broken heart, mild hysteria crept into her lungs. Who am I kidding?

*Only me.*

The inward reply brought on fresh anguish. She didn't belong in Kristopher's world. She felt like a small-town girl with big dreams and a horrendous past. If she knew a way out, she'd leave and never see him again. But she couldn't leave him. She loved him, truly loved him.

The hours had passed by slowly, but Kristopher still hadn't returned. Maybe he's left me, she thought. Laughing at her own stupidity, she sat on the bed and read the instructions for use of the phone. Dialing Stephanie's number, she waited patiently for an answer.

"Hello," Stephanie greeted cheerfully.

"Hey, big sis, its Sass. I wanted to let you know we arrived safely. The helicopter ride was wonderful. I didn't feel frightened once."

"Glad to hear it, Sass. I hope the rest of your time away will be just as pleasant."

"Have you heard from Mom and Dad? If so, is Justin okay? I miss him so much."

"They've called. Everything's just fine. I know you can't wait to get him back home, but Mom says Justin's having the time of his life."

"Kristopher is missing him, too. He'll be leaving for Paris not long after we get back. I still have a few doubts where he's concerned: trust issues. I want to be with him and I know for a fact that I love him, but I get so nervous and become unsure when I think of what happened to me before. I got my hopes up so high, only to have them dashed to nothing. I won't survive another serious disappointment like that last one, not from the same man I love with all of my heart."

"Sass, don't do this to yourself. You've told us a hundred times that he's nothing like he was before. I don't think you should keep on expecting to get hurt again. Maybe he was just scared to death of his feelings for you. Don't let the present slip through your fingers by focusing too much on the past. Since he's only going to be here a short time, get the most out of each second so you can make a wise decision. You don't have to rush into marriage before he leaves. He doesn't expect that of you and he's already told you that he plans to be patient."

"I know that. I appreciate you and all that you've said. But Stephanie, there's so much that he doesn't know. I want to confide in him about every detail of my life, but I'm scared. Marriage between us won't happen if I don't learn to fully trust him. He's given me no reason not to trust him thus far, but practicing denial is what got me into trouble before. I have to open up before we walk the aisle."

The door opened and Kristopher walked in, smiling brightly. The slight swelling of her eyes had him again wondering if she'd been crying, or if something had gone wrong at home.

"Stephanie, I have to go now. Kristopher just came back from his meeting. I'll call you tomorrow. Goodbye."

"Bye, Sass. Take care. While you're at it, let go of the past. I think you have a bright future ahead of you. Now that you've got us rethinking our opinions of him, you should practice what you preach."

"I deserved that. Love you, Stephie." Sass smiled as she hung up the phone.

Kristopher walked over to the bed and dropped down beside her. He looked her over. "Is everything okay, Sass?"

"Just fine. How'd your meeting go?"

After pulling his shoes off, he stretched out on the bed and propped a pillow behind his head. "It was okay; just the usual corporate board meeting. Rather boring in some ways, especially when you have a beautiful woman waiting in a hotel room for you. Just as I thought would happen, I couldn't stop thinking of you."

She laid her head against his chest, relieved that he was back. "I missed you, Kristopher."

"I missed you, too. I'm here now. We'll be together for the rest of our stay in Carmel. Kiss me, Sass Stephens. I'm hungry for the taste of your sweet mouth."

She offered her lips to him and Kristopher kissed her softly. The more intense the kisses became, the more he realized he'd never be able to satisfy his hunger for her mouth or her gentle touch. He held her away from him and gazed into her eyes. "Did you sleep the entire time I was away?" He gently smoothed back her hair, loving the softness of it.

"If that's what you want to call it. I had a bad dream that seemed so real. I woke up an emotional mess. But I'm okay now." She began to look a little despondent.

He caressed the nape of her neck. "I'm sorry, Sass. Wish I'd been here for you."

"You *were* here for me. Knowing you cared about me helped me get through it."

"It's more than caring, Sass. It's love and a genuine concern for your well-being. Why don't we go for a drive around Carmel and see what this place has to offer. Then we can come back and dress for dinner."

"I'd love to look around. I've heard a lot about this cozy coastal city. I'll hurry and slip into my clothes."

They engaged in another passionate kiss and the heat emanating from him reached inside Sass's robe, stroking her nude body, causing her pores to seep sweat. Kristopher moved slightly away. Opening her robe, he blew his sweet breath over her, cooling her overheated body.

Too drained to withstand another passionate assault, she slipped from his embrace. Grabbing her clothing, she ran into the bathroom. Closing the door behind her, she pressed her back against it. Emotionally spent, she slid down to the floor from the sheer exhaustion of it all. Sass felt whipped.

Twenty minutes later, dressed in white jeans and a red-and-white striped polo jersey, Sass checked her appearance in the bathroom mirror. After brushing her long hair back from her face, she secured it with a red scarf. Seated on the floor, she pulled white canvas shoes onto her small feet and tied the laces.

As she stepped out of the bathroom, Kristopher gave her a sweet smile, making her heart gasp at the appearance of his body clad in tight jeans and a soft-blue Italian knit sweater. "Hunk" didn't begin to describe him. With stars in her eyes, she crossed the room to go into his outstretched arms.

He kissed the center of her forehead. "If you keep running out on me, I'm going to think I have bad breath."

"My emotions sometimes get a little carried away. There are times when I need a little space. Your breath is as fresh as a spring morning. If it wasn't, I wouldn't have any problem telling you."

He grinned. "I'm glad you're so honest and forthright. Let's get out of here."

She smiled. "Wait, I have to put on my Sunlit Sass."

Smiling lazily at her comment, he watched her take flight again. Her retreating back sent shivers of longing and fear down his spine. Sass had agreed to become his wife, but she had him a little fearful. He still sensed doubt in her, yet he understood. Loads of patience was what he had to exhibit at all times. It was imperative to gain her full trust. He was in no doubt of her love. Nobody ever loved him like Sass did.

The short tour of Carmel led them to many exciting and beautiful places, but there wasn't enough time to do all of their hearts' desires. Most of the time was spent at the Barnyard, a shopping and dining complex offering many specialty shops and fine galleries in an extraordinary garden setting. The entire place had a country atmosphere.

Sass had a fit when she saw a Thomas Kinkade art gallery among the rows and rows of quaint shops and small businesses. She positively loved the man's brilliant work. He had a way of breathing life and light into everything he created on canvas. He was a master artist.

"Can we go in here for a minute? Mr. Kinkade's work takes my breath away, but not nearly as much as your wonderful smile does."

Grinning, he swatted her gently on the behind. "You sure know how to work on me. When you look at me like that, I'll agree to take you anywhere. What about a trip to the moon or perhaps an excursion to paradise?"

She wiggled her nose. "We just came from the moon and we've been in paradise for days now. Let's walk inside this gallery, where we can allow our imaginations to take us somewhere we haven't been yet. We can just use our imaginations to step into one of Mr. Kinkade's paintings. That'll take us to another uncharted place, somewhere where only love and peace exists."

He pulled her into his arms. "Sass, you titillate me in so many unsuspecting ways. I love your colorful sense of adventure. I can't wait to take you to all the exotic places the world has to offer. I know that you'll appreciate any corner of the universe. You have a way of finding beauty in all things. I love that about you. I love the beauty inside you, the beauty that speaks to your gentle, untamable nature. In fact, I love everything about you. I just hate that it took me so long to come to terms with the impact you've had on me."

They stepped inside the place where Sass knew the union of light and shadows would abound. His magnificent use of the gift of light was what made Kinkade's works so special.

Sass led Kristopher around the gallery, stopping at all of her favorite works of art. Instantly, he was able to see why she was intrigued with these particular works. They weren't only magnificent; they spoke to the heart and soul of nature, to the creative works of the Father up above.

"Look at this one! 'Stepping Stone Cottage,'" she read aloud from the engraved nameplate. "I can see us living in this beautiful cottage for the rest of our lives. Look at all the fine detail of the trees and the sparkling brook. Though there's snow on the roof of the cottage, which indicates winter, the trees come alive with a splendid mixture of the colors of spring. Check out the shadow of light coming through the trees."

Kristopher smiled at Sass's enthusiasm. "I'm not so sure that's snow on the roof, Sass."

Sass took a closer look at the painting. "What could it be then? It's white like snow."

"To be honest, I don't know. The grass is much too green and there are too many flowers in bloom for winter."

"Let's leave it up to our imaginations. It can be anything we want it to be. I like the idea of snow in a spring setting. How's that for creativity? Can we go there for a visit?"

Kristopher kissed the tip of her nose. "Certainly. Look over here at 'New Day Dawning.' That's a fitting title, wouldn't you say?"

Smiling, Sass nodded.

He pointed out the details in the painting. "See how the waves crash against the rocks. If we close our eyes, we can probably hear the sounds of the pounding surf smashing into the coastline. Look at how the sky and ocean appear to meet in almost the same exact space. There's also a path leading into the forest of beauty beyond the cottage."

"Kristopher, let's walk across the 'Bridge of Faith,' and into the peaceful world of nature lying in wait on the other side. I feel the peace emanating from this painting."

Back at the inn, they dressed without much enthusiasm for the dinner engagement. Both were tired and wanted nothing more than to spend a quiet evening in front of the fireplace. For Kristopher, that wasn't an option. When an important business associate extended an invitation to dinner, he made every effort to attend.

Sass looked stunning in a black and white trapeze dress with a large white bow in front. The lens in Kristopher's eyes shuttered wildly as he photographed her beauty. The strapless dress, white at the top, flowed into a black trapeze bottom. Her hair looked windswept, piled loosely in a cascade of curls on top of her head. Matching the center of the bow on her dress, small rhinestone earrings in the shape of bows dangled from her ears.

Dashing in a black silk moiré suit, Kristopher's high-fashion statement dripped with charisma and style. Sass's heart created a thunderstorm after taking one long look at him. Flashes of lighting were visible in her eyes as she inhaled his appearance. Proud of each other's evening attire, they strolled out of the room arm in arm with the look of love in their eyes.

# Thirteen

At the door of a magnificent house set high above the pounding swells of the ocean, the host, Steven Anders, greeted Sass and Kristopher. A medium-built man with pasty-white skin, he would have no color at all if not for those bright cobalt blue eyes, Sass mused as the introductions were made.

Mrs. Anders suddenly appeared in the doorway. Smiling, her husband draped his arm around her thin shoulders, introducing her to Sass as Reva. She was beautiful but too skinny, with bleached golden-blond hair and ivory skin. Even with all the cosmetic dentistry available, she still had somewhat of a crooked smile. While looking into her grayish-green eyes, Sass saw a splash of what appeared to her as envy.

Steven extended is hand to Kristopher. "Welcome back to our home, Mr. Chandler. We're honored to have you and Miss Stephens as our guests. Come, I'll announce your arrival to the other members of our party."

Heads turned as Kristopher strolled confidently, proudly into the room with Sass on his arm. He knew most of the people there, but Sass was a bit nervous. As she was introduced, her natural people-person personality took over, allowing her to easily make the acquaintance of the others. Impressed with how well she handled herself, Kristopher smiled.

Rewriting her resume in his mind, Kristopher closely studied Sass during the introductions. Beautiful, confident, makes friends easily, and can intelligently discuss a variety of topics. She was sensitive, caring and passionate. With his entertainment calendar as full as his business one, all of these things were important to him in his line of work. He was proud of how comfortable she seemed with the people in his circle, those who led a fast-paced lifestyle.

Reva Anders called everyone into dinner.

Seated next to Kristopher, Sass took the napkin from his place setting and laid it in his lap. To show his appreciation, he kissed her hand. Sass noticed right away that a blessing hadn't been said, yet everyone had already starting eating. Taking Kristopher's hand, she closed her eyes and said a quiet blessing over their meal. He smiled at the way she'd taken the lead on something as important as prayer. It didn't matter to her who witnessed her giving thanks.

Having devoured the exquisite prime rib and seafood dinner, the guests were now gathered in the main salon of the great house. While engaging in conversations with several different people, Sass found herself enjoying the company of what she considered the elite. But to her, Kristopher was the crème de la crème. He had made everything come together for her over the past few weeks.

Seated on an ivory-beige French provincial sofa, Sass talked with Reva Anders, who held a wineglass in one hand and a champagne flute in the other. With Reva's eyes so glazed over, Sass was fearful that the hostess might tip over at any moment.

"Sass, what do you do for a living?" Reva's question had come with forced politeness.

"I'm a communications specialist."

"Oh, so you're also in the media. I'm sure you have a satisfying and rewarding career. I thought you might be one of Kristopher's secretaries." She sounded totally unimpressed by Sass's profession.

Uncomfortable with Reva and the snub she'd just directed at her, Sass looked across the room at Kristopher. When he winked at her, she blushed.

The look of love on Sass's face caused Reva to further envy the obvious sparkle of passion in Sass's eyes.

"You and Kristopher seem to have a special relationship."

The half-smile playing around the older woman's mouth made Sass feel that Reva might have more than a casual interest in her personal relationship with Kristopher.

"Very special, Reva."

"Be careful! From what I hear, the Bachelor Chandler gets around quite a bit."

Reva's smile was insincere, reminding Sass of Grace's phoniness. Noticing the winter storm that had suddenly appeared in Reva's eyes, Sass decided the subject needed to be changed.

"You have so many beautiful works of art in your home. How do you acquire them?"

"Steve and I travel all over the world looking for great works of art. We have brought things back from every corner of the world. I understand that your boyfriend also has quite a collection of art work from around the world . . . and quite a collection of broken hearts."

Sass sensed that Reva had intentionally baited her, but she wasn't about to react negatively, as Reva probably hoped. "Yes, both of his residences are filled with the most breathtaking sculptures, paintings and several of the most sought-after photographs from the most exotic locales in

he world. As for his collection of broken hearts, I haven't
een those yet. I'll be sure to ask him about them later."
ass had cleverly disguised her anger at Reva's comment,
ut it hadn't come easy for her.

Reva looked stunned. "He's taken you to his place in
rance?"

"Oh, gosh, yes! He flies me there whenever I have time
ff. We've spent many romantic nights together in both
laces." Sass felt no guilt at purposely telling an untruth.
f Reva Anders wanted a bit of gossip to chew on, she'd
ome to the right place. "The next time I'm there, I must
emember to ask him to show me his broken heart col-
ection. I'm glad mine won't be added to it." Sass wanted
o much to boast of her engagement to Kristopher but
hat was inappropriate since Mr. Anders was a colleague of
is. At any rate, Kristopher should be the one to announce
t to his circle of friends and associates.

Reva paled, slightly annoyed with the cheekiness of
er guest. "Oh, dear, that won't be necessary. I was just
aving a little fun. Kristopher is a wonderful person."

The thought of Sass telling Kristopher about her com-
nents appeared to make Reva cringe.

Sass smiled. "He is definitely wonderful."

Walking up behind Sass's seat, Kristopher smothered
he nape of her neck with warm kisses. As Sass looked
t Reva, smiling mischievously, Reva's blood rushed to
er face.

"Are you having a good time, my beautiful Sass?"

Reva looked uncomfortable with his obvious display of
assion toward Sass.

Sass smiled impishly. "I'm having a wonderful time.
teva and I've been having a conversation filled with in-
rigue." Sass looked from Kristopher to Reva.

He eyed Reva curiously. "And what were you talking

about, Reva?" He narrowed his eyes at her, sending a hot jolt of discomfort through her.

Nervously, Reva fingered the double row of diamonds about her slender neck. "Just a little girl talk." Reva practically jumped to her feet. "It's been nice talking to you, Sass, but I'd better tend to some of my other guests. Excuse me."

As Reva stumbled off, Sass's soft laughter followed after her, causing Reva's feet to move even faster.

"Seems like this conversation was filled with more than just a little intrigue. Has Reva been telling you what a heartbreaker I am?"

"How perceptive! However, I think she met her match in me. There's more than one way to clip the sharp claws of a she-cat. That Siamese just ran up against the master declawer."

Amazed at how easily Sass had read Reva Anders, he laughed heartily. "What's her story?"

Lowering her chin, Sass looked down her nose at him. "Maybe should tell me. Reva Anders seemed to show more than just a casual interest in your personal affairs."

Coming around the sofa, Kristopher sat down next to Sass and took her hand. "Reva thinks she's romantically interested in me, but she just wants a boy-toy. I've never been one of those. I don't fool with married women, either. It's not my style. Nor do I mix serious business with physical pleasure."

"I'm glad I'm not married. So glad."

Her statement tickled him. "I'm glad, too. But I may have made you an exception to that rule had you been married."

Sass looked puzzled by Kristopher's comment. "What makes you think that, Monsieur Chandler? How could you possibly know that I wouldn't have had a happy marriage?"

Holding her face tenderly between his hands, he kissed both of her cheeks. "Because you weren't married to me; we're soul mates. Now that we've found each other again neither of us will ever be happy with anyone else. It's true. I hope we never attempt to find out."

Sass leaned her forehead against his. "You're absolutely right, my love. How could I have ever thought otherwise?" Laughing gently, she kissed him deeply.

He held her at arm's length. "Speaking of marriage, have you decided on a date yet?"

Inwardly apprehensive, Sass wrinkled her nose. "Not yet, but is that okay? Are you asking me to set a date before you return to Paris?"

He shook his head. "I can see that you're not ready. I promised not to pressure you . . . and I won't. Is it okay for a guy to indulge himself in a little wishing and lots of hoping?"

She placed her forefinger in the center of his chin. "Kristopher, are you angry with me?" Her voice came out child-like. The pain in the question made it sound as if her defenses had somehow broken down.

"I could never be angry with you, Sass. I love you, remember? Anger is not an emotion that I willingly give in to. If it were, I still can't imagine being mad at you."

*I hope you remember that when you learn everything about me.* "In that case, you're free to indulge in your heart's desires, but I'd rather you take me home and make me your woman."

He grinned, happy to see her mood brighten. "I intend to do just that. But let's take an evening walk first. Come on. We'll tell everyone goodnight."

Offering their heartfelt thanks, Sass and Kristopher said their farewells and left.

\* \* \*

After changing clothes in haste, they headed for the garden behind the inn to take in the moonlight. Sass wore a pullover and a pair of black jeans. Kristopher was also dressed in a sweater and jeans and a dark blazer. He carried a blanket under his arm.

As Sass snuggled up to him, he lifted his arm and placed it around her shoulders. "It's a beautiful night, Sass."

Sass looked up at the silver moon. "It is. The air is so clear and clean. Look at how tall all these magnificent trees are. This cobblestone path must be centuries old. The stones are well worn but they've been kept up beautifully. That white wooden swing hanging among those trees has probably been there a long time, too."

Kristopher pulled her along with him to where the swing was hung. As he held the seat in place, she sat down and placed both hands on the weather-beaten yet sturdy ropes. She laughed like a little girl when he pushed her high into the trees. His joy at seeing her happy was uncontainable. Pulling her up from the swing, he sat down and she dropped down on his lap. With the evening breeze playing harmoniously about them, they just sat there and drank in the beauty of nightfall.

"Seated among all these trees rather feels like we're in one of the Kinkade paintings we saw this afternoon."

He stroked her cheeks with the pads of his fingers. "I think you're right. Why don't we imagine a little, white steepled church beyond the clearing over there? Do you want to get married in a church, Sass, with all the wedding trimmings?"

Sass gave a minute's thought to his question. "I think a small chapel works better for me. I used to dream of a large wedding, one with all the lacy, flowery trappings and such. My bridal gown would have a train that ran the length of the church and the veil would be made of fresh flowers and pure lace." Her expression was soft and wistful. "There'd be a full wedding party of bridesmaids, groomsmen, a ring bearer, flower girl and all. My handsome father would glow with his love for me as he walked me down the aisle. My mother would look like a beautiful angel as she sat on the front pew crying softly into her lace handkerchief. I've dreamed of candelabras, harps, white doves, and a multitier wedding cake decorated with delicious butter-cream icing. But that can't happen now."

Tilting her chin up, he looked into her eyes. "Why not?"

Sass dabbed at the sentimental tear escaping her right eye. "You know that I'm not a virgin. My ideal wedding is reserved for the pure women, at least that's how tradition has it. I also have a child, which further disqualifies me for the traditional white wedding."

Lifting Sass from the swing, Kristopher spread the blanket down on the grass. After seating himself, he lowered her onto his lap. "I wouldn't concern myself with tradition if I were you. I find it hard to believe that every woman who has a large wedding is a virgin—quite the contrary. We're living in the twenty-first century, not the dark ages. It seems to bother you that you're not a virgin. You looked sad when you mentioned it. Does that trouble you?"

She raised an eyebrow. "Does it bother you that I'm not? Wouldn't you prefer that I was one? Don't all men prefer virgins?" Sass gave no thought to the fact that that she had been a virgin the first time they were together.

Kristopher stood up and removed something from his pants pocket. "Maybe this'll answer your question for me." He flicked open the small velvet box in one fluid motion.

Sass's mouth fell open as Kristopher placed the three-carat emerald cut diamond on her finger. There were no words to describe how she felt. Her insides had melted like candle wax. Instead of her voice, her eyes spoke for her. Glistening like the precious stone Kristopher had just placed on her finger, her eyes spoke to her deepest emotions. Her mouth opened against his. Bringing her closer to him, he deepened the kiss, his tongue eagerly searching and finding hers.

Their mouths still united, he lifted her off his lap and set her down on the blanket. He then got on his knees. "Marry me, Sass Stephens. Unite our hearts together forever. Please grant me the honor of becoming a real father to Justin. You've already become my best friend and my lover. I promise to love Justin as though he was my own. If his father permits it, I'd love to adopt Justin and give him my surname. This is my covenant unto you. Will you become my bride?"

Sass's tears streamed from her eyes. "Kristopher, I, Sass Stephens, would be honored to become your wife. I will be delighted to unite our hearts forever. I will grant you the honor of becoming a surrogate father to my precious Justin until he's old enough to make a decision on his own about the role he wants you to play in his life. I would be proud to become your bride. These things are my promises to you."

His lips found hers and then sealed their promises with a staggering kiss until each was practically breathless. He wiped her tears with his fingers and she dashed his away with her knuckles. For several minutes they just sat there and quietly basked in the magic of the most precious moment in their lives.

Lifting her, he placed her back on his lap. "About all that traditional stuff, I think we should make your dream wedding come true. It would make me very proud to take you as my wife in front of all your friends and family members. We can even invite some of my Parisian friends. There are a few people that might not forgive me if I don't include them in our day of celebration."

Sass shook her head. "I don't need tradition. All I need is you and Justin. We'll find a charming little wedding chapel for us to wed in. I'm sure we can find one that has a steeple. The only people I'm interested in coming to my wedding are family and close friends. Would you mind too terribly if we kept it small and quiet?"

"As you wish, the soon-to-be Mrs. Kristopher Chandler. Anything you desire is only a request away from your tender lips. As I've said before, I aim to please."

After a hot, leisurely bath, the night continued to grow in excitement. Kristopher showered Sass with love and affection. As he catered to her every whim, she kept wondering if he was really back in her life or was he just a figment of her imagination. On the carpet in front of the fireplace, he made her his woman over and over again. Since their first intimate encounters years ago, Sass had never forgotten all the ways he'd taught her to please him. He was thrilled at being the recipient of the newer discoveries she'd made about herself. Lying back on the carpet in a relaxed position, he let her rule.

At times she was hesitant. Then she'd shock him senseless; he found both personalities exciting and pleasurable. Making him drunk with desire, she teased him by pulling back and then advancing on him. Paying close attention to the things that drove him insane, she found pleasure in using them to her advantage. "Does that feel good? What about this?"

He moaned. "Don't stop, Sass. No, don't pull away now. Sass, you're driving me wild!"

She lowered her face to meet his. "That's my intention, lover. Tell me what you want?" Darting her tongue in and out of his ear and then nibbling on his hardened nipple, she made him tremble all over. When he could no longer stand the taunting foreplay, he turned the tables on her, making her all but beg for his slow hand to take her all the way there.

Explosion after explosion occurred before they finally fell into an exhausted sleep.

During their last day in Carmel, they learned more and more about one another. Sass and Kristopher had fallen head over hills in love all over again. Kristopher had a hard time keeping his hands off Sass. Each time she touched him he wanted to make love to her.

At Point Lobos State Reserve, where wildflowers and sea lions abound all along the rugged coast line, Sass and Kristopher lounged about under a giant Monterey cypress tree, talking for hours. Kristopher had brought with them a picnic lunch from one of the delicatessens at the Barnyard, which consisted of a variety of cold shellfish, salads, fresh raw vegetables and ripened fruit.

After a satisfying lunch, they walked for miles over the rugged terrain, taking in the beauty of the land. He pointed out the different types of trees and plants to her and she named several of the wildflowers for him.

Their last night was filled with passion as Kristopher took her to places she'd only dreamed of. He spent the entire night verbally drawing beautiful pictures of foreign lands for her, sharing with her the history of some of those most romantic spots in the universe. Each one of them touched her deeply. From the balcony of their suite, they'd watched the flaming orange sunset. Without sleeping, they held each other closely through the bright yellow sunrise. Each time they'd come together it was like kerosene being poured on a highly combustible fire.

* * *

After a few hours of early morning sleep, Sass awakened to ready herself for their return trip, but Kristopher was nowhere to be seen. Climbing out of bed, she went out onto the balcony. The skies looked clear and the ocean appeared calm. This has been a wonderful two days, she thought, as she loved being this close to nature. Thinking about their passionate nights made her shiver with delight. This man had her addicted all over again. Sass was ready to go right back through the fire for him. Risky as it was, she was ready to jump into the fiery furnace with him and wager it all. She could only hope that this time around didn't turn out to be a case of her not being able to live with him and at the same time unable to live without him.

She silently vowed to love him for the rest of her life, no matter what.

Laughing inwardly, she rushed into the bathroom to shower. A large vase of red roses and a colorful card greeted her before she stepped inside the stall. Smiling, she ripped the card open and sat down on the floor to read it.

SASS, I TRIED TO WAKE YOU, BUT YOU WEREN'T HAVING ANY OF IT. I'VE GONE OUT FOR A FEW MINUTES. IN CASE YOU FIND THESE BEFORE I GET BACK, GOOD MORNING. I LOVE YOU.

Hugging the card to her heart, her face became illuminated with a huge smile. Lifting the vase, she inhaled the heady scent of the roses. With tears of joy in her eyes, she got up off the floor and climbed into the shower.

Upon returning to the room, Kristopher found the bed empty. After searching the balcony, he went into the bathroom. He smiled as he looked through the glass at her nude silhouette. Pulling back the shower door, he climbed inside, fully clothed, shoes and all. Sass couldn't believe her eyes as her rose-petal laughter echoed about them.

Kristopher steered the car away from the helicopter terminal and out onto the busy streets of Los Angeles. Looking over at Sass, he grinned. "You were marvelous on the trip home. I'm glad you weren't scared."

"I did do pretty well, didn't I? Maybe I'll learn to fly one day. Wouldn't you like to have your own personal pilot?"

Kristopher threw his head back and laughed. "That might be nice. But I've never flown with a female pilot."

She threw him a haughty look. "There are pilots and *then* there are pilots. Not one of the aviators that you're referring to can soar you through the friendly skies like this one can. I'm sure none of the male fliers are as sexy and bright as the female ones. And, for sure, none of them will be willing to wed you and bed you for the rest of your life."

"You've made a point, lady, even if is was a female-chauvinist one. Would you really like to learn to fly?"

Laughing at his comment, Sass shook her head. "Not really. It's one thing to fly as a passenger, but I'm sure it's an altogether different story as the pilot. No, I think I'll stick to communications, something I know about."

"Is there something you'd like to do before we get to the apartment, Sass?"

"I need to buy groceries, lots of them. I didn't ask Lillian do any shopping while I was gone. Since you'll be leaving soon, I'd like to cook for you this evening. My parents won't get back with Justin until tomorrow. After dinner, we can watch a couple of the Arabesque movies adapted from the books, since you now love to read romance novels. I tape them when they come on BET."

His hand found her thigh, caressing it gently. "Afterward, we can make our own romantic film. I still have a few lessons to teach you yet. Are you ready for the advance course in Lovemaking 101?"

Sass blushed like crazy. "Maybe it's *me* who should be teaching *you* that course. But I have learned a lot in your class. Some of it still astounds me. I think I'd make a pretty good instructor, though, don't you?"

"If last night was any indication of your skill level, where do I enroll?"

Leaning across the seat, she brought her lips to within a breath of his. "Put your signature kiss right on these starving lips of mine. But that's not all you'll need to do to sign up for my course. First off, no cutting classes. Then you have to promise to be a willing student, to give me full authority over your sexy body, to surrender to my every desire. I must have the power to exercise complete control over you."

"Even though you sound like a dominatrix, I'm ready to sign up, Sass. Your request for complete control is hereby granted."


The grocery store was practically empty of customers, which was strange since it was just before noon. Grabbing a buggy, Sass placed her purse in the child carrier portion of the basket. Kristopher then took control of the cart.

Making the meat department their first stop, they scanned the rows of fresh meats before Sass picked up a hefty leg of lamb. "This looks great. If I recall correctly, lamb is one of your favorites, isn't it?"

Kristopher nodded. "My very favorite. I can show you

how to prepare it so that anyone you ever cook it for will beg you to fix it again."

Sass wagged her finger at him. "Not tonight you won't, my love. I'm doing the cooking and the teaching. You're just the window dressing this evening. I just want you to sit around in your silk pajamas and look gorgeous for me. As a matter of fact, I'm going to bathe you in aromatic oils and give you a full aromatherapy body massage while the lamb is in the oven."

"Your plans for this evening keep getting better. Let's hurry up and get out of this store before I'm tempted to pull you behind one of these food displays and ravage you."

"Sounds a little kinky to me, Kristopher. But I must admit to being more than intrigued with the concept, even though we'd probably get arrested."

While rushing through the different food aisles with Kristopher right beside her, Sass picked up Justin's favorite cereal, Honey Nut Cheerios. She only allowed him to eat it in moderation even though he loved it so much. It was rough on the delicate tissues in the roof of her mouth, so she was aware of what it would do to his tender flesh.

Kristopher took the cereal box from her hand and put it in the cart. "I see you remembered that Cheerios is my favorite cereal?"

"I'd forgotten, but it's Justin's favorite, too. You two are going to get along fine."

The basket was filled to capacity by the time they reached the checkout counter. Kristopher unloaded the groceries and Sass watched the cash register's screen as the purchases were rung up. She'd picked up enough groceries to last for a week.

A lot of Justin's favorites were among the food items. Sass made sure he ate a balanced diet of meat, vegetables and grains. Other than milk in his cereal, she fed him very few dairy products. There was something about the heavier dairy products that didn't settle very well on her or Justin's stomachs. Also careful about giving him too much sugar, she kept lots of fresh fruit in the refrigerator instead of candy. Justin loved white grapes and pineapple chunks.

When it came time to pay the cashier, she and Kristopher both handed the clerk the money at the same time. Their eyes met with a questioning look.

Gently, Kristopher nudged her hand away. "I'll take care of this for us. You've been a gracious hostess since I've been here." He winked at her to ease the tense look on her face.

She liked how tactfully he'd made his intentions known. The reference to "us" made all the difference for Sass. "As long as you're doing it for us. I don't want people thinking I'm a *kept* woman." She flashed a smile at the cashier, who looked puzzled. Holding her hand up, she showed off her three-carat diamond ring. "Just a private joke between me and my fiancé. I'm not a kept woman." Sass laughed heartily. "We're actually engaged."

The clerk laughed, too. "Oh, that's nothing compared to some of the conversations I hear from customers. They talk about everything from cereal to condoms in my line. That's a beautiful ring. Congratulations to both of you!"

Simultaneously, Sass and Kristopher voiced their thanks.

The clerk was surprised when Kristopher told her to keep the change, which was more than twenty-five dollars. When she continued to protest, he told her to give it to her favorite charity.

Sass stood by watching as Kristopher loaded the groceries into the trunk. "That was really nice of you to let her keep the change. I thought she was going to faint."

"She probably didn't want to take it because of some

silly company policy about employees not accepting tips. I thought about that after we walked away. I hope I didn't force her to do something that could cost her the job."

"I don't think so. Besides, she might give it to her favorite charity. Because she's a cashier doesn't mean she's not making decent money. She could also have a doctor for a husband, for all we know. I have a friend back east that works in auto mechanics. Her husband has plenty of money since he owns several garages. He also owns the one she works in. She was working there as a senior mechanic when he purchased it from the previous owner. She stayed on as his employee and they fell in love. After they married, she refused to give up her good-paying job to stay at home and look cute all day. She's a real go-getter."

"That's a nice story, Sass," he said, opening the car door for her.

"I think so, too," she responded, as he slid into the driver's seat.

"I haven't heard you mention them before. What are your friends names?"

"Ramona and Larry Smith. And they're nice, fun-loving people. They go out dancing until all hours of the night. Ramona loves to play games over the Internet. Larry's very sweet and generous, but he works way too hard. His sense of humor is a riot. He'll keep you laughing."

"You sound as if you're very fond of these people."

"More than you can imagine. You know how some people can come into your life and leave an indelible mark. You come to understand that everyone touches your life for a reason, good or bad. Everyone who comes in isn't necessarily meant to stay. But there's a lesson to learn from each person that crosses your path. You just need to be willing to sit still and listen to what's being taught by them."

"I know someone like that, someone who left an ineradicable emblem on my heart. When I first saw her walk past my studio window, I thought I was seeing things. I didn't think there was anything in the world that was so beautiful. Then I came face to face with her at a social function. Her graceful beauty nearly brought me to my knees. She nearly broke my heart when she refused to dance with me. Then, a short time later, destiny stepped in and worked its magic. I saw her again at one of my fashion shows. Talk about the third time being a charm!"

Sass smiled at the memory. "It was definitely the charm. You weren't so arrogant the second time around. Then, a few weeks later, you dumped a bucket of ice water on me while I was wearing the red ball gown you insisted I try on. Oh, the memory of that event."

Kristopher had never forgotten that evening. He'd finally gotten her to model for him while he took pictures of her. There had been an assortment of shots of her in array of fabulous clothing, but the hot red ball gown was the most sensuous of all. After he got off all the shots he wanted, he'd released the bucket of water rigged above the set. His camera had gone crazy while shooting the numerous, priceless expressions that had crossed her face. His mind suddenly flashed to the image of her looking so beautiful. In the next instant, the image popped into his mind of her soaking wet, looking bewildered and unable to believe what was happening.

"An unforgettable one, Sass! You were simply mesmerizing. I can't tell you how many times I've looked at those pictures from the best photo shoot I've ever done. I even had a couple of them matted and framed. A few hang on the wall in my office and there's a couple in my home, which you've so far refused to visit. Since we're officially engaged, I'm hoping that will change. My home is going to become your home, too."

Stretching across the seat, she kissed him full on the lips. "I've never forgotten that incident either, especially how you made wild love to me while I was still soaked."

"Yeah, you were definitely wet; in more ways than one."

To make sure the water was just the right temperature, Sass dipped her hand in. While the bath continued to run, she removed a jar of ice-blue bath crystals from the bathroom caddy and poured a generous amount under the faucet to assure proper agitation. Reaching for the bottle of Skin-So-Soft, she flipped the lid and squirted quite a bit under the running water.

After wiping her wet hands on a towel, she went to the bathroom door. "Kristopher, the water is ready for your bath. Are you undressed yet?"

Naked as the day he was born, Kristopher met her at the door, wearing nothing but a smile. "Is the water the only thing in here that's ready for me?" He raised an inquisitive eyebrow.

She leveled him with a seductive look. "No, but that's all you're going to get for right now. Get into the tub before the water gets too cold for you to enjoy."

"Does that mean you're not getting in with me?"

She clapped her hands. "Kristopher gets a gold star for his great perception. Come on, ease down in there, big boy. I don't have any Calgon, but I'm going to take you away."

Laughing at her comment, Kristopher slid down into the hot water and rested his head on the back of the tub. "This feels nice, Sass. You really should join me, you know."

Taking the bath-sponge, Sass squeezed hot water over

his shoulders. He moaned with pleasure. After applying some Skin-So-Soft right on his anatomy, she rubbed it all over him with the bath-sponge. Massaging his muscles gently at first, she then scrubbed him hard, like her mother used to scrub her. She ended her somewhat rough treatment on his neck and elbows.

"I know you're probably used to professional massages, Roman baths, Swedish dips, steam saunas and such, but this is as good as it gets here in my apartment. The nice thing about getting it done here is it's free."

"*Mademoiselle*, you're much too kind. How can I ever repay you?"

Lowering her lips against his, she kissed him passionately. "Paid in full, my love."

Before allowing him to get out of the tub, Sass washed his hair and massaged his scalp vigorously. Just as she was about to rinse his hair with warm water, he reached up and pulled her down into the tub with him. The silk gown she wore got soaked through and through. As it clung to her like a second skin, her erect nipples strained against the damp material.

"Kristopher," she screeched, "look at me. How could you do this? I'm all wet."

He silenced her protest with a deep, moist kiss, rendering her helpless against the fiery sensation of his mouth on hers. Kristopher always kissed her as though it might be the last: hard, deeply and passionately. She relaxed against him and savored the delicious assault on her lips.

His smile was charming as he pressed her hands against his hairy chest. "Yes, you are, my darling, and you look beautiful all wet. I felt lonely and cold in here by myself. Am I forgiven?" He nipped at her lower lip.

"I'll have to think about it, boy."

He captured her lips in another fiery kiss. "Have you thought about it, girl?"

"Another kiss like that and I won't be able to think, period."

"Good."


Later, wearing nothing but a towel, Sass held open a white fluffy bath sheet for Kristopher. As he stepped out of the tub, she wrapped it around him. Guiding him into the bedroom, she requested that he lie in the center of the bed. Crouching on her knees beside him, she completed her tender care of him, providing him with the hot oil massage she'd promised.

With soft music playing on the stereo and scented candles providing the only light in the room, Sass enraptured Kristopher with her newly acquired teaching skills. Her enchantments were all he'd hoped for and more. Though he had high hopes of aceing Sass's Lovemaking 101, he still planned on repeating the course several times.

# Fourteen

It was late afternoon as Sass sat at her desk editing her story on September 11. In about an hour or so she was to meet with Rebecca Walsh, the anchorwoman who would narrate her story over the air. Knowing Rebecca was a stickler for perfection, she had worked and re-worked the story numerous times.

Mandy Wells, the office coordinator, entered Sass's office. Smiling, she plopped down in the overstuffed chair across from Sass's desk. Mandy was a very intelligent woman in her early thirties. As she'd always been a big help, Sass respected her, often looking to Mandy for guidance. She was a large woman who would've been considered pretty if her face wasn't so scarred with pockmarks from a childhood disease. Even the heavy layer of make-up she wore wasn't able to completely cover the damage. Despite her deep and piercing hazel eyes and her beautiful cropped dark brown hair, the scars were what people noticed first.

"Hey, Stephens, how's it going?" Mandy spoke in a lazy southern drawl and her thin lips didn't appear to move at all.

Sass smiled. "It's going okay. I've been working so hard on this story, but I'm still not satisfied. Rebecca will have my head if she doesn't like the way I've written it." Feeling a little bewildered, Sass reached across the desk and handed her story to Mandy. "I'd like to hear your opinion. What you think of it is important to me."

Mandy quickly scanned the story. Her wide smile made Sass feel more confident about what she'd written. When Mandy finished the story, she propped her feet up on Sass's desk, looking intent. "I think it's very good. About Rebecca Walsh: that's why I came in here to talk with you. Rebecca won't be doing the story. She's out with a serious sore throat and is not expected back for several days. I've recommended that you do the story on the air."

With her heart beating wildly, Sass's eyes widened with disbelief. Had she heard Mandy right? "Mandy, if I heard you correctly, thanks for the vote of confidence, but I've only done bit pieces here and there on the air. I'm not nearly good enough to handle this lengthy piece," Sass said breathlessly, stunned by the gracious gesture.

Giving Sass a crooked smile, Mandy stood up and leaned on the desk. "You heard me right, Stephens. You can't get good if you don't get the experience. You have interviewed all of these people and you know first hand how desperate they're feeling. You've experienced their pain and shared in their sorrows. This story is written with deep compassion and I can only imagine that your empathy for their situation will come through even more when you tell the story. Trust me, Stephens, I wouldn't have considered it if I didn't think you could do it." Before returning to her chair, she gently patted Sass's hand.

"I'm in shock . . . over . . . here. Never in my wildest dreams did I imagine I would get the opportunity to do this story. With your help, I'll accept the challenge."

Mandy clapped. "Now that's the Sass Stephens I know! I'll do all I can to help you through this one. By accepting this challenge, you'll be opening the doors to broaden your horizons. I think you're more than up to the challenge. I'll be rooting for you. I have another piece of good news. I was able to get the okay for you to do the story we discussed regarding Dr. Daniel Davis's house calls to the elderly. If you do the 9/11 piece with the compassion and professionalism I know you're capable of, who knows . . . you might be able to deliver that one also. I'm of the mind that you're the only one who should do the story."

Sass grinned. "You're too good to me, Mandy Wells. I appreciate you so much. Thanks for everything."

"You're easy to be good to, Sass. Tomorrow is your big day, Stephens! Get a good night's rest. Call me at home tonight if you need anything. I'm only a phone call away." Giving Sass the thumbs-up sign, she strode out of the office.

Whirling her swivel chair around and around, screeching from excitement, Sass maniacally tapped her feet on the clear plastic runner under her chair. While reading her story over and over, she ended up changing it several times before she was satisfied.

Two hours later, Sass yelled out her good nights as she passed by the different office areas.

Sass entered her apartment. Upon sniffing the air, she was rewarded with delicious smells wafting through the room. Throwing her briefcase down on the sofa, she ran into the kitchen. Seeing Kristopher standing over the stove with one of her mother's aprons on, she couldn't help laughing out loud. Then her expression suddenly changed. She now looked very troubled.

Seated at the table, Justin was licking something from a large spoon, something that looked like chocolate cake batter. Most of it was on his face. He scrambled from his seat when he heard his mother's laughter. Jumping into Sass's arms, ruining her silk dress, he smeared her face with chocolate kisses, making her laugh hysterically despite her sudden bout of annoyance.

Returning Justin's messy kisses, Sass strode over to Kristopher and gave him a hug. She had the urge to share the chocolate mess with his waiting lips, but not with Justin in the room. "What are you up to in here? And where is Lillian?" Sass didn't know why Kristopher was alone with Justin, especially since she hadn't given anyone her approval.

Wetting a paper towel, Kristopher tenderly wiped off Justin's face and hands. He then wiped off Sass's face and his own. She sat down in the chair and settled Justin onto her lap, bouncing him up and down. Giggling softly, Justin mashed his nose against Sass's, moving it around in circles over hers.

"I gave Lillian the rest of the day off. She, Wes and your other family members are joining us in celebration of our engagement," Kristopher enlightened. Sass frowned heavily, making him wonder if he'd been too presumptuous. "You don't seem too thrilled at the idea."

Sass's frown turned into a hard scowl. "I just can't believe you told my family something that important without me being present. I'm sure everyone will be overly excited about our news," she said with heavy sarcasm. "I'm not at all thrilled over the idea of an engagement celebration. This matter needed to be handled with extreme care. Besides that, I thought we agreed to keep Justin out of our relationship for the time being."

When she looked down at Justin, her heart nearly broke. He looked so scared. Her tone of voice had frightened him; he'd never heard her raise it to him or anyone else. Sass smiled to put her child at ease, kissing him to wipe away the anxious look on his face.

"Sass, everyone may not be jumping for joy about our news, but I think it's time for them to understand that we're going to be a family. However, I only asked them to dinner. I didn't share the reasons for it. Everyone accepted the invitation, so doesn't that count for something?" Sass couldn't believe her family had accepted the invite, but that was the least of her concerns.

"We shouldn't discuss this in front of Justin. Besides, I have a lot of work to do before my story airs tomorrow. Kristopher, the network is allowing me to do my own story on the air. I'm so nervous. I guess you can overdo preparations and end up screwing things up badly. I think I'll just chill out. Maybe relaxing with my family and friends is exactly what I need, but I don't think now is the right time for telling them we're engaged."

Kristopher was so excited by her news that he decided to wait until later to challenge her. He lifted Justin from her arms, hugging him tightly. "Did you hear that, Justin? Mommy's going to be on television! You and I are going to watch our favorite girl together."

His excitement passed on to Justin, who bounced up and down in his arms, as though he understood. Crystal clear tears arose in Sass's eyes at the touching scene in front of her. Justin hugged Kristopher's neck. As he'd seen Kristopher do, Justin kissed him on both cheeks, making both Kristopher and his mother laugh. Perhaps she'd been taking too hard of a line regarding the two men in her life getting to know each other.

Sass sniffed the air as Kristopher handed Justin back to her. "This room smells like a French restaurant. What else are you two cooking besides the obvious chocolate cake?"

Justin wiggled down from her arms and sat down on the floor in front of her chair. Reaching for his truck, he crawled around on the floor, pushing the toy out in front of him.

Kristopher smiled broadly. "You have a sensitive nose.

I'm preparing scallops in saffron butter, colossal shrimp in herbed butter, and a variety of lightly steamed vegetables. And because everyone isn't crazy about seafood the way you and I are, I have a large goose slowly roasting in the oven and a casserole of macaroni and cheese waiting to go in. Is your mouth watering yet?"

"I'll be drooling in a second. It sounds delicious."

"I found this apron in one of the utility drawers," Kristopher expressed happily, twirling around to show off his cooking attire. Justin stood up and imitated Kristopher's movements. Sass laughed at her guys, giving both of them a warm hug.

Kristopher kept surprising Sass. This side of him was warm, loving and so caring. He cooks on a grand scale, too, she thought, amused by his cooking attire. More than any of his other newly acquired qualities, she loved Kristopher for being so patient with Justin.

"You look adorable in your apron. How long were you alone with Justin before I came in?" When Justin heard his name, he wrapped his arms around Sass's legs and stuck his thumb in his mouth.

"Less than thirty minutes. After Lillian finished cleaning, I told her to take the rest of the day off. She seemed reluctant, but I convinced her that it was okay. Before she left, I invited her and Wes for dinner. Justin and I have been here in the kitchen ever since. Justin didn't want to take a nap, but he seems pretty sleepy right now. I hope I haven't overstepped my boundaries."

"I think you already know that you have. Lillian should have cleared this with me before she took off. This is not like her, but I understand how hard it is for any woman to resist your charm." Sass shook off her rising anger, but she didn't like him making those kinds of decisions.

She stood up and lifted Justin from the floor and carried him into his bedroom. Kristopher followed after them. Justin was asleep before she could lay him down. "He needs a good nap before everyone arrives. It was sweet of you to want to take care of Justin, but that's not what we agreed on. To come home to my two guys slaving in the kitchen was a real treat, but the timing's all wrong. Please take Justin's shoes off for me. You can leave his socks on." She would've never let Kristopher get this close to Justin had she been aware of his plans. There were too many kinks that had yet to be worked out between them.

"Since you've already decided to marry me, doesn't it seem silly for you to continue making a big fuss over Justin and me spending time together? I don't get it."

"Everyone needs time to adjust to our relationship. We may be moving too fast."

"Too fast for who, Sass? Your family . . . or you?"

"Both, I guess." She threw up her hands. "I don't want to fight about this, but it looks as if we have a lot more to talk about. Maybe we should really talk after dinner tonight. It's past time."

"That's what I've been telling you all along. Tonight, after everyone has left, we'll talk, and we won't stop until all the obstacles standing between us are removed." Kristopher suddenly noticed how tired Sass looked. "I'd like to see you take a shower and then lie down until shortly before our guests are due to arrive."

"You'll get no argument on that. Do you need me to help you with any of the dinner preparations before I take a short nap?"

He kissed her forehead. "I have it all under control. Sleep sweetly, Sass."

Kristopher made his way back into the kitchen, where he immediately checked on his meal. Opening the lower oven, he basted the goose. Taking the cakes from the upper oven, he placed them on the racks to cool. Once he'd mixed up a light whipped-chocolate-cream frosting to serve on the double-layer cake, he sat it in the refrigerator. After washing his hands, he went over to the sofa and lay down, dangling his long legs over the end.

Kristopher didn't know when he'd ever been happier. Being here like this with Sass and Justin felt so right; just a few days ago he thought he'd lost her to the pain of their past. Glad that he hadn't given up on her, he wondered if Sass was sure she could get through all the hurt. He wondered if she wanted more children. He would be content just having Justin in his life. They could always adopt later if they wanted more children, but the issue of children wasn't the biggest hurdle to leap.

Kristopher made mental notes of all the things he needed to do before leaving for Paris. Talking to Justin's biological father was high on his list of priorities. He had to come to terms with this man about Justin if they were going to live a peaceful life. He only had a short time left before he had to leave, which meant he had to work fast. While he still questioned Justin's paternity, he didn't think Sass would lie about something like that. If he were Justin's father, he was sure she'd tell him. When the timer went off in the kitchen, he leaped up from the sofa.

Kristopher stood at the door quietly, watching Sass's sweet, sleeping face. With her leg protruding from under the sheet, he raked his eyes over its even tan. As she turned over, the sheet fell away. He inhaled deeply as his eyes devoured her in the jade silk camisole and hipster panties, scalloped with lace edging. She had a magnificent body. He liked the fact that she didn't flaunt it like some women that he'd known. She was still so young and innocent. When she finally came into her own, the world better look out. Amusement twinkled in his eyes.

Walking over to the bed, he knelt down beside her, kissing her awake. Slowly, she opened her eyes. Their sheer nudity physically aroused him.

"Sass, it's time to get up. Our guests will be here momentarily. You wouldn't want them to find you still in bed, right?"

Sass stretched her arms high over her head. Pulling his head against her breasts, she brushed his hair back with her fingertips. "I don't want to get up." Sticking out her lower lip, she pouted for a couple of seconds. "But I know I have to since I still have to dress Justin before I dress myself." Swinging her legs out of the bed, she sat on the side of it.

"I'll take care of Justin. You just tend to yourself." He kissed her nose and left the room.

Wesley Jones and Lillian were the first guests to arrive. As Wes handed Sass a dozen pink roses, she hugged him warmly. While thanking him, she inhaled their gentle scent. He and Lillian had also gotten together on a purchase of a toy car for Justin, and Wes had chosen a bottle of fine French wine for Kristopher.

The rest of the guests arrived as the others sat in the living room enjoying the wine. Jason and Amantha were dressed handsomely in casual clothes fit for dining in or out. Jumping up and down with glee, Justin showed them how much he desired their immediate attention.

Dressed in white short pants and the red shirt Kristopher had picked out, Justin's red knee socks were turned down neatly at the top and his white high-top shoes looked freshly polished.

Jason held out his arms. "Come here to Papa," Jason said merrily. Running to his grandfather, Justin leaped into his arms. Lifting him high into the air, Jason hugged him closely.

Everyone began chatting away, since Sass's family had already been introduced to Wesley Jones at the previous dinner she'd had for him and Lillian to get acquainted. However, Sass didn't know what to expect from her family when in the presence of Kristopher. Thus far, they'd been cordial to him. The fact they'd accepted not only one, but two, dinner invitations from him was definitely a great stride in the right direction.

Coming out of the doorway of the kitchen, Kristopher announced that dinner was ready to be served. Sass couldn't take her eyes off him. Dressed in dark dress slacks and a light yellow shirt, she thought he looked scrumptious. A shock of wet hair hung down on his forehead, damp from the heat of the stove. Everyone noticed how Sass stared at him. Both her sisters looked amused at the way her eyes appeared to undress him, yet each was fearful of Sass's future with him.

As the entire group held hands, Jason passed the blessing. Once the chairs were quickly pulled out from the table, everyone took a seat, eyeing the delicious-looking food. The goose had been cooked to perfection. It looked tender enough to melt against the palate; the scallops and shrimp looked just as tender as the fowl.

Within minutes, the platter the seafood had rested on was emptied. The macaroni and cheese was prepared in a delightful way that everyone enjoyed. The vegetables, crisp and crunchy, still carried their healthy color. Kristopher had also made a delicious cheese sauce to pour over them.

"I have to know the recipe for this cheese sauce before you return to Paris," Amantha said, attempting to make polite conversation with the man she felt a little better about.

"Kristopher, I have to tell you this. No woman could outdo you in the kitchen," Gerald offered. "You need to come over to our house and give Stephanie some cooking lessons. This girl burns the water for our morning coffee." Stephanie playfully slapped her husband's wrist.

"That is a compliment coming from Gerald," Eugene stated. "Before we got here, he was skeptical about your ability to even cook a decent meal. I can see that you've changed his mind."

Kristopher was completely surprised by the compliment, and thrilled by it, as he joined the rest of the group in laughter. He felt himself begin to relax, but he had to remain on guard if the unexpected occurred. Her family wouldn't be easy to win over, but he had to keep the faith.

"Gerald, I'd give you one week eating my food—and you'd want to hire me as your personal chef. My father was the one who actually taught me how cook. According to him, my mother wasn't very creative in the kitchen," Kristopher advised, laughing. "I've also heard from Sass that you refer to French cooking as 'sissy meals,' but you'd really go crazy if you had the opportunity to eat any of the French dishes I've learned to prepare."

"I was stationed in France a long time ago. I was soon put on a restricted diet by my commanding officer. I ate so much of that sissy food that I could barely get into my uniform," Wes contributed.

"I wish someone could put Eugene on a restricted diet," Staci chimed in. "Every time I turn around I find him at the refrigerator. He always says, 'I'm just looking,'" Staci added in a gruff, manly voice. Everyone laughed at her great imitation of her husband.

"Staci, not everyone can eat nonstop and not gain an ounce. Just wait. One day all those mashed potatoes and gravy are going to lodge themselves right onto those thighs of yours. You're going to regret making some of those fat jokes you like to tell," Eugene interjected.

"Daughters, you'd better listen to your men. Take a good look at me and you'll know what they're saying. Jason fed me so much when we were dating that I started to believe he was fattening me up to keep anyone else from wanting me. After all these years nothing's changed. He's still stuffing me with his delicious cooking." Amantha poked her husband in fun.

Jason couldn't help noticing that Sass was unusually quiet, wondering if she might not be feeling well. He hadn't seen her this withdrawn in a long time. He wondered if she was regretting the decision she'd made about starting a new relationship with Chandler.

Kristopher had noticed Sass's mood, too, which also caused him concern.

"Sass, are you alright?" Jason asked. "You haven't said two words since we sat down at the table. Are you sick?"

Amantha reached over and put her hand on her daughter's forehead, checking her for any signs of a fever. "You don't feel warm. Does something hurt?"

Embarrassed by Amantha's motherly hovering, Sass gently pushed her hand away. "I'm sorry, but I've just been thinking about the story I'm going to narrate tomorrow. I'm feeling a little anxious about it."

As Lillian gasped loudly, everyone turned to look her.

"Sass, are you saying you're going to do your own story on the air?" Lillian asked.

Sass saw that Lillian was the only one who'd really caught what she'd said. "You got it right, Lillian. The person who was supposed to do it is out ill and the program coordinator has recommended me. I'm ecstatic that she has such confidence in my abilities. The show taping is tomorrow. I only found out today so that's why I'm a little preoccupied."

With their hearts bursting from pride, Sass's parents looked at her with adoration. Watching Amantha and Jason's loving reactions toward their daughter, Kristopher was thrilled for Sass. She seemed embarrassed by all the attention as everyone voiced their sincere congratulations to her.

Stephanie nudged Sass playfully. "You're the only person I know that could've held this wonderful news in for so long. How do you do it? I would've screamed it out the minute everyone walked in the door. You always were good at keeping secrets."

Sass frowned. *Perhaps too good at it.*

"That's because you have a big mouth," Staci joked. "You missed your calling, Stephi. Acting as a Hollywood gossip columnist, you would've made a great reporter."

"I know you didn't say that, Miss Staci! Who is it that calls me every night to give me all the latest gossip? Who knows about all the Hollywood stars and their love affairs? You're all up in everybody's business and can't take care of your own," Stephanie charged haughtily.

Shaking her head, Sass held up her hand, laughing at the way Kristopher's eyes darted from one sister to the other. "Time-out guys! With all this bickering between you, you're going to scare Kristopher right back to France," Sass scolded lovingly. They'd probably like nothing better than to have him gone, Sass mused, laughing inwardly.

Kristopher grinned. "I don't scare that easily, Sass. I think it would be nice to have sisters and brothers to bicker with. Our house was too quiet. That's why I did so many incorrigible things. I always felt this need to generate excitement. Our house was full only on holidays and other special occasions. Once everyone left, I immediately felt lonely again," Kristopher stated, his tone melancholy.

"No one in this family gets a chance to be lonely. We often find ourselves looking for a quiet place far from

this maddening crowd. We're raving maniacs every time
we get together. During sports telecasts, we're wild," Eugene said, laughing. Everyone agreed with him.

Sass laid her fork down. "Kristopher, let's get the
dessert. I'm in need of one of those quiet places Eugene
just spoke about," Sass joked.

Kristopher stood up and pulled her chair out. Grinning
widely, he left the table with Sass pulling on his hand.


Sass fell into Kristopher's arms. Tilting her head up
for him to kiss her, he obliged her with a hot, passionate
kiss. Quickly, they released one another when Justin appeared in the doorway. Neither of them had any
intention of exposing Justin to adult situations.

Kristopher picked up Justin and carried him back into
the dining room.

Staci came into the kitchen to help her sister when she
saw Kristopher's arms full of Justin. After opening the refrigerator, Sass got out the topping for the cake, eating
a spoonful before carrying it into the dining area.


Kristopher knew his dinner was a success from all the
praise he received. It was even suggested that he could
cook for the family anytime he desired. He couldn't stop
smiling as he made a fresh pot of hot coffee and some
hot tea for Sass. Things were looking better than ever.

The guests didn't stay too long after dessert, knowing
Sass needed to get a good night's sleep. Jason had bun-
dled Justin up good before carrying him out into the
night. Excited about the upcoming telecast, everyone
promised to be glued to the television. Amantha and
Jason had even invited Kristopher to watch television at
their home along with the rest of the family. Though in

total shock over the invite, he managed to graciously accept the kind offer.

Sass had stripped off the gold silk wrap-around skirt and matching blouse as soon as the door closed behind her guests. While Kristopher cleaned the kitchen, she slipped under the hot shower. As she thought about the telecast, her stomach fluttered nervously. Leaning her back against the cool tile, she gave way to anxious tears.

"I know I can do this," she cried. "Then why am I so nervous?" *Because America is going to have their eyes on you, babe.* She hoped that she didn't disappoint her colleagues and fellow Americans; especially those who'd been directly affect the events of September 11. Glad that she'd accepted the challenging assignment, Sass felt relief wash over her.

By the time Kristopher returned to the bedroom, Sass was dead asleep. Deciding not to disturb her for the time being, he kissed her forehead. Grabbing a few things from his bag, he went into the hall bathroom to shower. After his quick and thorough shower, he stepped into gray silk pajamas and then rushed back to the bedroom. Deciding that their conversation could wait until the next day, he slid into the bed next to her. Lying perfectly still, he began to reminisce about his past relationship with Sass. There were many things he needed to say to her, but he had to choose his words very carefully. Who fathered Justin was the topic he was most interested in discussing with her. He couldn't think of anything he wanted to discuss more than that.

Deep down in his heart, he believed that Justin Brian Stephens belonged to him. Despite the fact that Sass had given no indication that Justin was his, Justin looked too much like him for Kristopher not to question his paternity. He'd love Sass no matter who the father was, but his desire to know for sure was a strong one.

Over the last few days Kristopher had had plenty of time to think about their past and present situations. Thinking about all the things he and Sass had done together during their brief affair made his flesh steam. He couldn't help remembering how stunning she'd looked at the fashion show. As he delved deeper and deeper into he past, his eyes soon began to burn from the hot, unshed tears.

There had been a lot of humiliation during the break-up, he recalled. Sass had been on the giving end, as well as the receiving end. She hadn't been able to let go without knowing why he'd hurt her so deeply. She'd shown up unannounced at his apartment on numerous occasions. At times, she'd scared him to death with her wild threats of damaging his personal property, as well as doing bodily injury to him. He didn't recognize her as the same girl he'd fallen in love with, but now he fully understood that she'd only been reacting to the horrific pain he'd caused her.

Her strange behavior disappeared almost as quickly as it had appeared. They saw each other off and on, but they were never able to get their relationship back on track. He recalled how comfortable and unselfish of a girlfriend Sass had really been. She hadn't been hard to please and he could only remember one time that she'd asked him for money—the money to get her hair done—but she'd paid him back in a couple of days. She'd been so different from many of the other women he'd dated. Rarely had she asked him what he'd been doing in his spare time and she'd always made herself available to him.

Maybe that was the problem. Had she been too available? Had that caused him to take her for granted? He'd gone out with more women than he could shake a stick at, so how was she supposed to have reacted when she found out? She really did try to accept it and stick it out when he told her it wouldn't happen again, but it must've driven her insane. Just thinking of her with another man gave him some idea of how she must've felt knowing. The pain must have been bottomless. He remembered her asking for the same dating privileges that he seemed to enjoy, but he'd told her if she dated other men it would be over between them. That was the selfish Kristopher Chandler. Thank God he was no longer the same man.

If a man other than himself had indeed fathered Justin, had Sass been in love with him? Was it possible that she still could be in love with him? He needed the answers to his questions and he knew there were numerous answers that she needed from him.

All afternoon the different crews at LABS television station made a fuss over Sass while preparing her for the telecast. Her hair was styled by Ingrid, the in-house stylist, and Eliza, from the cosmetology department, had applied her make-up very carefully and skillfully.

Wearing a red suit, white linen blouse, and navy linen pumps on her feet, Sass looked great. The red, white and blue attire was perfect, a symbol of patriotism.

Sass sat down in the assigned chair, crossing her legs. With her palms sweating, she waited for the signal to begin her broadcast. Silently, she prayed for courage. Thoughts of Kristopher and Justin calmed her nerves almost instantly.

Mandy gave Sass a lot of encouragement, laughing and joking as she tried to put her nervous reporter at ease. "Stephens, just keep your chin up and look into the camera. Speak distinctly and try to keep your mind off your nerves. You've had some airtime so just remember that the same rules apply here," Mandy said cheerfully.

Sass scowled. "If you can call two seconds here and there airtime, then I guess I've had airtime. It was easy when we did it for class assignments, but this is the real thing. Mandy, I won't let you down. Count on me," Sass said, her confidence rapidly growing.

"I know you won't. Okay it's show-time." Mandy hugged Sass and quickly moved out of the eye of the camera. The countdown was made as the cameras zeroed in on a close-up of Sass.

"Good evening. I'm Sass Stephens reporting live for LABS Television in Los Angeles. Thank you for joining me this evening. Together, we will explore the plights of our military families who have been left behind while their loved ones were deployed to Afghanistan and parts unknown to bravely avenge their country in the wake of the horrific events of September eleventh.

As the war rages on in the hot deserts of the Middle East, where temperatures reach unbearable degrees, the devastating effects are felt here at home as family members wait daily to hear the slightest news from the men and women they love. While battling a ruthless, seemingly fearless enemy, many of our American troops are faced with what some call insurmountable obstacles and formidable opponents who are under the leadership of a madman. Unfortunately, the American families left behind are fighting obstacles of a different kind, a fight for survival . . . and one that's no less real."

Her gaze was steady. "Often our young men have been referred to as boys at war. We've often before heard expressions like 'bring our boys home,' and 'our boys are dying over there.'"

Sass took a barely noticeable breath before continuing. "Our young men and women may have left their

homes, jobs and schools as boys and girls, but they became men and women from the moment they landed in
the Middle Eastern war zone. Throughout the past few
weeks I've had the special privilege of visiting a few families whose loved ones are proudly serving their country
in Afghanistan and other Middle Eastern locations. I
have also met with families who've already suffered the
loss of loved ones during these unpredictable times and
volatile battles. In coming together as a nation, we must
keep these families in constant prayer.

"I've heard numerous heart-wrenching stories of the
terrifying and painful experiences that these families are
having to cope with. One family informed me their
young son was killed two days before his assignment was
up. Another couple informed me that their son was
killed while being airlifted out of the war-torn area. I've
talked to wives who have had problems getting their husband's earned pay because of the improper filing of
papers, which makes it impossible for them to buy food
and other essentials needed for the survival of their families. Some have seen food stamps as an embarrassment,
but they take them willingly in order to feed their children. Is this not a sad commentary?

"These families have tried to get assistance from the
Welfare departments, but are being turned down because their husbands are employed, employed by a
government who has seemingly turned its back on the
families of those employees who are fighting against ter-
rorism to preserve democracy."

Sass's compassion showed clearly in her sepia eyes.
Everyone in the studio felt the intensity of her heartfelt
sympathy. Trembling slightly, she folded her hands in
her lap.

"We, as Americans, need to ask many questions. Whose
democracy are we trying to preserve . . . and at what cost?

Who's protecting the homefront while our protectors are in the Middle East? Why are our young men dying in foreign lands? What cause are they dying for this time? We need to insist that our government supply us with the answers to these thought-provoking questions *before* we ever send our people off to war, not after its over."

Sass shifted slightly in her chair, uncrossing her legs. "One family told me of their plight when they tried to have a loved one's remains returned home. They've been fighting bureaucratic red tape for months. They remain unsuccessful. Another family had the wrong remains returned to them, which caused a mother to suffer a near fatal heart attack." Sass's insides were trembling hard, but her voice remained strong and clear. "Our troops are dying away from their homeland, while their families are suffering greatly right here at home. In an era of hard times, in a society divided by unemployment, racism and unanswered questions, we Americans must band together in a united front. We must put our differences aside to help solve these problems. We need to help one another, neighbor to neighbor. War isn't just a problem for some. It is America's dilemma!

"If you would like to give us your opinion of this broadcast, or have any comments on how to help the plight of fighting men and women and their families, please call 1-800-555-LABS. We are interested in your opinion! Thank you and good evening. This is Sass Stephens, reporting live for LABS Television, Los Angeles."

The minute the cameras panned away, Sass leaped from the chair and ran into the ladies' room. Her tears couldn't be held back another second. Her thoughts were on the tragedy of September 11, those troops deployed to the Middle East and the families left behind.

Mandy entered the bathroom right behind Sass. "Come here, Sass Stephens." Mandy was also in tears as she held her arms out for Sass. Falling into her arms, Sass cried broken sobs. Holding Sass away from her, Mandy tilted her chin up. "Stephens, you did a great job. Look out, Rebecca Walsh! The network may have just found themselves a new dynamic anchorwoman. You were very professional. Your heart was right out there on your sleeve for all of America to see. Anyone watching could see your deep compassion was heartfelt." Excited by the success of the piece Sass had created, Mandy hugged Sass again.

As they emerged from the bathroom, arm in arm, the cheers went up from the crew. Sass was repeatedly congratulated on a job well done and was hugged until she felt like a lifeless rag doll. Emotionally drained, Sass begged off from a celebration. Grabbing her things, she headed for the parking structure, anticipating the feel of Kristopher's and Justin's arms around her.

Sass reached the front porch of her parents' home, but before she could open the door, Kristopher swung it back. Gathering her into his arms, he showered her face with kisses and hugs. He then handed her Justin and she squeezed him gently.

"Sass, you did a fantastic job for your first lengthy piece! There was not a dry eye in this house. I'm sure all of America is still crying. You were charismatic and highly professional. Your breaking heart would've been obvious to a blind man. It came across strongly in that sexy voice of yours."

Putting her arm around his waist, she allowed him to guide her into the living room, where her entire family waited.

"You were great, Sass!" everyone chimed in at once, as planned.

Sass smiled brightly. Then her tears became uncontrollable renegades. "Thank you! I'm glad everyone thought I did a good job."

Her voice trembled as she spoke about the telecast and her tired legs felt unsteady. Clearly seeing her fatigue, Kristopher pushed a folding chair under her. Gently, he nudged her into the seat.

Smiling weakly, Sass looked over at her family members. "I'm so emotionally exhausted. If I lose any more tears, I won't have the strength to wipe them away."

"I'd wipe them away for you," Jason said softly. "Kristopher, why don't you take her on home? We can celebrate later. We'll put Justin to bed. He's half asleep, anyway."

Sass's car was left in the driveway at her parents' house. Kristopher got her home as quickly as possible. He could only imagine how draining a first telecast was. With Sass's success, he felt her fatigue would only last a short time. He suspected that the subject matter had more to do with her fragile emotions than anything else. Or had something else declared war on emotions?

Inside the apartment they split up. She entered the bedroom and he went into the bathroom. While running a hot bath for her, he poured perfumed crystals into the water.

Fully clothed, she was lying across the bed when he entered the bedroom. After undressing her, he carried her into the bathroom. Once he'd settled her into the water he turned to leave, concerned that she hadn't spoken a word within the last half-hour.

"Kristopher, could you light the candles, please? I'm too tired to lift my arms. You might have to wash me, too." She knew she was acting like a spoiled brat, but she needed all the pampering she could get.

Wondering if she'd read his mind, he smiled, lit the candles and turned off the light. "My pleasure. Call me if you need me. I'll be in the bedroom."

Seconds later, he came back into the bathroom with her robe, laying it along with her towel across the pink wicker clothes hamper. Blowing a kiss her way, he exited the room. As her eyes were closed, she missed the loving gesture.

Sliding deeper into the hot water, she laid her head on the back of the tub, her thoughts taking her back to the telecast. Before she could even ponder it, she fell into a light sleep.

Kristopher lay across the bed, reading a magazine. Looking at the clock, he wondered what was taking Sass so long. Getting up from the bed, he went into the bathroom. With her head tilted to one side, he could tell she was asleep.

Stooping down in front of the tub, he outlined her face with his forefinger. "Sass," he whispered, "you need to get out of the water. It's surely cold by now."

Reaching for her robe, he held it open for her to drape herself in. As she stepped out of the tub and into the warmth of the terrycloth, he closed it around her and tied the sash belt.

"Thank you. I don't have any energy left for anything. So many people in this world are in trouble. I wonder how this world has gotten to where it is."

Walking slowly into the bedroom, she fell across the bed.

Lying down beside her, Kristopher pulled her full against his body, dropping kisses in her hair as he stroked her legs. He wanted so desperately for them to talk, but the timing always seemed wrong. Would there ever be a right time? Time and his patience were running out.

"I guess we have to put our talk off a little longer. I see how exhausted you are. Try to go to sleep, Sass."

"Thanks."

# Fifteen

Sass opened the door to her apartment, and she and Kristopher stepped inside. While walking through the place, Sass found Justin and Lillian seated in the living room watching cartoons. The second Justin spotted Kristopher he jumped up from the floor and came running. Leaping into Kristopher's arms, Justin twisted his tiny fingers in Kristopher's hair. When he kissed Kristopher on both cheeks, the three adults burst into laughter. Kristopher shouted his greeting to Lillian from over the top of Justin's head.

Justin shimmied down Kristopher's leg and then pulled him toward his bedroom. "Football," he shouted with glee.

Kristopher caught Justin by the seat of his pants. "Wait a minute, Justin. You didn't kiss Mommy yet. She's been waiting all day to get a big hug and a kiss from you."

Justin turned to look at Sass, giving her his wide-toothed grin, the one that had a way of lighting up her world. "Mommy," he shouted gleefully, "I miss you." The same as he'd done to Kristopher, he leaped into his mother's open arms. Looking at him with adoration, Sass gently kissed her little boy on the mouth, tousling his golden-tipped hair.

He pressed his lips onto her mouth and then onto her

nose. "I wanna play football. We can go to the park, Mommy?"

Smiling, Sass looked over at Kristopher. "Did you hear that?"

Kristopher came to stand in front of Sass. "I certainly did. It would be my pleasure to take Justin to the park. I'd like to see you rest while we're out."

Lillian touched Kristopher's arm. "If you two would like some time alone, I can take Justin out to the park."

"Thank you for the generous offer, Lillian, but I've been looking forward to going back to the park with Justin. In fact, I told Sass that over the phone earlier. You're welcome to come along with us if you desire to do so."

"Thank you, Kristopher, but I'll pass. I was just trying to kill a little time. Wes is coming over to my place for a late supper this evening."

Kristopher smiled in a knowing way. "It seems that you and Wes are spending a lot of time together. I'm happy for you. Do you hear wedding bells in your future?"

Lillian blushed. "I think it's too soon to tell. However, we're definitely talking of having a future. We enjoy each other so much."

Sass gave Lillian an affectionate squeeze. "I knew you two would take to one another. He's a wonderful man, Lillian. I've got first dibs on maid-of-honor; that is, if you don't already have someone special in mind."

Lillian kissed Sass's cheek. "With no close blood family to speak of, I'd have to say that you and Justin are it. I feel as though you are my children. Should it come to down to a wedding, I'd revel in having you stand with me."

Kristopher hugged Lillian. "The wedding will be on me should it happen. I wish you the best of luck. I like your choice in a companion. Wes is a good, strong man."

"I think so, too. Thank you for being so kind, Kristopher."

Justin tugged on Kristopher's hand, interrupting the conversation. "Park!"

"Okay, partner. Go get the football." Justin took off for his bedroom. "Lillian, we'll talk again soon. Can't keep my star quarterback waiting any longer. Have a good evening."

"I hope you three do the same," Lillian remarked.

Kristopher turned his attention to Sass. "Are you going to lie down, Sass?"

"I don't think I can rest. I'm too keyed up. Would you mind if I came to the park with you and Justin?"

"Mind? You've got to be kidding. Perhaps the fresh air will do you some good. We can bring along a blanket and some of your reading materials. You can relax while Justin and I act like children."

Sass smiled gently. "Sounds like lots of fun to me. I'll go change clothes while you get Justin together." Sass looked at his expensive suit. "Did you bring a change of clothes along? I can't imagine you playing football in that beautiful suit."

Pulling Sass to him, he kissed her earlobe. "I guess you haven't really looked at everything that's hanging in your closet." Stroking her face with a single digit, he grinned.

"Why do you say that?"

"I left my mark by leaving a change of clothes in your closet. I wanted to be sure I had a good reason to come back here. Are you angry at my devious act?"

Sass threw her head back and laughed. "Are you sure you haven't been hanging out with Eugene and Gerald? That sounds like something they would've done while dating my sisters."

He looked abashed. "I actually saw it in a movie. I thought it was kind of odd; that is, until I saw how I might benefit from such a clever act."

"You're too adorable. But I hope you don't try everything you see in the movies. A lot of that stuff just won't work, especially with us sister-girls," she joked.

Kristopher didn't get a chance to respond to Sass since Justin was tugging at his pant leg, pointing at the door. Lifting him up, he carried him into Sass's bedroom, where he retrieved the clothes he'd left behind. Carrying the toddler in his arms, he went into Justin's room to change into his sports gear.

Sass and Lillian smiled at each other. "Those two are quite a pair," Sass remarked.

"Quite a pair indeed," Lillian agreed, looking at Sass with concern. "Can we talk for a few minutes?"

"Sure, Lillian. What's on your mind?"

"Are you okay, my dear? You haven't seemed yourself these last few days."

Sass sighed wearily. "I'm much better now that the telecast is over. Anything to do with death really upsets me. I'm glad Kristopher could stay on a few days longer. He's been so good to me and Justin."

Lillian gripped Sass's hand. "You can tell me to mind my own business if you like, but have you told Kristopher all the things you're keeping bottled up inside?"

"I haven't told him much. This whole matter is really complicated. I know Kristopher has to be told the truth about everything, but I need a little more time."

"Don't take too much time, Sass," Lillian warned. "Mr. Chandler seems like a very patient man, but every human being has a certain tolerance level. Perhaps you should tell him everything before he becomes intolerant of you and your secrets. While you've never told me what your secrets are, you have talked of them bothering you numerous times."

Sass brushed Lillian's cheek with her fingertips.

"Thanks for the advice and for caring about me and Justin. You've been good to us. Don't worry, I won't wait too long."

"Glad to hear you say that. I'm going to be off now. I still need to pick up something for dessert. I'm going to take a bubble bath so I'll be fresh when my handsome guest arrives."

Sass giggled. "Sounds like there's love in the air to me. I wish you both the very best."

"Thank you, Miss Sass. Enjoy the rest of your evening, darling child."

There were still several more hours of sunlight, Sass figured, while waiting for Kristopher to spread the blanket out under a large oak. With the cover all smoothed out, she sat down and removed her white Nike sneakers. When Justin took off across the park with the football, Kristopher had to make a hasty departure to catch up with him.

Taking off her socks, she rolled up the legs of her jeans. Keeping an eye on Justin and Kristopher, she made her way to the lake in the center of the park where she sat down and dipped her feet in the cool waters. Sass realized she should've stayed at home and rested. Instead, her mind took her to a place where peace ruled, a place where she, Kristopher and Justin would one day live happily ever after.

Several ducks came so close to Sass that she had to scoot over to the side to let them pass. She laughed at the way they strutted their stuff before diving into the lake. When she heard laughter other than hers, she looked up and saw Kristopher standing there with Justin in his arms.

"Did they scare you? I saw how close they came." Kristopher dropped down beside her. Mindful of the lake and Justin's quickness, he held Justin firmly on his lap. Justin squirmed in his grasp, but Kristopher wasn't about to loosen his grip.

"Not really. I was a little surprised they weren't afraid of me. I guess people have spoiled them by feeding them despite the signs that say not to. They seem so unafraid."

"They do seem pretty tame. Weren't you able to rest?"

"I didn't try. The lake looked so inviting I decided to get my feet wet. Why don't you take your shoes and socks off and get yours wet, too?"

Kristopher handed Justin to her. "Hold on to him. Justin is quicker than greased lightning. I don't relish jumping into the lake after him. He loves the ducks and he might try to follow them into the water."

Sass took Justin's shoes and socks off. Holding him tight, she moved closer to the water's edge to let him bathe his little toes. Justin giggled with joy when Sass dipped his feet into the water. "Does that feel good to Mommy's baby?"

Justin nodded, wiggling his toes in the water. Sass put Justin's right foot up to her mouth, kissing each of his toes, tickling the bottom of his foot. Justin squealed with delight, squirming like a fishing worm in Sass's arms. Joining in the fun, Kristopher stuck his feet in the water and met Sass's. Winking, Kristopher gave her a bright smile.

Sometime later, after returning to the blanket, Sass took out a book to read. Justin and Kristopher headed for the sliding board and the swing set. She watched as Justin hopped and skipped across the park with Kristopher holding his hand. When it appeared they'd entered into a race with each other, Sass couldn't keep from smiling at how fast Justin's short legs carried him across the ground.

Sass closed her book only minutes after opening it and looked in the direction of where her guys headed up the steps of the slide. She laughed hard when Justin threw up his hands as he whizzed down the slide on Kristopher's lap. Her heart leaped with joy at hearing their melodious laughter tumbling through the fresh air.

Kristopher was so good with Justin. She saw how important they had become to each other. That wasn't what she'd intended to happen, but now that it had, she couldn't see it any other way. She didn't even want to imagine her life without Justin and Kristopher in it.

*What if it doesn't work out? What if our relationship doesn't have the right ingredients to withstand the unending challenges of marriage?* Although her heart would be broken, she was more concerned about Justin's little heart. Kristopher had become so much a part of his life. He had gained her little person's love and, for sure, his trust.

Sass closed her eyes, envisioning the three of them living in one of Kristopher's homes. The high-rise in Paris didn't work for her, not as a family abode, but his home in the Hollywood Hills would be a good choice for the three of them. Then she thought about the French countryside, a place Kristopher talked about loving enough to live there one day.

Kristopher had so much to offer both her and Justin. She could only hope their plans didn't go awry, thinking of all the advantages Justin would have culturally and socially. Living abroad would give him a sweet taste of so many of the magnificent things that the wide, wide world had to offer. Historically, Europe was a cache of wealth, a bounty of intrigue.

Tired from running and playing with Justin, Kristopher flopped down on the blanket.

When Justin plopped down on Sass's hip, he startled her, awakening her from her short nap. "Justin, look at you. You're all dirty," Sass exclaimed, laughing heartily.

"You look like a little ragamuffin." She turned to look at Kristopher. "And you don't look much better. How did they taste?"

Kristopher looked puzzled. "How did what taste? We haven't eaten a thing."

Sass cracked up. "The mud pies. You two look like you've been dining on wet dirt."

Kristopher grinned. "We *are* pretty dirty, aren't we? Oh well, that's part of the fun. We've had a request for McDonald's from our little one, but we may be too dirty for that now. What do you think?"

"I think, yes. However, I've brought along a change of clothes for Justin. They're right here in this bag. As for you, you'll be okay after washing your face and hands." Sass pointed to a building a few yards away from where they sat. "The park bathrooms are over there. I also have a couple of face cloths in here." Digging around in her bag, Sass came up with two washcloths and a couple of hand-towels.

Kristopher laughed. "What else do you have in that large satchel? You certainly walk around well equipped. With a small child to care for, I guess you have to be ready for anything."

"Anything and everything! The things I don't have to worry about anymore are diapers and bottles. Justin was potty-trained before he even turned two . . ."

"McDonald's, Mommy," Justin interrupted. "I'm hungry."

"Okay, sweetie. I'm going to take you into the bathroom to wash you up and change your clothes." As Sass started to get to her feet, Kristopher drew her back down.

"I'll take care of Justin. Stay here and enjoy the cool breeze coming from off the lake."

\* \* \*

Rubbing his stomach, Justin stuffed a long fry into his mouth. Looking on, Sass and Kristopher sat across the table from one another.

"Ketchup, please, Mommy." Sass squeezed ketchup over all his fries. "Thank you, Mommy."

"You're welcome, sweetie pie. Here's your drink." Sass pushed Justin's orange drink in front of him. "How's your Big Mac, Kristopher?"

Kristopher wrinkled his nose. "I like Fat Burgers better."

Sass laughed, remembering how Kristopher used to wolf down the tasty burgers that he'd introduced her to when they first began dating.

"How's your fish sandwich, Sass?"

"Kind of dry."

"That's because you don't like tartar sauce."

"I have ketchup on it, but it hasn't made much of a difference. Maybe I'm just not that hungry. This isn't my favorite place to eat, either."

Kristopher jumped out of his seat. In looking all around him, he saw that Justin had gotten down from the table and was heading for the McDonald's play area. "I told you he was quick," Kristopher shouted over his shoulder. "We have to stop mooning over one another when he's around. Neither one of us noticed that he'd gotten down."

Sass didn't get a chance to tell Kristopher that Justin was just practicing his normal routine because he was already out the door. Justin always took off for the play area when he finished eating. While keeping an eye on him, Sass would clean the table and then follow after him. After disposing of the trash, Sass joined Kristopher and Justin.

Entering the colorful play area, Sass could see that Kristopher was enjoying himself as much as Justin. Unfortunately, for Kristopher, he was too tall to climb or crawl through the bars and tunnels Justin loved to wander about in. The multicolored balls were one of Justin's favorite things to toss about and jump up and down in, which he did with much enthusiasm. This McDonald's took extra precaution in making sure that the play area was safe and clean.

Justin climbed all the way to the top of the structure. He waved at Sass and Kristopher before hitting the slide. As he slid off the end of the slide and into the heap of balls, he giggled, clapping his hands together. Justin patiently climbed to the top of the structure several more times. He laughed louder and louder each time he came in contact with the plastic balls.

Sass sat on the three-legged stool by the side of the bubble-filled tub while Kristopher bathed Justin. She could almost feel the tenderness in Kristopher's touch as he lathered Justin's tiny body from head to toe with liquid soap. This family-oriented scene reminded Sass of how Jason and Amantha used to take turns bathing their three girls while the other parent looked on. Those had been very happy times in the Stephens's household, she mused, recalling how the loud giggles and the sound of splashing water had echoed off the walls back then.

While she and Justin were every bit a family, the absence of a man in their home had kept the family circle incomplete. Kristopher had filled the part quite nicely, but would their dreams of marriage and family ever be fulfilled?

The small red, yellow and blue boats bobbed up and down in the water as Justin thrashed his hands about. He splashed water out of the tub and onto his mother and Kristopher.

Sass wiped her arm off with a towel. "Calm down,

Justin," Sass gently admonished. "You're getting water everywhere."

Wrinkling his nose, Justin looked at his mother and smiled broadly. "Okay, Mommy. I be good. I won't be bad anymore."

"Mommy didn't mean to suggest that you're being *bad*, Justin. You're just a little over-excited. You could never be bad. You're too sweet," Sass soothed lovingly, kissing his forehead.

"I love you, Mommy," Justin sang out.

"I love you, too, sweetie."

Looking up at Kristopher, Justin's large eyes grew soft. "I love you."

Both Kristopher and Sass's eyes misted at the tiny little voice confessing something as large and wonderful as love. Sass quickly dashed away the sentimental tear running down her cheek. Neither of her guys could imagine the magnitude of what she felt inside for them.

*"Je t'aime, Justin."* Kristopher held the sides of Justin's face, placing a moist kiss in the center of his forehead and on both his cheeks. *"Je t'aime, mon fils."* *I love you, my son.*

Kristopher allowed the meaning of his remarks to Justin settle in his heart. *Not only do I feel as though you are my son, I feel as if I'm your natural father.* Kristopher felt both a physical and spiritual connection to this child; he could explain neither. For a man who'd never had a desire for children, his heart had done a complete one-eighty. He had a hard time imagining his life without Justin in it.

Sass washed Justin's hair with tearless shampoo. Before towel-drying it, she applied a deep conditioner to his soft curls. Kristopher held the towel open as Sass handed Justin to him.

With Justin all wrapped up in the fluffy linen, Kristopher carried him into his bedroom, bouncing him down onto the bed. Justin's childish giggles filled the room.

Kristopher took delight in drenching Justin's arms, legs, stomach and back with baby lotion. After working the lotion deeply into his baby-soft flesh, he dusted baby powder all over the little boy who was looking up at him in adoration. Kristopher's heart grew full as he picked Justin up and held him close to him, rocking him from side to side.

Sass took Justin away from Kristopher. Smiling at her little angel, she dressed him in his favorite Disney-character footed pajamas. Kissing his tiny mouth, she settled him into bed. "Justin, close your eyes so Mommy can say a prayer for you."

"A story," Justin said, looking at Kristopher. "The animal story."

"He's referring to the biblical story of Noah's Ark," Sass informed Kristopher. "It has become one of his favorites. *The Children's Bible Book* was a gift from my parents to Justin on his first birthday. I often read to him before he goes to sleep."

Smiling, Kristopher picked up the book and found the right story. He then began the story. Justin had a hard time keeping his eyes open from the first line. As his eyes periodically fluttered open and shut, Kristopher kept reading. A few minutes later Justin was fast asleep. Sass and Kristopher took turns kissing him goodnight before the bedside light was turned out. They left the room quietly.

The entire apartment was so silent that they could've heard a pin drop. Justin was all tucked in and tuckered out from his romping good time at the park and at McDonald's. But Sass's bedroom was filled with apprehension as she and Kristopher were stretched out on opposite ends of her bed. Unhappy that she'd reneged on the promise of them talking things over, Kristopher's eyes seemed to demand her full attention.

Quietly, she sat waiting for him to tell her to go to hell. He hadn't spoken a single word in the last three minutes, not since she'd refused to discuss the past with him as she'd promised to do earlier. Kristopher couldn't believe that Sass was determined not to get things out in the open so they could move on with their future. This conversation should've taken place several days ago and she was still stalling for time.

"I don't think I can wait any longer for you to talk to me. Time is running out for us. I have to get back to Paris. As much as I'd hate to leave California with our future unsettled, I have to fulfill the commitment that I made to finish my photography project. We can't hope to have any kind of future if we don't stop dodging our issues."

"Kristopher, I can't do this now. You're pressing me incredibly hard. You've always made me believe you'd be patient with me."

"For God's sake, Sass, I'm not Job. I've been patient enough." He nudged her gently. "Sass, it's time for us to have that long overdue talk. In fact, it's past time."

Waiting for her heart to restart so she could speak, she sat up in the bed, chewing nervously on her lower lip. Her brain felt numb. She ran her tongue across her teeth as she buried her head in the pillow. She suddenly began to cry, as though her heart were breaking.

Hating the sounds of her anguished sobs, he moved to where she was and pulled her head onto his chest. Kristopher gently stroked her hair. "What's wrong, Sass?"

She sighed hard. "I'm just so darn confused. I've wanted to talk to you for so long, but now I'm not sure it's a good idea." She lifted her head from his chest and stared into his eyes. "I no longer know what to say."

He could almost feel the softness of her voice on his face, but he also felt the hard knocks of her anguish. Kristopher pushed her hair back from her face. "We have to do this, Sass, no matter how much we may not want to. You already know how I feel about you, but neither of us is really sure if you can get beyond the past." He gently wiped the tears from her eyes. "We'll never know if we can move on with our lives if we don't get our issues out in the open. If you marry me without settling the old scores, you'll always wonder if you did the right thing or not. The lack of that knowledge will keep you discontent. If the pain of the past isn't eradicated before we move forward, you can bet it'll show up in our future."

"You've really become an understanding person and you continue to astound me, but the person you were is still one of the problems for me. We should've had this talk years ago, at the time healing was needed. All I wanted you to do was talk to me, but you refused. I wanted to know what I did wrong so I'd never again do whatever it was. I needed you to tell me where I went wrong and what it was that I should avoid ever doing again. I could call you all kinds of names if I thought it would serve a purpose. There were times when I did call you terrible names. But you know what I thought and you know what you were. Was I too good or too bad? Why wasn't I enough for you? Why couldn't I satisfy you?"

Sass's heart-wrenching sobs came from deep within her.

He shook her. "Stop it, Sass. Stop doing this to yourself. You were too good for me but I was nothing but bad for you."

She threw up her hands. "*Now* you tell me! Why couldn't you have told me that before you broke my heart? Your wall of silence kept me imprisoned. If you didn't want me, why couldn't you just say that? Why'd you have to act it out? Why all the women? Why'd you have to torture my spirit? Damn you! I loved you—still love you. I couldn't sleep, couldn't eat. The tears in my eyes eventually dried up, but my heart still cries. I saw you in every man I came in contact with, smelled your cologne on every man that I passed. Men scared me. I trusted none of them for the longest time. Do you have any idea how much pain you caused me, how much questioning of myself came into play? I racked my brain trying to figure out why you could no longer love me. Was I unlovable or just unloved by you?"

Trying hard not to show how much pain and misery he felt inside, he brushed her face with the back of his hand. "You are lovable and I did love you. I love you now. I didn't know how much I'd really devastated you until now."

Looking like she wanted to hit something, she clenched and unclenched her fists. "Too bad you couldn't help me understand what you needed from me. Day in and day out, night after night, I sat and stared at the four walls, looking for answers. I prayed, I prayed, and prayed some more. 'Talk to me, Kristopher, talk to me now,' I used to beg you on the phone. 'What's there to say?' was always your comeback. How about this? I'm sorry, Sass, sorry that I didn't respect you, that I treated you like a second-class citizen. Sorry I lied to you, cheated on you, and denied you my support when you were pregnant. Then I turned my back on you when you refused to abort our child. Sorry I was such a big coward!"

"Bingo!" Kristopher shouted. "Core issue! You've finally hit the release button on the deadly poison stored up inside of you. Asking you to have an abortion went against everything you believed in. That's the one thing that hurt you the most. Am I right?"

"Only half right, Kristopher. More than the withdrawal of your support, the alienation of your love hurt the most. You made me believe you loved me; you did it with such ease. You told me that you loved me, repeatedly, told me I was the only one. Then you betrayed me, broke my heart, and nearly destroyed my spirit. Sorry, but I have to ask again. Why?"

"Because I was stupid, insensitive, and I didn't have a clue what you wanted or needed from me. You were different from the women I usually dealt with. That scared me. I wasn't ready for your innocence and your way of melting my heart with your soft expressions and wide-eyed wonder. I fought my feelings for you. I battled my desire. Sass, I wasn't good for anyone back then. I was selfish, careless and reckless with my emotions. Being involved with you the way I was, on such a deep emotional level, was something I hadn't experienced."

"Then why didn't you just sit me down and say that? I could've let you go had you asked me to, and I would've waited until you were ready for a committed relationship."

"Kings don't bow to anyone or anything outside of their passion for success and their desires to take without the thought of giving back. In short, the material trappings of this world blinded me. And I gave no thought to the spiritual realm. I now understand that there are more important things in life for me to concern myself with. I realized something was missing before I achieved real success. Afterward, I came to know what that something was. You, your love."

"I'm not convinced."

He eyed her intently. "I understand that. But if you don't give me or us a chance, I'll never be able to convince you. I can't give you the world because it's not mine to give, but I can promise you all of me. Unlike before, you'll always know where I'm coming from. I'm not going to press this issue any further, but would you at least think about it before you make a final decision about our future?"

"I should've done that before I ever agreed to marry you. I've loved you for so long and I always will. But there are many things I still want the answers to. I need to know how much of my love for you is coming from the heart and how much from my memory. You're right. I can't begin a future with you if I don't take care of the past."

She tried to smile through her tears as she moved off the bed and walked over to the window and looked out. Only seconds had passed when she returned to the bed and sat down beside him. Sass lifted Kristopher's hand and pressed kisses into his palm.

He kissed her eyelids. "I know this is difficult for you. I'm right beside you."

She explored his mouth hungrily, knowing she was only delaying the inevitable. Once everything was out in the open, she didn't know if she could stay with Kristopher. That scared her silly since she'd fallen so hard again. The resurrection of the past could very well end their journey into the future. That was the real reason she'd put this discussion off for as long as she had. It couldn't be put off any longer, but she feared that someone was going to get hurt in the process. The fear of her being the one who gets hurt had her insides trembling.

He felt her tremulous heart next to his. He held her closer to him to soothe the fear he knew she felt. She was a woman enslaved by the past. Freeing herself was a difficult task, but she had to do it even if it meant an undesirable outcome for their future. If that were to occur, he'd just have to find a way to deal with it. Everything that had happened was his doing.

"Do you want to stay in here or go into the living room, Sass?"

Pressing her body deeper into the plush mattress, she wished she could curl up on it and just go to sleep. "I'm comfortable where I am."

While closely watching her expressions, Kristopher wondered how to move on with the conversation. There was a lot more to get out in the open. When it didn't look as if she was going to take the reins, he decided he should go ahead and break the awkward silence.

"I don't know where to begin to address all the things that have been said, so I'll just let the words come to me as I go along. I still love you very much, Sass. I've never stopped. I'm aware that I've messed up big time. There's an even better word to describe my horrible actions, a very strong expletive. I still don't know what I was thinking back then. I never meant to hurt you."

Like a professional flame-thrower, her eyes threw hot flames at his in an expert fashion. If his comments hadn't induced another bout of anger, she would've laughed at his eyes trying to dodge the deadly flames.

"You never meant to hurt me? What did you think you were doing to me? How do you break someone's heart without intending to? How do you tell a woman you love her and then sleep with someone else behind her back? I'll tell you how. You did it callously, disrespectfully and knowingly. There was no conscience at all involved with it, because you didn't have one. I tried to hold on with as much pride and dignity as I could muster up that night, the same way I did when I later realized how much I'd let you mentally and emotionally abuse me in the name of love," she ground out.

He cracked his knuckles, something he did when nervous. "Sass, that's not how it was, and you know it."

Her laughter was brittle. "That's exactly how it was, Kristopher. I don't lie to myself anymore. I blocked out all of these things for so long because they were too painful to deal with, and I was too damn weak to face the truth. They're not blocked out any longer. You hurt me needlessly and you'll have to take serious possession of your own defects of character. I'm personally not looking for any retribution, but you can bet it's going to be demanded by a much higher authority. The debt will be paid in full."

Her tears burned an angry path down her face. What she had feared most was already happening. She knew her anger would come when they discussed the difficulties in the past relationship, but she hadn't expected it to consume her. Knowing the potential for her to become unreasonable in her rage was another one of the reasons she'd kept putting this discussion off.

He ached to hold her and wipe the sadness from her eyes. "I knew our talk would bring up many unpleasant memories, but I don't want you to think that I have no remorse for the things I did to you." He raked his hand through his hair as he shook his head. "Sass, why didn't you tell me how you really felt back then, how much you'd been hurt? You didn't say any of what you just said when we talked about what had happened. You hardly opened your mouth at all. Why?"

"If you'd been listening, you'd know why. I was devastated. I was scared to death of what I was faced with, not to mention how embarrassed I was about finding you in your apartment with another woman. I felt so desperate. I guess I ended up staying with you because it seems that I may have loved you more than I loved myself. Kristopher, I'm not trying to defend the course of action that I took that night. My actions need no defense."

Sass pulled a pillow across her lap. "Oh, Kristopher, you took me all the way to the mountaintop. A short time later you dropped me off the highest peak and left me to fall down into the depths of dark despair."

The anguish in Sass's sweet voice made his heart pound abnormally. He knew she'd been through hell, yet he'd still had the nerve to ask her why. He berated himself inwardly for being so insensitive. "I honestly don't know what else to say, Sass. I was young and reckless. Like you, I was scared to death; only I was scared of commitment." He felt deep regret at the pain he'd caused her and he feared that she couldn't get past it. It was overwhelming for both of them.

The expert flame-throwers re-appeared in her eyes. "Don't you dare use youth as an excuse for ripping my heart to pieces," she openly challenged. "Where was your decency? Was your conscience on holiday? I learned in kindergarten to respect the rights and property of others, so age is a lame excuse. My heart was my property and I entrusted it to you, but you did everything but show respect for something so precious and fragile."

"I'm guilty, Sass."

Ignoring his admission of guilt, she wiped her tears. "When I first met you, I didn't know some of the things about life that I do now. I never understood what happened that night. I blamed myself for a long time. All I could think of was how I had embarrassed you and the mystery woman you were with, yet later you seemed oblivious to my suffering. Do you really blame me for what you did to me? Did you do the things you did because I was pregnant with your child, a child that you didn't want?"

The last question knocked him the rest of the way off balance. There was a time he'd honestly thought she'd been telling him the truth when she'd told him she wasn't really pregnant. That information, coupled with how much Justin looked like him, meant there had been a baby. His baby.

Moving even closer to her, he took her hand in his and looked deeply into her sepia eyes. She lowered her lashes to try and sweep back the falling tears.

"Sass, not long after you told me you were pregnant, you said there never was a baby. You lied about that, didn't you?"

She studied his face closely. At that moment all she

wanted was for him to hold her in his arms. "Kristopher, I lied."

"Is Justin my child, Sass?"

She stared right into his eyes, yet hid her total surprise at his question. "Justin's father is dead, Kristopher. He never saw his son." She had no idea that Kristopher thought Justin was his. He hadn't given her a clue to make her think he might believe that.

Kristopher had no comeback whatsoever for her leveling response. She'd completely floored him with that revelation. If Sass was telling the truth, that meant she'd aborted his child, and had immediately gotten pregnant by someone else. It was so unlike Sass to get involved that quickly with another man, especially sexually. But that was the only way it could've gone down when he considered Justin's age. Perhaps her unmanageable pain had pushed her into the arms of another in order to try and find comfort.

Taking her into his arms, he kissed her forehead and wrapped up her tightly in his arms. It didn't matter who Justin's father was or wasn't. He still wanted to take on the responsibility for both the child and his mother. He still wanted to marry Sass.

She gently pushed him away. "Kristopher, who was the woman in your apartment in what seems like a lifetime ago?"

He looked ashamed. "It was Grace, Sass."

She inhaled deeply, feeling the same burning pain on the inside as she'd experienced on that miserable night.

"Sass, I'm truly sorry."

She wanted to light into him like a deadly thunderbolt, but his apology knocked the hot wind right out of her sails. Why did she suddenly feel lighter? "I'm sorry" were the hardest words in any language for people to say. When spoken sincerely, they became monumental and

could heal the entire world. Kristopher's apology had
been genuine.

Sass got up and walked over to the window overlooking
the pool where she saw her lifeless body floating face down
in the ice-blue waters. "Just recently, I began to suspect it
was Grace. I'll never forget that night as long as I live.
Daniel had dropped me off at your place, but he waited to
see if you were home. After you shocked me into realizing
what was going on, I felt like I'd been murdered in cold
blood. I recall walking back to his car in a zombielike state.
I remember Daniel telling me that I looked like a ghost. I
responded to him by telling him that I was one, that I'd
just been separated from my spirit."

She laughed nervously but the vision in her mind was
making her instantly ill. "I remember telling Daniel to
take me home because I needed to wash all the blood off
me. I told him I'd just been murdered in cold blood . . .
and that the only weapons used were lies and deceit. He
looked at me like I was crazy. Of course, there wasn't any
visible blood, but my heart was hemorrhaging badly.
Blood had even settled behind my eyeballs, making me
see every shade of red there is. I told Daniel that you had
a woman with you and how bad I felt for embarrassing
her. He was so angry that I was even concerned about
the other person at all. He told me that I'd been right
about being killed—and that you were guilty of murder
in the first degree."

Kristopher could see how much this was costing Sass.
He wanted to stop her anguish, to fall down on his knees
and beg for forgiveness, but he sensed her need to keep
talking. She had to release all the toxic waste in order to
cleanse herself from within.

After CPR was administered to her lifeless body, she
sat back down on the bed, still not sure if she'd survived
the drowning. "I had so many questions. I was going to

demand the answers from you, but when you came over to my place that night I couldn't tell you how I really felt. I wanted to scream at you and rip your heart out, but it wasn't in me. I found myself just wanting to understand you, wanting to understand what it was about me that made people want to hurt me. I actually blamed myself for what had occurred.

"If only you had come to me and finalized our relationship, I don't think any of the bad stuff that followed would've happened. If you'd only shown me a little respect, I would've somehow managed to get through it all. These issues could've been easily resolved by talking. By doing that then maybe we could've remained friends. You apologized earlier and I now accept that apology with all my heart and soul. Your apology has worked wonders for me."

He'd been struck with lightning and thunderbolts all at once. His eyes flashed from the burning sensation in the pit of his stomach. How could a mere apology make up for all the things he'd done to Sass? The only wrong thing she'd ever done was to love him unconditionally. It had been wrong for her to love him only because he hadn't deserved it.

He took her hand again. "Sass, at first, I used to sit and think of all the reasons why I loved you. Then I thought of all the reasons why I couldn't let myself love you. But my head took the decision out of my hands. Now I know all the reasons why I loved you—and still do. You're kind and gentle, caring, unselfish and incapable of hurting or deceiving anyone. You've suffered indignities you should've never had to. You're forgiving beyond my comprehension. With all that has happened to you, if you were vindictive, angry and bitter, you'd be more than within your rights to be so, yet you're none of those. Again, I'm sorry, Sass Stephens, for causing you so much grief. I just can't adequately express how sorry."

Lifting up her face to his, he drew her bottom lip into his mouth. He then lost himself in the sweetness of her tenderness. Tangling her arms around his neck, she gave in to his amorous advances, desiring him to hold her until the jagged pain was completely eradicated.

But something about the moment felt very different. Her heart began to rebel.

Sass suddenly realized she wasn't about to let Kristopher Chandler wave his magic wand over her without a major battle of wills. This time she planned to fight back and win, hands down. Sass Stephens had finally learned something about self-respect. If she ignored everything she'd just heard, she may as well jump in a hole and heap the dirt on herself; he'd surely murder her again if given the opportunity. She could save him the trouble by burying herself alive, which is what she'd be doing if she continued with this relationship.

He'd apologized and she'd accepted. Closure had been achieved. Now it had to be over between them. It was important for her to know whose bed her man was going to be in when night fell. She had to get with the program and walk away from him while her dignity was still intact. Sass considered herself forewarned. She'd have to settle for loving this man at a safe distance. If she didn't get away from him in a hurry, she feared that all hell would break loose in her life. She also had to think of what was best for Justin.

Kristopher tried to read her eyes, but there was something strange about them. He'd never seen this expression in them before. It wasn't anger or disgust, but it was something he'd hoped to find for himself, he finally realized. What he saw shining brightly in her eyes was peace, the kind that passed all understanding.

Sass sighed in relief, thankful that it was going to be easier to walk away from him than she'd expected. She didn't have to be made a fool of again before she found the nerve to leave him. Her heart might not be able to stand the pressure of being destroyed again. She felt grateful that she'd grown into a much stronger woman.

"We can't do this, Kristopher. We have to end our relationship now. I'm glad we were able to get everything out in the open. I'm happy we've made peace with our past. Kristopher, I'll always love you. Tonight I'm saying good-bye to a presence of the past that has haunted me for too long now. My future is out there just waiting for me to find it," she said tearfully. "I love you." She kissed him once more and ran out of bedroom.

He was too stunned to move and the tears would've blinded his way. Burying his head into the pillow, he cried for Sass, knowing she'd never again return to him. All of her words rang in his ears as anguish took over his entire body. Too much said, much too late, he thought sadly.

Why hadn't he heard her out before now? No woman could ever give him what Sass had. He'd let her love fly out the window like an untamed canary whose owner had been too ignorant to secure the cage. He'd had her precious heart locked up, but like the stupid bird owner he hadn't valued it enough to secure its future and keep it safe within the confines of his own heart and within the safety of his arms.

His body wracked with sobs as he thought of Justin. Wondering what had happened to the baby they'd made in one of their heated passionate nights made his head spin like a top, but it also made him sick with grief. Something was wrong with her story. Sass had said she'd lied, but she hadn't revealed the part she'd lied about: the fact that she was pregnant, or never was. Out of all that she'd said—and more important, all that which she hadn't said—he believed more than ever that Justin was his biological child. Sass had lied to him again and she was still running away from the past. Tears blurred his vision, but pictures of them as a family were etched deeply in his photographic memory. The family circle was still incomplete.

Tears also blurred Sass's vision, but they weren't tears of relief as she'd hoped. How could she have a future as a free woman when the only man she'd ever loved belonged to her past? Would she ever be free, free of the past that had held her bondage, free of the man she loved more now than ever?

# Sixteen

Kristopher couldn't relax as he sat aboard the jetliner. He lowered the seat back and let his thoughts take him to a place in time when he thought his future with Sass was settled. Seated in a candlelit booth in back of the cozy Hollywood restaurant Poor Richard's, he and Sass had shared twin Australian rock lobster tails from one fork. Each time the drawn butter clung to her succulent lips, he'd lean over and tenderly kiss it from her mouth. The skin around her golden-brown cheeks was slightly flushed and the candlelight beautifully enhanced her sepia eyes.

Kristopher had seen into her heart through her eyes that night. She'd been stunning in the chic black pants suit and gold silk blouse she'd worn. He recalled how the gold necklace and matching earrings had accented her coloring. He remembered wearing dark brown dress slacks and a brown turtleneck sweater. Sass had complimented him with enthusiasm. She had told him how much she loved that color on him. Everything about that night was crystal clear in his mind. Everything about every moment he'd spent with her was no less than lucid.

He placed his hand over hers and massaged it gently. "Are you enjoying yourself, Sass?"

"Tremendously. I love this restaurant. It's so romantic. It'll remain in my memory always."

He lifted her hand and pressed it to his lips. "I'll always remember that I brought you here, Sass. How was work today?"

"Very good. Since my job helps me feed J.B., I have to love *it*, too." When she spoke of Justin, he saw the midnight sun in her eyes.

He felt engulfed by the beauty of her sheer eyes. "I've forgotten . . . what does the B stand for? I've never heard you call him by that nickname before now."

"Brian. My father's middle name is the same."

He felt relieved that it wasn't any part of Justin's father's name, which made him curious about the child's first name. "What made you decide on the name Justin?" He held his breath while waiting for her answer. Justin could be a junior.

She laughed. "You're going to find this silly, but I used to watch the soap operas. My favorite male character was named Justin."

Her laughter was contagious and he was immediately infected by it. "I don't find it silly at all. I find it quite charming." He hadn't kissed her in more than ten minutes and the urge to do so was overwhelming. She'd been a little standoffish when he'd picked her up from work so he had backed off. She later mentioned how much better she felt, right after she'd taken a hot bath.

Her eyelashes fluttered wildly. "Do you have a middle name?"

"Bradford. It's my mother's maiden name. I recall that yours is Ashley."

Sass smiled. "Bradford. Nice surname."

He nodded. "Yes, it is. Since it's Friday night, why don't we go dancing so that you can show me some of that incredible sass on the dance floor?"

When she nodded her agreement, he crushed his dying lips against hers and felt new life being kissed into them. His lips met with hers just as the seat belt light came on to wake him from his reverie.


Sass would've taken it as a good omen had she known that her thoughts mirrored Kristopher's as she lay in bed missing him terribly. Justin was with her parents, which made her feel even lonelier. She still felt anguished over how unhappy Kristopher looked before he'd left her home. She had the worst feeling about his departure. It was wrong of her to have sent him away like she had. She'd been horribly unfair to him regarding his past misdeeds. But had he stayed in her life, it would've only led up to the one-million-dollar question. Who was Justin's father? How could she tell him something she didn't even know herself?

Wasn't it already enough that Justin would never know his biological father? Because she'd agreed to something she wasn't sure she should have, Justin had to pay the price. Secrets were sometimes destructive. But her word was her bond.

"Slow down, my heart," Sass cried into her pillow.

She tried to count the tears as they fell, but realized it was useless and downright silly. She then muffled her sobs into the pillow, though no one was there to hear them. *I love you, Kristopher. I know I do.*

Memories of their first magic carpet ride after all those years rushed in to embrace her. She couldn't have given herself to Kristopher the way she did if she hadn't loved him. She had mourned the death of their love for so many moonless nights. She'd searched starless skies to discover why they had to be separated. Then her skies were suddenly filled with shooting stars and silver moons.

After all the anguish, she'd finally discovered the magic of having him back in her life. The feelings she'd experienced with Kristopher were foreign and wonderful. She'd felt his laughter in her heart, she'd heard his smile and she knew when he was near before he ever appeared. When she looked into his eyes, she'd been able to hear his heart whispering how much he loved her. She could feel his emotions and she knew that he felt hers. When she looked into his heart, she could touch the color of the sky and see the four seasons of the wind. But now he was gone forever.

"Kristopher," she whispered into the night, "can you stop the rain in my heart? Or will you cause it to pour again? Can you offer solace? Or are you once again going to rip away the last vestiges of my sanity? Whatever happens, know this: I'm going to love you no matter what. My heart has decided that you are the only man I will love . . . forever. Goodnight, my love, my forever soul mate."

In her dreams Sass relived one of their most spectacular nights.

Kristopher positioned one hand on the back of her neck and fanned his fingers through her wavy hair, drawing her nearer with the other. While they moved as one with the music, she felt like she was on the magic carpet ride that he'd promised earlier. Breaking the sound barrier, they drifted into space and danced an exotic ballet on the Milky Way.

His fingers racing through her hair intensified the heat from the brilliant constellations. She searched the heavens for a sign of the still waters she desperately needed to lie down in. They stayed entwined together through slow songs and fast songs. She never wanted this night to end. She felt his warmth all through her. She moaned when he tilted her chin upward, lowered his head and lost his mind in her inviting mouth.

While entwining their feelings, she looked at him with tears dazzling in her sheer eyes. He was suddenly in need of CPR. Feeling his struggle for air, she placed her mouth over his and softly blew her sweet breath of life into his lungs, extracting him from the jaws of cardiac arrest. Her crystal tears splashed against his face to cool his skin.

Gasping for breath, he whispered into her ear, "Come in out of the rain sweet, Sass. Use my smile as an umbrella on your way in."

After several hours of dancing, weightless in their flight to the car, he saw that she was comfortably seated before securing her door. His brief departure left her feeling cold. He could be lying next to her soul and it still wouldn't be close enough.

Driving high into the hills, he reached a flat ridge and parked the car. The shimmering panoramic view of the city took her breath away. The City of Angels was shrouded in glory, haloed with dazzling lights.

"This is as close to heaven as I want to get for now, Sass. Have you ever seen anything so beautiful? Present company excluded, of course."

"No, I haven't. Being in your arms is the closest I've ever come to heaven. This magnificent view definitely deserves a close second."

He exited the car and ran around to open her door. "I want to share this piece of heaven with your delicious mouth meshed against mine. Our only spectators will be the wind, the moon and the starlit skies."

He slowly ground his mouth over hers and the stars twinkled merrily to the sweet tune of the wind's chimes. Their interlude could've lasted forever and it would've been over too soon. Locked in the safe haven of one another's arms, they swiftly returned to the car.

Sass raised up with a start. Wantonly, she looked at the empty side of the bed. The telephone rang at the same exact moment she reached for it to call Kristopher.

It was Kristopher. It had to be. She felt it.

"I've arrived back in Paris safely. Did I wake you?"

Hearing his loving voice over the phone confirmed the genuineness of what she'd perceived. She blew out a deep breath. *I awakened the moment you first smiled at me in Paris. I've been awake ever since.* "Did you have a good flight?"

"A very restless one. I couldn't get you out of my mind. I kept thinking of all the things you said to me. I'm scared, Sass, scared for you, for us."

"I know you don't understand now, but I hope that you'll eventually come to that end. I wish we could've settled this differently, but I had somehow convinced myself that I had to let go of you. I no longer know if that was the right thing to do. I'm scared, too."

"How would you feel if the shoe was on the other foot? How do you expect me to be understanding when you refuse to deal with our problems?"

"I'm trying to."

"Are you, Sass? Is that really what you're doing? If it's true, why aren't you able to convince me of that? You don't sound like you actually believe what you're saying."

She moaned with exasperation. "Maybe we should talk later. You're too emotional about this. You were less than tactful in your anger the last time we talked."

"Should I apologize for having human emotions? Should I not care that you're taking away our chance for happiness by keeping so many secrets? Should it not concern me that you refuse to discuss Justin's biological father? What are you hiding that has you so fearful?"

"Oh, Kristopher, it sounds like you don't trust me."

"I don't trust your uncertainties. There are so many things you haven't told me, which is why I'm wondering if you're hiding something. Give me a reason to trust you, Sass, by telling me the whole damn truth."

Sass blinked hard. He was angry enough to swear. It hurt that she was the reason he was so upset. "I can't. It would help if you'd stop asking me to do so. Is it okay for me to call you back tomorrow? I don't want to fight anymore."

"I didn't think we were fighting, Sass. I thought we were having an adult discussion. At any rate, suit yourself about calling. If you can't trust me with your deepest secrets, then what would be the point?"

"What, indeed? Goodbye, Kristopher." She hung up before she lashed out at him in anger, before they both said something they'd more than likely regret.

Wearily, Kristopher dropped down onto the plush chair next to his bed. Before he could grind out another thought, he picked up the phone and redialed Sass's number. But he cradled the receiver before it even had a chance to ring. It would be of no use to call back now, he decided. At this point, they were both too upset to have a calm discussion.

Kristopher took off his silk robe and laid it at the bottom of the bed. He picked up the towel he'd removed from around his hips earlier and dried his hair with it. Before climbing into bed, he gazed out the high-rise window and up at the sky above. All the nights that he and Sass had once spent looking up at the stars and the moon blew into his mind like a summer breeze.

Lying nude under the lightweight bedspread, Kristopher's thoughts were much calmer than they'd been earlier. The deep breathing exercises had helped. His mind's eye began to paint portraits of deep-blue seas, colorful seashells, and a nude Sass, astride a bottle-nosed dolphin. The sea winds wove passion flowers in her heavy hair as the dolphin carried her across the mysterious crystal waters to deliver her into his waiting arms.

While waiting for her and the dolphin to reach him, he promised to introduce her to a world filled with romance. Red roses, sensuous nights, burnt-orange sunsets and bright golden sunrises would become a part of her daily diet. The camera lenses in his eyes photographed her in skimpy bikinis, lacy see-through lingerie and flowing satin evening gowns. Sparkling diamonds graced her soft, elegant neck and her dainty wrists and ears.

Visualizing her standing knee deep in the pounding surf, he imagined her in nothing but a soaking wet T-shirt. Her pouting, salt-kissed lips summoned him to taste her. Diving into the deep waters, he carried her to the ocean floor, where they explored the colorful caves and played among the starfish. Her rose-petal laughter rang out when she noticed how the mermaids were even greener in their envy of her.

He entwined several strands of black pearls around each of their necks to bond a never-ending link between them. "Sweet Sass, I'm lost in the tranquilizing sea of your sepia eyes. I wonder if you will throw me a life raft, or allow me to drown in your eyes? I love you," he whispered against her lips in the picture.

Sass looked at the legal papers she'd just been served. Seconds later she was screaming like she'd been stabbed. "Lillian," she screamed, "Lillian, I need you in here." Her hands trembled as she reread the document that had been served to her by the local marshall's office. Kristopher had only left a few days ago, but he'd certainly been very busy.

Lillian came running. "What is it, Sass? You look like you're about to croak."

Sass was in a state of shock. "Read . . . this," she stammered. "I can't believe this is happening to me. I just can't believe it."

Lillian rapidly read the documents and her reaction was

pretty much the same as Sass's. "Oh, dear. This is awful. I can only imagine how devastated you must be feeling."

Sass's color had drained from her face. "That's an understatement!"

Lillian wrung her hands together. "Do you really find it so strange that Kristopher might think that Justin is his child? The baby looks so much like him. I have to admit that I've been wondering about that possibility myself. I can't tell you how many times I noticed Kristopher staring at Justin in an odd sort of way. I've wondered if Justin belonged to Kristopher ever since I came here to work for you."

"Why would you wonder that back then? You'd never seen him."

"You had plenty of pictures of Kristopher laying around here when you first moved into this place. Even though you've never said whom Justin belonged to, I've been of the mind that Mr. Chandler might be his father. Sass, is Kristopher Chandler Justin's biological father? Is that why he's suing you for custody?"

"This is incredible! I'm not prepared to discuss Justin's natural father, but Kristopher Bradford Chandler had no part in creating Justin. He's bitten off way more than he can chew. He's going to regret the day he ever rang this particular chime. Not only am I going to answer the bell, I'm going to silence it forever." The doorbell rang just as Sass finished her statement. "Speaking of bells," Sass mumbled under her breath.

Lillian rushed off to answer the door, hoping Sass would be okay while she was gone.

Staci came into the room at the same moment that the hysteria had nearly concluded its hostile takeover of Sass's emotions. Dropping her purse, Staci ran to where Sass was seated and gathered her sister in her arms. The look on Sass's face had Staci terrified. "What has happened?" Frantically, her eyes searched the room for Justin. "Tell me it's not Justin." Staci shook Sass, trying to bring her around. "Where's Justin, Sass?"

Getting her mental hysteria under control, Sass stood up and paced the floor. "It's . . . not Justin, Staci. He's out . . . with . . . Mom and Dad." Sass looked to Lillian. "Would you excuse us for a moment? I need to have a private discussion with Staci." Her voice quaked with anxiety.

Though curious about Justin's biological father, Lillian felt sorry for the predicament Sass was in. "Of course. In fact, I'm going to go out and do some shopping. If you need me, please call on the cell phone." Sass nodded as Lillian hurried toward the back of the house.

By the time Lillian left the house, Sass had made up her mind not to tell Staci about what had occurred. She saw no need to concern her with it since she wasn't at liberty to explain the entire situation. But what reason was she going to give Staci for her emotional turmoil?

Staci took Sass's hand. "What has you so upset, little sister?"

"I'm sorry for being so emotional. It's just that I haven't had time to settle down since Kristopher returned to Paris. I'm afraid it's starting to come down on me." That was actually part of the truth. Sass hated herself for being a coward where the other part was concerned. She was in no doubt that soon her entire family had to be told every secret she'd ever kept regarding Justin.

Staci looked at Sass with concern. "Go in your bedroom and lay down. You've been burning the candles at both ends ever since you came home from Paris. I have a few phone calls to make regarding a business trip I have to take, but I'll come in and check on you shortly. Would you like me to fix you something hot to drink? Or perhaps a glass of wine?"

Sass smiled weakly as she fought off the next wave of

tears. "A glass of wine would be really nice. I'm going to go on into the bedroom and get out of these clothes."

Staci decided to follow Sass to make sure she was okay. "Would you like me to get a hot towel to wipe your face off? It's a little tear streaked and your eye makeup is all over the place."

Sass shook her head. "I'm going to go into the bathroom and wash my face and hands. You don't have to bring the wine until you finish your calls. I don't want you to have to make two trips."

Staci smiled at Sass. "Your needs come first. I'll return in a few minutes. If you're still in the bathroom, I'll leave the wine on the stand by the bed."

Sass thought about the legal papers at the same moment that she doused her freshly washed face with cool water. Oh dear, she thought, hoping Staci wouldn't see them. Though she'd accidentally left the documents in plain sight, she didn't think Staci would look at them. There'd be no reason for her to do so. She probably wouldn't even notice them, Sass tried to convince herself.

As Staci passed through the living room, the legal papers fell from the sofa table when her jacket brushed against them. The documents flew to the floor. Setting the wineglass down on the table, she picked up the papers. Staci had no intention of prying into Sass's private affairs, but she could see that these were legal documents. Though she tried hard to ignore the content, the part of the bold black print that read "child custody suit" seemed to leap right out at her.

Staci's chest hurt as she drew in a deep breath to steady her pulse. She folded the papers and put them back on the table, but she'd never be able to ignore what was written on them. It appeared that Sass had lied to her about Justin's father. If that was the case, she now understood why she never wanted anyone to talk to or get to know the man who fathered her son—especially if Justin belonged to Kristopher, as the papers seemed to suggest. It still didn't make sense as to why she would lie to the family. Didn't Sass know that it didn't matter to them who Justin's father was? They all loved both mother and child unconditionally.

Staci composed herself before she went back into the bedroom. The look on Sass's face told Staci that her sister was in deep despair. But unless she willingly shared her sorrow with her, Staci wasn't going to force the issue. Sass would have to come to her out of her own volition.

Staci sat on the side of the bed. "You look so tired, baby sister. Your fatigue is plainly written on your face."

Sass wanted to cry, wanted to scream out the truth to Staci, needed to explain everything to her, but the vow she'd made long ago held her back. In fact, it held her in bondage.

"Do you want to come home with me, Sass? You need someone to look after you since Kristopher has gone back to Paris." Staci hadn't intended to bring Kristopher up, but not to would have seemed suspicious since Sass hadn't mentioned any difficulties between the two of them. The lawsuit certainly spoke to the existence of a huge problem.

Sass squared her shoulders and sucked up the pain as she realized what she had to do. "I'll be right back, Staci. Please stay right where you are."

Sass came back and handed Staci the legal documents. She could see the anguish in her older sister's eyes as she completely read and reread the papers. When Staci finally looked up at her, Sass saw "liar" written boldly in Staci's eyes.

Staci got to her feet. "I don't understand this, Sass.

Didn't you tell the rest of the family and me that Kristopher wasn't Justin's father?"

She reached up and took both of Staci's hands. "Come and sit back down. I need you to understand something."

"Understand what? That you have lied to all of us from the start? That you have looked your family straight in the eye and denied that Kristopher fathered Justin? Why would he sue you over a child that wasn't produced from his seed? Why?"

Sass looked dejected. "Just because he thinks it's his child doesn't make it so. I need to ask you to bear with me regarding this matter just a bit longer. Staci, I need you to trust me. I can't deal with this alone. I need you more now than I've ever needed anyone."

Staci couldn't figure out what was going on with her sister, but she knew that Sass was either lying to her—and possibly to herself—or she was hiding something. Her concern for Sass's mental stability outweighed the anger she felt inside at what seemed like blatant deception on Sass's part. A large part of her didn't believe her sister was capable of dishonesty. But Staci couldn't rule out that when a woman suffered the type of hurt that Sass had, she might be in total denial. Denial and unyielding pain made people capable of things way beyond the norm, Staci knew; things way beyond the borders of sanity.

The fact that Justin looked a lot like Kristopher wasn't something that had been ignored. The family had often talked about how much Justin looked like him. It was never mentioned in front of Sass, but everyone knew there was a strong possibility that Justin belonged to Kristopher Chandler. Sass's denial had obviously kept her from facing the truth.

Sass gripped Staci's upper arm, bringing her out of her thoughts. "What are you thinking, Staci?"

To ease the knotted tension, Staci stretched her arms high over her head. "I don't know what to think, Sass. I have to tell you that none of this makes any sense at all. How are you planning to fight this custody matter? What is your first course of action?"

Nervously, Sass rubbed her cheek with her palm. "I'm going to go and see Kristopher and try to make him withdraw this silly suit. I'm sure I can convince him to drop it."

Staci looked skeptical. "What makes you so sure?"

"Because I have to. Kristopher has to see that he has to leave us in peace."

"Why does he have to do that?"

"Because he has no rightful claim to Justin."

"Rightful claim or biological claim? Which is it?"

"As far as I'm concerned, he has neither."

Sass had no idea how curious her inconsistent denials made Staci regarding Justin's biological father. Justin belonged to someone. If it wasn't Kristopher, then who was it? Until Sass provided the family with the answers, there was no way for them to help her. Staci couldn't stand the thought of Justin being taken away from them should Kristopher win the custody suit. Justin had already become an important part of his life. Justin was also too important to the Stephens family for them to want to see him caught up in some unexplainable custody battle.

"Why don't you just submit Justin for DNA testing? If you know for a fact that Kristopher's not the father, then it would all be over very quickly." Sass's discomfort at Staci's suggestion further contributed to Staci's uneasiness.

"I think I can handle this without subjecting Justin to any physical unpleasantness. I want to keep him out of this for as long as I can. DNA will be my last consideration, not my first."

Looking puzzled, Staci scratched her neck. "What possible reason would a man have for doing this, especially if he knew the child in question couldn't possibly be his?"

"Revenge!" Sass claimed. "Oh, Staci, how in the world did I fail to see that Kristopher and Grace were sleeping together? In the beginning, Grace made no bones about how she felt about him, but then she seemed to understand that we were going to be together whether she liked it or not. I thought she and I had even become friends. With the possibility of her being there to support him and sneer and jeer at me in court, how am I going to get through this ugly custody battle?"

Staci placed a calming hand on her sister's shoulder as they sat face to face on Sass's sofa. "Sweetie, you're still so naive even after all you've been through. Befriending you was part of her lecherous plan. If she won your confidence, it would be so much easier for her to deceive you. It wouldn't be so easy if she showed herself to be the enemy. Lately, a lot of so-called friends are betraying one another by sleeping with each other's man. Don't you ever watch Jerry Springer or Ricki Lake?"

Sass gave Staci an intolerant glance. "I never watch that kind of garbage, and you know it. What I should've been watching is my back."

"Why are you suddenly concentrating on the story of Grace and Kristopher when your world is falling apart over the possibility of losing Justin? Shouldn't your son be your main focal point right about now? Grace happened a long time ago. It's called history."

"To keep from dealing with the facts, I suppose. If I focus on something other than losing Justin, I just might be able to get through this. I can't lose Justin, Staci. I just can't. I couldn't bear it. I'd curl up and die if someone took him away from me."

Staci couldn't sit still. Something about Sass's entire demeanor bothered her, but she couldn't pinpoint any specific thing; other than the fact that she thought her sister was lying to herself regarding Justin's biological father, had been lying to herself for years, and to the entire family. Sass wanted everyone to believe she'd lost Kristopher's baby, but she'd never tell anyone who the actual father was. It made even less sense than it did when she first came home from San Jose with Justin. The whole family thought she had completely wigged out back then.

Sass broke into tears. "I have to tell you a gut-wrenching story, Staci. Can you promise not to reveal to anyone what I'm about to tell you? I desperately need your word."

Staci grew even more concerned for her younger sister. Sass looked like she'd rather die than let go of the secret story she'd mentioned. Sass's hands shook uncontrollably as Staci took hold of them. "You never have to worry about that with me. I'd never compromise your confidence. You have to know that."

Sass closed her eyes as she began to share her sacred story with Staci.

The heavy smell of ether permeated the air. Hazy clouds of smoke shrouded the darkened room in mystery. Her head felt like cotton and her eyes felt wild, unfocused, and burned with a frightening intensity. Then she began to float upward.

Far off in the distance she saw a bright beam of light, brighter and whiter than she'd ever seen before. As she floated toward the light, she saw a blinding white door with a huge golden knocker shaped like a cross resting in the center of it. Out of nowhere a fluffy band of clouds came and surrounded her. They appeared to dance above her head and below her feet. The light brought the sort of peace she'd never known before. The clouds seemed to lift her and carry her closer to the white door. She relaxed and floated along.

At the door, the knocker seemed to lift of its own accord. The gospel music that came from behind the door sounded like a full mass choir in concert. All of a sudden she began free- falling, down and down she fell, where space was totally devoid of light. She shivered in the darkness. In a twinkling of an eye, she was whisked back to the land of light.

Staci gathered Sass into her arms. Sass cried and cried. For all that she'd gotten off her chest she didn't feel the slightest bit relieved. Her burden was a heavy one. The consequences she'd eventually bear would be even heavier. Attempted suicide was an unforgivable sin.

Staci lifted Sass's head so that their eyes met. "This is a such a complex situation, but I'm so glad you finally shared it with me. Please trust that I understand. I'll never tell anyone your secret. I think everyone should know the truth, but it has to come from you, only when you're ready for it to be known. I'm sorry that you felt you had to go this alone. I'm so sorry."

An hour had passed when Staci got up to leave. "I've got to go. I hate to run, but I have something important to take care of. I'll call you later tonight. Are you going to be okay?"

Sass smiled weakly. "I'll be fine. Mom and Dad will be bringing Justin home in another hour or so. Justin is always great company." Sass started to cry again. "If I lose Justin, I stand to lose my life. Justin is my life. He's my everything, my all."

Staci lifted Sass's chin. "Don't even think about losing him. It's not going to happen. That's all you have to hold on to." Staci saw that Sass looked ready to bolt. She'd seen that look before, the time when Sass had run away to San Jose. "Calm down, sister. Don't think of doing anything irrational, anything that could hurt your chances of winning this suit. Kristopher is back in Paris, Sass, so how are you going to try and talk him out of this suit? Are you planning to fly to Paris?"

Sass pushed her hair back from her face. "I haven't figured that out yet. He is so upset with me because I've never told him the truth about Justin's father. He once said that it didn't matter to him who Justin's father is. What matters to him is that he thinks I'm keeping something terribly important from him. He doesn't like to be deceived. Who does?"

Staci held up her hand for Sass to stop. "Wait a minute. Are you telling me that you haven't told Kristopher what you just told me? I know you're not saying that. I don't even know why I asked that silly question. No sister of mine is that stupid."

Sass looked abashed as she pushed a few strands of hair behind her ears. "You have at least one sister that stupid. I didn't tell him because of the vow I'd made. Even if I wanted to tell him, I wouldn't have known how after so much time had passed. The fewer people who knew . . . I thought it would be better that way. I hated hurting Kristopher, but I was so scared to tell him the truth. I didn't want him to leave me again."

Staci grabbed Sass by the arm and marched her right to the telephone. "Call him. Now, Sass. He loves you and I can't imagine him not wanting to be here for you once he knows the truth. You have to come clean with him, but you have to do it now. Do you love Kristopher Chandler, Sass Stephens?"

Sass had no choice but to smile. Her heart wouldn't have it any other way. "Unconditionally . . ."

"Make the call. Don't let this go any further than it has." Without further comment, Staci left Sass alone in the apartment. Sass wasted no time in picking up the phone.

Kristopher answered the phone on the first ring. Sass let the sound of his voice seep into her soul before she announced herself. "It's Sass. How are you?" She heard his sharp intake of breath.

"I'm fine." He hesitated momentarily. "I don't have time to talk with you at the moment, Sass. I have a flight to catch."

Her heart crashed and burned inside her chest. "May I ask where you're flying off to?"

"I'm coming back home, Sass. We need to talk. I should have never left with so many things unresolved. I also need to explain to you why I felt it necessary to file a custody suit. Are you now ready to talk about all of this with me?"

Sass knew that she couldn't put this off any longer. Not only was her heart in danger of breaking, so was Justin's. "I . . . don't see that . . . I have much choice," she stammered. "I thought . . ." She cut the rest of her sentence short. What good would it do for her to tell him she thought he loved her? What he was trying to do to her wasn't a sign of love. Besides, he'd promised to never, ever hurt her again. Were all men degreed liars?

"Sass, are you still there? Do you not want me to come back there so we can try to work this out?"

Sass's heart did it's best to leap out of the burnt ashes. "That's what I want before any more damage can occur. I'm more concerned about Justin than I am about me."

"Then it's settled. I'll see you when I arrive. Is it okay to come to your apartment?"

"I'd rather meet you somewhere else. Justin misses you so much already. I don't want to compromise his heart any more than it already has been."

"Do you object to coming to my house? I'll E-mail you the directions."

"That will work. It'll have to be in the evening, after I get off work."

"I'll see you tomorrow around seven." *May the memory*

*of my love keep you safe until my arms are there to take over.* He wanted so much for him and Sass to be together. If he didn't believe with all his heart and soul that Justin was his child, he wouldn't have filed the lawsuit.

Sass screamed into the silence of her apartment when she thought of how she had so willingly betrayed him. He had all but healed her heart with the mere mention of his love for her, but he still hadn't earned her complete trust. Would he understand her when she told him the truth? Would he still want to marry her? The answers to her questions were coming—and very soon, she concluded.

# Seventeen

Wearing blue jeans and a white-cropped T-shirt, Sass was seated on the freshly cut lawn, right next to the gray granite headstone. It was early morning, so she wasn't frightened that there seemed to be no one on the grounds but her. Birds chirped in the trees overhead and a slight breeze blew across the lake. The majority of the cemetery plots teemed with colorful flower arrangements fashioned into crosses, hearts and other decorative shapes. It was peaceful enough.

She ran her finger over the letters in the name on the headstone. "I've broken the promise I made to you. I think you'd understand if you knew my reasons. In fact, I'm sure you would've given me your blessing. I know you wouldn't want anyone to take our child from me. I hope you can forgive me for what else I have to do. About your family, they haven't learned about our child and, after four years, they probably never will. He's safe from them. Now I have to ensure that he stays safe from the presence of my past. I love you. I'll bring Justin here to pay homage, when he's old enough to understand."

Sass made it back to her car and slumped into the seat. She put her head down on the steering wheel and cried over all that had happened in the past, all that might occur in the present. She could only pray that her future looked brighter than her past or the present.

* * *

The rest of the day turned out to be extremely busy for Sass. With several research projects coming due, she had spent a lot of time at the library. The more research she did, the more the ravenous hunger for truth and justice raged inside of her. Unable to quench her thirst for knowledge of the black experience, she had checked out several books to read at home.

Inspired by the stories of slavery, rallies for civil rights and the tremendous forward strides that had been made, as well as the recent setbacks to the civil rights laws, Sass spent the earlier part of the evening singing old Negro spiritual hymns to Justin. Many of the same songs had been sung to her as a child. From time to time, her thoughts would rebound to Kristopher, causing her to reflect on the wonderful nights they'd recently spent together stampeding out the pain of the past and building fresh, sweet memories.

Wanting more attention, Justin climbed onto her lap. Fastening his chubby hands around the shiny button on her sweater, he pulled hard enough to pop it loose. Sass hated to do it, but she smacked his hands lightly. As his heartbroken sobs filled the room, she wanted to hug him so bad it hurt, but she had to be firm with him. Her heartache deepened when she thought of what had happened when her parents had brought him home after Kristopher had left for Paris.

Justin had run all through the apartment searching for Kristopher. Recalling how sad Justin looked when he didn't find him caused Sass to wince. He'd smashed his little face against the picture taken of the three of them at Disneyland and kissed Kristopher on both cheeks, one of the many French customs he'd learned from his new friend.

Had she been wrong to let her son and Kristopher get so close to each other? She'd tried to keep their meetings at a minimum, but Kristopher had insisted on the three of them spending as much time together as possible. He loved bathing and dressing Justin, making an art form out of combing and brushing Justin's curly hair. Most of all, he loved to cook for him and read him stories. Justin had never spent a night in the apartment with them, however. Kristopher and Sass had made it a point to put him to bed at her parent's house, where Kristopher had read Justin bedtime stories.

Sass rocked Justin in her arms as he continued to cry. "Justin, stop crying now. You're going to make yourself sick. Mommy smacked your hands because you aren't supposed to pull on her clothes that way." As she kissed his forehead, he wound his fingers up in her hair.

Exhausted from crying, Justin fell asleep in Sass's arms. Glancing at the clock, she saw that is was eight-thirty, which explained why Justin had grown so cranky. It was half an hour past his bedtime. Sass held him tightly as she carried him into his bedroom.

Justin hardly moved a muscle as Sass put his pajamas on him and settled him into bed. Turning off the light, she knelt down beside his bed and whispered a prayer up to heaven for the angels to provide watch-care over her son as he slumbered throughout the night.

Showering first, Sass then prepared herself for the same end as Justin. Feeling lonely in the big apartment with Kristopher gone, she slipped into a peach camisole and tap pants. While brushing her hair out, she thought about putting Justin into bed with her but quickly changed her mind. It would be selfish of her to disturb him simply because she felt lonely.

Comfortably seated in the rocking chair in her bedroom, she read for a short while. Forty-five minutes later, she climbed in between the cool sheets, where her last awakening thought was of Kristopher. Her night began with sweet dreams of crystal champagne flutes, delicious hot bubble baths and baskets of fresh spring flowers.

Unexpected rain fell over the southland as Kristopher Chandler sped toward his Hollywood Hills home. Trying to make it home before the rain got any heavier, he drove a little faster than normal. Tired from the lack of sleep over the past couple of days, his eyes started to droop shut. When a vision of Sass's tearful eyes peered into his own, he suddenly felt alert.

Wondering what she thought of him, now that he'd sued her for sole custody of the little boy he felt so sure belonged to him, he had a burning urge to call his lawyer and withdraw the lawsuit just to keep from causing Sass any more pain and suffering. But he quickly realized he couldn't do that. No, he couldn't deny his child his rightful heritage.

If Justin was his, both father and son deserved to know the truth. He'd once made the mistake of not wanting the child they'd created but wasn't inclined to make the same mistake again. This was a chance for him to get it right, a second chance so to speak, a chance to try and repair the gut-wrenching pain of his past mistakes. As much as he didn't want to hurt Sass any further, he couldn't walk away from anything that could possibly bring him closer to his own flesh and blood. And perhaps, he dared to think, closer to the child's mother.

The memories of his last encounter with Sass washed over him, nearly drowning him in the anguish he'd seen in her eyes on that occasion. She'd been so determined not to discuss the things she'd promised to keep secret. He wasn't sure she'd keep her word this time either.

Something had a strong hold on Sass, something that she was scared to reveal. He could only hope that their anger wouldn't come full force when they got together to talk. Looking up at the roof, when it seemed that the rain had somehow gotten into the car, he realized the water came from his own eyes.

While dialing Sass's number, Kristopher prayed that the answering machine wouldn't come on. When she picked up the phone, he found himself unable to speak. Imagining himself lying next to her helped to relax him.

"Is anyone there?" Her voice was husky with sleep.

"No, Sass, someone is definitely not there." *And I'm having a big problem with it.*

Her breath caught at the sound of his deep, sexy voice. "Hi. How are you? I see you got my message."

"What message?"

Inappropriate as it was, she felt like giggling. *The one I sent to you by mental telepathy.* Inhaling deeply of the fluffy pillow he'd once laid his head on, she was able to catch a hint of the sexy smell of him. *Oh, how I wish you were here beside me.* "The one I left on your answering machine at your house."

"I'm afraid I haven't checked my service yet. I just arrived. Is Justin still asleep?"

"He is. Justin doesn't get up quite this early. I was sleeping, too. Are you tired?"

"Very much so. What if I come by your job for lunch? Is it possible to eat at the studio's commissary."

"That would be okay. If you come to the studio, you can meet Mandy and the rest of the crew. They're all dying to meet you. Mandy loves your photos. I've shared several of them with her. I usually go to lunch at twelve-thirty. Does that give you enough time to get some rest in?"

"Plenty of time. In fact, I'm going to come sooner so I can meet everyone. I don't want to cut into any of the brief time we'll have for lunch. Would you like to have Justin come along with me?"

She frowned. "I don't think that's a good idea. I don't want to keep him out of school for that." She took a moment to ponder her next comments. "I think it's best to keep you and Justin apart until we can discuss this lawsuit. He misses you so much already. He kisses your picture everyday. After you left for Paris, he ran all through the apartment looking for you. It affected him badly when he didn't find you. Our future together is so unsettled at this point. We don't want to confuse Justin, nor do we want to see him get hurt."

"Sass, don't be ridiculous." The silence on the other end told him of her hurt feelings. He wished he'd bitten his tongue. "I'm sorry, Sass. I didn't mean to hurt you. Justin is not going to get hurt, either, least of all by me. I understand the need to be cautious, but let's not overdo the precautionary measures. I certainly agree that he shouldn't be taken out of school for something as trivial as lunch, but I hope you'll rethink the decision you've come to. I had high hopes of taking Justin back to the neighborhood park. We had such a good time my last visit."

Sass sighed wearily. "Kristopher, have you've forgotten that you're suing me for custody of him? I'm keeping Justin out of this until we decide what to do. That's my final word on it. If you're still interested in lunch, I'll see you later."

"Sass, since you still want to be so obstinate about this, it's probably best that we don't have lunch. It seems to me as if our situation needs to be settled by the courts. You and I aren't going to be able to make any headway on our own. I can see that now. You're determined to keep Justin away from me and I'm just as determined to be in his life. I'll see you in court." He hung up the receiver without giving her a chance to respond.

Sass was mortified. That they couldn't work this out between them upset her to no end. To have custody settled in a court of law scared her in ways she'd never be able to explain.

Shaking like a leaf, Sass reached for the light switch and turned it off. Since it was still very early, she thought it might help her calm down if she could go back to sleep for a bit. In trying to get comfortable, she tossed and turned until she figured out it was of no use. She wasn't going to get back to sleep. There was too much on her mind. Kristopher's decision to go forward with the custody suit weighed heavily on her heart. This lawsuit had her entire life on hold.

What if by some fluke she ended up losing Justin to Kristopher? What if the judge decided to put her baby in foster care until the facts could be presented? She immediately rejected that dreadful thought. Besides, the facts were all on her side. Kristopher didn't have a leg to stand on. Confident that she'd be victorious in this ludicrous lawsuit, she scooted down in the bed and relaxed her head on the pillow.

Staci's expensive cologne reached Sass before her sister did. Jumping up from her chair, Sass rushed from behind her desk. The two sisters nearly crashed into one another as Sass reached the corridor right outside her office. They both laughed while embracing.

"I'm glad you could come out here for lunch, Staci. Thanks so much. I needed someone to talk to and you always fill that bill so well."

Staci smiled gently. "That's what sisters are for, Sass. Are you ready to go over to the commissary? Or do you want to grab something and bring it back here to eat in your office? If we eat here we won't have any interruptions."

"That sounds like a great idea. I hadn't thought about interruptions. With that in mind, I can just call over and have one of the pages deliver our lunch. What do you have a taste for?"

"I love the spaghetti that they serve over there. I'll also have a tossed salad with Italian dressing and a slice of French bread."

"I think I'll have the same. Come on into my office and get settled in, Staci."

"I'm going to run to the bathroom first."

"Do you remember where it is, Staci?"

"Around the corner and to the left."

Only twenty minutes had passed when the lunches Sass had ordered were delivered to her office. Everything was still piping hot when the women opened the Styrofoam containers containing the delicious-smelling spaghetti dinners. As they sat at the round table in one corner of the office, Staci offered the blessing. For several minutes the two sisters ate their food without attempting to make conversation.

Staci looked up from plate. "Have you been able to settle anything with Kristopher?"

Sass scowled heavily. "I'm afraid not. You already know that I took your suggestion about calling him. He's back in town for us to talk, but I upset him again when I refused to allow him to see Justin until things are settled. Realizing that we're not going to come to an agreement on our own, I made the decision to make contact with my lawyer again. Much to my dismay, she has advised me to get the DNA testing out of the way, voluntarily so. She says I need to appear cooperative, at least as far as the judge is concerned. The DNA results might already be in. She called me before I left for work, to tell me we're due in court Friday morning. Supposedly, the results are sealed. It seems that Kristopher's lawyer was able to pull a few strings to get the case on the calendar this quickly."

"Money has a way of doing the talking. Do you want me in court with you on Friday?"

"Want you there, need you there, you name it. I'm so glad you're here for me, period."

"Are you afraid of the outcome?"

Sass looked at Staci strangely. "You still don't believe what I told you, do you? I can see that you still doubt me. But I'm not surprised. You're not alone in that department. I think our entire family doubts me. Kristopher certainly doubts me. I'm even having doubts and I know better. I know the truth."

"What's that supposed to mean, Sass?"

"Nothing, Staci. I don't want to talk about this now. I promise we'll talk about it before court. Is everything okay with you and your sweet hubby?"

Sass's approach, or rather nonapproach, to this particular subject exasperated Staci at times, but she didn't drive all the way across town to pick a fight with her. She had come to support her and to let her know how much the family loved her. The Stephens clan would stand behind her no matter what. Still, she couldn't help wishing that Sass would tell them the entire truth.

Upset by her own naivety in her situation with Kristopher, Sass slapped an open palm down on the part of her bare thigh exposed by the short skirt she wore. Her flesh stung like fire. Looking down at her thigh, she saw the fresh, reddened handprint she'd branded there, wincing at the self-inflicted abuse she'd leveled against her own body.

Sass got to her feet. "Maybe I haven't been tough enough on him. Maybe I should turn into a female Kristopher Chandler to fight fire with fire," she ranted. "Pretend to love them, lie to them, then walk away and leave them. Women can play these games, too, you know. I know some women who are poignant masters of deception. That's it," she exclaimed. "Since he claims to love me so much, maybe I'll just go back to pretending I still love him and ask him to take me back. That should have him running for the hills. I can see him withdrawing the custody suit in a hurry. Egotistical men like Kristopher Chandler don't want to be bogged down with the responsibility of a family. He only thinks he does. If I hadn't decided to resist him and not to continue our relationship, he wouldn't be going to all this trouble to prove he's Justin's father, which he's not. No way, no how. His ego is at stake, plain and simple."

Dr. Ford cleared her throat. "Maybe you should sit back down. You're starting to sound irrational, Sass. I'd like to see you take a minute or two to calm yourself down before you force yourself into cardiac arrest."

Sass laughed with bitterness. "Starting to? I've been irrational through this entire bizarre mess. Getting back involved with Kristopher is the most bizarre of all. How can I be rational when my rationale has been destroyed? I sometimes feel that I can't trust anyone or anything. The only loves I trust are my Creator's and Justin's. There are times when I don't even trust you."

Dr. Ford raised an eyebrow sharply. "In that case, we may have a big problem. If you don't trust me, then perhaps you should change therapists. Trust is important between doctor and patient. I'm under a moral obligation, as well as a legal one, to keep your issues in confidence. What you tell me stays with me and me alone."

Sass sighed deeply, hating the statement she'd made unjustly. If she'd been a smoker, she would've lit her tenth cigarette by now. "Dr. Ford, I don't mean it in that context. Call it paranoia if you like, but I can no longer trust without question. I'm back to having issues of trust with everyone. I thought I trusted my parents implicitly, yet I still chose a man erroneously, which means that I've distrusted some of the things they've told me. This is what happens when you experience repeated acts of betrayal. The previous duplicity goes much deeper than the obvious. I don't know if I'll ever be able to explain all that's happened to me. There's so much more to my pain than what meets the naked eye."

Dr. Ford looked puzzled. "I don't understand. Please explain your last statement."

Pushing her hands through her hair, Sass stared blankly at her therapist. Looking confused and defeated, she reclaimed her chair. "I can't explain it. I don't know why I said what I did." She felt herself closing up on the inside, protecting her inner-self like a delicate flower shriveling from the heat of the sun. The withdrawal came easy for her. "Oh, boy," she cried, "I need more time. Can we move past this? I'm starting to block parts of the past out again."

Dr. Ford wrote something down in Sass's medical chart. "I'm beginning to think this request to move on has nothing to do with a block. You're purposely holding something back. I think you carry a deep, dark secret inside of you. I believe it's largely responsible for your inability to conquer your fears. You've grown comfortable with those fears. To release them now would move you out of your comfort zone. Without your fears to cling to, you'd feel that your soul has been stripped bare. Reality would have to be faced at that point and I don't think you're ready to enter an unsafe world. For reasons only known to you, reality is anything but a safe haven for you. How am I doing so far?"

Sass looked down at the floor, amazed at how close Dr. Ford had come to the truth. She did have a deep, dark secret, one that could never be revealed. Not unless . . . no, that can't ever happen, she told herself. "I'm going to get there, but right now I'm only rowing with only one oar in the water. Once I find the missing oar and get a firm grasp, I'll arrive much faster."

"Did you make a promise to someone that you'd never reveal a certain secret?" Dr. Ford asked pointedly.

Sass averted her eyes from Dr. Ford's. "We all have secrets. I'm no different from any other human being."

Thoughtfully, Dr. Ford rubbed her thumb across her chin. "I see. I'm going to leave this alone for now. This subject will have to be revisited somewhere down the road, the sooner the better. That is, if you still want to retain me as your therapist."

Sass looked shocked. "Of course I want to keep you on. You've brought me so far. I'm sorry that I offended you earlier. I really didn't mean it the way it sounded."

"That's good to know. But let me ask you this. When did you become such a man-hater, Sass Stephens?"

Another shocked expression crossed Sass's face. "I have a father who loves his wife and daughters. I also have a son who will one day grow up and take a bride. I could never hate either one. I'm no man-hater, far from it. I wouldn't have gotten so involved with Kristopher again if that were the case. However, I admit to now being extremely man-shy."

Dr. Ford got to her feet. Coming around her desk, she sat down in the chair next to where Sass was seated. "I believe you, Sass. The question was asked for shock value. I needed your response in order to further evaluate your emotional stability. This madness with Kristopher, how do you plan to handle it?"

Anguished, Sass twisted around on her wrist the gold bracelet he'd given her. "I don't know. I haven't talked to him since the conversation I told you about. He was angry with me for not wanting to bring Justin around until our issues are resolved. 'I'll see you in court' were his last words. I've phoned him a few times but he hasn't returned my calls. He's really hurt."

"Do you understand why it would hurt him not to see Justin? He thinks your child is his."

"Yeah, especially after he asked me how I would've felt had the shoe been on the other foot, but I can't do anything about it. His pain is going to increase when he learns the truth."

"A truth you're not ready to reveal. You already know the cliché about the truth setting you free. You might want to try it."

Sass laughed. "I have, believe me. Yet I'm still in bondage. Maybe I haven't revealed the truth to the right person. I'm having a hard time facing the facts, so I can't expect anyone to understand what I'm going through." *The day in court more than likely will reveal it all.* Sass wished that she and Kristopher could've worked this out without legal assistance.

Dr. Ford glanced at her watch. "We've gone overtime by a half-hour. I have an appointment that's been waiting at least that long. You won't be charged for the overtime, Sass. Make an appointment for the same time next week. If you need to see me sooner, call Fiona. She'll see what we can do to accommodate you."

"Thanks. I hope this custody issue is settled by my next appointment. Take care."

\* \* \*

A blood-curling scream ripped free of Sass's throat as she tried to make sense of the Judge's comments, though she wasn't sure she'd heard her right. Kristopher couldn't possibly be Justin's biological father. Somebody was pulling a terrific prank on her. They had to be. That was the only explanation for what she thought she'd heard Judge Mildred Waters say.

Sass threw herself into Staci's arms. "This outcome is crazier than I could've ever imagined," she sobbed openly. "You have to believe me. He's not the father of my child. My child's father is dead. Staci, please . . . don't let . . . them take . . . Justin from me," she cried brokenly.

The Judge slammed her gavel down to gain control of her courtroom, but all it did was send Sass further into hysterics.

Staci did her best to bring Sass comfort, but she was inconsolable. In fact, she believed that her sister had gone off the deep end. If Justin was adopted, how could she claim that the child's father was dead? It was just proven through DNA testing that Justin biologically belonged to Kristopher Chandler. Staci feared that Sass was having a nervous breakdown from all the stress she'd had to endure. She herself felt confused by it all.

"Miss Mitchell, you must bring your client under control," Judge Waters shouted above the buzz of the spectators.

Sass's screams grew louder and louder, heightening Kristopher's desire to rush to her side and offer her comfort as he looked on. Knowing he wouldn't be welcomed in her camp kept him in his seat, where he squirmed with discomfort for the added pain he'd brought to her life.

As Staci led Sass away, Sass dropped down to her knees. Her head fell forward until it touched the floor. Stretching her arms out in front of her, she began pounding the floor with her fists.

Kneeling down beside her sister, Staci knew that Sass was in big emotional trouble. "Sass, let me get you out of here. Unwittingly or not, you're allowing the judge to assess your mental stability. We don't want her to think you're mentally unstable. Pray for strength, Sass."

Sass looked up at Staci and then over at Kristopher. "I will not allow you take my child from me. I will see you burn in hell first," she screamed at the top of her lungs.

The Judge's gavel pounded up and down like crazy. "Miss Mitchell, getting your client under control is a must. We have serious decisions to make here today."

Sonja Mitchell, a thirty-something African-American, with wide hips and lean shapely legs, rose to her feet. "Your honor, I request a short recess. My client is obviously distraught. She's going to need a few minutes to pull it all together."

"Very well. This court will take a forty-five-minute recess. Court will reconvene at ten-thirty sharp." After sounding her gavel, the judge left the bench.

Sonja bent over to talk to Sass. "Honey, I need you to calm down so we can go somewhere and talk. This time we need to talk the truth and nothing but the truth. We're already in scalding water with the judge." Sonja Mitchell gave Sass a compassionate look and helped Staci get her client to her feet. After gathering up their personal belongings, the three women headed out of the courtroom.

"Staci, will you wait for me?" Sass asked, sounding weak and unhappy. As though she felt horribly guilty for all that had occurred, her eyes pleaded for her sister's forgiveness. "This shouldn't take long." Looking as confused as Sass felt, Staci nodded in the affirmative.

It had taken Sass less time than she'd thought to tell her incredible story to her attorney, once she'd pulled herself together. Sonja Mitchell cried as much as Sass did while listening to one of the most amazing stories she'd ever heard or read.

Sonja got to her feet. "This changes everything, you know. I'm going back in there to ask for a continuance. You have to bring me everything you have on this matter of adoption. I need a birth certificate, the death certificate, and all legal documents pertaining to this case. From what you've told me, we have to subject Justin to another DNA test. Though I find it hard to believe, these test results can't possibly be right in view of this new information . . . unless Kristopher was somehow involved with the biological mother. Is that a possibility, Sass?"

"Highly improbable, I'd say, especially with both of us living in San Jose when we met. However, she told me she was a model before she became ill." Sass thought of the possibility of Kristopher being involved with Justin's biological mother. "Oh, no, that can't be. That's just too much of a coincidence. No, I can't ever accept that possibility. It's just too unbelievable."

"Coincidence . . . or perfect explanation as to why the DNA came out in his favor? He cheated on you with one of his own models, so why not another model from another area? Let's get back in there before the judge finds us in contempt for being late. We'll get this all figured out before we have to appear again."

Once the court was called back into session by the bailiff, Sonja Mitchell stood and asked for the opportunity to approach the bench. Permission to approach was granted by Judge Waters. Minutes later, after Attorney Mitchell and the Judge had put their heads together in conference, Lawrence Chance, Kristopher's attorney, was called to the bench for a sidebar meeting.

While biting her nails, Sass wondered what was going to happen next. Staci hadn't said a word to her when she'd returned from her meeting with Sonja, nor had she even looked at her. As she sat motionless on a spectator's bench to the right of the defense table, Sass stole a guarded glance at her sister. She appeared deep in thought, probably thinking her baby sister a liar, Sass mused painfully. Her entire family would think her a liar after they got wind of the DNA news.

Sass saw that Sonja didn't look too happy when she came back to the defense table. "What's going on?" Sass whispered.

Shaking her head, Sonja sighed heavily. "Kristopher's lawyer has made a motion that might gain his client temporary custody of Justin until this matter can be revisited. The Judge hasn't made a ruling yet, but his attorney gave a convincing argument, citing the near breakdown displayed by you here in the courtroom. He's conferring with his client now."

Trembling all over from the fear of losing Justin, Sass looked horror stricken. "But Kristopher doesn't know that I adopted Justin. He thinks I'm Justin's natural mother."

"From the way he's looking at you, I'd say he knows now. The angry glare suggests he may see this as a ploy for you to further deceive him, Sass. He probably doesn't believe you. His anger might influence his decision to seriously take you on regarding permanent custody."

Judge Waters sounded the gavel. "I have reviewed the facts as well as the arguments both attorneys have presented to me regarding temporary custody of said child, Justin Brian Stephens. This is a very unique case and has yet to be tried in a court of law in the full sense of the word. This can only be achieved once all the extenuating circumstances are presented before this court. From what I understand, there are many facts yet to be considered.

"Though I found myself faced with a very tough decision, I have reached one. While I believe that a child belongs with his biological parent, Justin doesn't know Mr. Chandler. I believe it would be devastating to the child to remove him from the only home he's ever known and place him in a virtual stranger's custody, in unfamiliar surroundings. Therefore, I move that Justin will remain in the custody of Miss Sass Stephens for the time being. However, Mr. Chandler has every right to establish visitations with the child, to begin forthwith."

The judge looked from Sonja Mitchell to Lawrence Chance. "Is this something your clients can work out between them? If not, I'd like to hear your objections, or your suggestions as to how we can achieve my recommendations."

Both attorneys put their heads together with their prospective clients.

Sass was not ready to concede such a major defeat to Kristopher. The fact that he'd never wanted the baby she'd once carried for him in the first place is what kept her so obstinate. If she had her way, he'd never get near Justin. A man so uncaring about human life as to demand an abortion had no place in her son's life, adopted or not. She willed herself to hold onto the possibility of her belief that the DNA testing was simply flawed.

Sass sighed in relief when the judge agreed to let the two attorneys work out the visitation agreement, which couldn't possibly be reached between their clients in an instant.

When Sass didn't get up from her seat after court was adjourned, Staci was concerned for her and came to where Sass remained seated. Sass had no idea she'd urinated on herself until now. When she'd first felt the warm wetness of her clothes, she knew something had burst inside of her. The strange trickling sensation had come when the temporary custody issue first came up.

Sass whispered her embarrassing situation to Staci. Taking off her suit jacket, Staci put it around her shoulders. The jacked was long enough to hide the large urine stain that Sass felt sure was on the back of her pants. Sass stood up and looped her arm through Staci's. Disappointment was in Staci's eyes as she looked down at Sass.

"I know what you're thinking, but you're wrong. I'm going to prove it to you, Staci."

"Sass, you have nothing at all to prove to me. After I drop you off at home, I have to keep going. You've managed to keep some very important details from me. I don't think I want to deal with this matter another second. There are some missing pieces to this crazy jigsaw puzzle. You made the conscious decision not to provide me with the complete picture when you could've easily done so. You told me a lot of amazing things, but you didn't tell it all. I will not allow you to prolong the agony going on inside of this family for another day."

Sass was somewhat surprised by the innocuous way in which her sister had spoken. She hadn't been the least bit offensive, though it would've been appropriate for her to come off that way. Although she understood Staci's feelings, she wasn't going to let her comments go unchallenged or without protestation.


It had been one of the most agonizing thirty-minute drives she could ever recall living through in recent times. Staci's caliginous mood had shown Sass how little her desire for communication was, so Sass had kept quiet. Now that they were in front on her apartment, Staci wasn't making any move to park and come inside, but Sass had something to say.

"Aren't you coming in for a minute, Staci?"

She looked down at her. "I need to get home. I already expressed that to you before we left the courthouse."

"Are you telling me that you're not going to come up and see Justin?"

Without expression, Staci looked at her watch again. "Justin won't be home for hours, Sass. I'm not sure I'll be able to hold up emotionally should I stay to see him. I feel horrible for my nephew. I couldn't love him any more if he was my own. This is a very difficult situation for the entire family. We've always had such high hopes for you."

"Sitting in a car outside my apartment is not an appropriate way for us to discuss these issues. Won't you please come inside for a moment?"

"You go on in. Once I've parked the car, I'll follow behind you."

Sass got out of the car and ran to the door of her apartment. Tears fell from her eyes as she inserted the key into the lock. She had hurt someone who meant the world to her, someone she loved with everything in her, and it hurt like crazy. Leaving the door open for Staci, she ran into the bathroom and shut herself inside. Turning on the shower full force, to muffle her screams, she bared herself and settled under the stream of hot water. Loud and painful screams rented the air. Her sobs came so hard that her whole body shook with the force of them.

The screams were so loud Staci heard them despite the shower water teeming at full force. Entering the bathroom, Staci pushed back the curtain and immediately took Sass into his arms. "Oh, Sass, don't do this to yourself. You've been through enough. If I've added to your grief, please forgive me, sweetie. I never wanted to hurt you, not in a million years." Wrapping Sass up in a towel, Staci wiped her sister's face off. "Don't cry anymore."

She looked at Staci through the blur of tears. "I remember Kristopher telling me to save my tears for passionate, joyous or sorrowful occasions. Now look what he's doing to me. I couldn't feel any more sorrowful than I do right now." After completely drying off, Sass donned a robe.

"I've cried in my uncontrollable passion for him. I cried joyously when my heart had won his again. Now I cry over losing all that a second time. It's a very sorrowful occasion. But the one thing I can't lose in this is Justin's love. Why does Kristopher want to do this to all of us?"

Staci forced back her tears. "Sass, only you have the answers to your questions. He explained to you that he doesn't like being in the dark. It's about trust, Sass. Your inability to trust in him leaves him with no hope for the future. He also looked so disappointed over the pending loss of your future. You were so sure that Kristopher wasn't Justin's father, but you never fully explained it. The things you did tell me, like your attempt at suicide, weren't enough of an explanation. However sure you were about paternity, it seems you were dead wrong."

Sass looked up with a start. "I wasn't wrong. The *DNA* is wrong."

So sure that Sass had fallen back into denial, or that she'd possibly misunderstood her, Staci blinked hard. "I don't think I understood you."

Sass choked back a sob. "I think you heard me correctly. I'm not Justin's natural mother and Kristopher's not Justin's father, regardless of what was reported in court today. I adopted him from someone dying of cancer. She was in need of a mother for her newborn baby and my own son had just died. My son by Kristopher died several hours after he was born."

Swallowing a gasp, Staci pushed her hand through her hair. "My God, Sass, this is very complicated." Staci wiped the sweat from her brow. "I know this is difficult for you, but would you mind too terribly if I asked to hear this incredible story from beginning to end?"

Sass shook her head. "Not at all. Just bear with me through the tragic pain that I know will surely come." Sass blinked back fresh tears. "First of all, does what I've told you so far change how you were feeling about me?"

"If it's even possible, my feelings for you have deepened. The fact that I love you with all my heart hasn't changed, will never change. I just wish you had trusted me enough to tell me from the onset, but I understand your resistance. Please finish your story."

She sucked up some courage from deep within. "I was pregnant with Kristopher's child. When I told him about the baby, he asked me to have an abortion. I couldn't do it, so that's when I told him I wasn't really pregnant and moved away to San Jose to carry and deliver the baby in secrecy. I planned on raising the child on my own. I didn't tell you all about my pregnancy until after the adoption proceedings had begun. I've never told anyone that Justin is adopted, not until I told Sonja. Back then, you all asked if Justin belonged to Kristopher, I told you that he didn't . . . and that I wasn't going to ever reveal the name of the real father. I don't think you guys ever really believed Justin wasn't his child, but we've never spoken of it again. I had planned to tell everyone the truth and get this nightmare out in the open, but it just didn't happen. I'm sorry."

After moving into the living room, they sat on the couch.

"Tell me about Justin's mother." Staci winced at her mistake when Sass grew deathly pale. "I'm so sorry, Sass.

That was insensitive of me. You *are* Justin's mother, in every way."

As though cold, in need of warmth, Sass rubbed her hands together. "Aria's stomach cancer had spread like wildfire. She was blessed to have made it through the delivery and to have given birth to a healthy child. We shared a hospital room because of overcrowding. Although she knew she was dying, she came and comforted me after learning my baby had died. The sorrowful news had come just a few hours after he was born."

Sass let the tears fall without bothering to wipe them away. "In the middle of the night, as I lay sobbing into my pillow, the nurse came in and sat down next to the bed. She told me that Aria had asked to see me. She'd been moved to a specialized medical unit because she was in so much pain. Despite my own agony, I leaped out of bed and the nurse took me to her. That's when Aria first asked me to adopt her child and raise him as my own. She knew she wasn't going to live much longer . . ."

Sass's brokenhearted sobs pierced Staci's heart and she drew Sass into her arms. "It is okay, love. Take time out to calm down. We can do this another time if you want."

"I can't hold it any longer now that I'm finally able to release it. I thought Aria was out of her head from the medication, but apparently she wasn't. She knew exactly what she was saying. When I asked about the child's father, she told me he had died from a drug overdose, never knowing she carried his child. Then I asked her about any other family that might want to take the child. It seems both of her parents were closet alcoholics who became very abusive when drinking. Aria was very beautiful and had been a model before the cancer eroded her health. I somehow saw that as a connection of some sort to my baby, especially since Kristopher owned a photography/modeling studio. I agreed to adopt her baby and the legal wheels were set in motion. She named him Justin, after the name I'd already given to my child before his death."

"I'm terribly sorry for you, for the loss of your child, and for Aria, Sass. It must've been a very difficult time for you both. My dear Sass, why do you think Kristopher dares to sue for custody of a child that couldn't possibly be his? Perhaps he *is* Justin's biological father. He may have been involved with Aria since she was a model. It's possible that at some point she may have contacted him, or someone close to him about the baby."

"My attorney is exploring the same issues. I truly believe that the first time Kristopher learned about Justin was from me when I was in Paris. He thinks Justin is his child because Justin is the very same age as our child would've been. He probably thinks I lied to him about the abortion, which is partly true. I told him I'd have the abortion, but I couldn't do it. When I decided to keep the child, I told him an even bigger lie: that there was never a baby. I didn't want him to feel guilty about the abortion later in life since I never had one."

Staci looked stunned. "A man who asks a woman to kill his child feels no guilt simply because he has no conscience. The last thing you should've concerned yourself with was how he felt about anything. For you to have kept this all to yourself and not to have included your family in your secret is indeed remarkable. As for Justin's biological mother, has she died?"

Sass's eyes refilled with tears. "Aria is gone. She died not long after the adoption went through. Justin was just a few months shy of his first birthday when she passed away. I wanted Aria to see Justin on a regular basis, but she didn't want to get attached to him, nor did she want him to become attached to her. She said it would hurt too much. She only wanted him to know me as his mother. Still, I didn't move away from San Jose until after her death. She was hospitalized about three months before her death, never to come home again. She's buried here in Los Angeles, where she was born. I periodically visit her gravesite."

Staci's smile was sympathetic. "I am sorry, Sass. Still, you have a bigger problem facing you now. I'm not sure you should continue to fight Kristopher. It's been proven that he's the father's child. You love Kristopher, Sass, and he loves you. I also think he has changed. If there's any way you can come together with him for the sake of your child, I urge you to do so. This custody battle doesn't have to ruin three lives. I believe you two should marry right away. United as one puts Justin in a win-win situation."

"As for me winning, it's a sure thing. Kristopher can't possibly win. The DNA results are dead wrong. He's not Justin's father, no two ways about it," she strongly reiterated. "The new test will prove it." Sass couldn't begin to deal with the idea that Kristopher had fathered Aria's child.

With Justin asleep, Sass finally decided to do what she'd been pushing to the back of her mind all day long, muse over the possibility that Kristopher could've been intimately involved with Aria. She was certainly his type. Tall, beautiful, sensuous Aria had been everything Sass wasn't. As she did now, she often wondered what Kristopher had ever seen in her. She was completely different from the types of women she'd seen him with in his many photo albums. Kristopher Chandler had a serious penchant for beautiful, sexy women.

*The other women,* she thought. Could Aria have been one of his other women? It didn't seem possible. But then again, none of what was happening seemed possible. She and Kristopher had parted a lifetime ago, yet here they were, locked in a custody battle that made no sense whatsoever. How more impossible could this whole thing get?

With different types of Kristopher on the horizon of her mind, she turned over on her side. Kristopher, she mused, the one who had recently shown himself to be sweet and reliable: Was he at war over their relationship, as she was? It seemed to her that a part of him wanted to run away from the complicated mess, but another part of him wanted to stay. She imagined the real conflict for him was his deep love for her. He loved her, without a shadow of doubt. How many times had he told her that? No matter what she'd been telling herself, deep down inside she believed that he did love her.

It was amazing to love someone the way she loved Kristopher. He was the only man she'd ever loved. Even through all the pain and suffering, her heart still wanted him. Curling the pillow against her body, she closed her eyes to savor his image, the new one. Perhaps there was still a ghost of a chance for them to salvage some part of their relationship.

# Eighteen

Feeling extremely nervous, Sass was seated on Kristopher's sofa waiting for him to come out of the bedroom. He'd let her into his home and then had dashed off toward the back of the house. He'd mumbled something to her, but she hadn't heard a word he'd said. She had come there to make another attempt at settling the custody matter out of court. As she heard his footsteps drawing near, she smoothed her white skirt and folded her hands in her lap.

He stopped a couple of feet away from where she sat. He stared at her for several seconds. She knew he was angry. The bulging vein on the side of his neck told her that much. "Why didn't you tell me about Justin, Sass?"

She jumped to her feet. "Why are you doing this to me? Why are you trying to take my son away from me? Haven't you done enough already?"

He turned around and slammed his hand into the nearest wall. "You're not going to dump this on me. You tell me why you told me there was a baby and then there wasn't one. That was a cruel thing to do. You sat in my face and lied about Justin."

Sass pursed her lips. "Really, now? How are you so sure that I'm a liar? Could it be that it takes a liar to recognize one of its own kind? I don't owe you the truth about anything, but if you go forward with this pathetic attempt at revenge, you'll be making a damn fool out of yourself. If Justin were your child, you'd have no claim to him anyway. You asked me to abort your child. Remember?"

His eyes became filled with rage. "Do you somehow get sick pleasure out of reminding me of the biggest mistake of my life?"

Her nostrils flared with anger. "Getting me pregnant? Or ordering a hit on your own flesh and blood?"

He grew deathly pale. Her poisoned arrow had flown straight into his heart. If a chair hadn't been so close by, he would've fallen to the floor. He finally managed to compose himself enough to try and speak. "I didn't realize you hated me this much. I can see that you're hell bent on making me suffer for this entire mess. Aren't you, Sass?"

She advanced on his chair like an angry typhoon. "I think you got that all wrong, Mr. Chandler. I've never set out to cause you one ounce of pain. Can you say the same thing in reference to me? You slept with Grace and God only knows who else while you were romantically involved with me. Didn't you know that would hurt me? Didn't you know that it would destroy my faith in love and in men? Did you even care? Drop the lawsuit, Kristopher. You can't win. I won't let you be victorious. Not this time."

He jumped up from the chair and stood toe to toe with her. "Wrong again, Sass. I *can* win. And I *will.*"

"Impossible. Justin's not yours. Just thinking of me having sex with another man kills you, doesn't it? This is all about your ego. You're a damn fool, Kristopher. You were a fool when we were together, and you're still one . . . an unconscionable one at that."

He glared at her. She was right. It did hurt imagining her with another man. It hurt like hell. "We'll see who ends up being the fool. We could've settled this out of court, but you're too damn stubborn for me to even consider it. All you had to do was admit that Justin is mine. We could've come to some amicable agreement. He's my son, and I had a right to know about him. I had to force you to admit it in a court of law. That little boy looks just like I did when I was his age . . . and his age fits perfectly for the time frame we were together. The second DNA test will also speak for itself, Sass Stephens."

He'd torn into an exposed nerve but she never flinched. "Maybe I was doing the same thing you were. If you had a chick on the side, why couldn't I have had another man?"

"Because you knew I'd walk out on you if I ever found out, and you loved me too much to even think of going there. You weren't and still aren't the type of woman that involves herself with more than one man at the same time. If you were, you would've shown that to be true when we were together. You wanted me as badly as I wanted you from the moment we laid eyes on each other in that Paris bistro, but you'd never admit to that. It's always been like that between us. We ignite the fires of our passion every time we breathe the same air."

"You no good, selfish bastard! How could I have ever thought I loved you?" She took a second or two to let her anger subside. "So, let's just say that Justin is yours for the sake of argument. How are you going to tell your son the reasons why you wanted him to die before he ever had a chance to live?" Sass cringed at the cruelty in her question. It wasn't like her to be so brutal. It was then that she realized her alter ego had somehow entered the boxing arena.

Kristopher nearly doubled over from the mean-spirited jab she'd launched right into his midsection. He couldn't say anything because he didn't know what he'd tell his son if he asked that question. All he knew is that he wanted to spend the rest of his life making it up to his child, and to her for coming to such a horrible conclusion as he had.

She saw the defeat in his eyes, heard it in his silence. "I thought so. I'll see you back in court. You'd better fire your present lawyer and hire Johnny Cochran. You'll need him since you're going to have to defend yourself against attempted murder. I guess we'll find out in court if the child you attempted to murder is Justin." Without a backward glance in his direction, trembling with rage, Sass walked out of Kristopher's home.

He stared after her, unable to believe the hurtful attack she'd mounted against him. Her words cut him into like a dull, rusty razor. He never thought Sass would come to hate him. Sass's lack of respect for him had been obvious in her heated accusations. *Attempted murder!* He flinched at the very meaning, admitting to himself that he'd never thought of an abortion in that way, and had never seen it as taking a life. But that's exactly what he'd suggested to her when she'd first told him she was pregnant.

Why hadn't he told Sass that he'd tried to reach her to tell her that he didn't want her to have the abortion, that he wanted her to marry him and have them raise their child together? Why hadn't he let her know that he'd come to her apartment several weeks later, only to learn that she'd moved away and had left no forwarding address?

He'd contacted Staci and Stephanie, but neither of them would even talk to him, let alone give him information on the whereabouts of their youngest sister. He hadn't dared to call on her parents since neither of them had ever seemed to trust him with their daughter from the very beginning; a lack of trust that wasn't unfounded. It wasn't until a year later that he'd learned that Sass had moved up north to San Jose. By the time he'd learned her northern California address, she'd already moved away from that particular apartment complex.

Now, years later, he was still at frightening odds with the woman he loved, would always love. Sass was the mother of his only child, a son and heir apparent to his small fortune, the only male child to carry on the Chandler bloodline.

Sass awakened to the delicious aromas of breakfast foods. Thinking of how supportive Staci had been made her smile. Staci and Eugene had come over and spent the night when Sass had called and asked them to do so. Stretching her arms high above her head, she got out of bed and slipped into her robe. Met at her bedroom door by Justin, Sass picked him up and carried him into the bathroom, where she washed his face and hands, as well as her own. She then offered a brief supplication to start their day out on the right foot.

Justin yawned as she sat him on the counter to brush his teeth. "We're going to eat, Mommy?"

Sass tousled his hair. "You smell the goodies, too, huh, Justin? We'll have to thank Aunt Staci for cooking for us." Justin nodded, rubbing his eyes with his tiny fists.

Once she'd brushed his teeth, Sass picked Justin up and stood him on his feet. With his feet firmly planted on the ground, he took off running. Justin was already in Staci's arms by the time his mother reached the kitchen only seconds later.

Staci kissed Sass's forehead. "Good morning, my precious sister," Staci enthused. "Did you sleep well?"

Lovingly, Sass pushed an unruly strand of hair back from Staci's face. "I did better than I expected to. I lay awake for a long time thinking of all that I'm faced with, but sleep finally came. How did you sleep?"

After pulling out a chair for Sass to be seated, Staci put Justin in his highchair. "I too stayed awake pondering these troublesome times. I've been awake for hours. As you know, Eugene gets up before the rooster crows. I couldn't go back to sleep after he left."

Staci sat a glass of freshly squeezed orange juice in front of Sass and poured cold milk into a plastic tumbler for Justin. The plate of French toast she placed on the table smelled heavenly. A pitcher of heated maple syrup accompanied it. Scrambled eggs and turkey bacon, garnished with sprigs of parsley, filled a round meat platter.

Sass smiled. "You've been busy in here. Everything looks and smells divine. Shall I pass the blessing?"

Staci sat down in the chair closest to Justin's highchair. "By all means, my dear sister. Bow your head so mommy can pray, Justin."

"I pray," Justin said excitedly. Staci prompted Justin to recite the short blessing of thanks that Sass had taught him. "Thank you, Jesus, for everything," Justin said.

Although the food tasted wonderful, Sass found that she didn't have much of an appetite. The aggravated gnawing in her stomach made her feel queasy. The symptoms were synonymous to those of the ulcer she'd once suffered with a while back. She suspected that all the worrying she'd done was the cause of the wretched condition. Despite the aching in her stomach, she forced herself to eat. The last thing she wanted to do was hurt Staci's feelings. After all, she'd spent a lot of time in the kitchen, had put much effort into preparing the food for them.

Justin's appetite was certainly good, she mused. Having eaten everything on his plate, he was now asking for more. Several minutes later, when he'd finished his seconds, and had drunk his juice, Staci took him out of the highchair. Laughing, Justin scurried off to his bedroom to watch cartoons and play with his toys.

Staci lifted Sass's hand and kissed the back of it. "You haven't eaten that much. Are you feeling okay?" Staci looked concerned over Sass's constant lack of appetite.

"You noticed, huh? My stomach is a little queasy this morning. I probably should take something to calm it down."

Staci raised an eyebrow. "You're not with child, are you?"

Sass cringed inwardly. "Of course not. Besides, that's the last thing I need right now. I've already got enough going on."

Staci looked thoughtful. "Sass, aren't you the least bit curious about the unusual set of circumstances surrounding Justin's birth and adoption? Something doesn't seem right to me."

Sass scowled. "I don't know what you're getting at here."

"For the sake of argument, let's just say that the DNA is correct. That would mean that either Kristopher had an affair with Justin's mother, or the babies were somehow accidentally switched at birth. It's possible that you may very well be Justin's biological mother. Has that possibility ever crossed your mind?"

Too dumbfounded to speak, Sass's lips trembled when she did try to open her mouth, her eyes instantly filling with water. To steady her racing heart, she took a few deep breaths. "Never, ever has that crossed my mind, not even for a fleeting moment. Are you saying that you think Justin is my natural child? Your theory seems to suggest that I may have buried Aria's child. But how could that be? How could such a thing like that happen?"

"Unfortunately, very easily, Sass. This probably happens far more often than we think. Considering all that you've told me, I believe it could've happened. Aria's child would've been more prone to illness than yours because of her own medical history. You even mentioned that the nursing staff was surprised when she delivered a perfectly healthy baby."

Sass shook her head in disbelief. "This is too incredible! Oh, Staci, do I dare hope for such an outcome? Do I dare to even embrace the thought that Justin could actually be mine?"

With the moisture in her eyes flowing, Sass thought back to the first time she'd held Justin in her arms, the sweetest moment of her life. His chubby little fingers had clung to her, as though he knew every fiber of her being, as though she was his very own mommy.

Sass looked at Staci with hope alive in her eyes. "Do I dare to challenge the hospital on the possibility of them having made such a horrendous mistake?"

"You must not only embrace the possibility of Justin as your natural child, you also have to challenge the hospital. We have to explore every possible avenue. As is the case with paternity, DNA can also provide us with the answer. Maternity can be proven through mitochondrial DNA just as easily."

Replacing hope, fear swelled in her eyes. "If Justin is mine, that means he's also Kristopher's." She shook her head in disbelief. "This theory is more incredible than I first thought. How am I going to come to terms with Kristopher parking himself in my life after all that has happened between us? How can I overlook the fact that he once wanted to kill Justin?"

"Maybe you're being too harsh on Kristopher. The abortion was certainly an irrational, insensitive request on his part, but he may not have realized what he was asking of you at the time. Your pregnancy may have come as a terrible shock to him. I don't think he considered his request as asking you to take a human life. Let's get all the facts first, and then we can decide how to handle Kristopher

Chandler. There's still the possibility that he's not the father and that Justin *is* in fact Aria's child."

Sass frowned, looking crestfallen. "There's also the possibility that Justin could be Aria and Kristopher's child. As both you and my lawyer have pointed out to me, she was a model. That would be the worst-case scenario since it would leave me without a blood link to Justin."

Staci lifted Sass's chin with her forefinger. "Don't despair. Let's take one thing at a time, Sass. With all the resources available to me as a nurse, we'll begin the investigation. We need to talk to your lawyer and let her sink her teeth into our new theory. The beginning of this investigation should start with the hospital in question."

Sass chewed on her bottom lip. "Do you think this investigation may end up with the remains of Aria and the baby having to be exhumed? I wouldn't want to disturb their final resting places. That would be just too awful."

Staci shook his head. "I see no need whatsoever for that. If neither one of you is the biological parents, there'd be no reason to go to that extreme. DNA from you and Kristopher will prove it one way or another. This case is just a blood test away from being solved. In fact, instead of starting with the hospital, we'll first get the results of the new DNA tests. We'll deal with the hospital when we find out if they'd possibly made a mistake."

Sass looked so exhausted by the whole thing. It appeared to Staci that Sass looked ready to fall apart. Leaning forward, Staci took Sass's hand. "Baby sister, I know this is the trial of all tribulations, but you must keep your wits about you. We have much work to do. In just a few hours we'll be well on our way to finding out if you're Justin's biological mother. I believe with all my heart that you are his and he is yours. We need to contact your attorney at once and inform her of this new theory."

***

Sonja Mitchell stood before the judge. "Your Honor, we have new evidence to introduce to the court. However, we *are* prepared to proceed with this morning's procedures. May I approach the bench to offer you the typewritten discovery?"

"Permission granted. Has the latest discovery been turned over to Mr. Chance and Mr. Chandler?"

"No, Your Honor. Since I've just received these results a few moments ago, I haven't had the opportunity to share the information with them. However, I'm now prepared to give Mr. Chance and his client everything I'm priviledged to." The judge ordered the bailiff to turn the copies of the results over to the opposition.

"May we proceed, Your Honor?" The judge nodded curtly, then gave a verbal approval. "I'm entering into evidence the DNA test results that we've just received from Lotus Laboratories. Before I read the results of the test, I'd like to say a few words that will in all likelihood clear up our initital motion."

The judge once again gave her verbal approval.

"Miss Stephens came to this court to deny the fact that Mr. Chandler was the father of her child. Because she believed that to be the truth with all her heart and soul, she made the decision to fight against Mr. Chandler gaining custody of her young son. You see, Miss Stephens adopted Justin Brian Stephens when he was just a newborn."

The judge looked like a black cloud ready to rage a torrential rainstorm on a unsuspecting community. The whispering ran rampant in the courtroom, causing the judge to louldy bang her gavel to regain order.

"I'm confused Miss Mitchell. How can a woman adopt her own baby, pray tell?"

"Your Honor, Miss Stephens was asked to adopt the

child by its biological mother, who was dying from cancer. Miss Stephens and Aria Thornton shared a room in the maternity ward at San Jose Memorial Hospital. Miss Stephens was in fact pregnant with Mr. Chandler's child, but her child died a few hours after he was born."

Kristopher looked at Sass in disbelief, wondering how she could continue with such a charade as the one her attorney was presenting. More than his disbelief, he feared that she might end up in contempt of court for submitting untruthful facts under oath, which could land her beautiful behind in jail. Justin couldn't be dead and alive at the same time, especially when the last DNA tests proved that Justin was very much alive and belonged to him.

"Miss Mitchell, while I like a good story of intrigue as well as the next person, I'm afraid I'm going to have to ask you to get right to the point. None of what you've said makes any sense to me . . . and I'm sure I'm not alone in this. Please get to the heart of the matter."

"Yes, Your Honor. After Miss Stephens was told that her baby had died, Miss Thornton asked her to adopt Justin, which she did. The adoption was handled privately. Miss Thornton died shortly after the perfectly legal adoption was final. I will present the court with the death certificate of Justin Brian Stephens, as well as the birth certificate and adoption papers for Justin Brian Stephens. Miss Thornton named her baby after the deceased child that Miss Stephens had already named."

Mr. Chance got to his feet. "I object, Your Honor!"

The judge's face showed intolerance. "On what grounds, Mr. Chance, since we haven't yet heard the entire story? Objection overruled. Please continue Miss Mitchell."

"Your honor, the DNA tests that have been introduced into evidence prove that Justin Brian Stephens is the biological child of both Miss Sass Stephens and Mr. Kristopher Chandler."

The courtroom spectators buzzed like a hive of busy bees, but Sonja Mitchell was not to be deterred. This was not her finest hour, but it was definitely a worthy runner-up for second.

Sass was silent as driven snow on the outside, but her insides screamed every victory cheer she knew. Along with everyone else, she had just heard the DNA results for the first time. She didn't look over at Kristopher, but she could imagine the expression on his face.

When she finally looked over at the man she'd come to love with everything in her, his tears caused the tears in her heart to overflow. Her tightly held breath tumbled free in a very audible sigh of relief. Justin was really her child, her heart heralded with glee. Justin Brian Stephens was her baby boy, in every sense of the word. She was Justin's biological mother.

"In launching a thorough investigation into this matter, we have learned that the Stephens baby and the Thornton baby were accidentally switched at birth. It appears that the hospital discovered the mistake shortly after Miss Stephens had buried the wrong child. Fearing a lawsuit, which we will no doubt pursue in the future, the hospital administration decided simply to do nothing to correct the situation since the other child was already living with its birth mother. Miss Stephens had no idea that what had occurred was even a possibility, not until someone very close to her posed the idea. All these years she simply believed that she'd adopted the baby of a dying mother. Your honor, in light of this new evidence, I'd like to make a motion that Mr. Chance and I work with our clients to bring this matter to a resolution that best suits their biological child. I think my client has been through enough emotional stress at this point."

Sass took a longer look at Kristopher. He looked pale and confused. Feeling the intensity of her eyes on him, Kristopher's mocha eyes met in a head-on collision with Sass's heart-rending gaze. Unable to stand the naked pain in her eyes, he wished he could take her in his arms and make all the hurt go away.

Sass didn't know what she felt for Kristopher at the moment, but it wasn't hate. When the judge began to speak, Sass turned her full attention on the female in the black robe, the woman that held her and Justin's life in her very hands.

Judge Waters folded her hands, laying them atop the bench counter. "Miss Stephens, it seems to me that this court may have misjudged you. I'm truly sorry for what you've had to endure. However, the fact that Mr. Chandler is in fact the biological father of your child entitles him to certain parental rights where custody laws are concerned. I'd like to give you the opportunity, here and now, to tell the court why you don't think he has a right to be involved in his own child's life."

Trembling badly on the inside, Sass stood up. *He shouldn't have any rights because he didn't want Justin in the first place. He wanted me to abort the child I carried for him because he never wanted children, but he forgot to tell me about it. He's incapable of loving anything that he doesn't want,* Sass cried inwardly. Sass couldn't voice those thoughts because that's what she thought of the old Kristopher and all his selfishness. The man seated across the room was a kind, loving man, one that she'd be proud to have as her son's father. He had been right to fight for a place in his child's life. But she hadn't given him any other choice but to battle her for custody. Though it was too late, she now realized it could've been worked out, had she told him the truth.

Turning, Sass looked Kristopher dead in the eye. Though her eyes only stayed on him a few seconds, to him it seemed like an eternity. "Your Honor, I believe that he does have a right to be involved in *our* child's life. The circumstances under which my precious Justin came into my life was my sole reason for fighting this custody battle in the first place. I had no clue that I was his natural mother. Maybe I should've known since I've felt like his natural mother from day one. I always thought that the instant bonding between Justin and me was nothing short of miraculous. I've really never thought of him as anything but my sweet baby boy, have never told a single soul that Justin was adopted, not until I was forced to do so. In my heart and soul Justin belonged to me, only me. The relationship I have with my child is wonderful, beautiful, eternal."

Sass turned her tearful eyes back on Kristopher. "As for Mr. Chandler, perhaps he and I can work out an amicable agreement where our child is concerned. I certainly hope so for Justin's sake." She directed her attention back to the judge. "In a way, I'm very happy that these proceedings have occurred. Otherwise, I may have never gotten to experience the joyous feeling of knowing the child I've adored actually came from my womb. That's all I have to say for now, Your Honor. The ball is now in Mr. Chandler's court. It's his serve."

The judge looked at Kristopher. "I believe you've heard Miss Stephens's address to the court. Do you have any comments you'd like to make, Mr. Chandler?"

Kristopher got to his feet. "I concur with her remarks. I believe Miss Stephens and I know one another well enough to come to a mutual understanding about our child. I have no desire to cause Miss Stephens any further torment. I only ask that we settle this matter as quickly as possible, at a time most convenient for her. My desire for us to become a family hasn't changed. Sass, I love you and I love our son. I desperately want us to be together."

Though moved by his profound speech, the judge encompassed Sass and Kristopher in her stern gaze. "Do you both desire to work though your attorneys to come to an amicable resolution?"

Both gave a verbal affirmative.

"So it is ordered. Miss Sass Stephens and Mr. Kristopher Chandler are found to be the legal and biological parents of said child, Justin Brian Stephens. Results of the DNA testing were submitted to this court by Lotus Laboratories. With the help of their attorneys, the above mentioned parties shall settle the custody issues regarding said child," Judge Waters summarized. "This court will hold another hearing approximately one month from today to hear and respond to terms and conditions in the resolution of this matter of custody. I'd like to see both attorneys in chambers. This court is adjourned." With that, Judge Waters left the bench.

Rushing to Sass's side, Staci entwined her fingers with her sister's, so happy for her and the outcome. Sass was the type of woman who would always do what she knew to be the right thing, no matter what it cost her, no matter how much it grieved her. For her to extend herself to Kristopher in the gracious manner in which she'd done made Staci love Sass all the more.

Her sister was also the kind of woman who would take on major hurt if it meant sparing someone else's feelings. Sass could've just as easily said to the court all the things she'd said to him about Kristopher wanting her to abort their baby, but she hadn't. That alone spoke volumes as to the depth of her compassion and character. By tuning down her own prejudiced voice, she'd raised the volume to a level so Justin's little voice could be heard. In her heart of heart's she knew Justin deserved to know his father, something she'd never think of withholding from him.

With her head held high, Sass left the courtroom holding onto Staci's arm, quietly commanding her tears not to fall, tears that obeyed. Enough humiliation had already occurred. She vowed not to shed one more tear. In fact, she had no more sad tears left for this situation.

Kristopher caught up to Sass and Staci as they stepped out of the Municipal Court building. "Sass, can we talk for a moment?"

She turned to face him. "Only through our lawyers, for now." Putting her hand back in Staci's, she started to walk away, fighting the demanding urge to turn back to him.

Staci turned Sass slightly toward her. "You need to do this for yourself. Talking through this is a good thing. Think of Justin and how he'll benefit from having both of you in his life. I'll be right over here waiting for you." Without waiting for her response, Staci moved away.

Sass walked back to Kristopher, who still waited with hope. "What is it that you need to say to me, Kristopher?"

He looked terribly chagrined. "I'm sorry, Sass, sorry that I didn't know what you'd gone through. I would've never brought this thing to court had I been aware of it. When I first saw Justin, I saw in him the pictures of me at that age. There's no way I could've believed that you adopted Justin. Instinctively, from the first moment I saw him, I knew he was mine. I know it won't matter to you now, but I did try to find you and tell you that I didn't want you to abort our baby. You were the only thing that made everything right in my life. I tried to find you to ask you to marry me so that we could raise our child together, but you had moved away."

Sass gulped down her anger, the acid in her stomach burning her insides. "Why is it that you're always sorry afterward? Why is it that you never intend to hurt others, yet you do just that, even when you can prevent it? I came to you, tried to get you to drop the custody suit.

You saw my pain, you've seen it throughout these proceedings, yet it didn't stop you from inflicting more deep cuts and hard to heal bruises on my heart."

Kristopher moved in closer to Sass. "Why can't you find the good in this? If I hadn't brought this case to bear, you'd still believe that Justin was yours only through adoption. Why can't you let go of the anger for the sake of our child? Whether you like it or not, Sass, Justin is my son, too. I couldn't live with myself if I didn't fight for my rights as his father."

Looking thoughtful, Sass pursed her lips. "You know what? You're absolutely right. I not only have to lose this anger for Justin's sake but for all of our sake. I'm ready to lose it, ready to move my things out of the past. I'm ready to give you every kind of consideration that I'm capable of. I'm prepared to face the fact that I'm bonded to you through Justin forever. Justin is my child, yours and ours. Call me later so we can decide where we want to go from here."

Surprising him, she kissed him fully on the mouth. "Until later." Sass walked away with a smile on her face and in her heart.

"I love you, Sass."

She turned around and smiled. "I love you, too."

# Nineteen

Offering a magnificent view of the city below, the Villa Estates Country Club sat high upon a steep hillside above Pacific Palisades. The grounds of the exclusive club were lavishly landscaped with acres and acres of trees and shrubbery and a large variety of colorful flowers and luscious green plants.

In the large room Kristopher had chosen for the surprise engagement party numerous buffet tables had been set up, each adorned with highly polished silver servers of all types and shapes. A large ice sculpture carved into lovebirds was stationed in the center of one table. Surrounded by dozens of hand-cut crystal champagne flutes, fountains poured Veuve Clicquot. Yellow Label Brut sat next to the ice sculpture.

Kristopher led Sass into the main entrance of the country club just as everyone scrambled into place. Lights were turned down to signal their arrival. Exchanging knowing glances with several of the employees on the way to the reception room, Kristopher smiled brilliantly at the gorgeous woman holding onto his arm. Clad in a white dinner jacket, he looked fabulous. His eyes showed deep appreciation of the delectable rose-pink, strapless, taffeta dress she wore.

As they entered the doorway, the lights came on at the same time everyone yelled surprise. Looking totally be-

SASS 387

wildered, Sass laughed until tears fell from her brightly shining eyes. While glancing around the room, she saw so many of her family and friends. Undoubtedly, she knew Kristopher was responsible for the party, just as she was sure Amantha Stephens had been in cahoots with her smiling fiancé.

Smiling gently, Sass kissed Kristopher softly on the mouth. "No wonder I saw feathers sticking out of your mouth all week, Monsieur Chandler! I hope you enjoyed the innocent canary you've been trying to swallow for the past several days." When Kristopher landed a kiss on her lightly painted mouth, everyone clapped, cheering boisterously.

As Sass's parents and sisters came over to embrace her, she smiled mischievously at Amantha. Reaching into Kristopher's inner pocket, she pulled out his handkerchief. While Sass dabbed at her mother's smiling mouth with the neatly folded hankie, Amantha stifled her laughter. "You also have a few feathers around your mouth," Sass teased. "You guys are terrific! Thank you all for sharing in this joyous occasion."

Carrying Justin, Eugene walked up to Sass. Her eyes launched a million skyrockets at the sight of her precious son. "You should be in bed," she scolded playfully. "Then again, this is your engagement party, too. We're all marrying into one happy family." She kissed Justin's sweet lips. Gripping the back of her hair tightly, Justin mashed his little mouth against his mother's.

While kissing his daughter's forehead, Jason removed Justin from Sass's arms. "You and Kristopher have a lot of ground to cover this evening. It's time you got started," Jason said gently. He was genuinely happy for his daughter and his future son-in-law.

Mandy Wells and her husband, Jack, sat at one table, along with several others from the studio, Sass noted, her eyes sweeping the seated guests. Dr. Daniel Davis and Denise Lawson were seated at the table with Wesley and Lillian. Much to her delight, Dr. Elise Ford and her husband, Stephen, were at the same table. As Amantha had invited many of her own personal friends, Sass's mother proudly introduced Kristopher to everyone he hadn't already met.

Sass nearly flipped out when she saw Gregoire and Lesilee beaming at her from across the room. "Lesilee, Gregoire!" Sass squealed in delight, dragging Kristopher along with her to their table. "Gregoire, I didn't think I'd see you again this soon." Turning to Kristopher, Sass playfully punched at his arm. "You think you've been very clever, don't you? I owe you one."

Interrupting the joyous reunion, the remake of the classic tune "Unforgettable" by Nat King Cole, now accompanied by his daughter, Natalie Cole, filled the air. Excusing himself and Sass, Kristopher pulled her onto the floor to dance and wrapped his arms around her.

"This is such a nice surprise," she whispered into Kristopher's ear, clinging to him tightly. "You have to stop indulging me with so many wonderful gifts. You're creating a new monster. I'm so glad we've been able to deal with all our issues, the old and the new."

He grinned. "Me, too. And I'm going to indulge you in your every whim for as long as I have life in me. Like the song, you are unforgettable."

Bringing his mouth to hers, she kissed him passionately. "So are you!"

The guests later enjoyed miniature crab cakes, spring rolls, sliced cucumbers with sour cream, and boiled iced shrimp for appetizers. The main course consisted of breast of chicken marinated in wild mushroom sauce, freshly steamed baby vegetables and lightly roasted new potatoes. Freshly baked French rolls were served with creamy herb butter. A gaily decorated three-tier cake, boasting sculpted sugar ribbons, was wheeled in for dessert.

After enjoying the scrumptious meal, everyone worked off the calories on the dance floor. Stephanie and Staci were talking with their spouses when Stephanie's mouth flew wide open. Looking in the direction of her eyes, the others looked as stunned as she did.

With her head held high, Grace Chapman strutted proudly into the reception room. By the look on Kristopher's face, he was more stunned than the others.

Leaping from her chair, Staci accidentally knocked her chair over. She rushed over to Kristopher and pulled him into the foyer. "What in the hell is going on? Please tell me you didn't invite her."

With his thoughts so jumbled, he could hardly speak. "Staci, I had no idea she'd have the nerve to show up here. I'd never do something like this to Sass. I don't even know how Grace found out about the party. I sure as hell didn't tell her."

"That witch never stops!" Staci spat out.

Kristopher felt as if Grace had slapped everyone hard across the face.

"Staci, you have to believe I had nothing to do with this. I don't want Sass hurt any more than you do. We just got through an extremely tough time. I have no desire to bring any more unrest to Sass's life."

"You need to get your lead model the hell out of here before Sass sees her," Staci advised him. "We can't let her turn Sass's engagement party into a fiasco."

Sass entered the foyer so quietly neither Kristopher nor Staci heard her approach.

As Kristopher and Staci turned around at the same time, the accusatory chill in Sass's eyes impaled his heart. "Grace is not to be denied, is she? How could you let her do this to me?"

The sorrowful look in his eyes spoke to his chagrin. "Sass, I didn't let her do anything. I had no idea she was coming here. Please don't let her cause us any more pain."

Grace came out into the foyer. Turning on Grace like a savage tiger, Sass grabbed Grace roughly by the arm, marching her right through the reception room and out into the lighted garden. Kristopher quickly followed, wanting to hear Grace's explanation as much as Sass did.

Sass pushed Grace into one of the chairs. Seating herself across from her archenemy, Sass stared coldly into Grace's eyes, wondering why Grace needed to bring her emotional harm. "Okay, Satan's daughter, let's have it. Why did you come here tonight?" Sass asked in a tone laced with cyanide.

Grace tried to move from the chair, but Kristopher loomed over her, his look daring her to move a muscle. "I simply wanted to wish you and Kristopher well. I saw Doc Davis's girlfriend a few days ago and she told me about the surprise party," Grace pouted.

Sass's eyes spit fire. "You didn't come here to wish Kristopher and me well. You came here to hurt and embarrass me. You're like a poisonous snake, Grace. The venom you release spreads like wildfire, killing everything in its wake," Sass spat out.

Concerned for her patient, Dr. Ford appeared in the doorway of the garden but stayed out of sight. Staci had informed her of what was happening. Elise wanted to be there if Sass needed her. Watching the scene intently, she stood at easy listening distance.

"Grace, why did you really come here tonight?" Kristopher asked dispassionately.

"For the reasons I've already told you. I also wanted you to know that I'll always be here for you should you need a friend. I *am* your top model."

"If he should need someone, you're hoping he'll turn to you for comfort, right, Grace?" Sass asked.

Grace glared viciously at Sass. "Right you are, Sass! If you hadn't come into his life, he would've eventually seen how much I cared for him. If you hadn't barged into his apartment that night so long ago, he would've been mine. He was so scared of his feelings for you he would've done anything to get you out of his mind," she practically wailed. "Yes, including sleeping with me. He would've made love to me had you not showed up."

Her cruel words assassinated Sass right through the heart. Putting her hand across her heart, Sass massaged it, as if she could rub out the sharp, stinging pain. That Kristopher hadn't actually made love to Grace brought Sass a touch of comfort.

The crowd grew larger as Jason emerged.

"Sass and Kristopher, you have guests waiting, but I can see now that you're quite busy. I'll take care of things until you're able to return," Jason said tenderly. His eyes were filled with disappointment at the uninvited intruder.

"Grace, how many times do I need to tell you I'm not interested in a relationship with you?" Kristopher asked impatiently. "This is the last straw. I'm not going to be able to work with you any longer. You're obsessed and it's hurting everyone involved."

"You were interested when you were using me to set Sass up. I would've gladly let you use me if little Red Riding Hood hadn't shown up and made you chase away the supposedly big bad wolf," Grace said vehemently.

Sass drew in a trembling breath. "I never knew you were the woman in his apartment until just recently, but I had started to put two and two together. I believe all this trouble you're causing is about being rejected by Kristopher. You worked with Kristopher long before I met him. I would think if he'd wanted you in his bed, he would've taken you there long ago. Why are you really so threatened by me?"

Grace snorted. "Don't flatter yourself, honey. All you high-yellow girls with long pretty hair are just alike. You think the sun rises and sets on your yellow behinds. You look down your near-white noses at anything darker than you are," Grace menaced.

A light came on in Sass's eyes. "So, that's what this is all about. My color bothers you. But I don't understand why. I can no more help the color I am than you can help the color you are. God made us all, so you'll have to take your grievance up with him. Grace, I'm black regardless of the color of my skin. I'm also very proud and comfortable with my heritage. Maybe you should try feeling the same way."

Grace raised her eyebrows. "If you're so proud and comfortable, why aren't you marrying a dark-skinned brother?" she challenged Sass.

"My heart sees no color. It fell in love with a kind, loving, sensitive soul. Kristopher isn't that light. Even if he was jet black, my heart isn't capable of discriminating against him."

"You're breaking my heart," Grace said sarcastically. "He's rich and successful, and that's your only reason for marrying him. If he'd been a poor black, you wouldn't have given him the time of day."

Sass saw that trying to reason with Grace was impossible, which deeply saddened her. "Grace, I truly feel sorry for you, sorry that Kristopher hurt you. I'm marrying Kristopher because I love him and because we have a child together. We have guests to attend to. This is a festive occasion, not a wake. I've simply run out of patience with this no-win situation. Kristopher, if you'll kindly escort Grace out, I'd really appreciate it."

"Grace came here on her own and she can find her

own way out. I'm sorry, Grace, for the part I played in you getting hurt, but you've always known that Sass was the only woman I've ever loved. If you need a letter of recommendation, I'll be happy to write one."

Grace, unable to stand the trouble she'd created, ran past everyone and out the exit door. Sass was astonished at the way Kristopher looked after Grace. She'd never seen him this angry, never saw his green eyes look like a fire-breathing dragon's. Sass felt bad for Grace and hoped that she'd one day find true love and happiness.

She gently placed her hand on his arm. "Kristopher, let go of it. We've made ourselves perfectly clear to Grace. She understands that I'm in love with you, that I'm going to marry you. We have come together for Justin's sake and because we love each other. It's also what we promised Judge Waters. We have an engagement party to attend," Sass said in a light, airy voice.

Sass smiled as Kristopher took her hand. "Despite all this, I *am* happy, Kristopher. I've come to the conclusion it doesn't really matter how long you've known someone, or how well you think you know them. I thought I knew you well, but you turned out to be a complete stranger. To live life to the fullest is to take risks, the bitter with the sweet. I'm not going to borrow trouble by wondering if you're going to disappoint me again. If you do, I'll cross that bridge should I ever come to it. I love you, Kristopher, and I'm positive that you love Justin and me. I have a chance at a stable life with you and I'm going to take it as it comes."

Kristopher was pleased at what she'd said. "I'm happy to hear you say that, elated that we're not going to let this latest episode ruin our future. I couldn't bear another breakup."

"I couldn't let that happen. I have a lot to be grateful for. Self-love is at the top of the list. No one can make me happy. I have to be happy with me. For the first time in my life, I'm truly happy and comfortable with me."

Kristopher put his arm around Sass. "I love you, Sass Stephens, with all my heart."

Sass linked her arm through Kristopher's. Smiling deeply at one another, they headed inside. Sass stopped abruptly and turned to face Kristopher. She then threw her arms around him, hugging him fiercely. "I'll always love you. You are the father of my child."

Kristopher held the back of Sass's head as he pressed his cheek into hers. "I promise to always do right by you and Justin. I do love you, Sass Stephens, always, forever. You will always be a presence of my past, a presence in my future."

The rest of the evening was spent dancing to the tunes of many celebrated recording artists, in a variety of music styles, including reggae and rap. All the guests had a chance to congratulate the betrothed couple. Sass was now back to her wearing her emerald-cut diamond, which looked like a large, sparkling ice cube on her slender finger.

Several of the males in the room danced with Sass, and many women danced with Kristopher. Dr. Davis was the last to dance with Sass, and he held her closely.

"Sass, it has been wonderful knowing you. I hope you'll be very happy. I've imagined myself in love with you, but I knew you only considered me a friend. Knowing you're so happy means a lot to me. I've talked with your fiancé. I think he's become a great guy. Denise is a great woman and I think she's going to be around a long time. Be happy, honey. I'll always be here if you need me." He kissed Sass before turning her over to her waiting prince charming.

As she looked after Dan, tears brimming in her eyes,

Kristopher pulled her into his arms, kissing her fervently. "This has been one extraordinary evening! I can't wait to get you alone. I'd like for us to stay at a hotel tonight. Is that okay with you?"

"It's fine with me, but I don't have a change of clothes."

He smiled knowingly. "For what I have in mind, I don't think you're going to need any."

"I love the way that sounds. Let's tell everyone goodnight and get out of here. I can't wait to get you out of all these stuffy clothes," she teased, tugging lightly at his shirt.

After making plans to see Lesilee and Gregoire the next evening, they headed for the door. As though they were off to their honeymoon, everyone waved, watching as they exited the reception room smiling at each other.

Inside the hotel suite, Sass and Kristopher showered together. After making love under the hot steamy water, they drank champagne, fell into bed, and made love over and over. They slept for short periods of time, only to awaken and arouse each other all over again.

Through the early morning sunrise, they held each other closely, speaking of the exciting life they would share with one another. California was chosen as their main residence, but Kristopher planned for them to spend every other summer in Europe so that Justin could get an education in world travel and see how others live. The wedding vows would be exchanged before Kristopher returned to Paris.

"Sass Stephens, are you as truly happy as I am?"

"Kristopher Chandler, I am truly happy!"

The happy couple sealed their confession with a passionate kiss.

Dear Reader:

I sincerely hope that you enjoyed reading *Sass* from cover to cover. I'm interested in hearing your comments and thoughts on the romantic story of Sass Stephens and Kristopher Chandler. I love hearing from Arabesque readers.

Please enclose a self-addressed, stamped envelope with all your correspondence.

Please mail correspondence to:

Linda Hudson-Smith
2026C North Riverside Avenue
Box 109
Rialto, CA 92377

You can E-mail your comments to:
LHS4romance@yahoo.com

My Website is www.lindahudsonsmith.com

# ABOUT THE AUTHOR

Born in Cononsburg, Pennsylvania, and raised in the town of Washington, Pennsylvania, Linda Hudson-Smith has traveled the world as an enthusiastic witness to other cultures and lifestyles. Her husband's military career gave her the opportunity to live in Japan, Germany, and many cities across the United States. Hudson-Smith's extensive travel experience helps her craft stories set in a variety of beautiful and romantic locations. It was after illness forced her to leave a marketing and public relations administration career that she turned to writing.

Romance in Color chose her as Rising Star for the month of January 2000. *Ice Under Fire,* her debut Arabesque novel, has received rave reviews. Black Writer's Alliance presented Linda with the 2000 Gold Pen Award for Best New Author. Linda has also won two Shades of Romance awards in the category of Multi-Cultural New Romance Author of the Year and Multi-Cultural New Fiction Author of the Year 2001. *Soulful Serenade,* released August 2000, was selected by Romance In Color readers as the Best Cover for August 2000. She was also nominated as the Best New Romance Author, Romance Slam Jam 2001. Linda's novel covers have been featured in such major publications as *Publisher's Weekly, USA Today,* and *Essence Magazine.*

Linda Hudson-Smith is a member of Romance Writers of America and the Black Writer's Alliance. Though novel writing remains her first love, she is currently cultivating her screenwriting skills. She has also been contracted to pen other Arabesque and New Spirit novels for BET Books.

Dedicated to inspiring readers to overcome adversity against all odds, Hudson-Smith has accepted the challenge of becoming National Spokesperson for the Lupus Foundation of America. In making Lupus awareness one of her top priorities, Linda travels around the country delivering inspirational messages of hope. She is also a supporter of the NAACP and the American Cancer Society. She enjoys poetry, entertaining, traveling, and attending sports events. Linda is the mother of two sons; she and her husband share residence in both California and Texas.

## COMING IN MARCH 2003 FROM
## ARABESQUE ROMANCES

### __HOT SUMMER NIGHTS
by Bridget Anderson     1-58314-333-5     $6.99US/$9.99CAN
When Bobbi Cunningham met Quentin Brooks at night school, his upright, honorable ways and killer good looks made for an irresistible combination. Quentin fears that once she learns about his past, he could lose her forever. Unless, together, they turn a sizzling summer romance into a love for all seasons . . .

### __NO MORE TEARS
by Shelby Lewis     1-58314-325-4     $6.99US/$9.99CAN
Stunned by her husband's unforgivable betrayal, art gallery owner Miranda Evans walked away from their upper-class life. Now she wanders the back roads of Oklahoma as an itinerant artist, determined to stay free of commitments—and hurt. But she never reckoned that her new employer, Brody Campbell, would show a gentleness—and hidden fire—that could prove an irresistible temptation . . .

### __THE MUSIC OF LOVE
by Courtni Wright     1-58314-268-1     $5.99US/$7.99CAN
Famous musicians are being murdered in Baltimore and Washington D.C. It's up to Montgomery County P.D.'s detective Denise Dory and her partner and lover Tom Phyfer to find the murderer. It isn't long before the tension from their investigation spills into their personal life, jeopardizing their love—and placing them in harm's way . . .

### __UNTIL THE END OF TIME
by Melanie Schuster     1-58314-363-7     $5.99US/$7.99CAN
Renee and Andrew have been fighting for years. Seventeen years to be exact—ever since Andrew accidentally saw Renee in her birthday suit. For him, it's an endless source of amusement; for reserved Renee, an endless annoyance. That is, until she gets a peek of her own, and suddenly sees him exposed in a totally new, totally desirable light . . .

Call toll free **1-888-345-BOOK** to order by phone or use this coupon to order by mail. *ALL BOOKS AVAILABLE MARCH 01, 2003.*
Name_____
Address_____
City _____State_____Zip_____
Please send me the books that I have checked above.
I am enclosing     $_____
Plus postage and handling*     $_____
Sales Tax (in NY, TN, and DC)     $_____
Total amount enclosed     $_____
*Add $2.50 for the first book and $.50 for each additional book. Send check or money order (no cash or CODs) to: **Arabesque Romances, Dept. C.O., 850 Third Avenue, 16th Floor, New York, NY 10022**
Prices and numbers subject to change without notice. Valid only in the U.S. All orders subject to availability. **NO ADVANCE ORDERS.**
Visit our website at **www.arabesquebooks.com**.

## COMING IN APRIL 2003 FROM
## ARABESQUE ROMANCES

**__IN A HEARTBEAT**
by Kayla Perrin          1-58314-353-X          $6.99US/$9.99CAN
Radio talk show host Diamond Montgomery is desperate to take refuge from the spotlight—especially after the man who was stalking her escapes from prison. But when her journey lands her under the protection of rugged ex-military man Michael Robbins, she finds the attraction between them sparking a trust she never thought she could feel again.

**__RECKLESS**
by Adrienne Ellis Reeves   1-58314-381-5          $6.99US/$9.99CAN
Maggie Rose Sanders has come home to South Carolina to open her own business. In need of fast money, she takes a job at a riding stable, lured by the high salary—and the charms of the stable's owner, Chris Shealy. But working at the stable means facing down her greatest fear—a secret fear of horses that has plagued her since childhood.

**__SINCE FOREVER**
by Celeste Norfleet       1-58314-402-1          $5.99US/$7.99CAN
International superstar Lance Morgan arrives in Stone Ridge, New Jersey, determined to obtain movie rights from a best-selling author. Unfortunately, the only person who knows the author's identity is former child actress Alexandra Price. Lance devises a plan to seduce the reclusive star into revealing the author's identity . . . but Alex has plans of her own.

**__REMEMBER LOVE**
by Altonya Washington      1-58314-407-2          $5.99US/$7.99CAN
Dominique Salem awakens in a Chicago hospital, with no recollection of how she got there—or of her life before the devastating plane crash that stole everything, including her memory. Desperate to put the pieces back together, she is stunned when a seductive stranger calling himself Trinidad arrives and tells her he is her husband.

Call toll free **1-888-345-BOOK** to order by phone or use this coupon to order by mail. ALL BOOKS AVAILABLE APRIL 01, 2003.

Name _____

Address _____

City _____ State _____ Zip _____

Please send me the books that I have checked above.

I am enclosing                                    $_____

Plus postage and handling*                        $_____

Sales Tax (in NY, TN, and DC)                     $_____

Total amount enclosed                             $_____

*Add $2.50 for the first book and $.50 for each additional book. Send check or money order (no cash or CODs) to: **Arabesque Romances, Dept. C.O., 850 Third Avenue, 16th Floor, New York, NY 10022**
Prices and numbers subject to change without notice. Valid only in the U.S. All orders subject to availability. **NO ADVANCE ORDERS.**
Visit our website at **www.arabesquebooks.com**.